MURDER
IN
CHELSEA

MURDERED IN CHELSEA

a Lily Cane Mystery

Ticky Hedley-Dent

QUARTET

First published in 2014 by Quartet Books Limited
A member of the Namara Group
27 Goodge Street, London W1T 2LD
Copyright © Ticky Hedley-Dent 2014
The right of Ticky Hedley-Dent to be identified
as the author of this work has been asserted
by her in accordance with the
Copyright, Designs and Patents Act, 1988
All rights reserved.
No part of this book may be reproduced in
any form or by any means without prior
written permission from the publisher
A catalogue record for this book
is available from the British Library
ISBN 978 0 7043 7351 8
Typeset by Josh Bryson
Printed and bound in Great Britain by
T J International Ltd, Padstow, Cornwall

To Dan who, refreshingly, knows
nothing about fashion

1

21 Manresa Road, 2.15am, 5th July 2007

Lady Zuleika Winters stepped out of the lift and strolled along the corridor to her chic, Chelsea apartment. Even though she only had to walk twenty yards, the seven-inch black rubber and gold-leaf platforms she was wearing made it an epic journey.

She took her front-door key out of her red, Fendi clutch bag and made a few attempts at stabbing it into the lock. After much swearing, she eventually slotted the key in and made her way into a huge, open-plan sitting room. The moon was shining high in the sky and cast a shadow across the cream, plump carpet. She opened the tall windows and let the warm, summer air into the room. She looked at her watch: it was a quarter past two. This was her favourite time of day, those early hours before dawn. She felt alert, alive and sexual. She flicked the lights on and checked out her reflection in the mirror. She smiled at what she saw. The recent plastic surgery had gone well and she told herself that she looked a natural thirty-three at most, nowhere near her actual forty-two years.

Zuleika walked into the kitchen, opened the stainless steel fridge and took out a bottle of Krug with a silver spoon in the top. She removed a green, stripy Venetian tumbler from the cupboard and poured herself a glass. She took a sip, enjoying the sensation of the first bubbles hitting her tongue. She slinked back into the sitting room and opened a wooden box with a mother-of-pearl unicorn inlaid in the middle of the lid, which was resting on top of the sideboard. She took out a silver snuffbox with her initials on it, a diamond-encrusted snorting stick (a new present from her latest paramour) and a glass coaster with a picture of herself at Paris Couture Week set inside it. She whipped out her Coutts card, opened the snuffbox and began to chop a generous line of cocaine on to the coaster.

She picked up the snorting stick and smiled, savouring the moment. She revelled in every tiny detail of the ritual – the texture of the fluffy cocaine, the tap tap of the card on the coaster. She touched the snorting stick down on to the coaster and hoovered up the coke like a true professional. Whoosh, the cocaine flew up her nose in one second (there was a reason she was nicknamed 'The Gilded Dyson'). 'I'm pretty damn hot right now,' she thought, and got up to dance with her reflection in the mirror, arching her back so that her pert breasts stood to attention. She loved the familiar bitter taste in the back of her throat. Swallowing again, she tasted blood. She tried not to panic, suddenly it began gushing down the back of her throat and out of her left nostril, in a single, crimson stream that ran down the left side of her mouth and on to her chin. She coughed, causing flecks to spray down over her Chanel blouse and on to the carpet. She threw her head back and pinched her dainty nose to try and stem the flow of the blood, but painful convulsions began to take hold of her body. The spasms followed thick and fast, causing her to twist in agony. Then her chest went tight, as if an iron clamp was squeezing all the life out of her; a violent pain ripped through her body and she couldn't breathe. She tried to reach out for her mobile phone on the sofa, but as she did, she fell to the floor in pain.

Her long, thin body convulsed on the thick carpet for ten minutes like a landed trout on a riverbank. Gradually, the life seeped out of her and she went limp. The highly-structured white designer dress, which everyone had complimented her on that evening, now looked like a collapsed meringue. The fashion maven had fallen.

In the street outside, a solitary figure stood concealed behind a parked van clutching a mobile phone. In the flat, Zuleika's mobile blasted out the lyrics of 'Good Girl Gone Bad'. The figure waited a minute and then called again. Rihanna's voice reverberated around the apartment for a second time, the vibrating phone in stark contrast to Zuleika's lifeless form. The person in the shadows replaced the phone in their pocket and slipped off into the darkness.

2

Lily Cane stood smoking outside *The London Evening News* office on Wright's Lane. She used to be a social smoker but, these days, she found she was constantly nipping out for fag breaks. She sucked on her Marlboro Light and exhaled the smoke into the balmy, July morning. A young couple sauntered past, looking like they didn't have a care in the world. The handsome boy, in black skinny jeans and a pork-pie hat, nuzzled the blonde girl's neck as they walked by. Lily watched them, envious. Her attention was brought back to her cigarette, it had given her a terrible head rush. The only reason she smoked was to get a few minutes out of the office. She surreptitiously stubbed the fag end out in a flowerpot of ferns and slipped a piece of chewing gum into her mouth.

As she walked through the revolving glass doors, she said 'Hello,' to Barry the doorman, who winked at her in exchange. With heavy feet, she went up the escalator to the first floor where *The London Evening News* was located. The mammoth *Daily Chronicle* took up the majority of the building. A huge plasma screen displayed the *Daily Chronicle*'s front page:

NHS must review overseas recruitment checks after Glasgow and London bombings

When she reached the atrium, which housed a revolting eighties water feature, complete with carp, she took a left and went through some double doors and along a corridor that led to the large, open newsroom. It was a vast sea of enclosed desks – a battery farm of mainly bald heads typing away. The fluorescent strip lights were throwing their unforgiving light on tired, pallid faces. Lily made her way over to the features department, an island of desks in the far left-hand corner. There at the largest desk in the corner, sat her new boss, features editor Kate Pollock, who presided over her kingdom like a military dictator. She had very cold, wide-set eyes, which on the right person could be a sign of exquisite beauty but on her doughy, plain face, took on a distinctly reptilian quality. Her tiny height and her tendency to scrape her lank, brown hair back into a high ponytail made her look almost school-girlish.

However, behind Kate's bland appearance lay a sharp intellect and a bitter, jealous personality. This thirty-nine-year-old was thought by many to be a future editor-in-chief and, as a result, she terrorised her employees. Kate dipped a finger of KitKat into her tea and licked off the chocolate in a suggestive manner.

'It's very naughty of me to have chocolate in the morning,' she said in a surprisingly low voice that jarred with her appearance. Nick Weston, the thrusting, twenty-six-year-old features writer, laughed sycophantically, raising his over-groomed eyebrow in a suggestive arch.

'Yolo,' he replied in his slow, Etonian drawl. Kate looked puzzled. 'You only live once,' he explained.

'There you are, Lily!' boomed Kate, happy to have a distraction from Nick's affected urban lingo. 'I've been looking for you everywhere.'

'I just nipped out for a fag.'

'It's so *accounts* to smoke, Lily,' mocked Nick. Kate let out her machine-gun laugh; Nick chuckled at his own joke, delighted that this one had been understood.

'Einstein, Hitchcock, Churchill, Wilde, Pacino, Bardot, Monroe, Moss, Hockney, and Bowie. Sounds just like a bunch of accountants to me, Nick.'

'Oh, OK, you're still smoking to be cool.'

'Got it in one; and now the ban has come in, it is cooler than ever,' said Lily, returning to her desk and thinking that it would never occur to him that she smoked to get away from them.

'It's so now to be common,' said Sylvester, the sixty-year-old books editor, winking at Lily as he headed outside for a gasper.

'Very cool,' said Nick drolly.

'Lily, what's the latest on Abramovich?' demanded Kate.

'I'm working on it. We're unlikely to get an interview. He's only recently divorced Irina and won't want to talk about his new girlfriend, Dasha. He feels no need to publicise the football club himself, he leaves that to the players.'

'Unlikely?!' shouted Kate. 'That isn't good enough, Lily. Try harder. I want an interview and if you can't get it, I'll put Nick or someone hungry on it. I want a story and I don't care how you get it. Do you understand?'

Lily felt her face burn and saw the sub-editors desk watching Kate laying into her. There wasn't a day that passed without Kate losing it with someone. Today, like most days, Lily was in the firing line. She looked at her computer and pretended to answer an email.

'Look at me while I'm talking to you! What am I going to tell Sam? I've been here for four months now and I said this was in

4

the bag. I'm not letting your incompetence make *me* look bad. I, unlike you, have never let a boss down,' said Kate, her soulless eyes boring into Lily.

'I never said it was in the bag,' she replied calmly. 'It was always a long shot. A slowly, slowly catchy monkey feature.'

'Well, Lily, slow might be fine on *Cats Monthly*, but if you hadn't noticed, this is a daily newspaper and I want results. When I was at *The Post* we got things done. My staff obeyed me and would go to any lengths necessary to get the story,' Kate got up dramatically and marched over to the morning news conference, her pedestrian kitten heels making a squeaky sound as she went.

Lily looked up and saw Nick shaking his head.

'Amateur, Lily. You've got to let the old girl down gently.'

'Or grow a penis, flatter her and agree to her every demand? I don't stand a chance. She's had it in for me ever since she arrived.'

'Oh, poor Lily! Does Kate not want you to play in her gang?'

'Whatever, Nick. I'm going to keep on working on my piece about whether people think Boris Johnson would make a good Mayor of London.'

Kate returned from conference an hour later with a spring in her step.

'What's the news from the top, Sarg?' said Nick, reverting to his role as obsequious pageboy.

'Sam LOVED the interview with the ex-jihadist yesterday. Serious brownie points. We've got to keep pushing the agenda.'

'I wish you'd let me write it,' said Nick, shooting Kate a flirty look.

'You'll be doing them soon, Nick, I promise. The news today is that Boris Johnson has announced he would like to be Conservative candidate for Mayor of London. This is great timing with the attempted London bombings as we can say Ken's not on it, blah, blah.' Lily shot Nick an, 'I told you so' smile.

'How funny!' laughed Nick. 'Lily and I were just talking about Bojo. She's not a fan. I like the Johnsons myself. I used to play rugby with his younger brother at school. Jolly good chap.' Kate lapped it all up, beaming at him.

'Shall I carry on with that then? I've already started it,' said Lily.

'Access, Nick, access. That's what it's all about.' Then she turned to Lily. 'I think Nick should write this as he's got the inside

5

track. Give him what you've done and then will you come and grab a quick coffee with me in the atrium?'

Lily sent Nick two email addresses; she was damned if she was going to give him all her hard work. Five minutes later she reluctantly followed Kate across the news floor and out into the atrium. They made a funny pair: plain, little Kate and willowy, blonde Lily. At five feet eight, she towered over Kate and, as a result, Kate did everything in her power to assert her dominance. They walked to the other side of the building where there was a canteen that sold coffee and school dinners.

'Grab a table, Lily. I'll get you a coffee. What do you want?'

'A skinny latte please.'

A few minutes later Kate strode back and sat down abruptly, causing the drink to spill over the top of the polystyrene cups.

'Lily, I've been having a think about how the features' team works and I am going to have a rejig. Darling, you know I think you are an absolute star. The thing is I want to bring a really experienced writer on to the desk. So I've got Annie Kilder, an ex-colleague from *The Post*, coming over – she will be writing the majority of the interviews. I just wanted to give you the heads up. I thought perhaps you could concentrate on obituaries and any list features that pop up.'

Lily swallowed, feeling sick to her core. 'Will I get to write any interviews?'

'Lily, it's not personal,' Kate replied with a mocking smile, her dark eyes flickering maliciously. She was obviously enjoying herself. 'We need more weight on the team and I don't think you have the drive of someone like Nick. He is chomping at the bit and on the fast track. I think you are a different kind of journalist, more suited to less hard-hitting features. And, of course, there will be the picture captions too, you do those so well.'

'Is this about Abramovich? No one has got that interview, Kate. It's not me being slack and off the ball. The interview just isn't possible at the moment.'

'No, it's not about that, Lily. Although I do think these oligarchs react much better to men. You were obviously the wrong person for that story. I was trying to give you an opportunity but I see it was a mistake.'

'Oh, so you've put Nick on it?'

'Forget that story. I've told you it's a reshuffle. Let's see how it works.'

'When is this happening?'

Tomorrow, when Annie starts. I'm going to need you to move desks as I need Annie right by my side. So can you slot in next to your smoking buddy Sylvester? He says you can help him with the book pages.'

'Tomorrow! How long have you known about this?'

'Don't make this difficult, Lily. You're making a scene. Would you rather take voluntary redundancy?'

And with that Kate got up and went upstairs. Lily was furious. She couldn't face going back to her desk. She knew she had to get out of the building before she exploded. She crossed the road and began pacing around Iverna Court. Her hands were shaking so much she could hardly take a cigarette out of its packet. Eventually she lit one. After two Marlboro Lights in quick succession and fourteen circuits of the court she'd calmed down sufficiently to go back.

When she returned to her desk Lily was relieved to find Kate and Nick had gone out to lunch. Her relief was short-lived as there in her inbox was an email from Kate.

> Hi Lily,
>
> I hope our meeting today cleared things up. The structure of the features' team has now changed. Annie Kilder will be the senior writer and I have promoted Nick to features writer. You are still a features writer but you will be focusing on lifestyle features, obituaries and assisting Sylvester. You'll also do research for any of the big writers we commission.
>
> Now that Nick's on the Boris Johnson piece can you do a fun A-Z of things to do in London this summer for Friday?
>
> Kate

It was three-thirty when Nick and Kate returned from what looked like a boozy, celebratory lunch. Kate darted off to a meeting and Nick sauntered to his desk.

'Look, old bean, I'm not going to pretend this isn't awkward. But you've got to play the game. I know you're bummed out about

7

Abramovich. Thing is, I've got an old pal from school who works at Chelsea and he's going to pull a few strings. It will probably be a glorified photo opp but it will still look good.' Lily scowled at him. 'Kate isn't Peter. I know Peter was your great mentor but he's not the features editor any more. He's retired. He was old school and in many ways too much of a gentleman. Times have changed. Kate's a new generation – she's all about results. And that's cool, man.'

'Bullshit,' said Lily, 'she's all about people sucking up to her. You keep blowing, Nick – you do it so well.'

'Christ, Lily. You're just like my girlfriend – so over-emotional. You think what you want. I was hoping you were going to be grown-up about this.'

She ignored him and spent the next hour cruising Facebook trying to block out his very loud telephone conversations to his contacts about Boris Johnson. At five o'clock she picked up her leather jacket, her navy blue motorcycle helmet and battered handbag and sloped out of the office. It was the earliest she had ever left the building. As she whizzed along High Street Kensington on her scooter, a tear rolled down her cheek. 'Don't be so pathetic,' she chided herself, pulling the handlebars towards her and upping the speed. She wasn't going to let the bitch get to her.

3

Lily turned her scooter into Nevern Square and parked outside number 8. The tall, red brick Edwardian town house had seen better days: black paint was peeling off the front door in large flecks and an electricity cable hung down from the roof and snaked its way across the building and furtively sneaked inside, just above the entrance. She opened the front door and walked up the stairs to the second-floor flat, let herself in and made her way along the shabby hall, her scuffed biker boots making a clipping sound on the green lino floor. She walked into the kitchen, which was littered with dirty pans and plates – evidence of her flatmate

Billy's late night cooking session. She took her phone out of her pocket and dialled.

'Bill. It's Lil. Call me back. I'm having a shocker.' She made herself a strong cup of tea, went into the sitting room and collapsed on to the well-lived-in, light blue sofa. The flat used to belong to Billy's late grandmother and most of her furniture was still *in situ*. Lily played the day's events over and over again in her head. Her mobile rang, interrupting her thoughts. She checked who it was before she picked it up.

'Lily, it's Bill. Are you OK? It's not your dad is it?'

'Hey, Bill. No it's not Dad. I'm having a nightmare. That devil woman Kate has demoted me.'

'Oh, Lil, I'm sorry. I've wrapped up this session so when I get back let's get drunk. How has that tosser Nick fared in all this?'

'Oh, he's taken my job.'

'That talentless little fuck! Ah well. They deserve each other. You'll do better in the long run. I know it.'

'Yeah right, Bill, because what all the papers are looking for right now is an unknown, twenty-eight-year-old journalist who writes the obituary pages and the odd picture caption.'

'You don't know that. This will cheer you up. Want to know what I've been doing today? Playing backing guitar on Faith Smith's attempt at a new single. Yup, that's why I went to the Guildhall. Who needs trained musicians when you've got ex-girl-band members doing their thang.'

'Rock 'n' roll baby,' said Lily half-laughing.

'I'm living the dream, Lily, living the dream. I'll be back in an hour. Sorry about the mess in the kitchen. I rustled up a fry-up.'

Lily lay back on the sofa and lit a cigarette. An hour later her dishevelled flatmate burst through the door. He scanned the scene, taking in the three, stubbed-out cigarettes in the china ashtray and ran a manly hand through his mop of unruly, black-brown curls.

'I see the giving-up is going well,' he teased.

Lily scowled at him.

'Come on then, let's go down to the Troubadour and I'll give you the Billy Treadaway therapy session, otherwise known as beer, red wine and neat vodka, drunk in any order you like.'

Ten minutes later they were sitting in the garden in the Troubadour, tucking into some cold beers.

'Hit me with it,' said Billy in his deep, throaty voice. He leaned back in his chair and slurped at his beer.

'There's nothing much to tell. Basically, because I haven't got an interview with Roman Abramovich, Kate thinks I'm useless. But no one has interviewed him. Every day Kate gives Nick or one of our freelancers the juicy stories and I'm left writing picture captions. If I come up with a good idea, she says, "Who shall we get to write it?" It's torture! She just doesn't like me, because I won't bitch about people behind their backs. She's wanted me out ever since she arrived. And now she has hired one of her old cronies to be the main features writer on the paper.'

'She's a bitch; we know this. You've been unhappy ever since she arrived. Maybe you should think about moving on?'

'I know, Bill. It's not that. It's that I've worked so hard to get to this point. Really, I've given it everything. And then to be humiliated by having Nick, my junior, essentially promoted above me... He's only been there two years. I've been working my way up for over five! I was so happy to be made a features writer and it looked like I was going places, until she arrived. And now she's destroying everything I've worked for.'

'She can't take what you've learnt away from you. Can you complain to anyone?'

'There's no point. She's the golden girl. Our HR only deal with contracts and, besides, Sam the editor thinks she's brilliant. Peter is long gone and I'm wholly dispensable.'

'It stinks, Lily, but you've got two options: suck it up and try not to care, or, find a new job. I don't think it helps that you're hot.'

'Let's stop talking about it and get hammered.'

'That's the flatmate I know and love. Drink your way out of the hard times. Time for a vodka shot I think,' said Bill, walking up to the bar. Lily's mobile rang.

'Shit, Bill, I think it's the orifice.'

'Don't answer. Screw her!' said Billy, trying to grab her phone. Lily answered, got up and paced round the garden.

'Lily Cane?' asked a chipper, Cockney voice at the end of the phone.

'Yes, that's me,' replied Lily.

'It's your editor Sam here.'

Lily's blood ran cold. *Could he be calling to fire her?* she asked herself. Surely he wouldn't bother with small fry like her.

'I think we met once when Peter was at the helm of the features team. You're the blonde, skinny one, right?'

'Yes,' replied Lily, surprised that he even knew who she was. 'Sylvester mentioned you're doing a stint on bodies. Well, darling, I've got you a belter of a corpse – a posh bird. Lady Zuleika Winters, the socialite and ex-wife of American Grapefruit retail billionaire Peter Paul Anderson, has overdosed on cocaine in her Chelsea flat.' Lily racked her brain trying to think who the hell he was talking about. 'I know it's not Madonna or Prince William. But this is a good story for us. She's a perfect poster girl for decadent London. Very lah-de-dah. We can tag this to Kate Moss's drug scandal last year and all the showbiz wankers who are hoovering up coke at Shoreditch House. We're going to take a moral stance on this, Lily. Is it the end of the day for the "It" girl, blah, blah. So, do you know who this Zuleika chick was?'

Lily could picture him pacing round his office in his slightly too tight Savile Row suit, smoking a cigar because, even though there was a smoking ban, he was the editor and could do what the hell he liked.

'I think I've seen her in *Catwalk*.'

'That's the one. Get down to her flat, see if you can get anything from an indiscreet neighbour, then call the friends. Sally's going to email you some info now. You know our deputy editor, Sally Shingle? She knows everyone. This Zuleika woman was a family friend, so tread carefully. The beauty of this, Lily, is that no one knows about it. The body was only found this morning and the only reason we know is because Sally was meant to have lunch with Zuleika's brother today. The family are trying to hush it up for as long as possible. So tell no one and we'll go big on it tomorrow. She lived at Flat 1, 21 Manresa Road. So, blondie, off you go.'

'Bill, I've got a corpse!' said Lily, grinning and doing a jig around the Troubadour. Billy looked at her, appalled.

'I think it's time you got a new job!' Lily downed the vodka shot, stuck her tongue out at him, ran out on to the Brompton Road and hailed a taxi.

11

4

It was nine o'clock when Lily got back from snooping outside Lady Zuleika's flat. Billy was nowhere to be seen. What she'd learnt from the neighbours was that Zuleika was very tall, always well dressed, kept strange hours and had a stream of admirers. Armed with this information she hit Google. A host of images from fashion parties and magazine articles sprung up. Lily clicked on a picture from a French *Catwalk* shoot, which showed a naked Zuleika Winters tied to a stake, wearing an oversized diamond choker with a cobra wrapped around her, protecting her modesty, her flame-coloured hair blowing in the wind. In a shoot from Italian *Catwalk* by famous fashion photographer Larry Lauzanne, Zuleika was pictured in a hot-pink leather catsuit and sequin Latex mask, straddling a bomb flying through a stained-glass window. There was another Lauzanne shot of Zuleika leaning over the turrets of a castle, pretending to be Rapunzel, with fifteen metres of hair extensions. She was wearing an anarchic, punk Givenchy gown. A topless, oiled, chiselled youth in red leather trousers with toned arms and a skull tattoo on his left shoulder was starting to climb her hair. The picture caption stated: Lady Zuleika shot at family seat Struthern Castle for *Society* magazine.

Lily checked her Blackberry and saw a message from the deputy editor, Sally:

> Sam wants to go big on this – a story of excess and glamour, reflective of our times. Look Zuleika up in Debrett's and speak to the family. Then get quotes from designers, her lovers (she went out with heartthrob James Purcell), her ex-husband, Peter Paul Anderson IV, and her friends. Make sure you speak to novelist Lucinda Norse. She based her book on Zuleika and they fell out. You better keep Kate in the loop about this story. We couldn't find her to see who she wanted to put on it but Sylvester says you're the girl for the job. I'll be overseeing it.

Come and find me in conference tomorrow.

Sally

Lily's internet sleuthing showed that Zuleika was the product of the late Earl Winters's brief third marriage to Australian Olympic swimmer Joanna Taylor. His athletic wife came to an unfortunate end, when she drowned while swimming in an eight-hour race around Manhattan. Zuleika's father went on to marry three more times and had gone out with a bang, suffering a fatal heart attack while driving the Paris Dakar rally aged seventy-five, with his sixth wife, Columbian socialite Delores Las Calobres, who was thirty-five years his junior.

Zuleika had three half-siblings as a result of her father's unions; the current Earl Winters (forty-eight), Zuleika's older half-brother, who lived between the family estate Struthern Castle in Dumfriesshire and a London residence in Mayfair; her vegan, younger half-brother the Hon Richard Winters (thirty) a zoologist living in Borneo and a younger sister, Lady Araminta Winters (twenty-six), a London socialite.

As it was nearly nine, Lily decided to bite the bullet and call Earl Winters. She dialled his London number on Green Street.

'Hello, the Winters's residence,' said a reedy, male voice at the end of the line.

'Can I speak to Lord Winters?' asked Lily.

'He is not answering calls,' said the man. 'Can I help?'

'It's Lily Cane from *The London Evening News* about Lady Zuleika's tragic death.'

'She only died this morning,' said the man, sounding shocked. 'How do you know about this already?' There was a stony silence and then he relented. 'Wait a minute please.'

Lily waited, after three minutes she lit a cigarette to calm her nerves. As she was getting down to the stub, the man picked up again.

'Lord Winters will not be speaking to the press at this time. All the family are terribly upset about this dreadful tragedy and hope that the press will respect their privacy. Lady Zuleika was a vibrant and much-loved member of the Winters family.'

'I'm sorry, sir, but can you confirm how she died? Was it a cocaine overdose?' said Lily, feeling like a louse.

'Madam, I do not wish to comment. I believe that she suffered a cardiac arrest. I have no more information and, as I said before, all of the Winters family have asked for the press to respect their privacy.'

'Of course,' said Lily. 'Will there be a post-mortem?'

'That's none of your business. I know the plan is to bury her as soon as possible.'

'Can you let me know when the funeral will be?'

'It's planned for next Thursday.'

'At Struthern Castle?' said Lily, pushing it.

'Of course,' he said, putting the phone down.

Lily went back to her computer, where the picture of Lady Zuleika tied to the stake stared back at her. Who was this bewitching woman? There was something weirdly compulsive about her. Lily found an interview Zuleika had given to *The Sunday Review*'s fashion supplement a couple of weeks earlier, to launch her latest collaboration with shoe designer Christof Canaletti. There was a picture of Zuleika naked, in the Christine Keeler pose, her long, well-oiled limbs clamped around a red chair, wearing a pair of black rubber and gold-leaf platforms. In it was a quote from Zuleika about the shoes: 'When Christof asked me to design a shoe with him, I just couldn't refuse. I see Christof as a visionary, a true artist, because it is my belief that fashion designers are at the coalface of creativity.' Lily glanced at a picture of Christof and Zuleika at a fashion party; Christof was stocky with a trendy haircut, and the flame-haired, six-foot Zuleika loomed over him like a mesmerising siren.

Lily continued reading. 'I said to Christof, "I want to design something extraordinary. I'm not interested in designing a stiletto that any old Jane can wear to the office. I want my shoe to be gothic and dark but with a hint of glamour and exquisiteness. That is why I opted for gold leaf. The Renaissance painters used it and I thought I'd like to bring it to fashion. I think fashion is a modern-day religion and shops like Christof's are temples to worship in.'

Lily raised an eyebrow, thinking about what her father would make of all this. 'Ridiculous woman! She's no artist!' she could hear him muttering in his no-nonsense, Northern accent while chipping away at a sculpture in his Cornwall studio. Then she had a sickening feeling of immense sadness when she remembered how he'd hardly recognised her last time she'd gone home and how he was slowly slipping away. She lit a cigarette and inhaled deeply,

14

staring into the middle distance, lost in memories. Here her mother was still alive and her father a sharp, bon viveur. The end of the cigarette pulled her out of her thoughts. It was quarter past two and time to call it a night. She set her alarm for six, excited about what the next day held. As she drifted off to sleep, the haunting face of Lady Zuleika tied to the stake kept popping into her head.

5

When Lily entered the newsroom the fluorescent strip lighting sprang into action. It was the only time that she'd been the first one in. 'This pretentious socialite couldn't have popped her clogs at a better moment,' she thought. She put her bag down on her old desk, which looked rather bare, before remembering that she'd been moved next to Sylvester. 'Least I won't have to look at Kate.' She headed down to the library where Neil, the spotty librarian, looked affronted to be dragged away from his morning coffee. After five minutes he returned, his stubby, pink hands holding four envelopes stuffed with press cuttings. She wanted the physical articles so she could see the pictures, which weren't on the computerised library system. Lily grabbed them and vaulted up the stairs – there was no time to lose.

First up was a small item entitled *Lady Zuleika's Luck Runs Out* from the *Daily Chronicle*'s Michael Duster's society gossip column from 1982, about the seventeen-year-old Zuleika being expelled from Roedean for creeping out of school to go to Annabel's nightclub, with gambling entrepreneur Timmy Greensleves, who was sixteen years her senior. There was a quote from her father, Earl Winters, saying, 'I really don't see why Zuleika is being expelled for this. I would have thought this showed initiative and planning! Timmy's a good catch. Surely Roedean is meant to encourage its pupils to marry well. In my opinion, Zuleika's time is much better spent with Timmy than pawing over her Latin books.' The snippet added that Zuleika would continue her education at a crammer in South Kensington.

Further research showed Greensleves had dropped Zuleika when his wife Georgina threatened to divorce him, but that he had taken up with an Italian countess, Lucretia Dorreno, not long after. There was another press cutting from the social pages in 1987 about Zuleika's twenty-first birthday. 'Lady Zuleika arrived at Struthern Castle, the family's Jacobean castle in Dumfriesshire, in a chariot pulled by horses dressed as unicorns, a nod to the family's crest of two unicorns locked in battle. Zuleika was dressed in a long, silver Bruce Oldfield gown and danced with her new suitor, the American multimillionaire Peter Paul Anderson IV.' There was a photograph of a normal-looking Zuleika with a handsome, twenty-six-year-old man, who looked a bit like Christopher Reeve.

Another cutting from Duster's column from January 1988 announced the couple's engagement. 'I'm so excited about marrying Peter Paul. I'm over the moon,' gushed Zuleika. Then there was a quote from Earl Winters. 'Zuleika has met her match in Peter Paul. We are delighted to welcome him into the family. At last someone who can keep up with her expenditure!' Next was an article about the wedding, with a picture of Zuleika and Peter Paul at Cranthorne Manor, the Winters's Sussex manor house. Zuleika was wearing a white silk Emmanuel wedding gown with a three-metre train, and a French lace veil held in place by a substantial diamond tiara. Apart from that picture and a few mentions of them at social occasions there was nothing of note until their divorce in 1997 and then there were reams of cuttings. It appeared that Peter Paul Anderson IV wasn't the clean cut, preppy American he appeared to be. The marriage had come to an end when he was arrested for having a 'lewd act performed on him' by an Afro-American transsexual prostitute, Candy Sweets, in a Brooklyn cinema.

There was an embarrassing mug shot of Peter Paul, taken by the New York police, of him holding up his crime number. In the photo he was wearing a garish, fluorescent yellow sweatshirt, a bestseller at Grapefruit, the family's popular fashion brand. His lawyers released a statement saying, 'They were just old friends from Peter Paul's charity work.' Zuleika had maintained a dignified silence. All Lily could ascertain from the cuttings was that up until that point Zuleika had lived a charmed existence, flitting between New York, the Bahamas and the West Coast. When not in the US she had spent time sailing the globe on Peter Paul's yacht, *A Slice of Paradise*. Peter Paul was the heir to the Anderson fortune, amassed from the family's highly successful retail chain, which

16

owned multiple fashion stores across the globe. When she divorced him, Peter Paul was estimated to be worth $1.5 billion. There were no details of the exact divorce settlement but it was thought she walked away with at least $100 million.

Then came the fashion stories – Zuleika burst on to the social and style pages with a bang in 1998, spending half a million pounds in Paris Couture Week. There was a brief romance with the Marquess of Sussex that lasted nine months, as well as a few would-be suitors mentioned here and there, but no serious relationships until the British actor and heartthrob James Purcell. The first cutting on their relationship was from 2002, when they were spotted together at Elton John's White Tie and Tiara Ball. There was a fabulous quote from Zuleika in *The Daily Record* from Duster's successor, David Mullion's, page: 'Yes, it's true, I am dating James. I feel like I'm in a movie every day. He has that wonderful English wit and excellent teeth, such an un-English quality. He's a great artist and just being around him inspires me.'

Then there was a striking picture of Purcell and Zuleika at the premiere of *It's Not You Baby, It's Me* where Zuleika was dressed like the snow queen with a crown headdress made from ice, designed by milliner Percy Quinn. The article was all about Purcell's American co-star Megan Rice's fury at being upstaged at her own premiere. Rice was quoted as saying, 'As an actress it's all about your performance. I am about much more than what I wear to a premiere. However, some people's only possible route to fame is to make an exhibition of themselves at public events – and ride on other people's success.' Zuleika's response to this was, 'Megan looked beautiful at the premiere. What I like about her is that she is a real actress, who is only interested in her work. She doesn't care about fashion.'

As Lily worked her way through the cuttings, Zuleika appeared in ever more outrageous outfits. A snippet about Zuleika taking up acting caught Lily's eye. 'It's true, I am thinking about learning the craft of acting,' said Lady Zuleika at the opening of the new Gucci store on Bond Street. 'I'm taking private classes with Peter Mahan, James's mentor from RADA. It's just a bit of fun but who knows where it might lead. I am a drama queen, after all, and I love Shakespeare and dressing up. I'd love to play Lady Macbeth. I'd get fashion god Marcel Marount to design the costumes.' That cutting was from May 2005 and Lily noticed that, in June, Purcell fortuitously landed a three-year contract filming a sci-fi trilogy in New Zealand and their relationship ended. Within a week, he'd taken up with the twenty-two-year-old lead actress Julia Sarington on set.

The Sunday Record had a field day with the break-up, running a massive story on James Purcell's roving eye and Zuleika's cursed love life. They blamed Zuleika's artistic pretentions for the split. They'd even dug up Zuleika's frenemy, novelist Lucinda Norse, who lived with her in the eighties. The pair had fallen out spectacularly when Zuleika accused Norse of basing her lead character on her in her 2004 hit novel *Fashion Addicts*. Norse didn't hold back: 'I'm sure James was the great love of Zuleika's life. He had glamour, wealth and artistic talent. Admittedly, an estate would have helped. In Zuleika's mind he could never quite be "one of us" because, even though Purcell was rich, he didn't have the super-wealth of Peter Paul or the grandeur of a title and an estate. But he had something Zuleika craved: talent. She lived for the premieres, the opportunity to upstage the young actresses and flaunt her extensive couture wardrobe. It's hard to know who she will date next.'

She's my lady, thought Lily, looking at her watch. It was eight thirty in the morning – just enough time to get a quick coffee before she hit the phone.

6

Lily was so glued to her computer screen reading the press reviews of *Fashion Addicts* that she didn't clock Nick walking over.

'One of the great things about demotion is you get to lie-in,' he said cattily, 'there's no point shutting the stable door after the horse has bolted, Lily. Although it is rather touching.'

'Thanks for the careers advice, Nick.'

'Pleasure, darling,' he said, strutting over to his desk like a well-hung cowboy. Lily took a gulp of coffee and smiled inwardly, Nick's arrogance fuelling her competitive spirit. Time to try her luck with Lucinda Norse.

'Hello,' said a fruity, posh voice at the end of the phone.

'Hello, it's Lily Cane from *The London Evening News*. I'm calling to talk to you about the tragic death of Lady Zuleika Winters.'

'Oh God,' she exclaimed, 'so it's really true. I heard this morning from a friend but I didn't want to believe it. I loved Zuleika. We were old friends and I'm sad to say we had not spoken for a while. We'd had a silly falling-out over my last book, *Fashion Addicts*, such a stupid misunderstanding. Don't put that in. I want to say something befitting the occasion. She was a society swan – a true beauty. We lived together for a year in the eighties, just before she married. We were two young girls around town. She was such fun, a free spirit. She really didn't have a care in the world. We did it all, you know – Annabel's, the Embassy club, skiing in St Moritz, even hanging with the Brat Pack in LA and summers in St Tropez. It's a tragedy.' Lucinda let out a contrived sob.

'Did you know about her cocaine problem?' asked Lily.

'Of course I knew! Everyone knew. She was known as "The Gilded Dyson". She collapsed at a party of mine once and pretended it was anaemia. Wherever she went there was a snowstorm. Don't quote me on that bit.'

'No, of course not,' said Lily reassuringly. 'You said you hadn't seen her for some time. Do you know who she was close to?'

'I bumped into her a few weeks ago at Scott's. She was with a very erudite gentleman, not her type at all, small and balding. I can't think who he was – certainly not a lover. Looked more like an intellectual. Poor dear. She did fancy herself as a pseudo-intellectual, which was a bit of a joke among the literary circle, and I had heard she had a weekly tutorial with some Oxford brain. You should speak to her dippy, half-sister Araminta Winters – she might be able to help you. She's the social editor on *Society* magazine. Oh Lily, dear, if you can, do plug my next book *Stiletto Sisters*. And give me a call if you have any other questions.'

Lily's next call was to Gerald, the building manager of 21 Manresa Road.

'Hello,' grunted a gruff voice.

'Hello, it's Lily Cane from *The London Evening News*. Gerald, I hope you don't mind me calling you? The night porter gave me your number when I came to Manresa Road last night. I'd like to talk to you about the tragic death of Lady Zuleika Winters.'

'What a terrible thing.'

'I was wondering if you could tell me anything?' asked Lily hopefully. 'I don't like to do it on the phone, miss,' said Gerald. It was obviously the most exciting thing that had happened to him in years.

'Shall I come and meet you?'

'Er, I suppose so,' spluttered Gerald.

'How about 10am at 21 Manresa Road?'

'All right, miss. Ring the porter's bell and I'll meet you in the lobby.'

Lily put the phone down and heaved a huge sigh of relief.

Lily met Gerald inside the vast marble lobby of the luxury apartments that made up 21 Manresa Road. He was a portly man in his fifties, with a podgy, pink face, steel-rimmed glasses and an ill-fitting, cheap blue suit.

'Oh, this is a tragedy,' he said.

'Awful,' replied Lily. 'Shall we go and get a coffee?'

She and Gerald walked down to the King's Road where they made their way to the Old Dutch café. Lily had a skinny latte and Gerald an Americano and a large pancake, which he proceeded to cover in lashings of thick, golden, maple syrup. When he'd squeezed out the majority of the bottle and taken his first mouthful, Lily began her inquisition.

'What was Lady Zuleika like?'

'She was a charming lady,' he said, smiling. 'Eccentric of course and a real character. There was never a dull moment with her.'

'How do you mean?' she probed.

'She was a restless soul and always had something going on, always jet setting round the globe for shoots, parties or events. It was exhausting just hearing about it! When she was here she was constantly redecorating her flat and getting me to move furniture and pictures around. Only last week she had me rearrange everything because she'd bought a wretched white grand piano – we had to get it in through the window on a pulley.'

'Did you know she took cocaine, Gerald?'

'I suspected, miss. She kept funny hours. She wasn't a morning person and I knew from the neighbours she was a night bird. And, of course, Jane Lemon, her assistant, would confide in me, because Zuleika was quite tricky at times. Jane would say to me, "She's a bit edgy today. She's had a late one." One time I went in to fix a leak in her shower and I saw a mirror on the bathroom ledge covered in white powder. I was shocked as I always think thugs and gypos take drugs, not beautiful aristocrats like Lady Zuleika. I pretended not to see the cocaine. She tipped me so well: £1,500 every Christmas! By far the most generous person in the building, and believe me, the residents of the building aren't poor. Her Christmas tip paid for the wife's present and our holiday! I'll miss her.'

'Did she have a boyfriend?'

'She dated that posh actor for a while, you know, the foppish one in the movies. I think she had a stream of admirers but I can't say I met any of them. Miss Lemon might know more about that.'

'Could you give me her number?' asked Lily, turning on the charm.

'Um, OK,' said Gerald, caught on the hop.

'Thanks, Gerald,' said Lily, typing the number into her phone. 'If you think of anything else, you will let me know? Could you rack your brain about any regular visitors, boyfriends and people she was close to in the last few months of her life. I'm sure I could bung you a bit of cash for it, enough to take the wife out for dinner.'

'I'll have a think,' said Gerald, scratching his head.

Once Gerald had walked out the door Lily called Jane Lemon: unfortunately she was not nearly as accommodating.

'Oh really, have the press got on to this already?'

'Yes. I'm afraid we have. Jane, I am writing an obituary and would love some positive information. Do you think you can help me?'

'Sure,' said Jane, pausing for a few seconds. 'Zuleika was a unique person. She was fun to work for. She lived life to the full and was in the fortunate position to be able to do whatever she wanted to do.'

'And what was that?'

'Fashion mainly. She lived for it and she had the money to make it her life. She has – well I suppose it's "had" now – a beautiful house in Hampshire and she turned one of the barns into a huge walk-in closet to archive all her clothes. It must be the biggest wardrobe in the world! All the clothes, most of them couture, are tagged with which collection they're from and when she wore them. Many have personalised notes from the designers. I'm a fashion student and we had so much fun organising it.'

21

'That sounds amazing.'

'Yes. She was truly addicted to fashion.'

'Was she seeing anyone?' asked Lily.

'I don't see how that is relevant. She had many admirers, many of whom you can find from the gossip pages. She was actually a very private person in that regard.'

'Why do you think that was?'

'She loathed the press attention during and after her divorce. She was of the opinion that her private life was her business.'

'Was there another reason she was so private about it? Did she have affairs?'

'Look, I only want to talk about my experience with her.'

'Were you with her yesterday?'

'No, I wasn't. I had the day off to look for a wedding dress.'

'Do you know who she did see?'

'Well, Dr Bone was due to see her in the afternoon?'

'Who is Dr Bone?' asked Lily, expecting him to be a plastic surgeon.

'He's an Oxford tutor, who came around once a week to talk to Zuleika about anything she liked, from current affairs to the Italian Renaissance. He's a brain on a stick. Zuleika and I had a joke about him as he had a huge crush on her.'

'Do you have his number?' said Lily. Jane ummed and ahhed and then gave her the number. Lily dialled it immediately. The phone rang for half a ring.

'Philip Bone,' said a clipped, pithy voice.

'Dr Bone, this is Lily Cane from *The London Evening News* calling about the death of Zuleika Winters.'

'I just heard. This is a tragedy, a real tragedy. She really was the most charming lady. How can I help you?'

'I am writing her obituary and wondered if you could tell me anything?'

'Well, she was a character!' he scoffed. 'I mean, of all my students she was certainly the most flamboyant. She wasn't at the university of course. I met her at the premiere party for *Charles II: The Decadent King* a few years ago. I was the historical adviser on the film and, at the time, she was stepping out with James Purcell who was playing King Charles. We got talking and she just said, "I am going to feed off you Bone," which I thought was rather amusing – she was wearing a feathered

22

corset and her auburn hair was cascading down her back in ringlets. She was a vision. So that's where it started. When she was in London I would come up and teach her once a week. She paid me handsomely and I loved tutoring her. She was such an eager student. I enjoyed our sessions. She knew everything and everyone! She liked to shock me. Only recently she told me a thrilling story about one well-known media couple who are, apparently, rampant swingers. Gosh! She knew things – such a thrill to hear and so far removed from what we chat about up here in Oxford. She did tease me, though. She'd wear the most revealing and outlandish outfits. I think she liked to see my reactions. Once, she wore a gold lame burka "in sympathy with her sisters in Afghanistan". On another occasion her breast fell out of her corset when we were talking about religion. It was most inappropriate!' said Bone, giggling.

'Gosh. That does sound fun,' said Lily.

'We'd always have champagne, either Pol Roger or Krug and she would nibble on those coloured mini macaroons like Marie Antoinette. Who, of course, was a great heroine of her's. She certainly wasn't New Labour,' he guffawed.

'Sounds more *Brideshead Revisited*,' said Lily.

'Yes! But she wasn't Catholic. No guilt there!' said Bone knowingly.

'Dr Bone, was there anything unusual about her on Wednesday?'

'Let me think. Well, she was in a great mood as she told me she'd sat next to Tom Stoppard at a dinner and had discussed at length the metaphysical poets. Then she rather worryingly told me she'd told Stoppard that she thought George Herbert was an atheist! I can't think where she got that idea from, certainly not me. I didn't want to point out she'd completely misunderstood our tutorial. There were a few things she wanted to cover over the next sessions – she was interested in the scandalous female aristocrats in history, French politics and she also wanted to learn how to play chess properly. So we had our usual bottle of champagne and played a leisurely game of chess while discussing women who have ruffled society's feathers through the ages. It was a hoot.'

The doctor over emphasised certain words for effect which gave a certain weight to everything he said, however trivial.

'Great. That's really helpful, Dr Bone.'

'Call me Philip, Lily, and if you need anything else, do give me a tinkle.'

Lily was on a roll and she followed this call with successful ones to the shoe king Christof Canaletti, the fêted fashion designer Marcel Marount, and Dr Hope, Zuleika's doctor who had been called to the scene. All the doctor would confirm was that the cause of death was almost certainly a cardiac arrest caused by excessive use of cocaine but that the coroner had ordered a post-mortem. She had no luck with half-sister Lady Araminta Winters, the social editor at *Society* magazine. The editor's personal assistant frostily told her she was out of the office on compassionate leave.

Next, she tried James Purcell's publicist, a slippery eel called Rupert Palmer.

'Palmer here,' said a waspish male voice.

'Lily Cane from *The London Evening News* calling to see if James Purcell will give a quote for Lady Zuleika's obituary?'

'James is deeply upset about this and he will not be talking to the press.'

Lily called the Grapefruit press office in New York, but unsurprisingly there was no answer – it was six in the morning there. So she emailed and was surprised to receive an immediate reply saying the Anderson family's thoughts were with the family. Lily looked at her watch. It was ten fifty-five in the morning. Tracey, Sam's PA, called to ask her to come through to the conference meeting.

Lily walked into the meeting room where the morning conference was held. The glamorous fifty-year-old deputy editor, Sally Shingle, was chatting to Kate, who scowled at Lily when she came in.

'Do you need me, Lily?' asked Kate.

'No,' she answered, relishing the moment. All the heads of department were sitting round the table.

'Come and sit here next to me,' said Sally, 'you've got the big one today.'

Kate's brow furrowed. Sam swaggered in in his grey pinstripe suit. Even though he was small – he couldn't have been taller than 5' 6" – his bulk and personality filled the room.

'Morning all,' he said, 'the biggy of the day is the cocaine overdose of Lady Zuleika Winters. It's a decadent London story, nobs snorting coke in gilded London while everyone else flogs their bloody guts out. So I want to run a picture of her on page one and run an obit style story on page three. Then next week we go hammer and tongs on decadent London.' There was a general nodding of heads.

'Do you want features to take this over, Sam? I am so sorry we missed each other last night. I've got two perfect writers for it, Annie Kilder and Nick Weston,' said Kate in a low, authoritative voice.

Lily's jaw dropped through the floor in disbelief.

'Get with the programme, Kate! You're miles behind on this. Lily's already started and has it under control. Sally's going to oversee this one as she knows the family. Hit us with it, Lily.'

Kate's eyes flashed black in anger. All eyes were fixed on Lily and she felt the colour spread from her neck right up to her cheeks.

'I've got quotes from friends, designers, her assistant, the manager of her building, her doctor and her tutor, who was one of the last people to see her alive,' said Lily confidently, seizing the moment.

'Great, we'll need that within the hour,' and he moved on to the business editor. Lily looked at Kate, who couldn't quite disguise her fury but flashed a fake smile. Lily slipped out of the meeting and, as she walked over to her desk, she replayed Kate's bid for her story in her mind and chuckled.

Sylvester came in looking like a teddy bear in a pale blue cashmere sweater, a blue and white checked shirt, moleskin trousers and pink, silk socks.

'Something amusing, Lily?' asked Sylvester with a twinkle in his blue eyes.

'Just Kate's reaction when she realised I had the scoop.'

'Divine justice this, Lily. I'm sorry the woman died but you should have seen young Weston's face when he realised this story has legs. Make it brilliant, babe,' he said in his gravelly, smoker's voice.

'No pressure! Thanks Sylvester – I think you had a hand in this.'

Sylvester patted her shoulder and then began sorting through his mail. Lily glanced at her notes and began to type vigorously.

7

Once she'd finished, Lily read over the article three times and then filed directly to Sally Singer. She looked at her watch: quarter past twelve. She'd written and filed within the hour.

'Sylvester, I've done it!'

'Do you want a celebratory ciggie?'

'Absolutely.'

The pair made their way across the newsroom floor. Unfortunately Kate caught Lily's eye. She beckoned her over.

'What now?' Lily muttered under her breath.

'I'll meet you down there,' Sylvester replied, shooting her a knowing look.

Lily walked over to the features desk. A dark-haired woman with a severe bob and an ample bosom, clad in a purple, sixties smock was sitting at her old desk.

'Lily, this is Annie,' said Kate, who was obviously enjoying introducing Lily to her replacement.

'Hello, Annie,' said Lily, smiling.

'Lovely to meet you, Lily,' said Annie in a jolly, plummy voice.

'Lily, have you finished your piece?' asked Kate aggressively.

'Yes,' replied Lily, purposefully not saying any more.

'Have you filed to me?'

'No need,' said Lily, savouring this small victory. 'I filed directly to Sally.' She smiled and began walking, before turning around and saying, 'You can read it in tonight's paper!'

She could see Kate's cold, dark eyes flash in fury. Nick raised a conspiratorial eyebrow at Kate. She knew the moment she was out of earshot the bitching would begin.

Lily joined Sylvester outside. He whipped out a pack of obscure, Turkish cigarettes and offered her one, taking another for himself.

'Turkish,' said Lily appreciatively, 'thanks, Sylvester.' She inhaled deeply and blew the smoke out like a zephyr. 'I just gave the old girl a dose of her own medicine. I'll pay for it later, but I don't care. I enjoyed it.'

'You know what, Lily, I think this 'move' will be good for you. Kate's plan has backfired.'

'Yeah, bring on the celebrity mass murderer,' joked Lily. 'Jesus, I sound like a ghastly hack!'

'There's nothing wrong with being a hack, Lily. In my day we were proud to be hacks! Don't worry about sounding shameless. We're all after the big scoop. It just so happens your story has popped her clogs,' said Sylvester, with a shrug.

They stubbed out their cigarettes and made their way upstairs. Lily sat down at her desk, wondering what she was going to do next. Then her phone rang.

'Lily, it's Sam,' he boomed. 'I just wanted to say good job. I'm putting this on page three with a picture of Zuleika on the front page. I like your tone. I want you to follow this up next week with a piece on decadent London and "the cocaine dinner party set" the Met is targeting. Really go for the fuckers. Let's give this paper some moral backbone.' And with that he put the phone down. Lily let out a whoop and mouthed 'Sam' to Sylvester, who winked at her in approval. Kate looked over puzzled and whispered something to Annie, who glanced over and then pretended to inspect her nails.

Lily was in a great mood when she left work that Friday night. When she saw *The LEN* seller holding a pile of papers with her front page story, she felt a warm glow inside.

Winters' End
Fashionista Lady Zuleika Winters discovered dead at Chelsea home after suffering suspected fatal cocaine overdose
By Lily Cane
FRIDAY 6TH JULY 2007

Aristocratic socialite and fashion muse Lady Zuleika Winters was found dead yesterday in her luxury Chelsea apartment after suffering a suspected fatal cocaine overdose.

The eccentric beauty, who was a regular fixture on the society circuit, was a much-loved member of the fashion community.

She was renowned for her flamboyant dress sense and was regularly photographed in cutting-edge fashion shoots for Catwalk and Society magazines.

She was known for being one of the largest collectors of couture clothing in Europe. Today the fashion world mourns one of its most extraordinary champions...

Lily burst into the flat twenty minutes later with a copy of the paper under her arm.

'Bill. I'm home!' she shouted.

'Hey, hey, hey. Who's got the big story of the day? The woman whose career was in tatters yesterday,' said Billy.

'Ooh, you should have seen Kate's face when she heard my story was going big. The dumpy bitch tried to steal it back! I enjoyed seeing her and Nick reading it. Especially when Kate found out that I am writing a piece about decadent London next week. Sam thinks I'm the girl for the job!' said Lily, twirling around the kitchen with a bottle of Pouilly Fumé. 'Are you coming to meet Jazz and Johno tonight at Favela Chic? I'll shout you a few drinks.'

'I'd love to, but I've got a date with the singer from the Plastic Foetus,' said Billy, grinning.

'Of course, the big date. You've been chasing her for long enough. She sounds as pretentious as my corpse!'

8

Kate was on Lily's back from the moment she arrived in the office on Monday morning.

'How's decadent London coming on?'

'Good morning, Kate. Did you have a good weekend?' asked Lily.

'Yeah. Whatever. Did you see all the articles on Zuleika Winters? I hope you can put your money where your mouth is on all this.'

'Don't worry, Kate! I'm on it. I have a list of people to call today. I have researched stories before you know.'

'Don't let Friday go to your head, missy, and don't pull another fast one. You file to me first. I'm still your boss and you better come and tell me who you're planning to call. I might have some suggestions.'

'Sure,' replied Lily, knowing full well that Kate wouldn't help and that she was only saying this so she could take the credit if the piece was any good.

'Morning, Sylvester,' said Lily walking over to her desk.

'Good morning, Lily. Listen, give my son a call about your London story. His girlfriend is a model on the scene and he said he'd chat to you off the record. He says everyone's snorting coke. Nothing has changed, of course; we took loads of drugs in my day. I spent the sixties and seventies in a drugged-out haze, babe. It's always been around,' said Sylvester.

Lily's first call was to Detective Chief Superintendent Peters, the police officer in charge of investigating Zuleika's death.

'Detective Chief Superintendent Peters, it's Lily Cane from *The London Evening News*. We spoke the other day about Lady Zuleika Winters.'

'How can I help you?' said a chirpy, confident voice.

'I was wondering if you could give me any more details about Zuleika's case?'

'Well, the coroner is almost certain the cause of death was a drug overdose. We have to wait for the results of the post-mortem to confirm this, of course. The family tried to prevent the post-mortem but the law is the law. They have said they were fully aware of Lady Zuleika's cocaine problem and they just want her to be buried as soon as possible. The funeral is planned for Thursday and they want the body transported up to Scotland ASAP. However, she can't be buried until the results have been analysed and they haven't come back from the lab yet.'

'Can I talk to you about cocaine in general, for a piece I'm writing on decadent London?'

'Sure. As you know the Commissioner is keen for us to clamp down on middle and upper-class drug users', said Peters, enjoying his moment in the limelight.

'Are there many?'

'I'd say!' he exclaimed, letting out a hearty laugh. 'The cost of a gram of coke has come down considerably. It can be as little as £40 a gram for those buying in bulk. Everyone is buying it, from estate agents to secretaries. It's no longer just the prerogative of the rich. While the economy booms the dealers are enjoying their day in the sun. We don't have the manpower to crack down on the drug dealers and criminal drug users, let alone the thousands of yuppies doing it on a Friday and Saturday night.'

Her next call was to ex-cocaine addict and 'It' girl TV presenter Sophie Hamilton-Bruce.

'Hellah,' said Sophie in the poshest voice Lily had ever heard.

'Sophie, it's Lily Cane from *The LEN*. I was wondering if I could get a quote from you about decadent London and how everyone is taking cocaine.'

'Everyone is on it apart from me. Is this tagged on to Zuleika's death?'

'Yes.'

'Poor Zuleika. I am so upset about that. I didn't know her that well but I filmed a show with her a few weeks ago at her house in the country and she seemed fine. She was very loved-up with some new man and she didn't really strike me as someone who was seriously on the blow, but I guess that just illustrates how blasé everyone is about it.'

'Sure,' replied Lily.

'Obviously you know I used to have a problem. The whole world knows after that ghastly sting in *The Sunday Post*. They did me a favour actually. My life has got so much better since then, especially my career. I don't touch the stuff any more – I don't drink either. Oscar and I work so hard on *Fashion Fix* there's no way we could keep to our production schedule and party like I used to. But shoot, Lily, what did you want to know?'

'I wondered if you think a lot of people on the social scene take coke?'

'Is the Pope Catholic? Christ, Lily! If I only socialised with non-coke taking people I'd have about ten friends. Also, it's not just the young. Lots of professional types in their forties and fifties are taking it. Coke is the most-invited guest on the bloody social circuit.'

'Do people worry about it being illegal?'

'God, no! I think they think that makes it sexy. They don't think they'll get caught or they think they're above the law. I've been at dinner parties where people openly snort it at the table and don't bother to go to the bathroom. But sometimes I think they forget it's illegal; I certainly did.'

'How does all this affect you as a non-user?'

'Well, it's awkward and I normally go home when the coke comes out, given my history. But I'd say there is certainly a division between the users and non-users. Those who don't partake can feel socially ostracised.'

'That's interesting that you think Zuleika wasn't a big user.'

'I really don't think so, but as I said I didn't know her that well. We had a great time filming *Fashion Fix*. I am shocked she died. She seemed very happy to me. It's very sad.'

'Do you know who the lover is?'

'No, sorry; she was very cagey. But please don't mention him in relation to me. That was something she told me in private.'

'OK. No problem. Thank you so much, Sophie. This has been really useful,' said Lily, wrapping up the conversation.

9

For the next two hours Lily blitzed the phone. When she let up for five minutes, Sylvester wiped his forehead and said, 'Just watching you is making me exhausted.'

'I'm cooking with gas.'

'Lily!' barked Kate from the features desk. 'Can you come over here?'

Lily walked over, taking as much time as was physically possible, to irritate Kate.

'Are you nearly ready? I'm about to go to conference and I need to let them know what you're writing about.'

'I'm writing about how London is in a cocaine blizzard. I've spoken to Sophie Hamilton-Bruce, the police, doctors, models, drug counsellors, Sloanes, socialites and city types.'

'That sounds great. Well, you better deliver. We need the copy by five if it is running tomorrow.'

'No worries,' said Lily looking over at Nick who looked peeved.

'Actually, Sophie's dad is a great pal of the old man's.'

'You should have written this piece,' said Kate bitchily. 'Is there anything else you can feed into Lily?'

'Yes, Nick, is there anything you can tell me about posh cokeheads?'

'No,' shrugged Nick. Kate made her way to conference.

'Nothing you want to tell me about your pals Henry, Rupert and Mungo having a bop in Boujis and then going back to their Chelsea pads to get on the gak?'

'Ha ha,' said Nick drolly.

Lily made a big sniffing noise and walked over to her desk.

31

Cocaine Blizzard Hits London

By Lily Cane
TUESDAY 10TH JULY 2007

Despite the Metropolitan Police Commissioner Sir Ian Redmond's declaration two years ago to crack down on middle-class drug takers, London still has the highest number of cocaine users in Europe. The tragic death of socialite Lady Zuelika Winters from a suspected cocaine overdose in the early hours of last Thursday morning, highlights how widespread recreational drug use has become in the capital. A blizzard of cocaine is falling on London, stretching from the Mayfair clubs to the terraced houses of Fulham, out to the Home Counties and beyond. Rock stars and the like have been snorting coke since the eighties but now, it has gone mainstream and lost its exclusivity. Detective Chief Superintendent Peters of Scotland Yard, who was called to the scene of Lady Zuleika's death, says that London is 'awash with cocaine' and that the number of professionals using it recreationally is on the rise…

10

Wednesday was a huge anti-climax and Lily spent most of the morning skimming debut fiction novels for Sylvester. At three o'clock Sally Shingle called.

'Hi, Lily. I've got a job for you.'

'Great.'

'Sam wants to carry on with the decadent London series so he wants you to go to the Serpentine Summer Party tonight and have a sniff around. See who's there. Try and infiltrate Lady Zuleika's world. He wants you to take the temperature of society London. I've managed to pull a few strings with the Serpentine. Go with Jonathan Kindel - he's covering it for the diary.'

'I'll be there. Thanks, Sally.'

'Get Kirsty on the magazine to call you in something to wear – you'll need to look the part.'

When Lily left at five-thirty, Kate and Nick smirked. Nick tapped his watch and called out, 'No more deaths or coke busts?'

'*Au contraire*, my friend,' said Lily. 'I am off to the Serpentine Party.' She waved a Giambattista Valli dress at them. 'Kirsty on the magazine sweetly called this in for me.'

Kate looked like she swallowed a bottle of Domestos. 'I haven't heard about this feature, Lily,' she spluttered.

'Sally just called me about it – it's a diktat from above!' said Lily, enjoying herself. 'Sam is keen for me to keep going with the debauched society pieces. I'm just heading off for a blow dry,' she said, sauntering off with a confident swagger.

Lily arrived at the Serpentine Pavilion in Kensington Gardens at seven, wearing a scarlet, silk mini-dress and killer heels. As she walked in, Jonathan, the urbane diary editor, wolf-whistled.

'I'm glad Sally put you on this,' he said with a wry smile. Lily blushed.

'Jonathan, you're going to have to help me with the society types here. It's not my world, I'm afraid.'

'No worries. What are you writing about?'

'I'm the new debauchery editor.'

'You sound like my kind of girl.'

'I am trying to infiltrate the world of the late Lady Zuleika.'

'Poor you!' exclaimed Jonathan. 'You've got a bit of luck. Lady Araminta Winters, Zuleika's half-sister and social editor of *Society* magazine, is here. *Society* has a photo booth over there in the corner and they've got Dennis Hopper taking photographs. Also, your friend Sophie Hamilton-Bruce and her very camp co-star on *Fashion Fix*, Oscar Rutherford, have just arrived. They *live* to give quotes to the media.'

Sophie and Oscar were posing for the bank of paparazzi at the entrance of the party. They joked about, basking in the flashlights for a solid five minutes, only stopping when Hollywood action hero Adam Bronwen and his glamorous wife walked in and stole the limelight. When Oscar and Sophie had got their drinks and settled in a spot, Lily and Jonathan walked over.

'Hello, Sophie. It's Jonathan from *The London Evening News*. This is Lily Cane.'

'Hi, Jonathan darling!' purred Sophie in her husky voice, air-kissing him on both cheeks. 'Hello, Lily. Didn't I speak to you on Monday?'

'Yes. Nice to meet you.'

'This is Oscar,' said Sophie, introducing her wiry companion who had mousy hair streaked with blonde highlights. He was dressed in a studded white leather jacket and tight, electric blue jeans. Sophie looked glossy and groomed. The only thing that jarred on her pretty face were her silicone lips that were just a fraction too big and pushed her, ever so slightly, into transsexual territory. She took a Marlboro Light out of a packet in her red Anya Hindmarch clutch bag. She struck a match and sucked on the cigarette, her cat-like eyes blinking.

'Hi,' said Oscar in a camp voice.

'Sorry, would you like one?' asked Sophie, offering Lily and Jonathan a cigarette.

'Thanks,' said Lily, taking one and lighting it.

'It's my last vice,' said Sophie. 'I've managed to cut down to ten a day.'

'So are you two regulars on the art scene?' asked Lily.

'God no!' shrieked Sophie. 'I don't know my Warhol from my Rothko. I've just come along for the party and to look for fashionable young things for *Fashion Addicts*.'

At which point Oscar interjected, 'Actually, I dig the art scene. I am a serious Damien Hirst fan. I just love his moth paintings.'

'Butterflies, Oscar, not moths. Oh look, there is that fabulous potter in a dress. We've got to go and talk to him.'

'Sophie, thanks so much for your quotes the other day,' said Lily.

'No problem. I've been thinking about Zuleika a lot since we filmed her. She seemed really together and excited about the documentaries she was about to produce. I'm just sad that everyone will remember her as a cokehead. She was a rare breed, a fantastic champion of the British fashion industry. We really need people like her. The only person who is as "out there" as Zuleika is *Society*'s fashion director Flavia Wilde. Now she is crazy.'

Oscar nodded and did a loop the loop with his diamond-clad index finger. Lily noticed he had a sheer gloss on his slightly too long fingernails.

'Oh, there's my cousin with Veronique,' said Sophie.

Lily turned around to see the most handsome man she had ever seen walk past the paparazzi. He was tall with strong, proud features. Thick locks of floppy, chestnut hair brushed the top of his chiselled cheekbones. Everything about him was perfect, from his buttery skin to his sharp, tailored, dark blue jacket, which showed off his athletic yet slim figure. On his arm was a small, coquettish girl with long, thick, dark hair and huge brown eyes. Lily realised she was the daughter of the legendary French actor Pierre Lapin. The press went into overdrive but the indecently good-looking man ushered the kooky girl along so they could hardly get any pictures.

'Your cousin is the sexiest man I have ever seen,' said Oscar, drooling. He leant over to Lily. 'Not only is he a count and a successful hedge funder, he has a polo handicap of seven and goes out with the coolest girl in Paris. Now *that's* what I call style.'

'Who is he?' asked Lily, shrugging nonchalantly to disguise her interest.

'He is the Count de Bourgogne. Sébastien is his name and, in my opinion, he is the best-looking man in Europe. He has turned down countless modelling contracts. He's rich to boot. Time to go and say hello, Sophie. I want his good looks to rub off on me by osmosis,' and they walked off arm in arm.

'He is annoyingly good-looking. Well, he's not getting any press from me,' said Jonathan. 'Oh, look I've just spotted Horatio Wesley; he's the dandyish chap in a pink suit over there. He's a diarist's dream. He had himself crucified for his crucifixion pictures and is the master of the one-liner. Want to come and meet him?'

They strolled over to a tall man in his forties with jet-black hair, wearing a pink suit, red nail varnish and lashings of black mascara.

'Hello, darling,' he said to Jonathan, in a voice drawn out with sandpaper and breeding.

'Hello, Horatio. This is my colleague Lily Cane.'

Horatio ran his eyes up and down Lily's lithe body and purred. 'Genitals prefer blondes. Lily Cane,' he said, repeating her name a few times, rolling the words over his tongue slowly and relishing every syllable. 'I like it. That is either hard or soft. Are you a hard-hitting bondage instrument or a soft sugar stick? Why on earth are you wasting time in journalism? With a name like that, you should be in the sex industry.'

'It's always an option if it doesn't work out.'

'Yes,' said Horatio, drawing out the word and looking at Lily. 'I think it would be very sound career advice.'

'So what do you make of the party?' asked Jonathan, tactfully changing the subject.

'I'd have more fun in my lavatory. I can't think why I came. I can't stand these Josephines, Arabellas and Victorias. Give me a prostitute and a shot of heroin any day. I detest the pretentious upper middle-class hangers-on in the art world. What a bunch of anally retentive bores and they're all rubbish in bed. I shouldn't have come tonight. I normally let people seek me out. I sit on the chaise longue of life and let the world come to my door. Unless I am in a brothel of course.'

'How is the novel coming along?' asked Jonathan.

'All finished. It's published in the autumn. Then I'm done. Write a book, commit suicide, then once you're dead you're made for life,' at which point he walked off, not wanting to waste an excellent exit line.

'Lily, that blonde, skinny girl in the tight, lime dress with the red wayfarer shades is Lady Araminta Winters. The woman she is talking to, wearing the crazy red orb hat and black corset, is *Society*'s fashion director Flavia Wilde.'

Flavia's 'hat' was the maddest thing Lily had ever seen at a party. It was a red perspex orb that surrounded her head with a section cut away for her eyes, nose and mouth. Lily estimated it was at least a metre in diameter. Guests kept having to move out of the way to let her pass.

'The mad hatter,' said Lily.

At this point Dennis Hopper popped out of the booth and did a double take at Flavia's outfit and immediately ushered her in. Jonathan redirected Lily's attention to a man in his sixties with a Dali moustache wearing a lavender, checked suit.

'That's art dealer and socialite Henry Marmsby,' said Jonathan. 'He's a serious fixture in society life, but no one in the real world knows who he is. Hello, Henry,' he bellowed across the lawn. Their gaze was quickly diverted by a skinny girl with very short peroxide hair and biker boots giving it some to the paps. As she walked away from the photographers, she lifted up her voluminous polka-dot dress to reveal a pair of shocking-pink, spotty, net knickers.

'Oh to be young and fabulous,' said Henry, who had made his way over.

'This is Lily,' said Jonathan and Henry nodded in acknowledgement.

At this point a very tanned woman in her early fifties, who looked like she had been stuck in a wind tunnel, tapped Henry on the shoulder.

'Rosemary,' said Henry gaily, 'isn't Botox great? You look fabulous darling, at least ten years younger than when we were in Mustique at Christmas.'

The woman's eyes flashed with fury but her face remained motionless. Lily and Jonathan did their best not to crack up.

'What on earth are you talking about?' asked the woman crossly.

'Oh come on, Rosemary, you're not eighteen any more. We had some fun nights out in the seventies, remember? We can all see you've had some work done. Good for you! It looks great. I've had a whole facelift, for Christ's sake, and I don't regret it one bit. There's nothing better for perking up the old sex life.'

The woman marched off.

'Ridiculous,' said Henry, thoroughly enjoying the rumpus he had created.

Lily made her way over to the booth where there was queue of people waiting to be photographed by Dennis Hopper. A dapper man in his forties was sharing a joke with Flavia, who cackled.

'We need some beauties in here, Jonty. Not these bland girls in fucking Monsoon,' she spat. The group of Prada and Gucci clad hedge funder WAGs who were lingering around the booth in the hope of being photographed for *Society* magazine promptly evaporated.

'Ha! That got rid of them. Just because they are wearing Gucci doesn't mean they are worthy of the booth,' said Flavia, whose attention was quickly drawn to a curvaceous blonde sharing a joke with Ryan Todd, the lead singer from hit eighties band Rock Shop. 'Claudia,' she boomed, 'stop teasing Ryan with your heavenly curves and find me some PEOPLE for the booth. You are meant to be working you know.' The blonde girl sauntered off, rolling her eyes.

Lily spotted Araminta Winters ushering a model and telephone entrepreneur into the photo booth. She waited for her moment to pounce.

'Araminta, I'm sorry to disturb you. I'm Lily Cane from *The London Evening News*. I wrote the obituary on your sister. I just wanted to pass on my condolences.'

'Hello. Nice to meet you,' said Araminta, her big blue eyes welling up. 'I'm sorry, I can't talk about it. It's too soon.' She pushed her red wayfarers back on. 'I am so shocked and upset. I shouldn't really be here tonight but I came to help the magazine out.'

A Rastafarian patted her on the shoulder. 'Minty, babe, please stop ignoring my calls. I've got to talk to you urgently. You've no idea how many strings I've pulled to get here tonight,' he said in a South London accent.

'Back off, Mo,' she spat.

'Minty, no, it's not what you think,' he said pleadingly, looking genuinely upset.

'Excuse us,' she said to Lily, walking off to a deserted bit of lawn with Mo, where they continued to have a very heated discussion.

Lily's attention was drawn to the girl with the short peroxide hair who had come up behind Flavia and pinched her bottom.

'Rocky! At last, some youth and looks,' shrieked Flavia. 'Dennis, darling,' she cooed at Dennis Hopper. 'There is no beauty without decay. I have a youthful siren and a veteran rock star for you,' she said, proudly pushing a disgruntled looking Ryan into the booth with Rocky. When Lily turned to see if Araminta was free she noticed that Sophie Hamilton-Bruce had joined her and the two of them were having a full on argument with the Rastafarian.

11

It was half past nine and the party was in full swing. Lily walked around drinking it all in. It was beginning to get dark and people were mooching about in their social groups. She spotted Brit artist Ron Smile who was famous for making huge, shiny, plastic sculptures of household objects. He was larking around with Hans Rikiv, a German artist who famously only painted in yellow. Araminta was successfully persuading them to come and pose for a picture.

'Only if you'll sit on my knee, darling,' said Ron.

Lily walked through the Eliasson and Thorsen designed pavilion that housed the dance floor where Sophie was dancing provocatively with the handsome black heartthrob Matthew Miles, wrapping her leopard-print Louis Vuitton scarf around his neck and pulling him towards her. Oscar, meanwhile, was leering at Matthew's friend a handsome, dark-haired actor called Toby Creswell. Oscar grabbed the scarf and began to capture Toby in it. Toby quickly fashioned it Laurence of Arabia style round his head. They all laughed and carried on dancing. Lily walked past and into the gallery itself where a throng of partygoers were watching two attractive girls eating baby food. The girls were Dutch conceptual artists Adalind Janssen and Hanneke Brouwer, and were performing their latest work, *Ages of Man*.

'I don't really get this performance art,' guffawed a red-faced hooray to another man in a suit. 'I bought a ticket because I heard the girls are hot. Those artists are damn strange but bloody attractive.' Lily went to see if she could find any evidence of Sam's 'decadent London' in the ladies. She opened the door and stood in line. There were nine women waiting. The door crashed open. It was Rocky, the girl with the peroxide hair.

'Ronnie. Are you in here?' she bellowed in her husky voice.

'Oui,' replied a soft, gentle voice from the middle cubicle. Rocky went over to the cubicle and knocked.

'Toot toot, darling.' The door opened and she slipped in.

Ten minutes later Lily emerged from the ladies. The two Dutch artists had now reached middle age in their life cycle and were watching a DVD box-set on a sofa. Their audience had, unsurprisingly, dwindled to three. Lily went on the hunt for Jonathan; it was dark now and the dance floor was pumping. As she walked around the side of the pavilion she noticed a couple kissing in the hay bales that had been fashioned into a chill-out area. It was Claudia, the curvaceous blonde from *Society*, and the artist who only painted in yellow.

Lily found Jonathan talking to a sexy redhead by the bar.

'Found any cokeheads?' he asked. The woman walked off looking miffed.

'Plenty! The loo is like Noah's ark. They all go in two by two.'

At that point Ron Smile came up to the bar looking dishevelled and ordered a double vodka on the rocks.

'Hello, Ron. Jonathan Kindel from *The London Evening News*. Are you enjoying yourself tonight?'

'Oh yes,' he replied, suddenly staring into the middle distance. He wolf-whistled. Lily turned to see Veronique walking towards him. She did a flirty little twirl on the way. She had the confident swagger of someone who knew they were beautiful.

'This man is a genius,' she said in her breathy French accent. 'He designed my last album cover as a favour and I loved it. It was so sexy.' She pulled out a packet of Gauloises cigarettes from her Chanel bag.

'Oh, give us a fag, darling,' said Ron.

'So, what are you working on at the moment?' Jonathan asked Ron.

'I'm working on *the* pair of tits. I intend to make the biggest, most perfect pair of tits in the world,' said Ron, raising his hands to squeeze a pair of imaginary breasts. 'In fact, I have been doing a little bit of empirical research this evening.'

'Ooh la la, baby,' Veronique laughed coquettishly.

'My God, you're sexy,' growled Ron.

'Are the giant tits a statement about celebrity culture?' asked Jonathan earnestly.

'That's right. An hommage to Jordan,' scoffed Ron, who walked off to join fellow hell-raiser Mark Spudd.

'How's the new album coming along?' Jonathan asked Veronique politely.

'I've just finished it. Who knows what it will be like,' she replied shyly. 'I only arrived in London today. I haven't been for a while, so it is nice to come and see everyone here.' Sophie Hamilton-Bruce had walked up behind her and was leaning on her shoulder, tickling Veronique's face with her scarf.

'Did you only arrive yesterday, V? I thought Seb said you came last week?'

'No; I was planning to but then I needed a bit more time to put the finishing touches on the album.' Sophie looked momentarily confused. Lily looked up and caught Sébastien's eye as he walked towards them with Araminta. Her stomach began performing somersaults and she felt uncharacteristically nervous. What the hell was happening? He kissed Veronique on the lips and immediately some photographers circled.

'I've managed the impossible, Ronnie. Flavia and I managed to get Seb into the booth!' said Araminta proudly.

'Only because I wanted to meet Dennis Hopper,' replied Sébastien. 'I squinted on purpose, so you won't be able to put it in your magazine.'

'Oh, the joys of Photoshop, my friend. We'll get you in,' joked Araminta. At this point, Mo the Rastafarian came up to them and gave Sébastien a high-five.

'Hey, handsome,' he said, smiling.

'Seb, Mo, this is the journalist who broke the story of Zuleika's death in *The London Evening News*,' said Araminta, shooting them a warning look. 'What's your name again?'

'Lily.'

'Hello,' they said. 'I didn't know Zuleika well, but what a tragedy,' said Sébastien.

'It's a fucking disaster and I think there are a lot of things we don't know,' said Mo with feeling.

'What on earth do you mean?' said Araminta.

'I think it is unlikely that she died of a cocaine overdose.'

'Well, you would think that,' replied Araminta.

'Let's see what the post-mortem throws up,' Mo said forcefully.

'By the way, there was one thing I didn't agree with in your article,' Araminta said, turning on Lily sharply. 'Zuleika didn't play chess. I'd never heard that before.'

'She did. She talked to me about a new chessboard she was getting that posh furniture designer Linley to make. I played with her a few times. She was surprisingly good,' said Mo. Sébastien and Araminta looked taken aback.

'Her tutor, Dr Bone, said it was a recent thing,' replied Lily, who noticed that Sophie was listening intently. The conversation was interrupted by the arrival of a man with a nimbus of ice-blonde hair. He gave Sébastien's hunky shoulder a hearty slap.

'Hello, Seb. Hello, Minty. Hello, Sophie, darling!' he said in a slick, velvety voice.

'Hi, George,' said Sébastien smoothly. 'We're looking forward to you and Torquil's party in Ibiza.' Lily made a mental note to text Billy that she had met someone who actually knew someone called Torquil.

'Oh my God,' replied George, waving his hands around in the air excitedly. 'We are going to get mashed up. Mo is going to introduce us to a "friend" in Ibiza.' At which point Araminta kicked him. He carried on oblivious. 'We've got lots of hot chicks coming. I've hired the biggest sound system on the island. I've got Dalston "Hot" Davis to come after his set at Space and also, Seb, I thought we'd spin some tunes. It's going to be crazy, man.' At this point Araminta interrupted and said pointedly, 'Have you met Lily from *The London Evening News*?'

'Hi,' said Lily, giving him a cheesy smile.

'Hi,' said George stonily. He immediately made his excuses and left. Araminta followed and George whispered in too loud a voice, 'Minty, why didn't you warn me she was a bloody journalist?'

'I tried to. Don't lay into me George. I'm fragile.'

'I know. Sorry, darling,' he said, not sounding sorry at all and began talking about himself. The whole group walked off towards the dance floor.

'No guessing what they're getting up to in Ibiza,' Lily said to Jonathan. 'Talking of which, I'm going to go on the hunt for some Bacchanalian behaviour for Sam.'

'Sounds fun. Mind if I join you?' asked Jonathan, running his hand down Lily's side. 'This is the last thing I need,' thought Lily. Jonathan dragged her on to the packed dance floor. Sophie, Araminta, Sébastien, the effete George, Veronique and Oscar were all dancing in a group. Sophie was still using her scarf as a dance prop, wrapping it around everyone. Rocky pushed past Lily and Jonathan and began dancing with Veronique. They hammed it up for the paparazzi who went into overdrive. Sébastien looked unimpressed, tapped Mo on the shoulder and they walked off.

'Who is that girl?' Lily asked Jonathan.

'Rocky is Wolf Star's daughter. She has followed in her dad's footsteps and is in a rock band.'

Rocky was breakdancing in the middle of the dance floor. Everyone was clapping and egging her on. The two young actors, Toby Creswell and Matthew Miles, came into the middle to dance with her, joining her in the breakdancing. Rocky revelled in the attention, encouraged by Flavia Wilde, who kept whooping enthusiastically. Rocky stood up and did a handstand so that her neon pink polka-dot knickers were on full display. Matthew Miles clapped in delight and when Rocky found her feet they began passionately snogging.

Claudia appeared, looking red-faced.

'What have you been up to? You look indecently flushed,' said Flavia in an accusatory fashion.

'Ha ha. We've just finished packing up the photo booth. Dennis Hopper has so much equipment. We just lugged all of it to the location van. I need a drink to recover.'

'And a back rub?' asked Ryan Todd, massaging Claudia's shoulders. She looked mildly embarrassed and shot Flavia a 'save me' look. Flavia cackled and floated off in the opposite direction to dance with Araminta.

'It's been a fun party,' Lily said to Jonathan. 'Much better than I thought it would be.'

'Want a nightcap? My flat's a five-minute taxi ride away.'

'Thank you, but I think I am going to call it a night.' Lily walked to the main gallery to get her coat. There was already a long queue and as she waited she turned around and saw George Lazarus, Mo and the two Dutch artists coming out of the disabled loo. As George walked out the door he gave a massive sniff and then his nose gave an involuntary twitch. Sam was right: society London was under a cocaine blizzard.

12

Lily was sitting in the kitchen with a stinking hangover, munching on a piece of toast, when her mobile rang.

'Lily, it's Sam. You've got to get to the Serpentine Gallery right now. Sophie Hamilton-Bruce's body has just been discovered. It looks like she's been murdered. There'll be a press conference at ten but get down there pronto. Say you were there last night and see if you can get the inside track. Did you talk to her?'

'Sam, this is awful. I can't believe it. Yes, I did talk to her.'

'Brilliant, blondie! We've got a scoop. Anything strike you as odd about her? Any weird behaviour?'

'No. Not that I noticed,' said Lily, trying to gather her thoughts. 'Actually, she was saddened and surprised by Zuleika Winters's death.'

'You know what, Lily, there might be a connection. See what you can find out. Make sure you file by lunchtime. I want it in tonight. Everyone will run it – the murder is on the wires. Also watch out for the crime reporters on *The Post* – they're ruthless bastards and will be all over it. The coppers always tip them off first as they pay the most. Ricky our crime guy will attend the conference so see what you can find out before. Oh, and try and befriend the coppers.'

The scene at the Serpentine couldn't have been more different from that of the previous evening: debris from the party was strewn all over the lawn and the whole perimeter of the gallery had been cordoned off with blue and white police incident tape. A couple of police officers were standing at the gate and others were combing the ground for

43

clues. The main hive of activity was around *Society*'s photo booth where Lily could see a few senior-looking policemen in white paper suits and masks standing outside talking to someone inside.

'Excuse me, miss, nobody is allowed access to this area,' said a young Asian police constable.

'Hello, I'm Lily Cane from *The London Evening News*. I think I might be able to help you, I was here last night - I spoke to the victim a few times.' The policeman scratched his head.

'Hang on a minute. Let me check with the Commander.' The policeman ducked under the tape and went to speak to a portly gentleman in his fifties. The man looked around at Lily and said something to a stocky, mousy-haired man in his early forties standing next to him, who began to walk over with the younger officer.

'Hello, miss. How can I help you?'

'Hello, sir, I'm Lily Cane from *The London Evening News*. I was here at the party last night and I spoke to Sophie. I thought I might be able to help you.'

'And get some information for your paper no doubt. Nice try, love. I've already turned away two reporters from *The Post* and one from the *Daily Chronicle*. As I said to them, the press conference is at ten at Scotland Yard. We're trying to work on a murder inquiry here. If you need to speak to someone, contact one of our press liaison officers.' The policeman looked up at Lily and then said, 'Lily Cane,' and repeated her name again. 'Didn't I speak to you the other day about Lady Zuleika Winters? I'm Detective Chief Superintendent Peters, Scotland Yard.'

'Yes, hello, that was me,' replied Lily, giving him a flirtatious smile, 'Are you sure this is murder?'

'Oh yes – one hundred per cent certain. It's a gruesome scene,' said Peters, relenting a bit. He had a kind face. His grey-blue eyes were surrounded by wrinkles. He looked like a man used to carrying stress on his wide shoulders.

'How was she murdered?'

'Everything will be revealed in the press conference. Come on, you know how this rolls, Lily. Are you new? I don't recognise you from the press pack. I'd remember a face like yours.'

'New to crime,' said Lily, smiling. 'I'll need a bit of help.'

'Hmm,' said Peters, as he took in Lily with his eyes. 'Well, as you're new…I'll help you out this once – she was strangled.'

'Strangled?' exclaimed Lily. 'With what?'

'I can't discuss that with you at the moment: it's sensitive information.' Lily nodded in acceptance and then suddenly she had a flashback of Sophie wrapping her Louis Vuitton leopard-print 'It' scarf around the actors on the dance floor with Oscar Rutherford.

'She was strangled with her leopard-print scarf, wasn't she?' said Lily.

The inspector's eyes flashed. 'Why would you think that, miss?'

'She was wrapping it around everyone on the dance floor. You know the kind of thing, throwing it around people's necks and then pulling them towards her.'

'Get the chief and forensics here now! Patel,' said DCS Peters to the junior officer, 'it looks like you may be able to help us after all,' and he ushered her under the tape.

The older police officer and a dark bespectacled man in a paper suit walked towards them.

'Jeffrey, what's going on? This is most irregular. We can't have press actually entering the crime scene,' he said authoritatively.

'Sir, this is Lily Cane from *The LEN*. She was here last night and says that Sophie was dancing with a number of people on the dance floor with her scarf.'

'You didn't tell her the suspected murder weapon?'

'No, she guessed it herself.'

'Oh yes,' said the man, looking over his spectacles at Lily. 'I'm Commander Jaggs from Scotland Yard CID. Lily, I need you to tell Dr Philips here, our chief forensic medical examiner, exactly what you saw Sophie doing with the scarf.' Lily repeated what she had told Superintendent Peters.

'How many people do you think touched the scarf?' asked the doctor.

'I saw her wrap it around Matthew Miles, Toby Creswell, Oscar Rutherford but then later on she was using it again on everyone in her group.'

'How many people roughly?' pressed Dr Philips.

'Well at least eight, if not more,' said Lily.

'Christ,' replied Dr Philips. 'I need a bigger team.'

'This is a bloody dog's dinner,' said the Commander.

'We need to find that scarf,' said Dr Philips with urgency.

'The scarf isn't there?' asked Lily.

'No,' replied Jaggs, 'but you have just helped us identify the most likely murder weapon. We suspected it was a scarf. What colour was it?'

'It was a red, leopard-print Louis Vuitton scarf. I'm sure their press office could send you some images and there will be photos of Sophie wearing it from last night.'

'Is there anything else you can tell us? What time did you last see her?'

'I left around midnight. Sophie had been dancing with her friends near where my colleague and I were hanging out, but then she walked off when this blonde girl began flirting with Matthew Miles, the guy she was dancing with. I don't think it was a big deal: I don't think they were going out or anything.'

'She must have been killed around that time,' said the doctor thinking aloud.

'You mean she was killed when we were all here? How? Surely someone would have noticed?'

'Well, you might have thought so,' said Jaggs, 'but no one reported anything and the body wasn't discovered until six o'clock this morning when they came to take the booth away. How loud was the music?'

'Very loud, you wouldn't have heard a scream from the dance floor. You could hardly hear yourself speak. It was all kicking off and people were really going for it.'

'Lily, I'm going to ask you to come and have a chat,' said DCS Peters.

13

DSC Peters and Lily strolled up the path to the gallery, Peters nodding at his colleagues en route.

'The gallery will be closed for the next few days; we've taken it over. We can't have the public traipsing through the murder scene.'

'Are you working on the assumption someone broke in?' asked Lily.

'No. We'll concentrate on the people who attended the party first because a lot of them would have known the victim. We're talking to the security guards but there are no reports of gatecrashers

– although they wouldn't know about the successful ones of course. Also, Sophie is much more likely to have been murdered by someone she knew. In ninety-five per cent of murders the victim knows their killer.' Lily looked at Peters. She couldn't imagine any of the people she had spoken to the night before being capable of killing anyone.

'How is the CCTV?'

'It doesn't cover the corner of the garden where the booth is,' replied DCS Peters, rolling his eyes. 'There isn't normally a structure there.'

They walked into a small room on the right-hand side of the gallery, which had been turned into a temporary police incident room. Lily and Peters sat down. At that moment a young policewoman came in with two hot instant coffees for them.

'Thanks, Jill,' said Peters.

'Was this a sexual attack?' asked Lily.

'No, it doesn't look like it. We'll wait for the pathology to be certain.'

'Could it have been an accident? Could it have been a sex thing that went wrong? It just seems so strange.' Peters shook his head vigorously; he was obviously holding something back. 'What is it?' asked Lily widening her big blue eyes.

'Hmm, I'm not sure if we're going to release this. The Commander's now saying we will, so I suppose there is no harm in telling you, but you'll owe me. Her body was arranged as if she was posing for a photograph in the booth.' Lily gasped in horror.

'How do you mean?'

'Well, her body was propped up on the sofa, one arm was resting along the top and the other was kind of propping her up with the help of a cushion. Her skirt was hitched up and she was made to look like she was showing her legs off. One shoe was artfully arranged so it was just hanging off her toes. She was arranged in a provocative manner. We think the murderer may have reapplied her lipstick, as it looked fresh and perfect – but there was no sign of it in her handbag. We did find a wrap of cocaine in her bag, which is interesting, as by all accounts she had stopped all that. So it will be interesting to see what the toxicology tests reveal.'

'Gosh,' said Lily taking it all in. 'She didn't seem like she was on drugs. This is like something out of a Hollywood movie. That arrangement of the body suggests to me that the killer is someone who knows this "society" world.'

47

'Perhaps,' replied Peters. 'Now, can you tell me who she was hanging out with so we can begin taking statements from people?'

'Yes, of course.'

Lily spent the next half an hour talking Peters through all the people she had recognised who'd been at the party. 'Will you speak to every guest?' she asked.

'Yes, Lily, they were at a crime scene. There'll be a lot of publicity about this case and it will give people the jitters. How many people do you think went into the photo booth?'

'I have no idea, a lot. You'll have to speak to the people who work at *Society* magazine. They were manning it all night. I suppose all their DNA will be in there.'

'Yup,' said DCS Peters. 'A lot of them sat on the sofa, touched the walls, etc. when they were posing for the photos. This is a very difficult case for the forensics.'

'Do you think there is any connection between this and Lady Zuleika Winters?'

'Why do you say that?'

'It's just I didn't get the impression that Sophie was convinced by the verdict that Zuleika had died of a cocaine overdose. I don't think she knew her well but she said she'd filmed her recently and that Zuleika seemed very together. Detective, Sophie having cocaine just doesn't gel with me. She didn't look like she was on drugs last night. She was so vocally anti-them. She seemed like a person who had come to the end of the road with all that. I think there could be a link.'

'I doubt it, Lily. Don't let the desire for a good story cloud your judgement. I suspect it's pure coincidence. Although, I admit it is a little odd that two women who were of such a similar profile have died in the space of a week. We will know more when the results of Zuleika's post-mortem are back. We're hoping to have them today. They got mislaid at the lab, unfortunately, which is why they are taking so long.'

'Well, I think we'll be interviewing the same people but for different reasons,' joked Lily. 'Of course you'll have an advantage because at least they have to talk to you!'

'That's true. Who will be your first point-of-call?'

'Her co-star on that fashion programme, Oscar Rutherford, and her cousin, a French count called Sébastien something-or-other, his girlfriend Veronique Lapin and Lady Araminta Winters, Zuleika's half-sister. All the people she was hanging around with.'

'Veronique Lapin that pretty singer?' asked Peters, his interest piqued.

'That's the one.' Lily looked at Peters, trying to gauge how much more information about the murder she could squeeze out of him. 'Do you think you're dealing with a potential serial killer?'

'I think that is rather dramatic at this stage. You hacks!' He chortled. 'I've already had Sean at *The Post* on to me about that. You've all been watching too many thrillers. However, we are dealing with a cold-blooded killer. The way he or she arranged the victim's body in that cruel, mocking way suggests a hatred for her or for this world. Also, the fact they chose to do this heinous act at such a public event might suggest that they get off on the danger of being caught, but I'm not a psychologist.'

'Maybe the killer thought there was so much going on at the party that no one would notice. They managed it, didn't they?'

'I can tell you are new to this,' said Peters patronisingly, 'give us a chance! We only found out about this murder a couple of hours ago. It's much harder than you think to kill someone, Lily. There were hundreds of people at this event, some of whom must know something. We will find out who did this. Also, crime scenes talk, as does the body itself. The murderer always leaves vital clues even if he or she thinks they don't. Commander Jaggs is a professional and we've got a crack team of forensics: they're world class. We'll do everything in our power to catch this killer.' He scratched his head then rather abruptly said, 'Thank you for your help, Lily. This is my mobile number. We may be able to help each other. You'll be running first on this so I hope you will repay me by keeping me up to speed with anything you think might be relevant.'

'Absolutely,' she said shaking Peters's hand.

Lily walked out of the Serpentine feeling ecstatic before reminding herself that someone had been murdered. She walked to where her scooter was parked and called Sam. Tracey put her straight through.

'Hit me with it, blondie.'

'Sam, she was strangled in the *Society* magazine photo booth with her Louis Vuitton scarf and her body was arranged as if she were posing for a picture.' Sam whistled.

'This is big, Lily. We haven't had a juicy case like this for donkey's years. Did they say it might be a serial killer?'

'Not yet, but they aren't ruling it out.'

'That's how you sell papers, baby,' said Sam. 'Sure you're not murdering them to get your name in the paper?'

'I was getting desperate,' said Lily, fantasising about pushing Kate down an empty lift-shaft.

'OK, I want two things from you Lily: a front page story with the facts for Ricky Flynn, the crime editor, and then an in-depth piece, "my night with Sophie Hamilton-Bruce at the Serpentine". Get the picture desk to get all the pap shots of her from last night. We've got to own this. Go and introduce yourself to Ricky the moment you're back. He's up to speed and will be overseeing all the coverage.'

Lily had been wondering how long it would be before the paper's crime reporters stepped in. She reassured herself that she had something none of the other journalists on the paper would have – she was actually there when Sophie was murdered. She jumped on to her scooter and whizzed down Hyde Park Gate like a bat out of hell.

Socialite Found Strangled at Serpentine Party
Police to question all the guests who attended last night's £400–a–ticket glitzy function
By Lily Cane
THURSDAY 12TH JULY 2007

Police launched a murder inquiry today after 'It' girl and TV presenter Sophie Hamilton-Bruce's body was discovered at the Serpentine Gallery following last night's summer fundraising party. The strangled body of the thirty-five-year-old Fashion Addicts presenter was found at six o'clock this morning in Society magazine's custom-built photo booth, where veteran Hollywood movie star Dennis Hopper, was taking portraits of the glamorous partygoers...

14
New Scotland Yard, 10am, Friday 13th July 2007

It was boiling hot in the press conference room at Scotland Yard. The windowless room was much smaller than Lily had imagined. There was a throng of male journalists all dressed in drab, grey suits, chatting with one another at high volume. Despite the tense atmosphere, Lily could sense the camaraderie among them – there was lots of jostling and ribbing. In the front right-hand side of the room stood the TV journalists with their cameras at the ready – they stood apart from the press journalists. The room was lined with tight rows of blue, plastic chairs, which faced a podium with three places and three microphones. Behind the podium was a very large white billboard, which was plastered with 'Metropolitan Police' in big blue letters and a repeated image of the New Scotland Yard logo.

Lily spotted Ricky Flynn, who she had met briefly the day before, holding court in the middle of the press throng. At 6' 3" he towered above the other hacks. She knew she had to infiltrate the throng so she pushed her way into the midst of them to go and say hello. Ricky was talking to a stocky man with a salt and pepper grade two buzz cut and a very strong South London accent.

'You guys have stolen a march on us this time, Ricky,' said the man, raising an eyebrow and pursing his thin lips.

'No tip-off for *The Post* and one pissed off copper who hasn't got his free summer holiday,' quipped Ricky. Lily detected an ever so slight Yorkshire accent. 'Bribery doesn't work every time, Sean! *The LEN* doesn't pay for stories. We get them through good, old-fashioned journalism.'

'Yeah right, Ricky. Pull the other one. You're just jealous you don't have any wonga to pay for tip-offs,' gloated the smug reporter from *The Post*.

'Hi, Ricky,' said Lily, interjecting.

'Hello, Lily,' he said, running his hand through his shock of blonde hair. 'Sean, this is the young lady who broke the scoop and, guess what? She doesn't even work on crime.'

'Hi, I'm Sean,' he nodded, shooting her a cursory glance. 'Good to have some more chicks on board. The coppers love a bit of feminine charm; we always have one bird on the crime desk for that reason.'

'Ricky, I haven't done one of these before. Is there a strict procedure?'

'Normally, the first half is on the record and is filmed and the second part is when the fun starts. That's the off the record part when we get to ask questions and try and build a story,' he replied.

'And cut out the TV guys,' interrupted Sean aggressively. 'Lily, it's all about the detail, the special angle. We all huddle round the police like the tough motherfuckers that we are and cut out the telly guys.'

'You're kidding me,' said Lily.

'No, he's right,' replied Ricky. 'The TV guys ask their questions and then we go in for the kill. It's called a pack job. We're all very mature here in crime.'

'Us crime reporters hunt in a pack. Then we all go to the boozer after and work on our line. There is nothing like a good murder to catch up with our partners in crime. It's a bit early today. They've done that on purpose so we don't take the coppers out for a swift one.'

Two female police officers walked in. One was in her early twenties, the other was older with severely cropped, sandy hair. A weary looking DCS Peters and an imposing Commander Jaggs followed. Jaggs's uniform was freshly starched and his long stride and portly frame lent him a certain *gravitas*.

'If you could all take your seats,' said the younger police woman. 'As per usual, the first part of the conference will be on the record and then we'll ask you to turn your cameras off. For those of you who don't know me, my name is Mary Liddiard and I am one of the press liaison officers working on this case. If you need any images do come and get a disc from me at the end of the conference.' She walked up to the podium and slotted large nametags identifying DCS Peters, Commander Jaggs and the family liaison officer, Detective Constable Helen Jones, in front of them.

All the journalists were now shoehorned into the tight rows of blue plastic chairs. Only the cameramen were standing at the front.

'Good morning,' said Jaggs in an imposing voice, 'I am Commander Jaggs. Can I start by thanking you all for coming here today. As a result of yesterday's conference the public have come up with some promising leads, which Detective Chief Superintendent Peters and his team are investigating at the moment. We have not yet found the murder weapon but we think that it was the red Louis Vuitton leopard-print scarf that the victim was wearing to the event. We have released an image of Sophie wearing the scarf at the party. Did anyone who attended the event see anyone other than Sophie with this scarf? If so, we would very much like to hear from you. We will be interviewing everyone who attended the party but we ask anyone who was there, who we have not yet contacted, to please get in touch with us. I am pleased to announce we have fifty officers working on this case, all of whom are committed to finding Sophie's killer.' He stopped for a breath and took a gulp of water.

'As we stated yesterday, the murderer arranged Sophie's body as if she was posing for a photograph in *Society*'s photo booth. We are also now almost certain that the killer reapplied Sophie's lipstick to her lips, after he or she murdered her. Like the scarf, the lipstick was nowhere to be found at the murder scene. We have found out that the lipstick she was wearing was by make-up brand Mac and was called Ruby Woo. This comes in a plain black case, like this.' He held up a nondescript lipstick and took off the lid to show the cameras its bright red colour.

'The press liaison officers have images of the lipstick and the scarf. We need to find these items and we ask the public and all who attended the event to be vigilant. Both these items hold vital clues. Finally, I can reveal that a wrap of cocaine was found in Sophie's clutch bag. However, the toxicology report shows that she had not consumed any. Would anyone who might have any information about why she might have this and how she obtained it, please contact us immediately.' Jaggs looked up at the TV cameras.

'Our primary objective is to find the killer who committed this senseless murder. I'm afraid I am unable to give any more details of the police investigation at this point, but I assure you we are following all lines of enquiry. I would like to make an appeal to everyone who attended Wednesday night's party at the Serpentine Gallery to rack your brains for any peculiar behaviour you may have observed, however trivial it may seem. It would have taken the killer at least seven minutes to commit this atrocity. Somebody at the party must have noticed someone acting strangely. Did someone you were with disappear for a short period of time between eleven and midnight? Did you see anyone hanging around the photo booth? Did someone you know have something, which could have been Sophie's scarf, hidden in their pocket or handbag? We need to hear from you as soon as possible. I am now going to hand over to the family liaison officer working on the case, Detective Constable Helen Jones, who has a message from the Hamilton-Bruce family.'

DC Jones looked up and gave a cursory smile.

'Good morning,' she said in a whiny, estuary accent. 'I want to start by saying our thoughts are with Sophie's family and the people who knew her. Her parents Major and Mrs Hamilton-Bruce have given the following statement. "On Wednesday evening our beloved daughter was taken from us by a ruthless killer. It is our belief that this was not a random attack and we think she must have known her killer. We beg all her friends and acquaintances to think if there was anything troubling her in the weeks and days leading up to her death. It doesn't matter how mundane it may seem, it could be important. All we want is for the killer to be brought to justice."'

DC Jones handed back to Jaggs who looked like he was about to drop a bombshell.

'Detective Chief Superintendent Peters, has some information on the recent death of Lady Zuleika Winters.' Peters stepped forward and gave a gruff cough to clear his throat. The unforgiving lights in the room illuminated the cluster of wrinkles that surrounded his eyes like tree rings.

'As a result of the autopsy performed on the late Lady Zuleika Winters, we can now reveal that the cause of death was a cardiac arrest brought on by strychnine poisoning rather than a cocaine overdose as previously reported. However, as the strychnine was mixed in with the cocaine, it is unclear at the moment whether Lady Zuleika was the intended murder victim or an unlucky victim of circumstance. What we need to establish is whether Zuleika bought some "dirty cocaine" cut with strychnine or if somebody added the strychnine to her cocaine on purpose at a later date. If you know who might have supplied her with the drug, please do not hesitate to contact the Metropolitan Police. Thank you.'

'I hasten to add that we do not think the cases are necessarily linked at the moment,' said Jaggs. 'However, we find the fact that a wrap of cocaine was left in Sophie's clutch bag suspicious, in light of the fact she no longer took the drug. Furthermore, the ladies had very similar, social profiles and it is strange that they have both been murdered in the space of a week. So we have put an additional team of officers on the cases to investigate if there is a possible link.' Mary Liddiard then signalled for the cameras to be switched off and the first half of the press conference ended. Lily looked at Ricky who whistled. Sean surged forward like a bull in the crowd at Pamplona, pushing everyone out of his way in order to speak to Jaggs and Peters. Ricky and Lily followed in hot pursuit. Lily found it hard to keep up as the other crime reporters elbowed their way forward. She had to duck under the arm of a lippy guy from *The Echo* to catch up with Ricky and Sean.

'Do you have any suspects?' boomed Sean.

'We have some promising leads,' replied Jaggs.

'Has anyone been brought in for questioning on either case?' interjected Ricky.

'We are conducting interviews at the moment with people who attended the event but, as I just said, we are still investigating the leads.'

'Just to be clear, Commander, you have no suspects at this time?' said Sean, obviously enjoying himself.

'That is correct,' he replied.

'Superintendent Peters, have you had any luck finding anything on the CCTV footage from Wednesday night?' shouted a man at the back of the throng.

'We have a team combing the footage but it is limited and, unfortunately, doesn't cover the photo booth.'

At this point Ricky interjected. 'Are there any forensic leads from the booth?'

'This is a very difficult case forensically as so many people entered the booth over the course of the evening. We have a list from *Society* magazine of everyone they photographed and we are interviewing them. We are dealing with a forensically aware killer,' replied Peters.

'Do you actually have any forensic leads?' asked the reporter from *The Statesman*.

'The team are working incredibly hard,' said Peters. 'The problem is most of the men at the party were wearing suits and the suit fibres are very similar. It looks like the murderer wore surgical gloves when he or she committed the murder. We did think this suggested it was a premeditated attack until we discovered the performance artists were using them in their artwork, so the killer could have taken a pair. We know a number of people touched Sophie's scarf on Wednesday night as we have reports that she was wrapping it around other guests on the dance floor. Some of their DNA may have transferred on to her clothes.'

'Do you have any possible motives for the murder?' interjected a bald man from *The Star*.

'Not as yet,' replied Peters, 'I can reveal that the inquest into Zuleika's death will be held next Tuesday.'

'Did they have any boyfriends in common? Anything like that?' asked Sean. 'Could it have been a jilted lover?'

'We are investigating all avenues,' replied Peters.

'I think that is all the questions we have time for today,' said Jaggs forcefully. 'Thank you all for coming and we will continue to keep you informed. The most important message to get out there is that somebody must know something. Also, as DCS Peters said, anyone who might know who supplied the cocaine to Lady Zuleika Winters or Sophie Hamilton-Bruce must come forward.' And with that he walked swiftly out, followed in quick succession by Peters and Constable Jones. Mary, the young press officer, stood at the podium handing out the discs with the images of the murder weapon and lipstick.

15

Half an hour later, Lily walked through the newsroom doors carrying her scooter helmet and a coffee. She spotted Ricky Flynn perching on the side of her desk talking to Sylvester. He was so tall that his long legs spilled over into Sylvester's side. They were discussing cricket scores.

'Hello, Lily,' said Ricky, running his large hand through his thick, blonde hair.

'Hi.'

'Interesting press conference, didn't you think? It's a bloody shambles, – the police obviously have no suspects and no idea what's going on,' he said confidently. He wasn't someone who held back his opinions.

'I think it's very tricky,' replied Lily. 'You should have seen how many people were at the party. She was letting everyone dance with that scarf and lots of people were in and out of the booth all night.'

'I forgot you were actually there.' Ricky bristled. 'I bet Dennis Hopper isn't happy that he was detained here for a few days. I've learnt he can now return to the US. I mean he is hardly a suspect.'

'Everyone has to be treated equally in a murder investigation, I suppose,' said Lily.

'Yes, that's the beauty of the English justice system, Lily,' he replied, throwing Sylvester a weary look. Lily hoped he wasn't going to be a problem. 'So, Lily, we've got to figure out how we are going to work together on this. I must say you have done a brilliant job. I think Sam has a plan. He didn't say what it is yet, but I know that man and he has the look of someone who has something up his sleeve. Obviously, my team are now taking over the crime reporting on the case. I think you'll be covering the features angles. I suppose you, Kate and I will have to keep in constant contact about what we're doing,' he said, lifting his shoulders. Lily's heart sank – was this a conspiracy? Kate would definitely try and get her thrown off the story.

'I haven't been dealing with Kate on this. I have been dealing with Sally,' said Lily sharply.

'Right,' said Ricky, looking taken aback. 'Well I'm sure she'll carry on overseeing it then. Listen, let's keep talking as you have a unique angle on this case and we need to milk that for all it's worth.' At that moment his phone went.

'Gregory Phillips, if it isn't my favourite pathologist. Thanks for calling me back, mate,' and with that, Ricky strode off down the office. Sylvester sensed Lily was downbeat and gave her a friendly, paternal squeeze.

'You shouldn't be upset about that Lily. It's his job. I would have been surprised if he didn't get put on the story – he is the crime editor after all. And he's a really nice guy. I think you'll enjoy working with him. You have made your mark with this. Sit tight – it's far from over.'

Lily and Billy were sitting in a couple of red deckchairs in Jazz and Johno's garden in Dalston. Johno, a gangly chap in his late twenties, was poking at some sausages on the barbeque with a long fork, every so often giving them sharp little jabs. Jazz, his raven-haired wife was perched on the table smoking a roll up. Lily was staring into space, moving her lips, when she suddenly said, 'What is the link between Sophie and Zuleika?'

'Not this again Lily!' said Billy, exasperated, 'She's been like this all weekend. She's covered the flat in spider diagrams trying to link these two murder victims. It's like living with Jane Tennison.'

'Got to love Helen Mirren,' said Jazz, trying to defuse the situation.

'Hmm,' said Lily, distracted. 'I was there Jazz – I was there when this girl was murdered. I probably spoke to the murderer and no one is any the wiser. The police know nothing. This happened on Wednesday night; it's now Sunday and there's no suspect, no answers. It's a mess. Can murder be so easy?'

'You've got to try and step back from it, Lily. You can't take it personally,' said Jazz giving her a friendly pat on the back. Lily flinched.

'What? Are you crazy? I am in it, Jazz! You can't just switch off murder. It's not some show on telly. This is the thing, guys: you are treating it like *Prime Suspect*, but I am living it. We are talking about two women who have been murdered for Christ's sake! I need to find out the truth. I'm on the scent. I know I must know something.' Lily nicked one of Billy's fags. Jazz rolled her eyes while Lily wasn't looking.

'Time for the steaks,' said Johno.

'I'll get them,' said Billy.

'Hang on. I'll give you the marinade,' said Jazz looking relieved for an excuse to escape into the kitchen.

Lily walked to the end of the garden with her fag and paced round and round. She felt bad for savaging her old friend but she couldn't think about anything else. Were they random attacks by the same person? Did Sophie know something that caused her to be killed? Or was there no link beyond the fact the women were so similar?

58

Lily wolfed down her lunch and, the moment she could, she jumped on her trusty scooter and left. She had some serious thinking to do. This story was hers and she was damned if she was going to let it go.

16

On Monday morning, Sam called Lily and Ricky into his office. Sally Shingle was there with the paper's associate editor, Piers Henderson, an incredibly thin man, with sharp eyes and a face like a buzzard. Sam had a crafty look in his eye and was buzzing with energy. Nothing got him going more than a good story. He still got the same excitement about running scoops as he did about breaking stories when he was a cub reporter on the *Finchley Express*.

'Right, guys, we have to own this society murders story. I am going to throw resources at it. It is clear the police are no further along. The first few days of a murder investigation are vital for the police and it seems they have diddly squat. It's a huge embarrassment – they have no suspects, no motives, nothing. Ricky, can you write a piece spelling out the forensic difficulties of the case? Explain again to our readers why it is so hard to get any clues because the murder scene was so contaminated. Lily, your task is trickier: you need to establish a link between the girls and come up with possible suspects.'

'Sam, it's harder than you think. We can't just begin naming their friends as suspects – we'll have writs flying round our ears. These are powerful people,' said Ricky.

'Patience, Ricky, my boy,' said Sam grinning, 'that is why I've come up with the idea of sending Miss Cane here undercover.' Lily couldn't believe her ears. 'OK, you two, I need you to work together. Leave your egos at the door. This paper is going to be the go-to publication for this case. It's clear the ranks are closing in. Society London is not helping the police or the press with this. It's beginning to look like Lord Lucan all over again. In fact, Sally, I'd like a piece on that for tonight from someone who was familiar with the Lucan case: a think piece from an old timer. Get Cobdon-

Manners on it.' He looked at Lily and Ricky again. 'Now, where was I? Yes, I was about to reveal my master plan: Lily, you are going to go and cover the position of features editor at *Society* magazine for a couple of months. I've swung it with the MD of Panther Publications, who owes me a favour and, as luck would have it, the features editor has glandular fever, so it will look legit. You will be in the heart of it, working there. One of the murdered girls' sisters works there, for Christ's sake! Find out the whos, the whys, the motives – and feed them back to Ricky. When you know enough you'll withdraw and bingo we'll have got our scoop.'

'Right,' said Lily, 'So will I be writing for them?'

'Yes: as far as they are concerned you are the new features editor. You write their stories but your real objective is these murders.'

'Brilliant, Sam!' said Ricky, thinking all his Christmases had come at once.

'When do I start?' said Lily.

'Next Monday,' replied Sam.

'Jesus,' said Ricky. 'You must have some sway with the MD.'

'Martin will benefit if we solve the case – I've agreed that you'll do an exclusive for *Society*, too, Lily. They're a monthly so it won't affect us.'

'What do I tell Kate and the features team?'

'I think we'll keep this arrangement on a need-to-know basis, journalists talk and the fewer people who know the better. Tell her you are off to *Society*.' Lily smiled. Kate obviously wasn't quite so in the inner sanctum as she thought she was. 'Ricky, when is the inquest into Lady Zuleika's death?'

'Tomorrow.'

'You'd better both go to that as you'll soon be going separate ways. Hopefully that might throw something up. Keep up the good work.' It was obvious the meeting was over and Ricky and Lily made their way out of Sam's office.

When they were along the corridor Ricky said, 'Put it here, partner,' and gave her a high-five. Lily humoured him, but she was unsure about this new arrangement. If she was going to put in all this effort she wanted recognition for her work.

For a bit of fun, Lily made her way over to Kate's desk to break the news of her imminent departure. To her delight Kate, Nick and Annie were all there – bitching about an excellent piece in *The Herald*.

'She's so overrated,' Lily heard Kate saying about the journalist who had written it.

'Hello, hello,' she said cheerily. Kate gave her a dismissive glance.

'Hi, crime cat,' said Nick. The other two cackled.

'Not for much longer,' replied Lily.

'Oh sorry, Lily,' said Kate jumping in. 'I heard that Ricky Flynn and his team are on the story now. He's the crime editor.' She turned to Annie and said, 'He's seriously talented and very experienced. You'd like him actually. He's a proper journo and he's single.'

'Oh well, old girl, you got some good mileage out of it,' said Nick. Lily shook her head in disbelief – she was beginning to enjoy herself.

'I think I may have some picture captions of the Olympic park for you to do,' said Kate maliciously. 'A bit of a bump down to earth for our budding crime correspondent.'

'Actually, I'm leaving.'

'Oh dear,' said Kate interrupting her, 'I thought this might happen, I have saved you a couple of times.' She stood up and went through the charade of giving her a sympathetic hug. Lily thought nothing could be further from the truth, if anything Kate would have put her name forward for the sack.

'No, Kate, I haven't been made redundant. I'm off to be features editor at *Society* magazine.'

'Wow,' said Nick, 'good for you.'

'Well done, Lily,' said Kate through pursed lips. 'I told you to go to a monthly – it's more your pace. I'm glad you followed my advice.'

'I've managed the deadlines on these murder pieces fine Kate. I don't know what you're talking about, but if you want to think that, you carry on. Anyway, Friday's my last day and I'm still working on the murders until then. I'll do the captions if you like but I'm sure Nick can help you out. He doesn't seem to be working on anything exciting at the moment.' Lily strode off and as she went she heard Kate say, 'Not so quick, missy. What about your three months notice period?'

'All sorted with Sam,' said Lily, turning round to shoot Kate an affected smile. 'If you have a problem you can always take it up with him.'

17
Westminster Coroner's Court, 11am, Tuesday 17th July

Lily and Ricky Flynn walked out of the portico of Westminster Coroner's Court.

'What do you think?' asked Ricky.

'Did Zuleika buy some dodgy coke or did a scheming murderer kill her? I'm going for unlawful killing. Your Dr Philips nailed it with the evidence – why would a drug dealer lace the drug with strychnine, a poison that's really hard to get hold of? He's hardly going to source the poison from India to cut it in with his cocaine – it's too much effort and too expensive. Also, why would a dealer want to poison his clients? And if it was a contaminated batch, why hasn't anyone else had a similar reaction?'

'He's a great forensic,' replied Ricky. 'He nailed the murderer of Lizzie Kemp last year. It was all down to some DNA he found in the guy's car. He's methodical, a perfectionist.'

'I'd never heard of opisthotonus before. Can you imagine the pain of being bent over in agony like that?'

'No, thank God. It was heart failure that did for her, though. I'm with you – it'll be unlawful killing but it will be flipped on to the Crown Court as it will become a criminal investigation. If they ever arrest anyone, that is. Let's catch Peters.' Ricky walked over to Peters. 'If it isn't my favourite Detective at the Met.'

'Hello, Ricky,' nodded Peters. 'All right, Lily?'

'Good thanks,' replied Lily.

'Well?' said Ricky.

'Got to be murder, hasn't it? For a while I thought it was dodgy coke but the fact the cocaine is from the same batch that was left in Sophie Hamilton-Bruce's bag is just too much of a coincidence for me. Both women wound up dead – there has to be a connection. We're treating this case as murder now.'

'Can you prove it beyond reasonable doubt though?' mused Ricky.

'Hmm,' replied Peters. 'These girls sure lived racy lives.'

'Any luck with the list of people *Society* gave you?' asked Lily.

'You are a terrier, Lily! I just come out for a breather and boom! Here you are. You've got to watch this one, Ricky: she'll knock you off your perch,' chuckled Peters. 'But, in answer to your question, we've interviewed almost everyone who went into the booth and everyone says the same thing: they didn't know her well and how charming she was – which is a fat lot of use. I've interviewed the close friends and no one can think of any reason why she would be killed.'

'Unless she knew something about Zuleika,' said Lily.

'Quite,' said Peters. 'We're with you on this, Lily. I think there must be a link. I think it was an impulsive killing, despite the arrangement of the body.'

At this point the court was called in and the three of them made their way back into the impressive red brick building.

'Here we go,' said Ricky. 'As you're heading off to *Society*, Lily, why don't you write up the inquest? I'll look over it to check the tone is right as it's a reporting job rather than a feature.'

'Thanks,' said Lily, smiling. Sylvester was right – Ricky seemed like a decent guy.

It was Murder! Lady Zuleika Winters' overdose overturned
Inquest records unlawful killing verdict for Chelsea Socialite

By Lily Cane
TUESDAY 17TH JULY

Tests on fashion muse Lady Zuleika Winters show she died from heart failure as a result of taking cocaine laced with strychnine a coroner revealed today.

Simon Shakespeare, of Westminster Coroner's Court, said: 'Although it has been widely reported that the most likely cause of death was a cocaine overdose it now appears that that is not the case. The evidence from the post-mortem suggests that the fatal heart attack was actually caused by strychnine poisoning.'

The verdict of unlawful killing now turns this case into a murder inquiry...

63

18
Serpentine Gallery, 9am, Thursday 19th July

Lily walked around the garden of the Serpentine Gallery to see if it jogged her memory about anything that happened on the night of Sophie's murder. She strolled through the Eliasson and Thorsen pavilion that was still erected and traced her steps to where the bar had been. She closed her eyes and tried to remember. She recalled standing there with Jonathan, the diary editor, talking to the obnoxious Young British Artist Ron Smile. Then it all came flooding back: Veronique sauntering over, Sébastien and Araminta joining them and then the Rastafarian. What had he said about Zuleika? 'There are a lot of things we don't know.'

'You idiot, Lily,' she cursed herself. 'What did he know?' She immediately called Peters.

'Peters.'

'It's Lily Cane from *The LEN*.'

'It's all right. I know who you are now, Lily,' he replied. 'How can I help you?'

'Have you interviewed a Rastafarian who was hanging out with Sophie's group of friends?'

'Hmm, let me check with the others. Do you know his name?'

'I can't remember it but I'll call Oscar Rutherford: he'll know. Look, he said something about Zuleika, which in retrospect was strange. He said something along the lines of "there are a lot of things we don't know." Then Araminta said "well, you would say that."'

'OK, I'll get the team to look into it. We'll call Oscar and Araminta too – and get an ID on him.' Peters hung up.

Lily called Ricky who told her to find out his name immediately. Lily phoned Araminta – there was no answer, just a breathy message. Next she called Oscar Rutherford, who picked up immediately.

'Hello, Oscar speaking,' said a sharp, camp voice.

'Hi Oscar, it's Lily Cane. I don't know if you remember me? I was at the Serpentine Party the other night. I work for *The LEN.*'

'Oh hi,' said Oscar, sounding as if he didn't remotely remember or care who she was.

'I was talking to you and Sophie at the party.'

'I remember you. Why are you calling me? I don't want to think about that ghastly night. I've said everything I want to say to the press.'

'Oscar, who was the Rastafarian who was hanging out with your group of friends?'

'Mo?' replied Oscar.

'Yes, that's him. Who is he?'

'He's a DJ and cabbie.'

'He said something which I want to follow up on. Do you have his number?'

'No.'

'What's his surname?' she pressed.

'I don't know. Look, I don't know him well. He's just someone who's around.'

'Do you know who might have his number?'

'No,' said Oscar abruptly.

'What about one of the others? They seemed like they knew him well.'

'Why don't you ask them? Look I've got a call on the other line. It's my agent – I've got to go.'

Lily tracked down Sophie's cousin, the Count de Bourgogne's number. She'd seen him hanging out with Mo and thought he might have his number.

'Sébastien de Bourgogne,' he purred in his French accent.

'Hello, Sébastien, I'm Lily Cane from *The LEN*, I was at the Serpentine Party the other night. I was talking to your cousin. I'm so sorry by the way.'

'Of course,' he replied. 'It is a dreadful thing.' There was an awkward pause. 'How can I help you?'

'I am trying to get a number for Mo. I think he is a friend of yours?' said Lily.

'Ah. He is what you English call "an acquaintance". I don't have his number, sorry. Why do you need to contact him?'

'I need to ask him something.'

'About the murders?' asked Sébastien.

'Yes,' said Lily.

'Well, you could try Araminta Winters. She'll probably have it.'

'Thank you. Also, Sébastien, I wonder, do you remember Mo saying to Araminta something along the lines of "there are a lot of things we don't know," regarding Lady Zuleika's death?'

'I don't recall that, Lily, but there was so much going on. I remember him saying he played chess with Zuleika.'

'Right.'

'Let me know if you need anything else,' said the Count politely before putting the phone down.

Lily was certain that Oscar and Sébastien were lying about Mo. Why? What were they hiding? She strode over to Ricky's desk. He was on the phone reclining back in his chair.

'Still no joy on finding the scarf? I bet. All of them dead ends? How many people bought this wretched scarf? The lipstick? Thought so.' He put the phone down and shrugged his shoulders. 'Bloody useless!'

Lily was so excited about her news she was bouncing on the spot.

'Out with it,' said Ricky, seeing her excitement.

'OK, our Rasta was called Mo and he is a cabbie and DJ. Interestingly, nobody has his number despite the fact they appeared to be very friendly with him on the night. I think Zuleika's sister Araminta should have it but she isn't answering.'

'Good work, Cane! We're beginning to get somewhere. What did Peters say?'

'He's seeing if they've interviewed him.'

'Let's call him now.' Ricky dialled the number at top speed. 'I was just speaking to one of the other coppers on the case: they're no further forward,' he whispered under his breath and then he nodded at Lily, 'Peters, Ricky boy here. What have you got for us on our Rasta friend Mo?' He hit the speakerphone button.

'We haven't fucking interviewed him. He obviously didn't get his ticket through the official channels. His name wasn't on the sodding guest list. I'm checking to see if the cabbie story stacks up.'

'Do you think he's driving a deregulated old hackney cab? My mate's just bought one for a couple of grand – it's dead easy.'

'We're checking for a profile like his with London Transport, but there are a hell of lot of cabbies in London, mate. I just hope he's legit otherwise it's going to be like looking for a needle in a haystack.'

'You thinking what I'm thinking, Jeffrey?' asked Ricky knowingly.

'Well it would be a great way to deliver drugs around the capital, wouldn't it? No one would stop you, whether you were a legit cabbie or not.' Lily began gesticulating to Ricky.

'Hang on. I've got Lily here. She wants to say something.'

'We need to see if anyone took his photo at the party. He could have been photographed with one of the celebs in his group or he might be in the background of a shot. Then we could release it.'

'Brilliant!' said Ricky.

'Good thinking, Lily! Could you identify him, do you think?'

'Absolutely.'

'If there's no joy there, we'll need you to do a description of his face for a photofit.'

'Sure,' replied Lily.

'Great. I'll get back to you,' said Peters, hanging up.

19

Lily and Ricky sat alone in Sam's office early the following morning. The atmosphere was tense. Ricky's long legs were crossed and his lower right leg and foot were bouncing up and down in a frenzied manner. Today's socks were a sombre maroon. On Sam's desk was a piece of paper with all his appointments for the day printed on it. On the left-hand corner of the desk sat a large, silver photograph frame with a picture of Sam's wife and three round-faced children, all of whom looked like carbon copies of him.

'We've got to get a proper ID on this guy,' said Ricky. 'We need to be running checks on him before anyone else knows his bloody name. Once the police have it, it'll be fair game and they'll release it all in a press conference.'

'What checks do you normally do?' asked Lily.

'I forgot you soft features lot don't run people down like we do. Lily, you, me and the crime team are going to be like a pack of hounds. We aren't going to leave a stone unturned,' said Ricky with the fire in his eyes. 'We're going to find out if Mo's appeared in the magistrates' court before. Does he have a record? Has he been in the nick? Where does he live? Where did he go to school? What were his GCSE results? Who are his parents? What kind of guy is he? We're going to talk to neighbours, talk to an old contemporary from school. We're then going to build a picture of him from the info we have. We'll take a line on him, for example "the outsider who penetrated London society". Sounds like he's a dropout: he probably left school with no grades, fell into drug dealing – the usual crap. We're going to press those toffee-nosed snobs and find out what they know. Find out why they are shielding him. You know as well as I do why they are shielding him: he's their fucking dealer and they don't want to be exposed in a grubby little scandal.'

'Right,' nodded Lily, feeling the pressure. 'We don't know that yet. Also, all we know is he has an opinion on the murder. I'm not saying I think he is the murderer.'

'Listen up, Lily. It's been a week and the police have sweet Fanny Adams. You have provided the only viable lead. We've got a paper to write here and for once we can steal a march on *The Post*, who will be practising dark arts to break the scoop. Sam is going to expect all this today. Did you not have any luck with the pap shots?'

'Not yet, but I've got hundreds more to look at,' said Lily feeling uneasy about the press onslaught that was about to hit Mo.

'You've got the picture desk doing an edit, right? They're just showing you ones with a Rastafarian in them?' checked Ricky.

'Yes. They've got two freelancers in to look through the thousands of pictures taken that night. The police are looking through the CCTV footage. He must be on that somewhere; he wasn't wearing an invisibility cloak.'

'The cops will release the information they have about him today. They are under huge pressure from the powers that be to arrest someone for this crime. The Commissioner is now calling them for hourly updates. Commander Jaggs is sitting on Peters big time. I know these two women appear vacuous but they were pure establishment,' said Ricky. 'That's what makes this case so juicy.'

At that moment Sam strode in, followed by Sally Shingle looking sharp in a black trouser suit.

'That's right, Ricky, this crime is at the heart of the establishment and we need this information yesterday. What the hell is going on? Lily, write up what you know and file to me by eleven. I want to run it in the early edition and get it online. We're going to mention who this Mo character was hanging out with at the Serpentine Party. Let's scare the shit out of these socialites! Lily, call them again and again and again; hound them until they crack. I want a name and a profile piece on this character by lunchtime. Ricky, make it happen.'

Lily stood on the office steps, smoking. Ricky and Paul, one of the other crime reporters, joined her. Ricky was so full of nervous energy, he couldn't stand still. Paul, a sturdy man in his mid-thirties, stood there calmly. He was the stabilising influence on the crime desk. He was known for being methodical and highly organised, bordering on obsessive.

'I don't even smoke,' said Ricky, taking one of Lily's fags. 'I'm trying Peters again. Paul, keep going with London transport – we want the names of all Rastafarian taxi drivers in the capital. Bribe them if necessary.' He whipped out his mobile and marched towards Kensington High Street.

'No problem,' said Paul calmly.

'I'll try Araminta for the thousandth time,' said Lily, inhaling again. To her amazement it began ringing.

'Hello,' said a tearful voice at the end of the phone.

'Lady Araminta Winters, it's Lily Cane from *The LEN*.'

'No shit, Sherlock. You and the police are fucking stalking me. I turned my phone off for a day on doctor's orders and all I have is hundreds of messages from you and the Met. What are you trying to do, send me to a mental asylum? It's driving me crazy.'

'I'm so sorry,' said Lily, trying to sound sympathetic. 'We're trying to find out who killed your sister and we think you might be able to help us.'

'The police yes. You're just after a story,' she hissed.

'We are working with the police to try and find the killer.'

'I know. I'm just really shaken up by all this,' she said, sounding a little calmer.

'I understand,' said Lily. 'So, look, when I saw your group of friends at the Serpentine Party you were hanging out with a Rastafarian called Mo. Could you give me his number?'

'Why are you and the police so obsessed with him?' spat Minty. 'You're all so fucking racist. Leave him out of it.'

'No we're not,' said Lily calmly. 'He said something to you, Minty, that could be relevant to the investigation. Do you remember?'

'No. Everything is a blur right now.'

'He said there were a lot of things we don't know about Zuleika's death and you said "you would say that?"' pressed Lily.

'How do you remember what I said? You weirdo. You people are beyond the pale. Are you making this crap up to get a story?' she retorted.

'Not at all – I'm a decent person, Araminta. I'm trying to get the information out there to the public so we have a chance of catching this monster.'

'I still don't see what this has to do with Mo. He's a cab driver for Christ's sake. Oh shit, the other line is going – it's probably the police. I better take it or I'll be in trouble.'

'Can I have Mo's number please?'

'I'll text it to you…'

'Thank you, Araminta. Before you go, can you tell me anything about Mo?'

'He's about forty and drives a cab. He's also a rocking DJ and plays at lots of funky parties. That's it.' And with that she hung up.

Lily sat at her desk, trying to think how she could turn the little that she knew about Mo into a story, when her phone rang.

'Lily, Peters here. I think we've found your guy. If he's the right Rasta, his name is Moses Brown and he's of Jamaican origin. I've got an address for a council flat in Clapham – I'm on my way there now. I've let Ricky know. I'm getting his London Transport ID emailed over to you now. Call me when you get it and let me know if you think it's him.'

When she got to her desk Lily began to draw a spider chart on a blank piece of paper. She wrote Mo in the centre, circled it and then drew off all her points. One – he knew Zuleika and was overheard saying 'there are a lot of things we don't know,' about

Zuleika's death to her sister Araminta, although she won't confirm that. Two – he was seen having a heated discussion with Sophie Hamilton-Bruce at the beginning of the Serpentine Party. Three – he had not voluntarily gone to the police to be interviewed about what happened on the night of the Serpentine Party, despite police appeals for anyone who had attended the party who had not been contacted to come forward. Finally, why were all these snobby, society types friendly with a forty-year-old Rastafarian cab driver who lived in a council flat in Clapham?

Lily dialled, adrenaline pumping through her veins. She was ashamed to admit it, but she was seriously enjoying this murder investigation. Mo's number didn't even go through to an answer service, it just went dead.

LEN EXCLUSIVE
What did the cabbie know? Could missing Rastafarian taxi driver Moses Brown hold the key to the two recent society murders?
By Lily Cane
FRIDAY 19TH JULY

A regular London cabbie, Rastafarian Moses Brown, may hold vital clues that could help the police investigation into the recent murders of socialite Lady Zuleika Winters and fashion TV presenter Sophie Hamilton-Bruce, The LEN can exclusively reveal. Moses Brown, a forty-one-year-old Hackney cab driver of Jamaican origin, was heard saying 'there are a lot of things we don't know,' about Lady Zuleika's death to a group of friends, including Lady Zuleika's half-sister Lady Araminta Winters and Sophie Hamilton-Bruce's cousin, successful hedge funder the Count de Bourgogne, at the Serpentine Party on Wednesday 11th July – although neither can recall this...

20

Lily was packing away the things on her desk. It had to look like she was leaving. She was in two minds about this move to *Society*. She felt like she'd made a significant breakthrough with the

71

investigation and she hated the idea of being taken away from the heart of the action. She was really enjoying working with Ricky and Sam, and for once in her career felt like she was on a roll. Ricky came striding over with a big grin on his face.

'We did it, Cane! We're all going to the boozer to celebrate and you're coming,' and he slapped her on the back. Just then Tracey, Sam's PA, phoned.

'Sam wants us,' said Lily. They made their way across the news floor and went out into the management corridor and towards Sam's office, following the trail of cigar smoke. Tracey was packing up for the day and ushered them through. Sam was sitting at his desk but exuberantly leaped up to greet them.

'Brilliant! Bloody, fucking brilliant. We're breaking the news. We're leading this. I LOVE it. Tracey, can you bring in the goodies?' Tracey walked in with two bottles of Veuve Clicquot and gave one to each of them. 'Just a small token of my appreciation,' said Sam.

'Thanks!' they chorused.

'Lily, are you all set for Monday?' asked Sam.

'Yes. I'm there to cover for the features editor.'

'That's right. If they ask why you left in the middle of these murders just say the move had been organised for a while and you fell into writing about it – which, funnily enough, is true. Now, the key thing is that you and Ricky boy here keep in daily contact – but you cannot let them think that you're a mole.'

'Sure,' said Lily, wondering how on earth this was all going to play out.

'And contact us whenever you think you have anything, however small,' added Ricky.

'Just like this Mo thing,' chirped Sam. 'We stole a march on everyone. They all have it online, of course, but it won't hit their front pages until tomorrow. We need to stay ahead of the curve. Well good luck, blondie!'

'Thanks.' With that she and Ricky walked out.

'I'll meet you in the Windsor Castle in twenty,' said Ricky. 'What you drinking?'

'A big glass of Sauvignon Blanc.'

'Coming up.'

21

On the morning of Monday 23rd July, Lily strode into the lobby of Panther Publications on Brook Street. A chirpy lady on reception wearing oversized glasses, asked her to take a seat while she called up to *Society*. The reception desk was white; in fact, everything was white, including the plump, leather sofas. There was a huge mirror running down one side of the lobby, and in it were the reflections of all of Panther's different publications, the recent issue of every title hanging on the opposite wall. Lily sank back on one of the sofas and picked up a copy of *Society* from one of the perfectly arranged piles.

Lily pretended to read the magazine but her eyes were glued to the constant stream of uber-glamorous girls walking into the building, many of them checking themselves out in the mirror as they walked past. The staff could not have been more different from the pale, male journos at *The LEN*. A rather camp man with a perfectly tailored magenta jacket and matching stripy shirt came in; a cream pug with a purple star-studded leather collar ran obediently at his heels. He waved at the receptionist and she blew him a kiss.

The phone rang and the receptionist answered.

'All right darling, I'll send her up.' She beckoned to Lily. 'Fourth floor, my love. Someone will meet you at the lift.'

Lily walked past the receptionist to the three lifts at the back of the lobby. One of the doors opened and she stepped into the mirror-lined lift. She checked her reflection in the glass and wondered if she looked glamorous enough. She was wearing a blue, Marc Jacobs day dress and some round-toed heels. The lift reached the fourth floor and the doors opened to reveal a dippy-looking girl in her early twenties. Her big brown eyes were ringed with black kohl and she was wearing tight, flared blue jeans and a black, Chanel blouse with stars on it.

'Hi. Are you Lily?' she asked, flicking her long, tawny hair. Lily smiled. 'I'm Molly, Jonty's PA. Follow me.' She teetered along the corridor in her tan wedges. 'Hmm, not sure about these. I bought them at the Chloe sample sale, but I can't really walk. Flavia was so rude when I wore Converse the other day; I thought I'd better make an effort.'

'Right,' replied Lily. 'I better get my feet ready for some serious pain.' They reached a white door with glass panelling, Molly pushed it and they walked in. The office was much smaller than Lily had imagined. Jonty's office was a glass cube that divided the room; on either side of it were twelve or so wooden desks arranged in neat rows.

'That's art and subs,' said Molly, waving an arm theatrically, 'and this is features, travel and beauty. Flavia's fashion fiefdom is next door. Everyone, this is Lily,' said Molly in a loud voice. A man in his sixties, wearing a blue sweatshirt, navy chinos and trainers jumped up.

'Hello, Lily,' he boomed enthusiastically. 'I'm Patrick Connery. I'm the drinks editor, among other things. Welcome to *Society*.' He beamed.

At that moment, a slight man in his forties wearing a blue suit came out of the glass office. Lily recognised him from the Serpentine Party. 'He must be Jonty McDougall, the editor,' she thought.

'Hello, Lily,' he said in a clipped accent.

'Hi,' said Lily, smiling, trying to make it look like she had met Jonty before.

'This is Lily Cane everyone. She has come to cover for Katherine as features editor. You've met Patrick and Molly. This is Claudia,' he said pointing to a curvaceous blonde who Lily immediately recognised from the Serpentine Party. 'And this is Lara Wimpole,' he said, gesturing towards a chic lady in her thirties with a pixie haircut and incredibly long eyelashes.

'Hi,' they said. 'Jonty, is Katherine not coming back?' asked Claudia.

'Not at the moment,' replied Jonty, shooting her a warning look.

'Right, Molly, can you set Lily up at a desk please?'

'Absolutely. I'm on it.' She teetered over to Lily, stubbing her toe on Patrick's desk en route. 'So, Lily, you are going to sit here, behind Lara. At the moment your login is your name and then your password is "password". Jessica, the managing editor, is the person to talk to about contracts, money, holiday, blah blah blah. She sits round the corner over there. She will chase you about your copy.'

'Money!' exclaimed Lara. 'Chance would be a fine thing. We do it for the love of it here.'

'Jessica will whip you for your copy, Lily. You better not be a week late like Lara was last week,' said Claudia. Lily chuckled internally. This office couldn't be any more different than *The LEN*.

Lily settled herself into her new desk. She thought it would be bling and modern, like the lobby, but it had a distinctly shabby feel. The beige carpet looked like a spotted dick pudding, beige and covered in coffee stains. The large, rectangular, pine desks were enclosed on three sides with wooden partitions with pin boards inlaid in them. Attached to these were amusing photographs of staff, looking glamorous with various celebrities and public figures.

A photograph of a tall, young blonde and a short, fat, wrinkly man caught Lily's eye. There was at least a foot's height difference between them.

'Ah, you're looking at my "true love" board. That is billionaire Dennis Kluckman with his fourth wife Lindsay.'

'The *coup de foudre* of money and beauty,' said Lily.

'Where did you come from? Did Jonty say *The LEN*?' asked Claudia, poking her head over the partition. Her mop of wild, blonde hair tamed by a tropical print, Pucci headscarf.

'Yes.'

'Haven't you written something on these awful murders?' asked Lara.

'Yes, I did write a couple of stories,' replied Lily, trying to sound vague.

'Why on earth have you left?' asked Claudia. 'We were actually there. I mean it just has to be someone who attended that party. It's been a nightmare – we've all been interviewed by the police and had our fingerprints taken.'

'The police coming to Panther Publications to interview *Society* staff about a murder, is one of the oddest things that has happened in the twenty-five years I've been here,' said Patrick, 'especially seeing them interview Flavia in her flying saucer hat. I'm surprised they didn't make her take it off.'

'They wouldn't dare!' Claudia interrupted.

'On a serious note, I find it amazing they don't have a suspect yet. They don't seem to know what they're looking for,' said Patrick.

'What was Sophie like?' asked Lily casually.

'Fragile,' said Lara.

Claudia nodded in agreement, 'I interviewed her a couple of times. Look, she was the typical society girl: privileged, indulged and she had plenty of time to think about herself. She was a lot more feisty than most of them, that's why she was on telly. She was an exhibitionist but basically OK. None of us can think why anyone would want to kill her. I mean Zuleika had serious money so maybe there is a motive there, but I don't think Sophie was mega rich; though I suppose she had a past.'

'Of course, you all must have known Zuleika?' said Lily, feigning ignorance.

'Yes,' said Lara, looking around her and lowering her voice. 'Well, we've been told we can't discuss it in the office because of Araminta. Although she's off on compassionate leave until next week.'

'Compassionate leave,' huffed Claudia. 'She hated her sister. There was such jealousy between them and they were hardly close. There was a sixteen year age gap, for starters, and they had different mothers. Now she's died, it's Zuleika this and Zuleika that. You'd have thought they were bloody twins.'

'They got on when it suited them,' said Lara diplomatically.

'When they could do a photo shoot together you mean,' scoffed Claudia. 'Not that Zuleika wanted to share the limelight. She'd only enlist Minty if she had to.'

'Whose this?' said Patrick who had just strolled back from taking a proof to the subs desk. It was obvious that the three of them enjoyed regular gossip sessions.

'The Winters sisters,' hissed Claudia.

'Oh,' he said, arching an eyebrow. 'The late Earl was a debauched individual, terrible womaniser and a drunk. He had sporting blood; he squandered most of their fortune, as is often the case with these old aristocratic families. There's always a rotten apple. I played backgammon with him once. Entertaining fellow.'

'I bet you won,' said Lara.

'I did,' smiled Patrick. 'He was a lousy backgammon player, average at cards but he was good at chess. I read in your article, Lily, that Zuleika played chess?'

'Yes, well, according to her tutor, but I think it was a new hobby.'

'Tutor?' scoffed Claudia. 'Poor man having to teach that pretentious woman. I bet he's glad she's dead.'

'Claudia! That's too much,' said Lara. Claudia was on a roll and wasn't going to back down now.

76

'Case closed! He probably murdered her so he didn't have to give her any more agonising tutorials.' She began to pretend to strangle herself – Patrick smiled. Jonty came out of his office and gave them all a bemused look.

'How is everyone getting on with their copy? Lara when am I going to get your Sting and Trudie piece?'

'Today.'

'Claudia, what about your interview with Ryan Todd?'

'That old perv,' retorted Claudia. 'Jonty, you're using me as a honey trap for the over-fifties. He was all over me at the Serpentine. I'm telling you: serious octopus.' Jonty rolled his eyes.

'Both of you, copy needs to be in by this afternoon. Lily, could you come in here for a second?' he said beckoning her towards his office. 'Molly, can we have two coffees, please?'

'Coming right up, boss,' said Molly, who then got distracted by a picture of Angelina Jolie in *Hi*.

Lily followed Jonty into his office. His desk was a sea of papers and she could see his spidery handwriting sprawled over various pieces of copy and proofs. A large white shelf ran down one side of the office and on it were various framed photographs of his wife and young children along with piles of books. The office was small, light and airy and felt rather like a greenhouse, thanks to the row of perfectly tended orchids that ran along the windowsill. The walls were lined with framed *Society* magazine covers, which featured celebrities and society types.

'My covers,' said Jonty, smiling. 'I like most of them, apart from that one of Megan Rice. I always think it looks like she's sniffing her armpit. Flavia loves that one of course.'

'They're great,' replied Lily, running her eyes over them. She noticed that Lady Zuleika Winters and Sophie Hamilton-Bruce had both been cover girls.

'Nice to meet you,' said Jonty in his public school accent. 'This is all rather clandestine.'

'It is rather exciting,' said Lily, laying on the charm. 'I feel like I'm in a John Le Carré novel but with beautiful people.'

'So, I gather you are here on an assignment from *The LEN*. I will help you with it as much as I can, but that is top secret. No one can guess why you are here and everyone is very inquisitive, as you would expect from a room full of journalists. If I can ask you to tread carefully where Lady Araminta is concerned – it's all very recent.'

'Of course,' said Lily. 'Do you have any thoughts on the case?'

'That's the weird thing. I was there on the night and I spoke to Sophie and most of the guests at the party and I have no idea who committed this murder. It's probably something to do with money or sex. Part of the deal is that you will cover the features editor position. So I will need you to edit and commission all of Katherine's pages while she is away. When the others ask how long you'll be here, be vague.'

'Of course,' said Lily. 'Which sections of the magazine will I be looking after?'

'You'll be responsible for the first third of the magazine which is called the front of book and includes the art section. I think most of the pages are commissioned for the October issue but if you could run through it with Claudia and Lara that would be great. Also, Lily, come up with ideas. We need some hard-hitting features to slot in around the social and arty pieces.'

'Absolutely. I'll get thinking,' replied Lily. As she walked over to her desk she thought how pleasant it was to deal with someone who had manners rather than the abrasive Kate Pollock. She noticed bound copies of old *Society* magazines lining the back of the office and made a mental note to find the ones with Zuleika and Sophie on the cover.

22
Tuesday 24th July

'Can the features team come into my office please?' said Jonty, looking a little manic. He was sitting with the smooth creative director Ben Smythe, who was wearing heavy, dark-rimmed glasses and a fitted blue Liberty print shirt, and Lucy Morris the picture editor who had a fierce undercut. Everyone traipsed in.

'You look worried, Jonty. What is it?' said Lara.

'Hang on a minute. Molly, get Flavia in here will you?' Molly went to her desk and called through to the fashion department and began muttering under her breath.

'They're just trying to find her,' said Molly, walking into Jonty's office.

'Jesus,' said Jonty. 'It's half past ten. Right, get me her mobile number.' He vigorously punched her number into his keypad – it went straight to answer phone. 'Flavia, it's Jonty. I need to talk to you immediately. Can you call me back?' He slammed the phone down. 'I've got a decision to make. Are we going to publish the Serpentine pictures or not? What do you think?' There was a sharp intake of breath.

'Absolutely,' said Patrick. 'I know it's a bit ghoulish but I think you'll find the sales will rocket. You should change the tone of the feature.'

'Obviously,' said Jonty.

'I think you should, but I'm not sure about publishing any of Sophie,' said Lara.

'Hang on a minute,' said Claudia. 'Jonty, of course you do. Patrick's right, turn it into a feature. You HAVE to publish the pictures of Sophie – that's what people will be buying it for.'

'Jonty is right to be cautious, though, guys. Do you think all these people want to be associated with a party where someone was brutally murdered?' said Lara.

'Dennis is cool either way,' said Lucy, in an annoyingly calm voice that made you want to strangle her.

'That's good of him,' said Claudia sarcastically.

'Well our coverage of the party is now going to be completely different. I think we should get some quotes from people who were there on the night about what happened. Claudia, can you take charge of that please? You know who we photographed that night. Lily, you were at the party, too, weren't you?'

'Yes.'

'So if you two can pair up on that.'

'This is no longer a frothy piece about a party but a piece about the murder and the victims,' said Patrick.

'We have to tread very carefully here because of Araminta. Also, the Serpentine is not going to be too pleased about it. Lara, can you write a few words about Zuleika? I know she was already dead but I think now the general consensus is that the murders are linked. I'll write about the party itself: the atmosphere on the night and the aftermath. Lily and Claudia, can you team up again on Sophie Hamilton-Bruce? Claudia, you've interviewed her twice so if you take the lead. Patrick, can you do a profile of the Hamilton-Bruce family?' Everyone nodded. 'Great,' said Jonty, 'all I need now is Flavia. Molly, any luck?' Molly shook her head. Jonty looked exasperated but the resignation in his eyes made Lily think Flavia going AWOL was probably a regular occurrence.

Lily and Claudia both drew up lists of people they had seen at the Serpentine and decided who was going to call who. Lily was just about to call society art dealer Henry Marmsby when her mobile rang. She saw it was Ricky and picked up immediately.

'Hi, Dad,' she chirped, while making her way along the corridor to the fire exit at the end.

'Can you talk?' said Ricky.

'Yes, I can now. What's up?'

'You were right about Mo. He is their bloody drug dealer. The police have had three anonymous calls confirming it. No one wants to go on the record as they don't want to admit they've taken drugs. So they're saying they've heard he's the dealer, which is no use at all. They need proof.'

'What about his cab?'

'Clean.'

'Tough one for the police then?' said Lily, 'But surely they can cut a deal with any informant that they won't press any charges. I mean look at the witness protection system for Christ sake. These toffs may take the odd line but they're hardly hardened criminals.'

'Sure, but none of them want to go in the witness box and say it. Why would they do that? They don't want the bad publicity. They'd lose their jobs, among other things…The police are pressurising Oscar to say something. He has admitted under duress that Mo was Sophie's dealer when she was on drugs, but he says he never saw him actually selling her anything. So it's just Sophie's word against Mo's. All this is irrelevant as the guy's vanished into thin air.'

'Still?'

'Not a peep.'

'Are you going to run that he is the suspected drug dealer?'

'Yes, we are, but we have to be damned careful about what we can print legally. This guy needs to be able to defend himself – but the fact he's on the run makes him look guilty as hell.'

'It's that comment Ricky. "There are a lot of things we don't know." Sure he supplied the drugs but I don't think he put the strychnine in Zuleika's coke.'

'Who knows? We need him to tell us that. And to tell us who his clients are, so we can work out who might have tampered with Zuleika's coke.'

'Good luck with that!' laughed Lily.

'The guy's good at his job. We've spent all weekend and yesterday trying to find some dirt on the fucker. He's got a caution in 1981 for having an ounce of cannabis on his person – but, Lily, that's a long time ago. I mean, it's something and it shows he is acquainted with drugs but the guy's been a legitimate cab driver since he was twenty-six. He could write that off as youthful folly. He left school at sixteen, he did a few courses, none of which he completed and he was in a band. He's actually a very good tenor sax player as well as being a DJ. We're running what we have tonight but try and do some digging over there. See what you can find out. How's it going, by the way?'

'Fine. They're very nice. I'm actually calling people who attended the party for quotes as we're writing a Serpentine Party article here. So I'll see if I can tap any of them about Mo.'

'What's the general feeling about the cases there?'

'Shock, and no one can believe that there hasn't been an arrest yet. How's Peters?'

'Under pressure. He's got more officers on the case and there is a serious manhunt for Mo. It's about to be on all the major news bulletins again.'

'Well surely that should throw up some information.'

'Let's see. Keep in touch.'

At three-thirty the door to the office flew open and Flavia Wilde strutted in, wearing a black Alexander McQueen corset and figure hugging skirt, skyscraper heels and a small pillar-box hat with a net veil that fell over half of her face. Her red lipstick blazed defiantly.

'Jonty,' she shrieked, 'you wanted me?'

'About seven hours ago,' said Jonty, shaking his head.

'Be gentle with me Jonty,' she said dramatically. 'I've lost one of my best friends. Zuleika was my twin soul.' She began to sob

81

uncontrollably. At that moment, Phil, the post room boy, walked in with a copy of the first edition of *The LEN*. Lily could see Mo's photograph staring out at her from the front page.

'Give me that,' said Jonty.

'What is it?' asked Lara.

'Have they arrested someone?' said Claudia. Jonty began to skim the front page and then quickly turned to the article inside.

'No,' said Jonty, and he began reading the article out loud. 'Police have confirmed that they have had a number of calls claiming that Moses Brown was not only Lady Zuleika's drug dealer but also Sophie Hamilton-Bruce's when she was on cocaine a few years ago.'

'Tell me something I don't know,' said Flavia.

'You knew this?' said Jonty, looking flabbergasted. 'Well I hope you told the police, when they interviewed you.' Flavia looked sheepish. Jonty ushered her into his office and they could see him giving her a real dressing down before picking up the phone and handing it to her.

Lily had spent all morning calling people who had attended the party but no one had said anything particularly illuminating. She hadn't managed to get hold of Henry Marmsby, so she tried again – it rang.

'Henry, it's Lily from *Society* here. I was wondering if I could talk to you about the Serpentine Party.'

'Lordy! Well that was a party we won't forget. It's a bit like weddings really, they all merge into one unless something dramatic happens. I will never forget Natasha Simmons-Smythe being jilted by Peregrine Lord – he just went ashen and walked out of the church. The party went ahead for the guests but none of the bridal party attended – it was a great do! But even I, a true veteran of society life, can't recall a party where there was a bona fide murder. I went to one in the seventies when someone overdosed but that was it.'

'Gosh,' said Lily. 'Did you notice anything out of the ordinary at the party?

'Hmmm.' There was a silence while he thought. 'Not at the time. I spoke to Sophie, naturally. Dominic, her father, is a good friend. She seemed very well. I don't believe for a second she was back on drugs.'

'No, she wasn't,' said Lily. 'The toxicology confirmed that.'

'You're very knowledgeable about all this. Anyway, what do *Society* want us to say? Look, I think the party was highly charged. There was a Dionysian quality in the air. I remember Rocky Star writhing around when she was dancing and Ryan Todd feeding off all the energy of the young – youth is such an aphrodisiac. I didn't think Sophie was particularly charged though – well, not compared to the old days, anyway.'

'Do you think the murderer was someone who attended the party?'

'I would have thought so – but it is a ghastly thought and it saddens me deeply. The thing about these two ladies is that I am sure they both have skeletons in their couture closets. I'm sure the answers lie in their pasts and private lives. Sophie was a Hamilton-Bruce and we all know how wild they can be. Just look at what happened to her aunt. These society swans can be butterflies on the wheel. However, in terms of the night itself, all I can say is there was a wild energy in the air. It's such a shame for the Serpentine, though, and I do hope it doesn't prevent them from having their summer party next year. That's all I want to say about it.'

'Thanks, Henry,' said Lily, thinking that he was going to be rather a useful contact.

23

Lily spent the rest of the week reading all the past press cuttings about Sophie and Zuleika. She scanned all the social pages to see who they had dated and who they knew, to see if she could establish any links between them beyond the fact they were both society girls. Patrick was in full swing on his Hamilton-Bruce family article. He had the energy of a much younger man and was hitting the phones with gusto.

'You're looking very dapper today, Patrick,' said Lara. He was wearing a suit and tie, which Claudia informed Lily was a rare occurrence.

'I'm off to Whites,' he replied with a wry smile.

'With Jonty?' asked Claudia.

'No, I'm meeting an old friend of Dominic Hamilton-Bruce's.'

'We'll be seeing you back at five?' quipped Claudia.

'Perhaps,' beamed Patrick. 'How are you two getting on with your Sophie piece?'

'Jonty's changed it. I am writing a celebratory piece about her and Lily's getting quotes from friends and people in the fashion industry. We'll meet the deadline.'

'So will I. I've never missed a deadline in my life. Even when I was being shelled in my Beirut hotel room.'

'Before he entered the genteel world of women's glossy magazines, Patrick was a war journalist,' said Claudia.

'Why did you give it up?' Lily asked.

'I loved it, Lily, the thrill, the danger, the camaraderie amongst everybody on the front line. There is an electric energy in the hotels where the journalists stay – it's as if real life is suspended. The feeling like tonight might be your last night on earth – it's charged with so many emotions. Everyone drinks and people fall in and out of bed with each other. Not that there were so many female war journalists in my day, but there were some and of course in Vietnam there were the locals. Then one day I just didn't care any more. I decided I'd seen enough human suffering for one lifetime and I came back. I've never missed it – but it's a young man's game and I couldn't think of anything worse than being in Iraq or Afghanistan at my age.'

Lily felt sad. This talk of war journalists, had made her think about the very person she was trying to forget – Oliver, her ex-boyfriend. He was in Basra on the frontline with the army. It had been three months since they'd last spoken. The murders were a welcome distraction from the heartache. She pulled herself together.

'Patrick, Henry Marmsby mentioned Sophie had a wild aunt. Who was she?'

'Anoushka Hamilton-Bruce – one of the biggest sluts society has ever known.'

'Don't hold back Patrick!' said Lara, laughing.

'It's true. I can't think of many like her. Usually, the man-eaters like that come from humble origins but, boy, did this one fall from a height. She had a few husbands, a multitude of lovers and a few children legitimate and illegitimate scattered here and there. Her beauty ruined her. In her time she was married to a

French count and an English earl; then she dated a movie star, had a high-profile affair with a married Tory MP, seduced a priest and ended up with an Arab oil sheikh. When she married she converted to Catholicism. She then reverted to being a Protestant after her divorce and then, I suppose, she must have become a Muslim when she married the sheikh. I'm sure he must have had other wives. Not that any of these religions would mean anything to a woman like that – they were mere labels and a way to get to the men. And she was all about the men – a proper nymphomaniac. She was in a very risqué art house French movie, where she cavorted around in the nude and she even posed for *Playboy*. The family were very embarrassed by her behaviour, they tried to laugh it off – but it rankled with Reginald, her father. The Hamilton-Bruces have always been courtiers and Anoushka's behaviour was outrageous and not the done thing.'

'I think she sounds quite fabulous,' said Claudia, 'that reminds me: I'm going to call Harry on *Gentleman's Monthly* and find out who I need to blow to get to the *GM* awards.' Patrick ignored Claudia and carried on talking.

'She's dead of course but she was the original "It" girl, I suppose.'

'You know, I think Sophie might have been pretty wild sexually,' said Lara. 'I know quite a few people who had flings with her, although I suppose that is the drugs too. You are more likely to get into those kinds of situations if you're off your head.'

'How did Anoushka die?' asked Lily.

'She fell out of a window of her Chelsea town house when she was off her head about seven or eight years ago. Or she may have thrown herself out of course – it was unclear and I don't think any of her children were speaking to her at the time.'

'How awful,' said Lily.

'It was a tragic affair really,' said Patrick.

'Horrendous,' said Lara.

'How is everyone doing with their copy?' asked Jonty, interrupting the conversation.

'Nearly done,' said Claudia who began typing dramatically, lifting her hands high above the keyboard and placing them down with force.

'One hour,' replied Lara. Jonty tapped his watch and widened his eyes.

'I'm done,' said Lily. Jonty beamed and walked over to her, patting her shoulder.

'See, people? Lily is used to meeting deadlines. Patrick?'

'I've written it but I'm meeting a contact at lunch who, I think, will have some useful information. You'll have it when I'm back.'

'Great. Listen has anyone heard from Minty? Is she going to be covering the Cartier polo this weekend?'

'I'll give her a bell,' said Claudia.

'Is anyone else going? I can't make it: I'm interviewing Salman Rushdie,' said Jonty.

'No, I hate that event,' replied Lara. 'It's not what it used to be. I remember when it was chic when the supermodels went in the nineties.'

'That's very helpful, Lara,' said Jonty. 'We are covering the Cartier lunch and, bearing in mind the Serpentine coverage is now a tribute piece, I think we could do with some light relief. Also, they are a major advertiser. Although it will be interesting to see what the atmosphere is like as a result of these murders. Claudia?'

'I can't, Jonty. I'm off to America to interview Lauren Bush.'

'Of course! Lily, I think you should go. I'm a bit nervous about having just Araminta covering it in her present mental state.'

'Molly, can arrange for Lily to take my place,' said Jonty. Molly nodded and applied some lip-gloss.

Ricky Flynn was sitting in the far right-hand corner of Don Zuko, a small, nondescript sushi restaurant on Kingly Street. The place was packed and the Japanese waitresses expertly navigated the black plastic tables which were tightly packed together. The maître d' was a fierce, Japanese lady in her sixties, with a slash of bright red lipstick. Lily made her way over to Ricky's table and he gave her a big smile.

'I took the liberty of ordering you a beer, as it's a Friday.'

'Thank you,' said Lily.

'How's it going at *Society*?'

'Fine. I've got a couple of pieces in the pipeline. I'm doing a cover story with Veronique Lapin and Rocky Star in Ibiza, which should be fun. They were both at the Serpentine and in Sophie's crowd so I hope to push them a bit on the murders. And I'm off to the Cartier polo on Sunday.'

'Lah-dee-dah! Brilliant. You're where you need to be. I was going to suggest you got yourself invited to that. I've heard they've really upped the security in light of what happened at the Serpentine. Peters and I had a few beers last night and he revealed that Araminta Winters confirmed Sophie was having an argument with Mo about the drugs he supplied to Zuleika at the Serpentine. You were right about them having an altercation.'

'Wow, how did you manage that?'

'They are under so much pressure to get this guy. The powers that be want this case wrapped up pronto. So, I called your little friend and said I knew she had been party to this argument. She tried to pretend she didn't remember but in the end I got it out of her. I suspect she is worried that he is going to blab that she is on the stuff, too, or maybe she's scared he'll come and bump her off.'

'They don't know that he murdered these women. Yes, he supplied Zuleika with the drugs but that doesn't mean he murdered Sophie.'

'It's the most likely explanation though. Where the hell is he? That's what you need to find out. I've been in touch with his sister in Kingston, Jamaica, but she hasn't heard from him for months. She insisted he isn't a murderer. We're running an interview with her tonight.'

'Excellent.'

'What else have you found out this week?'

'That Sophie's aunt was completely wild and had shagged the United Nations. Apparently Sophie was promiscuous. Perhaps her killer was a jilted ex-lover? I'm going to look into her love life. I also discovered that both of these women dated the ageing rocker Ryan Todd. I have seen pictures of them both with him at parties but I don't think he was a great love for either of them and I'm pretty sure he was on the dance floor at the time she was murdered.'

'OK. I'll get on to him this afternoon. What we need to do is look at who the key people were in both of their lives and see if that takes us anywhere. I think the most logical explanation is Moses Brown but we can't leave any stones unturned. I've been in touch with the lawyers looking after their estates – the sole beneficiary of Zuleika's will is her daughter, Lucile. I can't get access to her as she is a minor. Peters went down to Bedales to speak to her with the family liaison officer and said she was pretty clueless about her mother. She had no idea who she was dating and obviously rather disapproved of her lifestyle. They don't appear to have been particularly close. Sophie, on the other hand, hadn't made a will – she's not married and has no dependents, so I suppose she didn't think about it. I think the proceeds of her flat and her money will go to her parents and her share of the Hamilton-Bruce family trust will go to other members of the family. However, estates take forever to wind up, but let's both keep our ears to the ground about the financials. Money is often a motivating factor in murder.'

24
Sunday 29th July 2007

Lily checked her reflection in her bedroom mirror: the pale pink Alberta Ferretti day dress the fashion department had called in for the Cartier polo match fitted perfectly. She teamed it with a pair of metallic, Jimmy Choo high-heeled sandals that Molly had kindly lent to her. Billy wolf-whistled from the corridor.

'You look hot, Lily, but how the hell have you persuaded me to come to this thing? I've borrowed this suit from Roger. He's a couple of inches smaller and a little wider – but I think it's OK. The retro tie is mine, though, for the record. How do I look?'

'Very handsome, but your hair's a bit unruly,' replied Lily, trying to tidy it up with her hands. Billy ducked his head and shook his dark, Byronic curls.

'I have Samson hair – live with it. I'm not slicking it back, if that's what you're angling for. If anyone in the band hears about this polo match I'll be toast – it will ruin my street cred.'

'Yeah. Whatever Billy,' said Lily, disinterested.

'So who are we going with?'

'Flavia Wilde, the fashion director, and Lady Araminta Winters, the social editor, who is also the half-sister of my first murder victim.'

'Jesus! I don't do society crap, Lily. I'm a musician who likes to go to dive bars and pubs.'

'Shut up, Billy. You love the high life as well. Don't worry, Flavia will love you – you're attractive and young.'

'I hope we're getting a car back. I don't want to be stranded in Windsor.'

'All right, my lordship! Yes, we've got one ordered for eight o'clock.'

'What?' exclaimed Billy. 'You want me to stay at this thing talking to horsey women for twelve hours? You've got to be kidding me!'

'I think it turns into a rave. China White have a tent.'

'Whoop-a-doop. The drinks better be free, Lily, or you're in serious trouble.'

Half an hour later the doorbell rang and Lily and Billy made their way downstairs to the Addison Lee people carrier that was waiting outside. Lily spotted Flavia's peacock feather headdress before she spotted Flavia, it took up the majority of the back seat.

'You get in the front, Billy.'

'Christ alive! What's she come as?'

'It's fashion, Billy.'

'Of course! Silly me,' he replied, and opened the front side door of the cab. 'Hello, I'm Billy.'

'Hello Billy, I see you have virility in your hair,' said Flavia provocatively. She looked particularly eccentric with the massive headdress balancing on her tiny head. It dwarfed her face and made her look like a tribal chieftain. She was wearing an electric-blue fitted dress that showed off her ample cleavage and her trademark crimson lipstick.

'See, Lily? Fashion is on my side,' said Billy, grinning. 'I do, Flavia! And I am delighted that you have pointed that out, as Lily was trying to get me to tame it but there is no taming a sexual beast like me.' Flavia let out an infectious cackle that reverberated around the car. Lily breathed a sigh of relief: she knew they were all going to get along fine. Flavia was a famous man-eater.

'Hi, I'm Billy,' he said, leaning back and shaking hands with Araminta.

'Minty,' she said, temporarily removing her hot-pink Ray-Bans.

'Loving the wayfarers, very eighties. My favourite decade,' said Billy, already beginning to enjoy himself.

'Oh me too,' gushed Flavia. 'The eighties were the decade of sex.'

'Not for me,' said Billy smiling, 'I was eleven when they ended but, Flavia, if I'd been older I'm sure they would have rollicked by. I like the music and terrible fashion.'

'Akmed are we going to get there for eleven o'clock?' asked Flavia who had obviously already charmed the driver.

'It will be tight lady but I'll do my best,' he replied looking at his watch. It was already half past ten.

'Get that foot down on the pedal,' purred Flavia, 'We're meant to be there to see Sébastien playing on the Prince of Wales team,' said Flavia.

'Such a shame that he's been dating Veronique for three years – a good-looking man like that should circulate,' said Minty.

'Absolutely,' agreed Flavia, 'bloody selfish if you ask me. Oh well Minty, the murderer might bump her off next and then you'll be in luck,' said Flavia wickedly.

'Flavia that's not even funny,' exclaimed Minty.

'Come on, Minty. Zu would want us to get on with our lives. She was certainly getting on with hers. That's the tragedy of it all. She was on a roll: she was fashion royalty and she had something else up her sleeve – I'm sure. Do you think it was Mo, darling? He always seemed so nice when I met him.'

'I don't know,' said Minty, 'I'm so screwed up over the whole thing. I don't know what to think. The obvious answer is Mo and the fact he's done a runner doesn't look good. But why would he do that to Sophie's body?'

'Well today is the last day for the murderer to strike as everyone will be heading off on holiday. So keep your guard up ladies,' said Flavia letting out another cackle.

By two-thirty the Cartier tent was buzzing, thanks to the free-flowing champagne. The marquee was filled with round tables, covered with crisp, white tablecloths that were surrounded by cream seats. Dainty white and cream flowers were artfully arranged on the tables and the tent poles were wrapped in green foliage. The overall effect was pretty, light and airy. A quaint, white, wooden fence surrounded the tent and, inside its boundaries, were wooden tables with large cream parasols where the celebrities and socialites could mingle together and observe the day, away from the hoi polloi. The enclosure was teaming with skinny girls with shiny, long hair who chatted with dapper Sloanes in suits and linen jackets.

Lily wandered round scanning the heads for Billy. She couldn't find him inside so she strolled out on to the lawn where she spotted Flavia chatting with the *Society* photographer Hamish Marlow and Oscar Rutherford, who was wearing far too much foundation and a candy-striped jacket that looked like a deckchair. Lily made her way over.

'Lily, do you know Oscar?' asked Flavia.

'Yes we've met,' said Lily.

'Hi,' said Oscar. 'Are you here on business or pleasure, Lily? I'm rather tired of answering questions about Sophie,' he said acidly.

'Ooh la la,' said Flavia. 'Keep your wig on. She works for us now.'

'Oh right,' he said, softening slightly. Hamish raised an eyebrow and excused himself to go and take some photos.

'So what will happen with *Fashion Fix*?' asked Flavia. 'Do you need a new presenter? I can think of a feisty fashion director with a beady eye and the gift of the gab who could make a seamless transition to telly.'

'Ha ha,' said Oscar drolly.

'I'm not joking, Oscar. I need the money, especially now Zu is gone. She used to bankroll me all the time. I wonder if she left me anything. She said she would, as she had a premonition she would die. She always said tragic things happened to extraordinary people.'

'Actually, Flavia, I am going to be presenting the show on my own. It is what I've always wanted. I know it's bad to speak ill of the dead but to be honest I have always done the lion's share of the work on *Fashion Fix* and I had to carry Sophie all the time. I'm just glad the producers have finally recognised that.'

'Surely you need a woman on a women's fashion programme?' said Flavia.

'Don't be so prescriptive, Flavia. I wouldn't expect it from you, but I suppose the older generation just don't get it,' said Oscar bitchily. Flavia was furious and stormed off. Oscar shrugged and went to talk to the actors of the moment, Toby Creswell and

Matthew Miles, who were hanging out on the thesp table with Hugh Dancy and Damien Lewis.

Lily found Billy sitting on a table in the sunshine with two Dutch girls.

'How do you manage it?' said Lily, smiling.

'My flatmate Lily,' said Billy, 'this is Adalind and Henneke and they are two performance artists from Holland.'

'Hi.' They nodded. Lily noticed they were wearing some seriously directional fashion; one was wearing a skirt that shot out half a metre at the hips and the other fluorescent pink harem pants.

'Were you two performing at the Serpentine Party?' asked Lily.

'Yes,' replied the blonde one, 'I'm Adalind. We performed our seven ages of man piece. It went really well, apart from the fact that the murderer used our surgical gloves to kill Sophie Hamilton-Bruce.'

'We had a box of disposable gloves stored behind a screen in the gallery for the birth scene and they think the murderer took a pair from in there. It meant there were no prints on Sophie's body.'

'Weren't there any prints on the box?' asked Lily.

'I threw the box away when we got home as there was only one pair left in there, we got through a few in the evening so I took those ones out and threw the box in the trash. The rubbish was collected the following morning and we didn't realise the significance of it until a couple of days later when we spoke to the police.'

'I feel terrible about this,' interjected Henneke, 'maybe we could have helped catch the killer.'

'We knew Zuleika,' added Adalind, 'we did a shoot with her for *Utopia*, the week before she died.'

'Why do you think she was murdered?' asked Billy, passing Henneke a roll up.

'I think she was a lady with many secrets,' she replied.

'Interesting,' said Billy, pretending to stroke an imaginary beard. 'Do you know what they were?' Henneke shook her head.

'We think Sophie was killed on the spur of the moment because she knew something. If the murderer had planned it, they would have had their own gloves.'

'It must have been someone who saw that particular bit of your act,' said Lily.

'We are not performing seals, Lily, but yes it must have been someone who saw our "art" or was familiar with our work. We performed that piece a number of times that night so we can't narrow it down. We stopped performing at about ten thirty and she was murdered around midnight.'

'Isn't that Ryan Todd?' said Billy, pointing at a man in his fifties.

'Yes,' said Lily.

'I used to love Rock Shop.'

'Let's go and say hello,' said Lily, shooting Billy a look.

'OK,' said Billy, 'I didn't like them that much,' he muttered.

'He went out with both the victims,' hissed Lily.

'All right, Poirot, I think I was getting somewhere with them.'

'What about your Swedish singer?'

'She's on tour and it's just a bit of fun anyway. Who are you? Mary Whitehouse?' Lily shrugged. They headed towards Ryan who was chatting up a girl in her twenties. Flavia rushed over to him, waving her arms in the air and the pair of them fell about laughing.

'That's a stroke of luck. Come on Billy,' said Lily who was beginning to get a little concerned about the amount of champagne Billy had consumed. 'You've got to pace yourself Bill,' he pulled a childish sulk face in response.

'Hi Flavia my friend,' said Billy cheerily.

'Samson,' roared Flavia who was equally charged on the Veuve.

'Ryan, this is Lily Cane one of my colleagues and her very shaggable flatmate Billy, who is a musician,' said Flavia.

'Hello,' said Ryan, 'What do you play?'

'The guitar and I sing.'

'He's pretty good on the drums, too,' said Lily proudly.

'He's sure got rhythm,' said Flavia cackling. Billy smiled – he had found a kindred spirit in Flavia. He liked people who didn't give a damn.

'Well we're lucky not to have been murdered,' said Flavia.

'I did notice some sniffer dogs here, actually,' said Ryan, 'They've tightened the security even more than usual, probably because of the Princes.'

'Do you think Moses Brown did it?' Lily asked Ryan, knowing she was pushing it a bit.

'I don't know,' said Ryan, a little taken aback. 'I knew both of the girls well.'

'You sex machine,' said Flavia, swinging her hips.

'The Mo story fits, doesn't it? He probably did sell her the dodgy coke and Sophie was on to him. I've never met the man. Zuleika did have a problem with cocaine – it's not a huge surprise.'

'Do you really think so?' asked Flavia.

'Come on Flavia you know it. She always looked great but she was very dependent on that stuff. It's really sad. Also, why would someone want to kill these women? They were hardly dangerous. They were both a little mad, granted, but to target them is odd. I had some reporter from *The LEN* calling me up about them as if I might know something about the murders. I was incensed. I told him if I knew anything I'd go to the police.'

'It wasn't you, Lily, was it?' laughed Flavia. Ryan looked at her coldly.

'No,' said Lily, trying to placate Ryan who obviously didn't like the fact that Lily had been connected to *The LEN*. He turned his head and scanned the lawn for familiar faces.

'Oh look there's Arnaud Bamberger. I really must say hello,' and he quickly walked off.

'He's the bigwig at Cartier,' said Flavia. 'I'd better try and find Minty. She has been glued to George Lazarus's side all day.'

25

The atmosphere in the China White tent couldn't have been more different from the genteel atmosphere of the Cartier one. It was six o'clock in the evening and all the polo goers were charged on alcohol and other substances. A celebrated DJ wearing neon wraparound shades, who Lily had never heard of, pumped out house tunes with loud, repetitive beats from a raised glass booth. A sea of orange bodies threw shapes on the dance floor and surrounding tables.

'Jesus,' said Billy. 'The women in here are scary. They're neon.'

'Fake tan, Bill,' said Lily. 'The men aren't much better: sleaze city. Don't worry, I've got some tokens to the VIP room.'

'Thank God for that,' said Billy mockingly. 'It looks like I've got used to the high life already.' They pushed their way through the throng to a long enclosed room with a bar at the far end where a crowd of people gathered like animals round a watering hole on the Serengeti. Lily spotted the French singer Veronique Lapin from the Serpentine Gallery Party. She was talking to Henry Marmsby the art dealer. She steered Billy in their direction.

'Ooh it's Veronique Lapin!' exclaimed Billy. They walked towards them but as soon as they got there Veronique pointedly walked off. Henry Marmsby was more polite.

'Hi, Henry. I'm Lily Cane from *Society*. We spoke on the phone the other day about the Serpentine Party.'

'Oh yes, hello. And who are you?' he said, running his eyes up and down Billy.

'This is my flatmate Billy Treadaway.'

'Hi,' said Billy charmingly, 'having a good time?'

'Well, I think it's pretty frightful in here. I'm a great observer of people, Billy, and I'm enjoying watching a few car crashes unfolding. It's quite amusing how many of the young have come up to me and complained about the lack of decent cocaine because of Mo's disappearance. Although young Lazarus seems to be in and out of the cubicle all night – it is most unbecoming. The young were more sophisticated in my day.'

'Mo had the monopoly did he?' asked Billy.

'Yes, he was an institution and everyone loved him too,' replied Henry. 'I've seen him at numerous society weddings, twenty-firsts, he was even invited to one ruby wedding party. A lot of people's noses are out of joint about the whole affair. I had Tabitha Monkton-Meller banging on about how her posh rave is going to be a washout next weekend because of Mo going AWOL. She didn't even consider the fact he is a prime suspect in a murder case. I mean really!'

'Do you think he did it, Henry?' asked Billy.

'I suppose he might have done it to cover his tracks. It is the most plausible explanation but why not take her out in her flat later? He knew where she lived from the old days when she was on the gear. I can't think who else would do it but as I said to Lily the other day I think the clues are in the ladies' pasts. This is all very morbid, let's change the subject.'

Lily sloped off leaving Billy to fend off Henry's advances on his own. She did a circuit of the room then popped outside for a cigarette. She took a cigarette out of the packet of Marlboro Lights in her pewter clutch bag and lit it. As she inhaled she surveyed the scene. The lead actress of a hit American teen show was holding court on one of the tables outside. A couple of boys with highly styled quiffs hung on her every word. Oscar walked up and joined them. The actress draped herself on him and Lily overheard him recruiting her to be a guest on *Fashion Fix*. George Lazarus and Minty were sitting close together on a table nearby violently snogging.

'What a sight,' said a confident French voice behind her. Lily swung round to see Sébastien de Bourgogne. He was no longer in his polo kit and had changed into a tailored, cream linen jacket, which he'd teamed with a blue shirt and black jeans. His chestnut-brown hair fell tantalisingly over his hard but perfect, jutting cheekbones. Through the tousled fringe, Lily could see his smouldering green, almond-shaped eyes and his straight nose. Lily's legs turned to jelly.

'Hi,' she said coolly.

'Lily, right?' he said taking a packet of Gauloises cigarettes from his jacket pocket, 'Do you have a light?'

'Sure,' said Lily, taking a box of matches from her bag. She lit one and, as he stooped down to put his cigarette in the flame, she caught the smell of his musky aftershave and the smell of his hot athletic body. Her stomach performed another somersault and her hands began to shake in excitement.

'I gather it was well played today?' she said, smiling.

'You didn't see the game?' he mocked.

'I'm afraid Flavia, Minty and I were a little late. I think Minty might have caught the end of it.'

'Oh well, you socialites don't come here for the polo. It was good fun actually and Prince Harry played really well. Pah! It's just a game. Don't worry, my girlfriend spent most of it gossiping in the stands.'

'Right,' replied Lily. 'We caught some of the afternoon match.'

'I'm glad you got to watch some of the polo. Lazarus and Minty are really going for it,' he said, looking over in their direction. They were snogging so ferociously they looked like a couple of rabid dogs fighting over a scrap of meat.

'Yes, it's almost teenage,' joked Lily.

'I think he may even have had a fling with Zuleika,' said Sébastien, 'English society is so incestuous don't you think?'

'I don't really know. I'm not a society girl. I'm just here for work.'

'You work for a newspaper don't you? Weren't you writing about the murders?'

'I was but I'm not any more,' replied Lily. 'I'm working at *Society* now.'

'Ah, well that should make a pleasant change. No doubt I'll be seeing more of you. I tend to be dragged to these events.'

'Of course you do. You'd rather be at home reading an improving book or having a pint down your local?' teased Lily. His eyes softened and he smiled.

'It depends who I am with,' he replied, staring at her with those bewitching eyes. Veronique and a girl with platinum hair with pink dip-dyed tips came up to them.

'Here you are,' she purred, 'you are as hard to control as one of your ponies. I will have to put you in a bridle and whip you.' The other girl giggled. Sébastien raised an eyebrow. 'Where is Prince Harry? I wanted to introduce Tilly to him,' said Veronique.

'I don't know, darling. You weren't so interested in him or your boyfriend when they were playing polo,' he teased. Veronique let out a soft, tinkling chuckle.

'Sébastien, you're not cross are you? Of course I watched you, my darling. You must have looked up while I was talking to Matthew and Oscar. Most of the time my eyes were firmly fixed on you.' Lily made her excuses and walked off.

After doing a couple of circuits of the VIP room, she finally found Billy hidden in the corner talking to a pretty girl with very long brown hair.

'Hi, Lil,' he slurred. 'This is Amanda.'

'Hi,' said the girl, equally drunk.

'We've been doing vodka shots,' said Billy, grinning.

'Evidently,' replied Lily.

'I needed something after your friend Henry Marmsby said I had soulful eyes and would I sit for a portrait for a "friend" of his.' The girl cackled.

'You still OK to leave at eight?' asked Lily.

'Sure. What are the others doing?'

'Minty is snogging a guy called George Lazarus and I think Flavia went back with Ryan Todd.'

'George Lazarus is off his face,' chirped Amanda. 'I heard some guys over there saying he is the only person with decent coke.'

'Drug addicts,' said Billy, shaking his head comically. The girl laughed again.

'Losers,' she said in a fake American accent. Lily humoured them.

'It's seven thirty. I'll find out if Minty is coming with us. Don't move, Billy. Stay here. We'll need to begin making our way to the car park soon.'

'Yes, sir,' replied Billy. 'Time for another shot?' he said, turning to Amanda.

Lily finally found Minty coming out of the portaloos. She was obviously drunk and off her face on George's marching powder. She stumbled in the grass and Lily caught sight of her enormous black and gold wedges.

'Cool shoes,' said Lily. 'I didn't notice them earlier.'

'Zu designed them. They're real gold leaf you know. She left me some of her clothes.'

'Oh right,' said Lily. 'That's quick isn't it?'

'Oh I'm not sure about the will. I asked Lucile if I could borrow some clothes. She doesn't care; she's a tomboy. Zu would have wanted me to wear them. She'd have hated her wardrobe to go to waste. I think I'm going to have to watch Flavia as she's already circling like a vulture for the couture. I doubt Zu left me any money. She didn't share her wealth with her poor little sister.'

'Right,' said Lily clocking Minty's slurred speech.

'It's so unfair. She was so rich and Lucile is rich in her own right. I hope I get something out of this damn will. Well, at least she won't get all the photo shoots now.'

'Minty, come on. I think you're upset.'

'What the fuck do you know?' she spat.

'Nothing,' replied Lily, taken aback. 'I came to see if you wanted a lift back but I assume you've probably got a ride with George.' Araminta began to laugh hysterically.

'Yes, it is rather out of the blue. We're having a great time. He thinks I'm hot and actually I think I like him. Don't you worry about me, Lily! I'll make my own way back. I'm quite capable of looking after myself. See you in the office next week.' She stumbled off like a newly born giraffe.

26

Lily was standing outside a warehouse in the East End, having a cigarette. She was having a stinker of a morning. She'd spent the past hour trying to persuade the son of a well-known entrepreneur to pose in some swimming trunks for a photo shoot. The photographer, who was equally egotistical, had thrown a queeny fit and stomped off the set saying his creativity was being jeopardised. Leyland Hooper, the twenty-year-old heir, was similarly recalcitrant. He may have been about to sail around the world in a boat that was shaped like a flying saucer but he flatly refused to get his kit off. It was a stalemate.

Lily's phone rang: Ricky Flynn. She picked up immediately.

'Lady Lily,' said Ricky in a thicker Yorkshire accent than usual. 'How goes it?'

'Good. I'm just trying to persuade a seriously hot young thing to pose in the some Vilebrequin's but it's not happening.'

'What are you talking about?'

'They're luxury swimming trunks for men – haven't you heard of them? Dear, oh dear, Ricky. Still getting your swimmers in M&S?'

'I'm an M&S man through and through. I could do with a holiday. Pity we didn't flog this story to *The Post* – we could be in the Caribbean now having a piña colada on the beach. Peters has thrown us an interesting lead. I winkled it out of him last night, after a romantic evening in the Fox and Hounds. So, on our fifth pint he revealed that the Met have got Zuleika Winters's mobile phone records for the last couple of months and there are two regular callers of unknown origin. Both these numbers are pay as you go. One of them matches the number everyone gave us for Mo but the other is a bit of a mystery. We've tried calling it but the phone's off. It makes me wonder if perhaps she had another dealer as well as Mo? It could throw the case wide open again.'

'Interesting,' said Lily. 'But why would some random dealer kill Sophie at the Serpentine? How do we even know if he or she was there? Also, why doesn't Mo come forward and say it wasn't him?'

'He's too scared and he doesn't want to do time for dealing. It's just a theory, as I say. Mo's still the main suspect.'

'Is this other number on Sophie's phone?'

'Peters is working on that.'

'Have you got the number?' asked Lily.

'They won't release it yet. What do you think of the theory that someone's hiding Mo? Maybe he knew too many secrets.'

'That's a bit far-fetched isn't it? As far as I can ascertain he was just a good coke dealer. They're not that hard to come by, surely? I don't think these people are that fickle that they'd shield a murderer in order to get high.'

'No, I don't mean that. Maybe he's blackmailing someone?'

'Possibly. Look, I'll ask around but everyone says they didn't know him well. I'm off to Ibiza on Thursday to do a cover shoot and interview with your heartthrob Veronique Lapin and another girl called Rocky Star, daughter of seventies hit singer Wolf Star. Can't say I know who he is.'

'You don't remember flower power Wolf of "Tame my Flame Baby" fame? You're making me feel old now. Try and get something in Ibiza, Lily, as Sam's beginning to lose interest. And you don't want to come back in September empty-handed.'

'Is he?' replied Lily, sounding worried. 'OK, well, I'll keep digging.' The last thing she wanted was to return to Kate's features desk.

The photographer walked down the alley to the warehouse and Lily hung up.

'Sorry about that,' he said in a mockney accent. 'The kid was getting on my tits. Let's shoot the fucker in a pair of chinos and a shirt, as obviously, that's what you'd wear in the middle of the Indian Ocean. I mean, it's not like we were trying to shoot him in a pair of Speedos. He's a good-looking chap, I can't see what the problem is.' They went inside to have one last crack at persuading Leyland to get into his swimmers.

Lily walked into Jonty's office triumphantly.

'After much persuasion, we got Leyland Hooper to strip down to his trunks.'

'Excellent,' said Jonty, looking up. 'I imagine it's different work here from what you're used to.'

'Coercing youths to strip is certainly a skill I have acquired since joining *Society*.'

100

'Hmm I'm not sure about that Lily,' teased Jonty. 'Are you all set for this cover story in Ibiza? It looks like it will definitely be Veronique Lapin and Rocky Star. Rocky has just finished the Australian leg of her tour and is back in Europe. Flavia is styling the shoot – she'll meet you out there. She's currently living it up on Peter Paul Anderson's boat sailing around the Greek islands. I want the cover to be full of energy – think young and buzzy. Make sure the interview is full of zip too. Take the angle that women now rule the music industry. Genevieve, Flavia's assistant, will fly out the clothes with you for the shoot. You might bump into Minty, she's out there with her new boyfriend. Good luck! Keep me posted on how you get on.'

'Of course,' said Lily.

'I'm off to Tuscany on my summer holiday but I'll be on my Blackberry. Make sure the art department sends the cover images to me as soon as they are in. Also, Lily, I don't want this shoot to go off-road. Ibiza's a crazy place and I don't want any half-baked schemes, dreamed up after the photographer, Flavia and the girls have been out clubbing all night. I'm trusting you to be the policeman.'

'Right.'

'Remember, no sunglasses on the cover. I want both the girls looking at the camera. And no black clothes. Oh, and Lily, make sure they smile.'

'Got it,' replied Lily. 'It's OK, Jonty, I'll keep the show on the road. Have a nice holiday.'

27

Lily and Genevieve drew up outside their hotel in Ibiza Town at dusk. The hotel was discreetly tucked away down an alley, just beside the imposing, old stone fortress. The building itself was nondescript but it was covered in thick, burnt-orange paint that gave it a warm glow in the final rays of the evening sun. Lily paid the taxi driver and helped Genevieve lug their five, heavy suitcases into the tiny entrance hall of the hotel. Ambient dance music pumped out of a tiny cube Bose speaker, the beats coursing through the air like a quickened pulse. The reception of the hotel was a rich, midnight-blue and there were little pieces of mirrored glass stuck to the ceiling. A sulky girl with indecently full lips, wearing a skimpy, knitted vest and a denim skirt, begrudgingly gave them the key to their room.

'Has another guest called Flavia Wilde checked in?' asked Lily. The girl shrugged nonchalantly. Lily repeated the question. The girl sighed, got up and called down the corridor in Spanish to a colleague. They heard the clip-clop of some flip-flops echo along the corridor. A man in his late forties appeared. He wore his long brown and grey streaked hair in a topknot on his head; a small, pointed bone went through his left nostril and he had a tattoo of Vishnu on his right, upper arm.

'Howdy,' he said in a transatlantic accent. 'Welcome to my pleasure dome.'

'Hello,' said Lily. 'I was wondering if our colleague Flavia Wilde had arrived?'

'Oh yes,' he smiled. 'I've seen some wild ones living here for the past twenty years but she sure is a kook. She arrived with a lobster on her head – brilliant. I told her we'd put it in the paella. She looked at me and said, "Young man this is couture!"'

'That's her,' said Genevieve.

'She's in Nirvana,' said the man shrugging.

'I bet she is,' said Lily rolling her eyes.

'It's the room next to yours. You're in Transcendence.'

'Brilliant. Any chance of Euphoria?' said Lily.

'Sorry that's taken,' said the man, 'but I'm sure you'll experience it while you're here. I'm John by the way. Welcome to my house of dreams. I think "hotel" is such a dirty word. I see my guests as global cousins I haven't met yet. You staying here is the cosmos's way of drawing us together in a circle of friendship. Let me know if you need anything, anything at all. I gather you're out here for a fashion shoot. An excellent choice of location: there is a magical light here. That's why it's called the white isle. It drew me here like Icarus to the sun and I've never left.'

'I've heard about the light,' said Lily politely.

'When's your shoot?' asked John

'Tomorrow. We'll be heading off at nine. Can we grab breakfast before?'

'Early birds, eh? I will make sure there is some breakfast for you on the roof terrace. Go forth and revel, ladies. José will bring your bags up. Your wacky friend is in the bar.'

Lily and Genevieve found Flavia in the bar, drinking a mojito. She was still wearing the lobster hat, which she had teamed with a Gaultier corset and cropped trousers.

'Darlings, what a relief it is to see you both,' said Flavia. 'I am having withdrawal symptoms from Peter's yacht. I was born to have staff. It's a tragedy I can't afford them. Genevieve, have you got all the clothes?'

'Yes,' replied Genevieve, through gritted teeth.

'Hmm. I'm thinking of taking the shoot in a different direction. This island is about hedonism. I smelled it the moment I disembarked from Peter's private jet. We must reflect that in the images. I'm thinking bikinis, heels, hats, jewels. If we use some of those dresses, let's have the girls jumping into the pool in them, waving them in the air or ripping them off seductively. This island is on heat!' Lily shuddered, remembering Jonty's request that they didn't go off-road with the shoot. 'There's a hot waiter here called José. I've persuaded him to come along tomorrow to pose as a pool boy in a pair of Speedos. Also, we're off for sushi tonight. I feel we should eat something with a pulse. Minty has suggested a great place twenty minutes from here up in the hills. John has booked it for us. Don't worry, we've got plenty of time – no one eats here until eleven o'clock. When in Rome, ladies.' She clicked her fingers to the barman, 'Cedric, two mojitos for the girls.'

28

Even though it was nine o'clock when they left the hotel, it still felt like the crack of dawn. The sun had only just dragged itself out of bed and the majority of the island was still asleep. Genevieve, Lily and José managed to squeeze four of the five suitcases of clothes for the shoot into the taxi.

'It's fine; we'll leave the last case,' said Flavia. 'We've got more than enough.'

The drive to the villa was picturesque and Lily drank in first the sea views and then the arid olive groves, as they headed inland. After half an hour they turned into an inconspicuous driveway. Flavia, Lily and Genevieve stepped out of the car and clocked Villa Roca – the house where the shoot was taking place. It was so stupendous that they laughed out loud.

'This is more like it. Sex on a stick,' said Flavia. The impressive, white modernist villa was nestled on the side of a mountain, which was stocked with pine trees and had staggering views of the island. Lily admired the stark, white lines, the multiple balconies and the inviting green pool.

'This is the kind of place you expect rap stars to be snorting coke off supermodels' buttocks.'

'Exactly, Lily,' said an enthusiastic Flavia. 'I'm sure it has happened. If this villa could speak, it would have as many secrets as Hollywood madam Heidi Fleiss. Your Dionysian thought is exactly the vibe we will channel in our shoot. So glad we're on the same page.' Flavia clicked her fingers and a good-looking butler dressed in loose, white linen clothes appeared. 'Hello. What is your name?' growled Flavia seductively.

'Santo,' he replied.

'Santo,' she said, repeating his name and smiling. 'Is Robert the photographer here?'

'He's up on the top balcony with his assistant. Welcome to Villa Roca, ladies. Can I get you anything?' replied Santo charmingly.

'Coffee and mineral water, please.'

'Breakfast? How about I rustle you up an egg white omelette or a fresh fruit salad?'

'Bring a selection of things, Santo, and we'll graze on those. Right, let's find Robert.'

They walked up the stairs to the roof terrace, taking in the hot tub, dance floor and red Bedouin chill-out tent. Robert was in his mid-forties and had short ash-blonde hair. He and his assistant were leaning over the rails of the balcony, surveying the scene, while having a fag. His faded, black jeans were slightly too tight for a man of his age.

104

'Roberto!' shrieked Flavia and let out her trademark cackle.

'Flavia,' he said with outstretched arms before giving her a big bear hug. He nodded to Lily and Genevieve who introduced themselves. 'This is Jerome,' he said, in a South London accent, pointing at his assistant, who beamed back at them.

'Great beard,' said Flavia.

'Thanks,' said Jerome, stroking his designer goatee.

'When are the rock chicks arriving?' asked Robert.

'Any moment,' said Flavia.

'I've spoken to their press people and they should be here now,' said Genevieve, looking panicked.

'No worries, no worries – we've got to set up anyway. Flavia, I think we should shoot one cover try inside. The master bedroom is quite something. It has its own jacuzzi for twelve people.'

'No jacuzzi, Robert, it's just too *Footballers' Wives*,' said Flavia sharply.

'Have you checked out the pool? It's like a lagoon.'

'Let's go down now and take a look. Gen, can you set up the clothes in one of the bedrooms? Have hair and make-up arrived?'

'Yes,' replied Jerome, 'they've set up in one of the back bedrooms.'

'Excellent. Oh to have a mansion like this. Robert, I want this shoot to be *alive*. Let's get some music pumping and get the creative juices flowing.'

At quarter past ten, a jeep with blacked out windows drew up outside the villa. Rocky Star and Veronique Lapin stepped out, both wearing shades. Veronique was dressed in a pair of cut-off denim shorts and a loose-fitting Stella McCartney top and Rocky was wearing a very short, black, gypsy dress with a brown, studded belt slung around her hips. They walked slowly up to the terrace, where Flavia and Robert were discussing the set up for the first shot.

'Yo, yo, yo,' said Rocky, finding some energy. Veronique followed behind her.

'Hi, I'm Robert.'

'Hi,' said Veronique, giving him her winning smile.

'Yo baby,' said Rocky. 'We've met before.'

'Hello,' said Robert who was still melting under Veronique's spell.

'It's rock 'n' roll today ladies,' said Flavia. 'The most important thing for me is that we capture the wild, feckless spirit of youth. Are you with me?'

'Oh yeah,' said Rocky jumping about. 'Don't you worry. I'm pumping, Flavia. We didn't get home until five in the morning and that was only because Ronnie dragged me home. Sébastien was absolutely furious! Ha.'

'Is Simone doing the make-up?' asked Veronique.

'Yes,' said Genevieve, who had just appeared on the balcony. Veronique looked relieved.

'Thank fuck for that,' said Rock. 'She's a genius who can hide a multitude of sins which is just as well. Flavia, this is one phat villa!'

'So, for the first set up, we want you up here with the view behind you. I'm thinking little dresses or evening shorts. Lots of attitude and va va voom,' said Flavia, authoritatively.

'OK, get us slapped up with make-up, babycake! Take us to the transformation room,' said Rocky in her husky, throaty voice.

By one o'clock, the shoot was in full swing. Rocky and Veronique were feeding off each other's energy and Flavia and Robert were delighted with the results. Rocky was wearing a bikini top, chiffon shirt and gold Prada shorts and Veronique was wearing a very short, purple and black Roberto Cavalli dress, with exceedingly high, strappy sandals. The sun was beginning to hot up and everyone was relaxing into the shoot and enjoying themselves.

'Shall I order some rosé?' suggested Robert.

'Yeah man,' said Rocky, taking a drag on her fourth cigarette of the day.

'Not for me,' said Veronique.

'I think we'll move downstairs and do a pool shot,' said Robert, who ordered Jerome to lug all the equipment downstairs.

'Veronique, I want you to be coming out of the water in the Chanel evening dress. Think Ophelia before she died,' said Flavia. Rocky howled with laughter. 'Right, you,' said Flavia. 'I want you in that amazing, red, Dior dress working some shapes. Are you familiar with the pictures Norman Parkinson took of Jerry Hall in Russia in the seventies?'

'The one with the flag?' asked Rocky.

'That's my girl,' said Flavia, beaming. 'Come on, let's get moving. We've got three more shots and the cover to do.'

'And the interviews,' interjected Lily, who was beginning to get slightly concerned about when she was going to get time to talk to the girls.

106

'Lily, you'll have to fit the interviews in around the shots and after we've finished. The girls will need their hair and make-up redoing after the pool. So you can grab a bit of time then – but today is about the images,' insisted Flavia.

Veronique and Rocky sloped back into the villa to get changed. Lily knew she had to befriend them both if she was going to get a half-decent interview and, more importantly, to get any information about Sophie or Zuleika.

29

Robert walked over to the sound system by the pool and pumped up the volume. Balearic beats reverberated round the pool. Everyone began moving to the music – even Wing, the fierce but silent Japanese hair stylist.

'OK rock stars, I want an iconic image,' said Robert.

'Icons aren't made – they are born,' said Rocky, jumping up on to the poolside bar and beginning to sing above the beat. 'We're going to get high baby, yeah, yeah, yeah. Move it to the beat,' she belted in her husky voice.

'What a pair of lungs,' said Jerome to Lily, who was watching the whole thing, bemused.

'Remember Jerry Hall, Jerry Hall,' shrieked Flavia. 'Anyone got a Union Jack?' Robert had grabbed the camera and was already snapping.

'Work it, Rocky, work it,' he said. She pouted and posed on demand. She was a true professional. Lily had never seen anything like it.

'I do actually have a flag,' said Genevieve proudly. 'I've worked with you long enough, Flavia, to have a bag of tricks by my side.'

'Gen, I love you,' said Flavia, kissing her on the nose. Genevieve tied her long copper hair into a ponytail and made her way back upstairs for the hundredth time.

Rocky strutted her stuff on the bar in a sexy, red evening dress that had a slit slashed up to the thigh. She threw her short, peroxide hair backwards and threw the Union Jack over her shoulder.

'Oh, the grand old Duke of York, he had ten thousand men,' she began to belt out in a cool, jazz voice, which went brilliantly with the house music. Veronique leapt up behind her wearing a short, silver cocktail dress and a diamond star in her hair. She threw her arms around her and gave a cheeky salute.

'Yeah, yeah, yeah,' said Robert, shooting them from below then leaping on to the bar and shooting them from above. 'Beautiful!' he shouted. 'Crank it up girls.' Flavia walked over with a cheeky look on her face.

'I have an addition to make for one of the pool shots.'

'Right,' said Robert, looking up from his camera.

'José,' beckoned Flavia. The handsome waiter from their hotel walked out. 'José is going to be the pool boy.'

'Hi,' said Robert, humouring Flavia. Rocky let out a huge wolf-whistle and José beamed.

'Veronique, in the next shot I want you in the Chanel, coming out of the pool. Rocky, you are going to be lying on a sun lounger in the Vuitton blouse and D&G bikini bottoms and José, can you stand in the background with the pool net?'

The shots got crazier and crazier and Lily was seriously worried it was not what Jonty wanted. She walked over to the table where Jerome was sitting, staring intently at a laptop. The digital images from the camera were coming through in quick succession and Lily leaned over to take a peek – they looked fantastic and were buzzing with youthful energy. Flavia may be mad but she had a magic touch.

'OK, I'm going in!' shrieked Rocky. Lily looked up and saw Rocky jump into the pool with a running leap, in the red evening gown. She waited for the image to come up on the laptop's screen. Bang! Robert had caught it. Jerome laughed.

'Bullseye! You got it!' he shouted excitedly. Everyone cheered and came over.

'Excellent,' said Flavia. 'Let's break for lunch.'

'Cool,' said Rocky. 'I need some fuel man. I'm beginning to feel last night.'

'Can we start the interview over lunch?' asked Lily.

'Sure,' replied Veronique.

Lily, Rocky and Veronique walked up to the first-floor balcony where the table had been laid up. An inviting avocado and prawn salad stood in the centre in a frosted glass bowl. A basket of warm bread stood next to it. Santo came out and placed a freshly prepared tortilla in front of them. There was a bottle of rosé in an ice cooler and two chilled bottles of sparkling and still mineral water.

'I'm moving in here,' joked Rocky.

'I'll join you,' said Veronique.

'It can be our place. It has my name after all. I'll change it to Villa Rocky: much better than Roca,' said Rocky.

'So how did you both get into music?' asked Lily.

'You go first, Ronnie. I'm famished,' said Rocky, biting into an enormous slice of tortilla.

'Well,' said Veronique, fixing Lily with her large brown eyes. 'I always used to sing at home with my father, when I was a little girl. He was an actor but also an excellent singer and guitar player. So, for as long as I remember, I have always sung. It's part of who I am.'

'Sure,' nodded Lily.

'Then, when I was fifteen, I was cast in a film where I sang a solo. It was a controversial film in France as it covered some grey areas. It was about desire and that time in a teenage girl's life when you are neither a girl nor a woman. Anyway, I sang this song and it became very popular and it went from there really.'

'Was that *China Doll*?' asked Lily.

'Yes, *Poupée de porcelaine*. So, after that, I recorded my first album and I've made music ever since. My mother is a folk singer; people always forget that because she is less famous than my father was.'

'What does Seb make of *China Doll*?' interrupted Rocky.

'He hated it – of course,' said Veronique, rolling her eyes.

'Seb is in a foul mood with us,' joked Rocky, 'because we got in the DJ box with rap god "Hard Wonga" last night at Pacha.' Veronique glared at Rocky who promptly changed the subject. Lily spent forty-five minutes talking to the girls. They were in full swing, regaling her with stories about the music industry, when Flavia marched up to them, with a forceful look on her face.

'Come on you two. We've got a cover to shoot. Lily, you can carry on with this later. Get into hair and make-up now.'

109

They got up and made their way inside. The villa was bright white and was mostly made up of glass; the overall effect was startling. The rooms were minimalist, but every now and then there were white sofas and stark glass and chrome furniture. They padded into the bedrooms where Wing and Simone were waiting to do their hair and make-up.

'Oh God,' said Wing in a Japanese accent, looking at Veronique's hair, 'It's going to take at least half an hour to get this back in shape, probably longer.'

'No worries,' said Flavia, 'as fast as you can. We're shooting the covers in the master bedroom, so come there when you're done. I've got the clothes ready and waiting.'

Lily sat down on the corner of the double bed and continued interviewing them.

'What motivates you?' she asked.

'Control,' said Rocky, not missing a beat. 'I couldn't do anything else. I feel alive when I sing. I love the nervous tension before singing in front of an audience. It's just crazy. I'm addicted to the high. This is what I'm meant to do – it is as simple as that.'

'For me it is a happiness thing. It gives me a purpose,' replied Veronique.

'Were you both at the Serpentine Party?' asked Lily casually.

'Jesus,' said Rocky. 'Yeah we were. I cannot believe they have arrested Mo. There is just no way he did it. I only found out about this yesterday, when Ronnie told me, as I've been in Australia and Asia touring. For a start, Mo liked Sophie, unlike some people,' and she shot Veronique a look.

'I was there, too. I obviously didn't notice anything on the night,' said Veronique, 'but it was very shocking. Sophie was Sébastien's cousin so it has been very hard for him.'

'Do you think it was Mo?' asked Lily.

'Probably,' said Veronique shrugging, 'it's the most likely explanation. You never know, maybe Sophie was back on stuff.' It was obvious that there had been no love lost between Veronique and Sophie. Lily didn't want to seem like she was pushing them on the murders and they talked about the party for a few minutes.

'I knew Zuleika,' chirped Simone, the make-up artist. Lily was delighted that the conversation was naturally going her way.

110

'Did you?' said Lily.

'I did her make-up all the time. I did practically all of the photo shoots and then whenever she went to an event, which was at least a couple of times a week. I saw her a week before she died. I think she was plotting something. I suspect she was bonking a married man – they did tend to pursue her.'

'I'm sure,' said Veronique. 'I knew her from Paris – she had a flat there. Sébastien and I had dinner with her once. She befriended me and lent me clothes a couple of times. I liked her.'

'I only ever met her at fashion events,' said Rocky. 'She was quite a bit older than me. I don' think she'd have wanted to hang out with a twenty-three-year-old girl who reminded her of her age. She loved younger men. I think she had a fling with George Lazarus.'

'Really?' said Veronique. 'Are you sure? I think she invested in his fund, Rocky. He gets amazing returns for people. Sébastien doesn't know how he does it.'

'I think so,' said Rocky. 'Mind you, I think she had affairs with everyone! Who cares? She's dead now.'

The conversation moved on to general gossip. Lily got some great quotes about the fickle nature of the music industry. Wing had waved her magic wand on Veronique's hair which now looked tousled, sun kissed and sexy. She crafted Rocky's peroxide mop into a quiff.

'We're going to look like lipstick lesbians,' joked Rocky. 'Simone, will you emphasise my eyes and lips? I'm thinking pop art. I'm thinking Andy Warhol's "Blondie".' Flavia walked in, carrying a long, gold evening dress and a short one, covered in thousands of pewter sequins and crystals.

'I was friends with Andy, back in the day. I had some wild times at The Factory. I want one hundred per cent rock chick from you two. Come on! It's time for your close up.'

30

Lily threw her head back in the shower and enjoyed the sensation of the warm water running through her hair. It was ten o'clock and they had only just returned to the hotel. She turned the knob to cold, so that icy jets of water ran down her body. She needed to wake herself up. All she wanted to do was go to bed but Flavia had insisted that she and Genevieve accompany her to George Lazarus and Torquil's villa party. Lily padded out of the bathroom wrapped in a fluffy, white towel and flopped on to her bed. Genevieve was knocking back the rosé, while painting her toenails orange.

'Better?' she asked, fixing Lily with her friendly, brown eyes.

'Yeah,' said Lily. 'You can't come to Ibiza and not party, I suppose. I'm looking forward to part two of the Rocky/Veronique show.' She did an impression of Rocky gyrating on the bar going 'ooh baby!' Genevieve laughed.

'Come on, it will be fun. We're going for dinner at half eleven at Las Dos Lunas with Flavia and the team. It's the best restaurant on the island. You know Flavia and her expenses. We deserve it, we've worked hard enough.'

'You're telling me,' said Lily. 'Are shoots normally this exhausting?'

'Yes. It's worth it: the pictures will be great.'

'The girls certainly liked posing. I've never seen anything like it.'

'Do you want some rosé?'

'No thanks, Gen. I am going to need something harder if I'm going to make it for dinner, let alone the party,' said Lily. 'I think I'll get José to bring me up a vodka lemon.' She picked up the lilac phone on her bedside table and ordered. 'Who is this Torquil character?'

'Torquil is the Earl of Launceston. You know Flavia: she loves a title.'

'Right.' She put her head on the pillow and shut her eyes in the hope of snatching a few minutes sleep. She was rudely interrupted from her slumber by a sharp knock on the door.

'Enter,' she said, expecting it to be José with her vodka. Flavia strutted in, wearing a skin-tight neon lime and yellow rubber dress and orange Dame Edna Everage style shades.

'Right, what are you two wearing?' she demanded.

'I thought I'd wear the McQueen gold sequin dress from the shoot,' said Genevieve.

'Good idea, Gen. What about you, Lily?'

'I've got a print maxi-dress which I thought I'd wear with some gladiator flats. I thought I'd channel my inner hippy.' Flavia looked horrified.

'You will do no such thing. Look at you, you have the body of a goddess – just as good as either of those girls on the shoot today – and you want to hide in a printed sack? No wonder you're single. You need taking in hand.' Flavia's eyes alighted on the suitcases of clothes from the shoot. She marched over and began rifling through it.

'McQueen, Chanel, Dior, Burberry, Prada, D&G, Giambattista Valli, Missoni, Pucci, Armani, Stella, Lanvin for Christ sake!' She began waving a pair of midnight blue, silk shorts around.

'Try these on,' ordered Flavia. Lily reluctantly put them on with a blue and black see through, silk blouse that Flavia flung at her.

'No,' she said firmly. 'This is too much – it's a villa party. I want something more low-key. I'll wear a dress,' she conceded.

'What about this Missoni jumpsuit with the Chloe wedges?' said Flavia, whooping in delight at her own suggestion. Lily took it from her and walked into the bathroom. She stepped into it. The knitted fabric clung to every curve on her body. The mirror was still steamed up from the shower so she stepped out of the bathroom to see the others' reaction. Flavia and Gen wolf-whistled.

'You're wearing that, Lily,' said Genevieve.

'You are. You have no choice,' said Flavia. 'Put on some make-up and meet me in the bar in half an hour. Robert and co are meeting us at the restaurant.'

31

Lily was so tipsy by the time they arrived at the Villa Margarith that she was no longer self-conscious about the catsuit. They followed the sound of the dance music around the sprawling villa and down to the party area, where there was an infinity pool, with multicoloured underwater lights and a chill-out zone with hammocks, giant cushions and banquettes. Fairy lights and hurricane lamps burned in the darkness and the smell of cigarette and hashish smoke clung to the warm air. At the far end, was a round hut with a thatched roof, where there were some turntables and impressive speakers. Lily recognised Araminta's boyfriend, George Lazarus, standing behind them wearing large, bug-eyed shades, huge DJ headphones and a T-shirt with 'Style Icon' emblazoned on the front in gold print. He was punching the air with one hand and pretending to mix the discs with the other. Every now and then he would shout 'tune' and a group of scantily clad girls on the dance floor would cheer and punch the air back at him. Araminta was in the middle of the group of girls, wearing a pair of black hot pants with a black, star-studded leather belt. She'd teamed these with a burgundy, brocade waistcoat and a skimpy, black vest. She ran over the moment she spotted them.

'Flavia!' she shrieked, throwing her arms around her. Then, she proceeded to hug all of them. 'I'm so happy!' She whooped and did a little jig. Robert raised an eyebrow at Lily, who stifled a giggle.

'Hi, darling,' said Flavia, giving her a kiss.

'You must get drinks. There's a bar over there in the corner. I recommend the Araminta cocktail – it has mint and lime and is utterly delicious like me!' She pushed them in the direction of a table, covered with a white tablecloth, where two tanned youths were serving drinks. As they walked over, they spotted Rocky and Veronique sitting with a slight, simian chap who was holding a guitar. Lily immediately recognised him as Irish crooner Andy Blake, who had had a string of hits popular with housewives. He was a constant figure of fun in Lily and Billy's flat because Billy knew him from the Guildhall and hated him with a passion.

'How are my rock stars?' asked Flavia.

'We're grand,' replied Andy, puffing on a joint and passing it to Veronique with a flirty look.

'Andy, this is fashion genius Flavia Wilde, Robert Simpkin the photographer and the team from *Society* magazine. We were doing a shoot with them today in the sexiest villa known to mankind. It was seriously bling and, rather appropriately, it was called Villa Rocky,' said Rocky.

114

'I know Villa Roca,' smirked Andy knowingly. 'I've had many a wild night there,' he said, gazing at Veronique with his grey eyes.

'I'm gasping for a drink,' said Robert and they followed him to the bar – apart from Flavia, who settled in next to Andy. As they walked away, they heard Flavia demand that Andy serenade her.

Lily flopped down on an enormous cushion next to Robert and Jerome and they spent the next hour people watching. Oscar Rutherford came and held court on the banquette next to theirs – he was wearing very tight, white jeans, no shirt, buckets of fake tan, a diamante crucifix and lashings of mascara.

'He certainly waxes his chest,' observed Robert, 'I did that once in the eighties. It was seriously painful. He's a funny chap; I photographed him the other day. I don't think he was remotely upset about Sophie dying. He seemed over the moon that he now has a solo show. It was all he talked about. He mentioned he was meant to be doing a telly job with Zuleika but he is doing that on his own now, too.'

A tall man in his late twenties with curly, auburn hair and blue eyes came up to their table.

'Hi, I'm Torquil,' he said.

'Hi. I'm Lily and this is Robert, Jerome and Genevieve. We've come with Flavia. I hope you don't mind us crashing your party?'

'Not at all,' he replied, smiling. 'As long as you enjoy yourselves I'm happy.' A young girl, who couldn't have been older than nineteen, walked up to him.

'Come on Torquil,' she nagged.

'No, Tansy. This is my younger sister,' he said, introducing her.

'Hi,' she said dismissively. 'Don't be such a dork, Tork. I'm nineteen not twelve. Anyway I'm on my gak year,' she joked. He shook his head at her - exasperated. She stormed off.

'Never allow your younger sister to pressgang you into coming to Ibiza on holiday with you. BIG mistake. I've spent the whole night being a policeman, preventing her from taking drugs or pulling my friends.' Robert laughed.

'Good luck with that!' said Lily. Torquil smiled and followed in hot pursuit of Tansy, who was now pestering Sébastien and George in the DJ booth.

'Nice guy, bad name,' said Robert. The others nodded in agreement.

More revellers arrived and the party was soon heaving with attractive girls and boys intent on having a good time.

'I'm going to have a wander,' said Genevieve. 'Care to join me Lily?'

'Sure,' said Lily, getting up. They made their way over to the bar to get a refill. An old school friend of Genevieve's cornered them. After twenty minutes of polite conversation, Lily left them to it. She strolled up to the villa and walked in. It was immaculately done up with hand polished stone floors, large windows and lots of chill out areas with wide, cream sofas with plump cushions in chic muted colours. Lily walked through the house and out to a terrace on the other side. A vine was growing up the side of the wall and there was a line of small, manicured, lime trees in large, terracotta pots. Lily thought she saw something out of the corner of her eye and she quickly turned round. In an alcove, at the far end of the terrace, a couple were making out. Lily turned away but then something made her turn back. She saw the girl's long brown hair falling down her back and saw a guitar resting on the seat nearby. It was Veronique and Andy Blake.

Lily ducked back into the villa in search of a bathroom. She was utterly confused. Why would a beautiful girl like Veronique, who had an equally handsome boyfriend, go for a joker like Blake? She walked down the hall and opened a heavy, wooden door at the end of the corridor. It led on to a spacious bedroom complete with a four-poster bed and white see through curtains. She crept across the room and opened the en suite bathroom door. There was a gasp and she saw Rocky Star snorting a line of cocaine off one of her own CD cases, which was resting on the turquoise sink tiles.

'Busted,' said Rocky laughing, 'Do you want one?'

'No thanks,' said Lily.

'It's OK, I won't tell anyone,' said Rocky. 'We can be partners in crime.'

'It's not my thing,' said Lily. 'I'd love a fag though. I've run out.'

'Sure,' said Rocky. 'Let's have it on the back terrace.'

'I think you'll find Veronique is busy out there,' said Lily, raising an eyebrow.

'Ah,' nodded Rocky. 'She and Sébastien had a row about the cover and us dancing with Hard Wonga last night at Pacha. She's just having fun – forget it. They're both French – that's what they do isn't it?'

'Probably,' said Lily. They flopped down on the four-poster bed. Rocky lit Lily's fag and then lit one for herself. Then, she lay back on the bed, stretched her arms behind her and sighed.

'It's nice to have a bit of quiet time,' said Rocky her eyes half-shut because of the cigarette smoke.

'I need it. It's been a long day,' said Lily. She looked at her watch: it was already four in the morning.

'Please don't mention your little drug bust to anyone,' said Rocky, 'I don't do it often. I'm just tired and having a few days off from touring. I'd hate you to think I was a cokehead.'

'Don't worry,' said Lily.

'Really?' said Rocky. 'Phew. You wrote about the murders didn't you? I googled you when we got back.'

'Yes I did.'

'For what it's worth, I don't think Mo did it. I left with him and he was normal. We went to a rhythm and blues night in Soho after the Serpentine. I don't think he would have been all cool if he'd just murdered Sophie.'

'Who did it then?' asked Lily.

'I don't know but lots of people didn't like Sophie. She was so hot and cold – a real Jekyll and Hyde. I know Veronique hated her. She thinks she purposefully introduced Sébastien to lots of pretty girls in London. Ronnie lives in Paris most of the time, so they see each other at weekends and stuff. Mind you, I don't think Sébastien liked Sophie much either. He was really embarrassed by her and was very relieved not many people knew she was his cousin. Minty loathed her because she rejected her from *Fashion Fix* and, of course, Oscar was nice to her face but bitched about her all the time. There are four people for a start!'

'What is the link between them and Zuleika? There is no credible motive for any of them,' said Lily.

'Hmm,' said Rock, sniffing. 'Well Minty didn't get on with Zuleika. I see your point though – you'd hope you wouldn't murder someone over a TV show or a dress. All I'm saying is that it wasn't Mo. You should talk to Lazarus, they were both clients of his – he might know something. I've got a bottle of vodka over there. Do you want a shot?'

'Now you're talking,' said Lily. Rocky got up and walked over to the ebony chest-of-drawers where the bottle stood. She

117

unscrewed the lid and took a big swig. She came back over to the bed and handed the bottle to Lily, who took an equally big gulp.

'That's my girl. Are you sure I can't tempt you to a line?' she asked, playing with the bottom of her ripped T-shirt, lifting it up to show her tanned washboard stomach.

'No I'm fine,' said Lily. Rocky looked at her and smiled quizzically.

'You look hot in that catsuit.' She lent forward and kissed her on the lips. 'Really hot,' she mumbled, lingering for a few seconds. When Lily didn't respond she got up and walked into the bathroom. Lily was incredibly relieved.

'I think I'll head back to the pool,' said Lily.

'See you down there!' shouted Rocky from the bathroom.

Lily walked along the corridor to the back terrace. Luckily, Veronique and Andy Blake were nowhere to be seen. She stepped out on to the terrace and looked up at the stars, which looked particularly vivid in the pitch-black sky. What the hell was happening? Had she given off lesbian vibes? She laughed and thought to herself that this trip couldn't get any weirder.

32

Lily returned to an electric dance floor. There were at least a hundred people going for it. She noticed that George Lazarus was no longer on the decks and a handsome man, with very tanned, brown skin and a zigzag shaved into his buzz cut, was rocking the party. One of the speakers had been moved out of the hut and was now on the edge of the dance floor. A progressive house tune with a deep penetrating beat was playing. The beat was so loud and hypnotic that Lily could feel it coursing through her body – it felt sexy. The song broke into a tune and there was a loud cheer, Veronique had jumped on the speaker and was pretending to be an air hostess pointing at the exit rows. She was wearing a little, sixties style hostess's dress and hat and was clearly loving all the attention. Torquil and George were dancing by the speaker, egging her on.

Lily spotted Robert and Jerome dancing by the side of the pool.

'Hello stranger,' said Robert with saucer-like eyes.

'Hi ecstasy eyes,' said Lily laughing.

'I'm too old, I know, but I feel young inside.'

Lily found Flavia flopped on one of the giant cushions talking to Araminta and Oscar Rutherford. Minty was so out of it, she was just lying there and every so often she would say, 'I'm rushing, I'm rushing.'

'What does that mean?' asked Flavia laughing.

'Pull it together, Mint,' said Oscar. 'It's not a good look.' He got up and walked off without acknowledging Lily.

'Hi,' said Lily, sitting down on a huge cushion with mirrors inlaid on it.

'It's the reluctant beauty,' said Flavia. 'Have you kissed anyone yet?'

'Rocky just tried to snog me,' said Lily, laughing.

'Ha! I told you you looked sexy,' said Flavia. 'I'm not hugely into this house music, I prefer rock 'n' roll.'

'Me too,' replied Lily. 'Where are Keith and Mick when you need them?'

'Now Mick is a proper pussy magnet. If he were here that dance floor would be having a collective orgasm. I know – I've seen it.'

'Get with the programme, you two,' said Minty. 'The Stones are for dinosaurs. It's all about electric beats now,' and she flounced off on to the dance floor.

'What rot,' said Flavia, 'dear Minty's not the brightest, she doesn't have Zuleika's brains. Poor Zu. I really miss her,' said Flavia.

'What did Peter Paul Anderson make of it all?' asked Lily, taking advantage of the fact that Flavia was obviously tipsy. Flavia lit a menthol cigarette and inhaled deeply, pausing for thought.

'He thinks it's dodgy. What is not known is that he and Zuleika were actually on very amicable terms when she died. Everyone thinks they were estranged but that isn't true. They made an effort to get on for Lucile but also because a lot of water had gone under the bridge.'

'Really?'

'He said rich people don't buy bad drugs. She was like Keith Richards in that regard – she bought good shit. Also, he said, and

119

I agree with him, that she didn't take huge quantities. He thinks someone spiked her coke to kill her.'

'Why would they do that?' asked Lily.

'Because she knew something. We both think she was about to reveal something. She was setting up this production company to make documentaries and we think she might have unwittingly stumbled on something.'

'Didn't she tell anyone what she was doing?'

'No. She was very secretive about it because she was fully aware that people thought of her as a fashion airhead and wouldn't take her seriously.'

'Would Dr Bone know?' asked Lily.

'Who?' asked Flavia.

'Her tutor.'

'Possibly, but I doubt it. I was one of her best friends and she didn't tell me.' It crossed Lily's mind that Flavia wasn't the best person to keep an explosive secret.

'Have you told the police?'

'We only came up with this theory on holiday. Peter and I are going to try and find out a bit more and then we'll mention it to them.'

'I think you should do it sooner rather than later, Flavia. It could be important and you might be putting yourself in danger, if you go renegade.'

'You go renegade, Lily,' said Flavia, shooting her a knowing look.

'I don't know what you mean,' said Lily, brushing off the comment.

'I think we should go soon. I loathe admitting it, but I'm too old for this. I don't take drugs and I need to go to bed. Can you get Genevieve to call the driver? My bed and John's house of dreams beckons – I must return to Nirvana,' said Flavia dramatically.

33

Lily found Genevieve propping up the bar. The drinks had run out and there were just a couple of bottles of warm lemon Fanta left on the stained white tablecloth.

'Have some of this,' said Genevieve, passing her a pale green drink. Lily took a gulp and then drained most of it.

'Steady on,' said Genevieve.

'Sorry. I was seriously thirsty,' said Lily.

'No it's not that, Lily. It had MDMA in it,' replied Genevieve, laughing out loud.

'You're joking.'

'Nope! Enjoy the ride. Don't worry. It's not that strong. Look at me: I'm fine.'

'How much have you had?' asked Lily.

'Just the sip I had taken before you wolfed it down!'

'Who gave it to you?' asked Lily, praying it wasn't Minty.

'Minty,' replied Genevieve.

'Have you seen her?' said Lily. They turned and looked at Minty gurning on the dance floor, waving her arms around out of time with the music.

'Great. Will that be me in half an hour? Also, Flavia wants to go.'

'What? Oh what a pain. I'll call the driver. Don't worry, he'll take at least an hour to get here, everyone on this island is on a permanent digression.'

'OK,' said Lily. 'I'm going to get some water.'

'Hmm, I'm not sure that'll help. Minty's had buckets loads,' she teased.

After much searching, Lily found the kitchen in the back of the villa. She opened the fridge, scanning it for mineral water, but all she could find was a half-drunk bottle of tonic water.

'Great,' she said, and opened various cupboards looking for a glass. She opened the freezer and found some ice. At that moment her mobile beeped. She knew there was only one person who'd text her at this hour. She nervously took the phone out of her bag and read the message.

> *Darling, I miss you. We were shelled today. I just made it but my translator didn't – dark times. Makes me wonder why I'm doing this and what I'm missing out on with you. Hope you're well sweetheart. O x*

Lily read it again and sighed; she was fed up of being sad. She looked up and saw Sébastien standing in the doorway. She had no idea how long he'd been there.

'You look beautiful. This way of dressing suits you.' Lily rolled her eyes. 'The English can't take compliments,' he said, shrugging his shoulders.

'Don't give me that crap. You're half-English, Sébastien.'

'Have you been researching me, Lily?' he asked. Suddenly Lily felt a rush of energy through her body, becoming incredibly relaxed for the first time in months. She laughed at Sébastien.

'Interesting though you are, I have actually been researching your girlfriend.'

'Ah,' he nodded, 'I didn't want her to do the cover. Why all this publicity?'

'She needs to sell albums.'

'Hmm. I don't want to talk about her. I want to talk about you. Who was your text from?'

'No one,' said Lily.

'Yeah right,' laughed Sébastien. He reached over and picked up her phone.

'Don't read it,' said Lily.

'I thought it was nothing,' he replied mockingly.

'It's my ex. He is in Iraq – he just got shelled.'

'I'm sorry,' said Sébastien.

'It's an occupational hazard,' said Lily bitterly.

'Are you looking for a hero, Lily?'

'No. I just fell in love with someone who loves his job more than me.'

'Hmm,' said Sébastien looking at her. The effects of the MDMA were now in full effect and Lily stretched her arms in the air and smiled.

'It's no big deal.'

'I see that. It just makes me wonder why a serious girl who is in love with a war journalist would be working on a fashion magazine. It just doesn't sit with me. I suspect you like to live on the edge too.'

'What?' said Lily, fixing him with her now very dilated pupils. 'It's a great job.'

'For an Oxford girl like you? I'm not buying it.'

'Now whose been doing their research?' said Lily.

'I have.' He stepped closer to Lily. 'And I've now got some empirical research to do,' he said, staring at her seductively. He began to run his hands up and down her body. He pushed her head back and began to kiss her. Lily began to kiss him back, slowly at first and then faster and more urgently. He pressed against her and she could feel his taught, muscular body. She ran her hands up and down his back and under his T-shirt to his flat, strong stomach. He grabbed her by the waist and pushed her back on to the marble table-top. Before she knew it he was on top of her, kissing her neck and working his way down to her chest. She ran her hands through his chestnut, brown hair. He looked up at her and fixed her with his green eyes. He was mesmerizingly attractive.

He began kissing her neck again and his hands slipped behind it to undo the tie on her catsuit. Before she knew it he was kissing her breasts, playing with her nipples with his tongue. Lily dug her nails into his back, seriously aroused.

'You're so hot,' he purred and then he moved back up to her mouth and carried on kissing her. Lily lay back and enjoyed the moment. The MDMA was coursing through her veins and she felt light-headed and elated. After a couple of minutes she began to gather her focus and pushed him off her.

'Whoa!' he said, looking confused.

'This isn't appropriate,' said Lily, coming to her senses. 'I'm out here to interview your girlfriend. This is unprofessional.'

'Don't stress. She won't find out. She's so off her head – she wouldn't notice.'

'That's not the point. Look, I've got to go.' Lily fastened her catsuit and jumped off the work surface.

'Please yourself,' said Sébastien. 'It's a shame, I was rather enjoying myself.'

34

The last two weeks of August were dragging their heels like an overworked lap dancer. The *Society* office was dead. Minty had stayed in Ibiza with George Lazarus, Flavia had returned to Peter Paul Anderson's yacht, which was now moored in St Tropez, and Lara was living it up on Harbour Island. Jonty was penning an opus on the Bloomsbury set from Lord Bilby's Tuscan villa but still managed to phone in every morning at nine thirty to check up on them. As a result, Claudia and Lily were taking it in turns to arrive on time. Molly had to be on time every day and didn't cease moaning about it. Claudia was taking full advantage of Jonty's absence and had spent the entire week having beauty appointments. This laissez-faire attitude to office hours was playing into Lily's hands, as she and Ricky had met a couple of times to discuss the murders, which had now completely disappeared from all the papers. They were following up Flavia's tip-off that Zuleika had inadvertently trodden on someone's toes with her planned documentaries. They had invited Dr Bone to join them for lunch at Scott's to see if he had any idea of what they were about.

'Don't you just love August?' said Claudia, swanning into the office in a pair of oversized, black shades and bouffant hair. She had spent the entire morning having her very blonde highlights done at Richard Ward for a beauty feature. She looked glamorous, in a low cut, cornflower blue tea-dress that showed off her ample bust. She'd upped the voltage with bright red Louboutin heels. She sucked in her tummy, stuck out her chest, lowered her shades and peeked over the top of them.

'Get me a coffee,' she barked at Molly. 'I'm channelling my inner Hesba Blair, editor supreme and ruler of the world.'

Hesba Blair, the editor of American *Catwalk*, was the most powerful woman in fashion and was much revered in the *Society* office. Molly shrugged, stuck out her tongue and ignored the command.

'Not even close, darling. I'm not remotely scared,' she said, stealing Claudia's thunder. Jessica, the long-suffering managing editor, rolled her eyes.

'Don't worry, Jess. We're still getting our quota of pages through. We seem to get more done when no one is here,' said Claudia.

'Fine. I'd be delighted to cut the salary budget,' said Jess. 'Then I can balance the books. Flavia's expense bill for July is beyond a joke. I just hope she economised in Ibiza.' Lily thought about the lavish dinner for all the shoot crew at Las Dos Lunas in Ibiza and shuddered. 'Lily, we need to wrap up the cover images and story by next Wednesday. It's bank holiday next Friday and everyone will begin buggering off if they haven't already done so.'

'I've been told the images should be in today and you'll have copy by Monday, I promise.'

'What's the delay?' asked Claudia when Jess had gone. 'Were they dull as shit? Most celebrities are. The real life stories are much better. What you want is a dissolute earl who's shagged around and has a huge grudge against his ex-wife and the enormous alimony payments he's shelling out; or an attention seeking artist who'd sell their vagina for some publicity. The emotionally incontinent are manna from heaven for us. Luckily, there are lots of these types in society.'

'Some people would pose in their lavatory for free publicity,' added Molly.

'Loose cannons make good copy,' said Patrick in his precise, clipped voice, 'or people with nothing to lose or something to prove. The rest, quite frankly, is wallpaper. Mind you, I don't read magazines. All my pals find it hilarious that I work here. I haven't read a magazine for over twenty years, if at all, and I wouldn't read a women's title.'

'How to get ahead in magazines,' quipped Claudia. 'Come on, Patrick, tell us you had a subscription to *Catwalk* when you were at Eton.'

'Certainly not,' said Patrick, looking appalled. Lily and Claudia stifled giggles. 'So, are the three of us going to enjoy a long, liquid lunch?'

'Absolutely,' said Claudia, 'and I've got a story to charge it against. Lily?'

'I can't today. I'm meeting an ex-colleague.'

'Where?'

'Scott's.'

'I think *The LEN* expense account is more generous than ours. Patrick, are you happy with a steak around the corner?'

'As long as there is wine and good company, Claudia, I don't give a damn. My taste buds got pickled years ago.'

Lily walked into the Audley on Mount Street at half past twelve. Ricky was hunched at the bar with a pint of bitter. He was wearing a pale blue shirt with a sharp collar and his usual grey suit trousers. There were dark circles under his eyes, which were unusually bloodshot. His face looked more wrinkled than usual, partly because he could hardly open his eyes.

'Late night?' asked Lily.

'You're good. Yes it was, actually. I was in the 606 club until three in the morning, catching some jazz and then the rest.' Lily gave him a knowing look. He waved his arm to brush it off. 'What are you having?'

'A coke, please. I'll have a glass of white with lunch. I want to keep my head clear.'

'I find it helps oil the wheels. I'm an old school hack. We're like old cars: we need filling up to get going.'

As it was a warm August afternoon, they made their way outside to one of the wooden tables that overlooked Mount Street. Ricky squinted in the bright sunlight and rubbed his head. He took a battered pair of tortoiseshell shades out of his pocket. Lily looked at them – they were almost rectangular and looked like something Joe Pesci would wear in *Goodfellas* but not in a cool, ironic way.

'What the hell are those?' asked Lily.

'Prescription. Couldn't get my lenses in today.'

'You look like someone's loser uncle.'

'Thanks, Lily! You're not at *Society* now. No need to call the fashion police.' Lily smirked.

'London is officially dead right now. The whole of the *Society* office is away. I tell you, I should be in St Tropez on Peter Paul Anderson the IV's yacht, digging away.'

'What is it with the Americans and the number thing? Are they trying to invent an aristocracy?'

'Something like that.'

'Come on then. What are we going to get out of this Oxford don? He certainly has expensive taste. I was thinking we'd go up to Oxford and take him for a pub lunch but, oh no, he wants to go to Scott's, don't you know!'

'Well, he got a taste for the highlife with Zuleika. You know academics, they're just like journalists: they love a boozy lunch as long as someone else picks up the tab. We have to find out if he knew about Zuleika's production company and, also, all the people and subjects they covered. It'll be fine Ricky – this guy loves the sound of his own voice. You just sit there and look pretty. I'll ask the tough questions.' Ricky smiled and gave her a little salute.

Lily and Ricky finished their drinks and strolled along to Scott's. The smart doorman ushered them in with a smile.

'Your guest is already here,' said an eastern European waitress with rust-coloured hair. Lily and Ricky looked over and saw a

126

balding, chubby, little man with round, black glasses, sitting back in his chair surveying the room. He nodded at them.

'Hello, hello,' said Dr Bone, enthusiastically, jumping up to greet them. He couldn't have been more than 5' 5" and both Lily and Ricky towered above him. He thrust his plump, damp hand into Lily's and shook it vigorously and then did the same with Ricky. Lily saw that he was immaculately dressed – he wore a striped, pale blue and white shirt that fitted him perfectly and went excellently with his cream, linen trousers. Doing up his cuffs were a beautiful pair of mother-of-pearl cufflinks.

'I must say, I do like this place,' he said, his sonorous voice reverberating round the room. Two chic ladies on the next door table muttered something under their breath.

'Are you a regular?' asked Lily.

'Well, Lady Zuleika and I came here a great deal. It is a bit like old times and wholly appropriate that I should talk about her here.' He studied the menu. 'I recommend the baked, spiced crab, the oysters and John Dory. And, if I can be so bold, the Rully Blanc, is absolutely excellent with fish.' Ricky raised an eyebrow at Lily.

'So, doctor, we think you may be able to help us in our investigations into Zuleika's death.'

'Well I am of course happy to help you, Lily. As I told you before on the telephone, I was a great fan of Zuleika's and I am so upset that someone did such an unspeakable thing to her. It is like the Borgias – quite horrendous and unbelievable. One thing we must get straight, though, is that you call me Philip. We are not in the lecture hall now. I understand you, too, were at Oxford,' he said, drawing out 'Oxford' so everyone on the surrounding tables would be in no doubt where he worked.

'Yes I was,' said Lily.

'English Literature at Hertford I believe?'

Lily smiled politely but she didn't want to get distracted with university reminiscences.

'Philip, I've been doing some digging around and I understand Zuleika had set up a production company and was about to embark on a career in documentaries. Did she mention this to you?'

Their waitress came to take their order. Lily and Ricky ordered sea bass and Dr Bone the John Dory. The doctor was keen to get a generous array of side dishes.

'Yes, she did mention it. She was worried people weren't going to take her seriously. She said the image of her as a society and fashion figure clouded people's opinion of her and meant everyone thought she was an airhead. She wasn't stupid, you know. She was a victim of class! I know how ridiculous that sounds, but it is true; a lot of upper-class women in the seventies and eighties were sent to dreadful boarding schools, where they learnt very little, apart from how to snag a man. As if that is the be all and end all of life.' The promised bottle of Rully arrived. The wine waiter filled their glasses. The doctor smelled the bouquet and put the glass to his lips. 'Delicious! How lovely to meet you in the flesh, Lily, and you, Ricky. You must have some fascinating stories being the crime man.'

'It keeps me interested,' said Ricky, who was obviously struggling with his hangover but trying not to show it.

'So what was Zuleika planning to do with this production company?'

'It was early days. I know she'd registered the company and, obviously, she had the money to indulge this interest.'

'Was she going to direct them?'

'No, I don't think so. In fact it's rather a shame everything has turned out the way it has, as I was going to be the historical adviser on them, which would have been a lucrative little affair and a lot of fun. I was looking forward to working with her. '

'Really?' said Lily, kicking Ricky under the table.

'Was Zuleika going to be in them?' asked Ricky.

'Well, I'm not sure. To be honest, I think she imagined herself as the new, hot historian! Oh dear, can you imagine?' he chuckled.

'So she was going to present them?' asked Lily.

'I'm not sure. As I said, she knew what people thought of her and I think she thought she would produce a couple and gently edge her way in front of the camera. But Lily, as I say, it was very early days – these were just ideas. Although, I must admit, I did encourage her to stay away from the camera for the first few. I said I thought they would need to have a credible, historical figure presenting them.'

'Like you?' flattered Lily. Dr Bone smiled and puffed his chest out.

'I don't really think I have the face for television but that doesn't seem to matter these days, especially with historians. I'm better looking than Simon Schama or David Starkey.'

128

The waitress arrived with the food and proceeded to place the fish plates in front of them. She returned with silver dishes filled with lashings of creamy, mashed potato, fried zucchini, buttered beans and creamed spinach.

'What a feast,' said Dr Bone, smacking his lips. Ricky proceeded to dig into the mashed potato, putting the majority of the dish on his plate.

'Excellent choice of wine, Philip,' said Lily, giving him her winning smile. 'I must say those are stunning cufflinks. Are they a family heirloom?'

'Thank you, Lily. Actually they were a gift from Zuleika. They are art deco. I think they may even be a Winters family pair. I'm not asking any questions. She was so generous.'

'Everyone has said that. Do you know what she was planning on making these documentaries about?'

'Vaguely. I think she was just throwing ideas around. There was no time pressure. She would ask to study different things each week. As I said on the phone, when we first spoke, at the time of her death she was interested in French politics, the metaphysical poets and scandalous women in history. They were mainly of an aristocratic bent.'

'That doesn't sound controversial,' said Ricky, shooting Lily a look that said why are you wasting my time here? 'It's unlikely you'd be murdered for making a documentary on a historical figure. I don't think any distant relatives of Marie Antoinette were going to come and poison her cocaine.'

'I never said I knew who killed her,' said Dr Bone defensively.

'Of course not,' said Lily soothingly, 'just out of interest, Philip, who was she interested in?' The doctor looked at his glass of wine, which was now empty.

'Well, as Ricky guessed, Marie Antoinette was indeed a favourite of hers but she wasn't planning on making anything about her. She thought there were so many things about her already out there. She was fascinated by the Mitfords.'

Ricky groaned. 'I don't understand the fascination with them. Two of them were fascists, one was all over Hitler like a rash and then people go on about them as if they're national treasures. If I see one more thing on them or the Duchess of Windsor, I'll scream. Real people don't care.' Dr Bone winked at Lily. He was finding Ricky's reaction hilarious.

129

'You're just like some of my students, Ricky. It's so nice to see that youthful passion in an older man. I hear what you say – not everyone can stomach the whims of the upper classes.'

'Who else, Philip? This is fascinating.'

'Let me think. She was interested in Diana Mosley and the Duchess of Windsor but I think she would have agreed with you, Ricky, that they were over-exposed. The Duchess of Argyll, Vita Sackville-West, Jane Digby, Lady Castlemaine and Caroline Norton were all of great interest to her. She was looking for subjects and she liked women with scandal in their lives. I must stress that the documentaries project really was in the embryonic stages and maybe she talked to other people about completely different ideas. However, I do think she would have run them past me. She respected my opinion on intellectual matters. Not on fashion, of course!' he smiled. Lily jotted all the names down in her notebook.

'You saw her on the day she was murdered, didn't you?' asked Ricky, who obviously thought the historical figures were complete red herrings.

'I did, Ricky. We had an early supper here and that's where I gave her the tutorial. I didn't go to her apartment that day.'

'Gosh. The police must have pumped you for information. You were one of the last people to see her alive.'

'Well, the last one people know about,' said Dr Bone, taking another gulp of wine. 'Initially it was fine, when they thought she died of a cocaine overdose, but when the coroner's verdict came back as unlawful killing, I suddenly found myself being a possible suspect! Can you imagine? Me, a fusty little Oxford don in the middle of a society murder. Well, Zuleika would have loved that.'

'So what did you tell them?' pushed Lily.

'Looking back, she was quite excitable that day. I didn't really notice it at the time but, with hindsight, I would say she had a frenetic energy about her, the energy of a woman in love. Actually, not a woman in love but in lust. I think Lady Zuleika found it hard to love and I am sure she may well have confused the two.'

'Do you think she was emotionally stunted?' asked Lily.

'I think she was damaged by her upbringing and the fallout from her marriage.'

'She was on good terms with her husband,' said Lily. Ricky gave Lily a quizzical look.

130

'Yes, she was, but I think there were scars. We don't come through the emotional quagmire unscathed. Otherwise, we might as well all be robots.'

'You're a romantic,' said Ricky, draining his glass of wine. The cheese arrived and Lily and the doctor dug in. Bone loaded an oatcake with a large dollop of smelly epoisses.

'Did you have feelings for her?' asked Lily.

'I was fond of her and I'd be lying if I said I didn't find her physically attractive. I certainly didn't kill her; apart from it being the act of a savage, her dying is a terrible state of affairs for the Bone finances. I'm substantially out of pocket. Not only do I miss out on my weekly fee but I was in line to do handsomely out of the documentaries, if they'd ever got off the ground.'

'Neither of us think you killed her, Philip,' said Ricky, in his frank, Yorkshire accent. The doctor shuffled in his chair and smiled.

'Good.'

Lily looked at her watch: three-fifteen. 'Do you have any idea who this paramour was?'

'I have no idea. Zuleika was so secretive about her personal life, probably because so much had been revealed in the press with the end of her marriage and the break-up from James Purcell. She simply wouldn't discuss it – she really did trust no one. She would hardly use her mobile phone with her lovers, as she claimed her and Purcell's mobiles got hacked when they were dating. This has been a big problem for the police as there are hardly any clues on her phone.'

'It's true,' said Ricky nodding. 'It's most unusual.'

'Do you think she had one lover or more?'

'I don't know. When I first met her, she was with James Purcell and I think she was very happy with him and, actually, she was devastated when that finished. Then, there were a lot of different men, I think, but she didn't talk to me about them. More recently, she'd make the odd passing comment but that was it.'

'What kind of comment?' asked Lily.

'She was funny because she liked to shock me. About eighteen months ago she said, "I am sleeping with an accountant. Everyone says they're dull but, really, they're very sexually adventurous." Then a few weeks ago she poured me an excellent glass of Muscadet and said, "I drink a cold glass of this before I blow my fella." I would stutter and squirm and she loved that!' Lily and Ricky laughed. 'I think she probably saw a few married men and thought I'd disapprove – but who am I to judge another mortal? She was an attractive woman who knew the power of her allure. She used it and good for her, but I hope it wasn't that that caused her demise.' Dr Bone looked very sad and Lily could tell that he had genuinely been fond of his exotic pupil.

Ricky called for the bill and paid before Bone could start on the digestifs. The three of them made their way out on to Mount Street.

'Well it was lovely to meet you,' said the doctor, shaking their hands. 'Do get in touch if you think I can help you any more.'

'Thanks, Philip, you've been most helpful,' said Lily. They watched the rotund figure of Dr Bone, waddle up Mount Street towards Grosvenor Square.

'Well that was a waste of time,' said Ricky, 'apart from the Muscadet anecdote.'

'You should call Peters and tell him he should be closing in on a kinky accountant,' said Lily. Ricky laughed.

'Jesus it's quarter to four! I've got to fly. Sam's back in the office and wanting answers.' He stuck out his arm for a passing taxi and leaped in.

35

It was a gorgeous August afternoon and Lily walked back through Berkeley Square, looking up at the refreshingly green leaves of the trees as she went. London was satisfyingly empty – it felt as if someone had pushed a pause button and time was standing still. It was four o'clock when she walked into the lobby of Panther Publications. Lily was slightly worried that she was pushing her luck. Her fears were allayed the moment she walked in, however, as Patrick had passed out on the sofa in Jonty's office and was snoring loudly.

'Sweet isn't it?' said Claudia who was flushed pink and looked like she, too, had had a boozy lunch. 'Ooh, you'll never guess what just came through.'

'What?'

'We just got an email from the Winters and Hamilton-Bruces' to say there will be a joint memorial service for Zuleika and Sophie on the 4th September.'

'Gosh. That's quite strange isn't it?'

'Well they are odd circumstances and I suppose a lot of the same people would have been asked to both. It will be a fascinating affair; more like a fashion jamboree than a memorial. You know what it's like when famous people die – every man and his dog wax lyrical about how wonderful they were and how they were their best friend. I wouldn't miss this for the world.'

'Do you think I can slip along?' asked Lily.

'Darling, anyone who is anyone will be going. That is the beauty of *Society*: you can just say it's work.'

'Perfect. I suppose I better begin writing this blasted interview. I'm finding it very hard to get started for some reason.'

The reason was Sébastien. Lily felt guilty about her dalliance in Ibiza. Even though she knew Veronique had been conducting her own infidelities with Andrew Blake, she felt she'd crossed a line professionally. However, this had not stopped her replaying the seduction over and over again in her mind. Often, she imagined how it might have played out. She'd received one text from him the day after. She'd read it repeatedly and each time she felt excited, very excited.

> *Hi Lily, I know I shouldn't but I keep thinking about you. S x*

After a day and much discussion with Jazz, who was in two minds about the whole thing, Lily had replied.

> *Naughty boy. Me too. L x*

That was over a week ago and she hadn't received a reply. This didn't stop her checking her phone every five minutes and complaining to Billy about it. He thought the whole thing was hilarious and teased her incessantly about getting off with one of the interviewees' boyfriend and being propositioned for a lesbian tryst by the other. Jazz was pleased that Lily fancied someone for once but thought the circumstances were far from ideal. Billy was sceptical, saying he didn't trust him as he was too smooth and played polo. Lily knew her father would be totally confused by a sweet-talking, French, polo-playing, hedge funder/playboy. She had never fancied anyone like this before. He couldn't be more different from the rugged, fearless, craggy Oliver who threw himself into deathly situations, daily, in order to reveal the truth.

Lily read through her transcript from the interviews with Rocky and Veronique and wondered what on earth she was going to write. She came to the conclusion that Rocky was a highly sexed, adrenalin junkie. She'd listened to their music and thought they were both talented. She'd also read all their press cuttings and now had no excuse not to write the article. She put on her earphones and began playing Rocky's album *Funk Me Hard Punk*. In the first track her husky voice declared, 'I'm a soul soldier and I'm searching for something'. Lily began typing.

> *Rocky Star and Veronique Lapin have a strategy about how to get ahead in the music industry: 'Never take no for an answer and write your own material.' In a world of manufactured girl bands, Star, twenty-three, and Lapin, twenty-eight, are a welcome breath of fresh air. This comes as no surprise, as both have music and charisma hardwired into their DNA. Lapin is the daughter of the late, legendary, sixties heartthrob Pierre Lapin and his folk singer wife, Camille Delacroix, and Rocky is the daughter of seventies crooner Wolf Star.*

Lily's phone beeped. She was happy for the distraction and immediately opened the text message.

> *I'm back in Ibiza in the same villa. Every time I walk into the kitchen I think about you and how you rudely pushed me away. Want to know how it was meant to end? X*

Lily smiled. She knew everything about this was wrong but it was exciting, forbidden and sexy.

> *You must be telepathic. I was just writing about you. Go on then, finish me off. X*

Lily pressed send. She had no idea if he'd text back or if he'd leave it another week. She could tell he was a game player and she didn't want to let him take control. She told herself to step back and just play it cool. If she'd learnt anything from her disastrous love life it was not to give everything away at the onset. She would no longer throw herself into things with wild abandon – her doomed relationship with Oliver had caused her far too much unnecessary sadness. In the end, she'd felt powerless and she would never let that happen again. She went to go and buy a coffee, purposefully leaving her phone on her desk.

When she returned ten minutes later the first thing she did was pick up her phone like a lovelorn teenager. The irony wasn't lost on her. There was a text waiting.

> *Don't write anything about me. Not yet. There is a reason and you'll like it. After I ripped down your catsuit and pushed you back on the table top kissing your perfect breasts, I picked you up and flung you over my shoulder, carrying you next door to the bedroom. I pulled down your catsuit, and you were naked in front of me – yes, I noticed you weren't wearing pants. Then I knelt down and began to kiss your thighs working my way gently upwards…*

36
Guards Chapel, 11am, Tuesday 4th September 2007

The atmosphere outside the Guards Chapel was more like that at the beginning of a rock concert than a memorial service. The majority of women were dressed in black but this did not stop them looking like they should be strutting down the catwalk instead of the aisle of a church. Most wore highly tailored dresses or jackets teamed with killer heels and statement hats – many of which were designed by Flavia's favourite milliner, Percy Quinn. The fashion crowd and socialites milled around outside the entrance of the chapel, posing and smoking in full view of the hovering paparazzi. Lily spotted supermodels Jocasta Jones, Marika Jablinski and Isla Bennet-Hughes chatting to the fêted fashion photographer Larry Lauzanne – the photographer who had taken most of the outlandish photographs of Zuleika that had been plastered all over *Catwalk*, *Society* and various other fashion magazines.

Jonty ushered Lily, Claudia and Lara along towards the entrance of the chapel.

'It sounds awful but we want a good seat,' he said apologetically.

'Absolutely,' said Claudia, 'I want a good view of fashion god and editor supreme Hesba Blair. Sorry, Jonty!' Jonty laughed.

'Has Hesba Blair flown over from New York?' asked Lily.

'Yes,' said Lara, 'Zuleika was a proper fashion maven. She has the editor of *Catwalk* and the world's best designer eulogising about her.'

'Jesus,' scoffed Claudia. 'Who has Sophie got? Will she be upstaged in death as well as in life by Zuleika?'

'She's got a good designer,' said Lara.

'Who?'

'Jethro Seward.'

'Small fry compared to Blair and Marount,' snorted Claudia.

'OK, enough,' said Jonty before adding, 'Sophie's godfather is speaking.'

'Hit us with it,' said Claudia.

'A king of screen and stage,' replied Jonty. Lara, Lily and Claudia all looked at him inquisitively.

'Kenneth Brannagh?' said Claudia. Jonty shook his head.

'Douglas Quail.'

'That's pretty cool. He has an Olivier and an Oscar,' said Lily, joining in. 'Does that make it thirty all?'

'No way,' said Lara. 'Zuleika is winning. This is a fashion memorial.'

They had reached the entrance of the chapel and walked in. As they did they were each given an order of service that had an elegant Percy Quinn sketch of both of the dead women on the front. Lily took in the enormous chapel with its high, wooden ceiling and the impressive collection of Union Jacks hanging majestically on both sides of the aisle. The chapel was already three quarters full. The Marquess of Sussex, an imposingly tall man in his late forties, who had dated Zuleika briefly after she divorced Peter Paul Anderson, waved at Jonty and ushered them in to sit with him. Lily spotted George Lazarus and Oscar Rutherford guarding the front rows for the families of the deceased. She looked over the congregation, taking in all the famous faces: Zuleika's ex, actor James Purcell, was near the front, sitting next to Marcel Marount and Flavia. She was wearing a black, tweed, McQueen jacket with a nipped in waist and huge lapels and a small, black hat with a cascading waterfall of black and red feathers that fell diagonally across her face. It was spectacular, and very Flavia.

Then Lily saw the back of his head. The unmistakable wave of dark, chestnut hair, his strong powerful shoulders and muscular lithe body, clothed in a sharp, Savile Row suit. She immediately got a flashback of him pushing her back on the kitchen worktop in Ibiza. Of course, Lily knew Sébastien was going to be there – it was his cousin's funeral – but the sight of him filled her with nervous excitement. He was with Veronique, who was clad in a neat, dark grey Chanel suit. His arm rested on the back of their pew and he was tapping his fingers restlessly. They were both deep in conversation with Ryan Todd and Henry Marmsby.

The chapel was now full and the latecomers were standing at the back. Lily scanned the rest of the congregation for familiar faces. She spotted Zuleika's assistant Miss Lemon, Dr Bone, Gerald the building manager at 21 Manresa Road, the writer Lucinda Norse and then two rows from the back were Detective Chief Superintendent Peters and Commander Jaggs. Lily discreetly tapped everyone she recognised into a note on her phone.

At eleven, on the dot, the Winters and Hamilton-Bruce families entered. Zuleika's elder half-brother, Earl Winters, led the Winters clan. He was a stocky man with thick, sandy hair. His face was doughy with a strong nose and a generous chin – his wife a tall, whippet-thin woman with short, brown hair and a pinched look, walked by his side. Behind them was a good-looking man in his late forties with jet-black hair laced with grey. Lily immediately recognised him as Peter Paul Anderson IV, Zuleika's ex-husband. He was holding hands with a pretty, teenage girl with very long, dark brown hair. The girl was Zuleika's daughter Lucile. She had Zuleika's dainty, pointy nose and lofty frame. Minty was behind them, wearing a sensational, black, Roland Mouret dress that looked more appropriate for a film premiere than a memorial service. She shimmied down the aisle, loving the attention. She was accompanied by her anthropologist half-brother Richard Winters, who was like a *Big Issue* seller in an expensive suit. He had a shock of unkempt, thick, mousy hair and a bristly beard. He looked in need of a jolly good wash.

The Hamilton-Bruce family followed close behind. Major Hamilton-Bruce was an imposing man with a stern face. He and his wife looked exhausted and broken. She was wearing a hat with a very large brim that obscured her face. Behind them was a man in his thirties who, Lily assumed, was Sophie's brother, Louis. He had his arm around a young girl who couldn't have been older than twenty. She was staring at the floor as she walked along but Lily could see she was an absolute stunner and wondered who she was; she knew Sophie didn't have a sister.

Once the families took their seats in the front pews, the congregation stood and the service began. They sang a hearty rendition of 'All Things Bright and Beautiful' and then the handsome film star James Purcell read an E. E. Cummings poem.

'To be nobody but yourself – in a world which is doing its best, night and day, to make you like everybody else – means to fight the hardest battle which any human being can fight; and never stop fighting.' Purcell looked up meaningfully, giving the congregation the dazzling effect of his performance and his piercing, blue eyes. The female half of the room swooned. When he sat down, magazine editor extraordinaire Hesba Blair walked confidently to the front of the chapel. She looked magnificent in a black, Dior suit, which had a discreet mink trim around the lapels. She had a thick mane of perfectly groomed, caramel, shoulder-length hair and buttery tanned skin. Her auburn eyes smouldered behind smoky grey eye make-up. She was the best looking fifty-something woman Lily had ever seen.

'It's interesting that James chose that poem to talk about Zuleika as, when I first met her at a party at Indochine in the eighties, she quoted it at me, a glass of champagne in one hand and her white pet rabbit, Albi, in the other. Albi was as immaculately dressed as Zuleika – he wore a ruby-studded collar and Zuleika looked statuesque in a matching red sequin power dress,' said Hesba in a transatlantic drawl, tinged with a slight English accent. 'Zuleika truly was a one-off in a world where we are constantly pressurised to conform. She came to New York to escape her very English upbringing and that she did. Of course, I have met many English society girls in my years of being a fashion magazine editor but Zuleika was different – she had that playful insouciance of the young and privileged but she also had a vivid imagination and a genuine, zany streak. She really didn't care what people thought of her and she embraced life. She lived in the now and didn't allow herself to be weighed down with thoughts of consequences. This made her a unique person to be with.

Over the twenty years I knew her I saw her develop a passion for fashion I have seen in only a handful of other, equally extraordinary individuals. She knew fashion didn't save lives, she knew it was superfluous but she enjoyed it for what it was. She saw fashion as more than the clothes we wear on our backs, she saw it as a method of self-expression and boy did she run with it! She championed young designers, bought whole collections outright and was a muse to many of the best designers in the industry. She would put herself in danger in order to catch that defining image. Who can forget her straddling a fake black bomb, flying through a window, with shattering, stained glass flying all around or hanging off a turret with metres and metres of heavy hair extensions?'

Hesba's eulogy lasted for ten minutes. She went on to talk about Zuleika's sense of humour and generosity to her friends. Then, designer Marcel Marount took to the microphone to honour his 'greatest muse'. Fifteen minutes into his eulogy, Claudia leant over and hissed, 'This is going on far too long! We've got Veronique Lapin's performance, some harp music, two more eulogies, a reading and a couple of hymns to go.'

'It's turning into a fashion wankfest,' whispered Lara. Jonty glared at them. Marcel Marount finally finished his eulogy and returned to his seat. Everyone clapped – more out of relief than anything else. Veronique walked up to the pulpit and began to sing 'Amazing Grace' in her sweet, haunting voice. Many of the congregation were discreetly wiping away tears. Halfway through the song, Lily turned around. She didn't know what made her look round but at that moment the door of the chapel quietly opened. Lily couldn't believe her eyes - it was Mo. He was perfectly turned out in a black suit, white shirt and black tie and his dreadlocks were pulled back into a neat ponytail.

37

Mo stood tucked away at the back of the chapel. Lily couldn't believe nobody seemed to have noticed him. Veronique had finished singing and the congregation stood to sing 'The Lord's my Shepherd'. Lily nudged Claudia. 'Mo, the prime suspect is standing at the back!' Lara and Claudia immediately swivelled round to see. Mo was singing angelically, looking calm. There was a look of intense peace on his face. They began singing the third verse:

> Yea, though I walk in death's dark vale,
> Yet will I fear none ill;
> For thou art with me;
> And thy rod
> And staff me comfort still.

It was in the middle of the third verse that someone tapped Detective Chief Superintendent Peters on the shoulder. Lily saw the man in the row behind whisper something into his ear. Peters immediately looked in Mo's direction. When he saw Mo, his face fell. He looked utterly astonished. He muttered something to Commander Jaggs who looked absolutely furious and the two men spent thirty seconds discussing what to do. They got up as discreetly as possible, Peters walked down the aisle and Jaggs went subtly down the left-hand side of the chapel. The majority of the congregation carried on singing the hymn, oblivious to what was going on. Lily, Claudia, Lara, Jonty and now the Marquess of Sussex were watching Peters and Jaggs, open-mouthed. Mo carried on singing, he must have known the police were coming but he stood firm and belted out:

> Goodness and mercy all my life
> Shall surely follow me;
> And in God's house forevermore
> My dwelling place shall be.

Jaggs and Peters were now on either side of him and were discreetly trying to persuade him to accompany them outside.

He was staying firmly put. A skinny man in his twenties, wearing a black pinstripe velvet jacket, grey skinny jeans and a thin, black tie had made his way to the pulpit of the chapel where the microphone was. He had bright red hair and thick, tortoiseshell glasses.

'I remember the first time I met Sophie. It was at a party in Hackney. It was two o'clock in the morning and a friend of mine had challenged me to make a dress for her out of one of the sheets on the bed we were sitting on. I ripped it and wrapped it round her and was writing "punk it" on it with red lipstick, when Sophie walked in. "Hey, flame boy. I'll have one of those but can you make it out of the curtain? Red's more my colour."'

Jethro Seward's reminiscences were rudely interrupted by a loud shout of, 'GET YOUR BLOODY HANDS OFF ME!' Mo was pushing Jaggs and Peters away. The whole congregation turned round – there was a collective gasp of horror.

'I promise you, I didn't do it. I am an innocent man!' he shouted at the congregation, 'God is my witness.' There were a few boos and hisses from various pews of the chapel.

'Come with us, sir. Please don't make a scene. Just come with us,' said Commander Jaggs firmly.

'Let me say goodbye to my friends. I loved those girls. I'd never do anything to hurt them,' said Mo, who was obviously charged with emotion.

'Moses Brown, I am arresting you on suspicion of the murders of Lady Zuleika Winters and Sophie Hamilton-Bruce and of drug offences. You do not have to say anything. But it may harm your defence if you do not mention when questioned something you later rely on in court. Anything you do say may be given as evidence.'

'You have no right to arrest me in the house of the LORD.' Mo flung himself down on to his knees and began to pray. 'I know I'm not a saint Lord!' he shouted, 'but I am a Christian and I promise you on my life and on the lives of those whom I love, that I would never commit such disgusting, evil acts.' Peters and Jaggs were beginning to haul him up. 'Dear God, help the police find the real killer. The true perpetrator of evil.'

'Come on, Moses, do you really want to be manually dragged out of this church?' said Jaggs forcefully.

'I recognise him – he was always round Lady Zuleika's flat. I'll help you get him out,' said Gerald, Zuleika's building manager, and a few other men came forward.

'OK, OK I'll come with you,' said Mo realising his time was up. 'I don't want to ruin this beautiful service – but I'm telling you all that I did not murder these women.' He stared at Jaggs and Peters and shouted, 'You've got the wrong man! I'll find the person who has set me up. Minty, Oscar, Sébastien, Veronique - I thought you were my friends? George is the only sound one among you.' Jaggs and Peters began to physically remove Mo from the church. Mo shrugged them off with force.

'I'm coming with you. Goodbye, Zuleika and goodbye, Sophie. I know you know the truth and that's all that really matters. Rest in peace my friends. The truth will prevail,' and with that he turned round and walked out with DCS Peters and Commander Jaggs.

38

The moment Lily was back in the *Society* office she slipped off to the fire escape to call Ricky. She'd already had four missed calls from him during the taxi ride back with Jonty, Claudia and Lara. Ricky picked up the phone immediately.

'Tell me you saw it all?'

'Yes. It was quite something. It beats Richard Mason's interruption of Rochester's wedding in *Jane Eyre* or Duckface's wedding in *Four Weddings* for dramatic church scenes.'

'How did he look?'

'Smart, serene and a little nervous. He has a lot of chutzpah! Not many men would walk into the memorial service of the two dead women they are suspected of murdering after being on the run from the police for six weeks. It's unbelievable.'

'Do you think the guilt got to him?'

'I don't think so. He certainly believes he is innocent – there is no doubt about that.'

'Lily, can you write up everything you saw and email me in the next twenty minutes? I know it's rough you're not getting a byline

142

but we can't blow your cover yet. I want every minute detail. I want the reader to feel like they were there. We've got some great photos of him coming out of the chapel – pure gold. Sam is over the moon. The paps caught it all.'

'What will happen now?'

'Well, they've got thirty-six hours to question him and charge him. I wonder if they have enough evidence to charge him for the murders? They'll certainly charge him for drug offences while they try and gather enough evidence to build a case. Peters is out of radio contact so I've been dealing with Detective Inspector Baradi – he's the office manager on the case. He is running the incident room. I don't know him and he's being very tight-lipped and by the book. They'll do a press conference when they've charged him.'

'Ricky, Mo mentioned that George Lazarus was the only one who stuck by him. He ranted about how all the others had deserted him but that George "was his friend". I'm sure the police will be on it – but I think we should both be looking into George Lazarus's affairs. We need to work out what Mo meant. Did George help him escape?'

'You've met this chap, haven't you?'

'Yes. He's not very friendly. He's a cokehead who's obsessed with house music. He's dating Araminta now.'

'This is all so incestuous. I'll look into him, too. Send me everything about the memorial and, then, work on George. Speak later.'

Mo's appearance at the memorial service was the only topic of conversation in the *Society* office that afternoon.

'I'm still flabbergasted,' said Lara. 'Even if he didn't do it, I think it was disrespectful to disrupt the service.'

'He's a drug dealing murder suspect, Lara – I don't think he'd have checked the *Debrett's Book of Correct Form* before arriving,' said Claudia archly.

'It was extraordinary,' said Jonty. 'I feel desperately sorry for the families.'

'I didn't think anyone would upstage Hesba – but Mo managed it,' said Claudia.

'I wish I'd been there,' said Patrick, 'I've never heard of anything like it. What do you think Lily? You've written about the suspect.'

'I think he didn't do it.' Everyone looked taken aback.

'Really?' said Lara.

'Listen. I think he supplied the drugs and they'll get him for that.'

'The drugs that killed Zuleika,' interjected Lara playing with an oversized, silver Tiffany bangle on her left wrist.

'They'll get him for manslaughter,' said Patrick. 'If he admits selling the drugs, he'll go down for the whole thing. And it sounds like he sold her the drugs.'

Jonty's phone rang. Molly answered.

'Yes. She is here. Do you want to speak to Jonty?' She mouthed 'police' to Jonty.

'Hello, Jonty McDougall speaking. Yes. Yes. She's here. Come up to the third floor.' He put the phone down and turned to Lily. 'The police are here to talk to you. Why don't you go into my office? Molly can you meet them at the lift and bring them in please.' The whole office began exchanging glances.

Two uniformed police walked in – one woman and one man. The policeman was of average height with acne-pitted skin and the woman was petite and sturdy. They looked very out of place in the *Society* office.

'Hello, Lily,' said the policeman. 'I'm DS Bond and this is Constable Smith.'

'Hi,' said Lily stretching out her hand. They shook hands.

'Why don't you go into my office?' said Jonty, ushering them in. The three of them walked in and shut the door. Lily took Jonty's chair and the two police officers sat on the two chairs on the opposite side of the desk. Constable Smith ran her eyes over the framed magazine covers that hung on the walls.

'You've got both the victims then?'

'Yes,' said Lily wondering what all this was about. Constable Smith took a black notebook out of her breast pocket. Lily could see Jonty talking to Lara and Claudia out of the corner of her eye but she knew they were all observing what was going on in his office.

'Lily, you wrote on Friday 20th July in a *London Evening News* article that Moses Brown was overheard saying, "there are a lot of things we don't know," about Lady Zuleika's death, to the deceased's half-sister and the Count de Bourgogne at the Serpentine Summer Party. Is that correct?'

144

'Yes,' replied Lily, feeling nervous.

'You were there at the Serpentine Party on the night of Sophie Hamilton-Bruce's murder?'

'Yes I was.'

'Could you swear in court that Moses Brown said that?'

'Yes I could.'

'You have some knowledge of the case. What do you think he was talking about?'

'I suspect, although I don't know, and this is just a guess, that he was trying to infer to Araminta that he hadn't sold Lady Zuleika dodgy cocaine. You should speak to Araminta.'

'We are doing so,' said DS Bond.

'Do you think Mo was inferring he had some knowledge about the murder?' asked Constable Smith.

'Perhaps. Although I think what he was trying to say, without saying it out loud, was that his coke didn't kill her. It must have seemed ridiculous to Araminta at the time, as everyone was under the impression Zuleika had died from a cocaine overdose.'

'On that night, did you see the suspect having an altercation with Lady Araminta and Sophie Hamilton-Bruce?'

'That was earlier in the evening,' replied Lily. 'I saw the three of them having a heated discussion but I didn't hear it. I imagine Moses Brown was saying more explicitly what he tried to imply later, when there were more people around.'

'Yes, that would tally with what we've been told,' said DS Bond, 'Thank you for your time, Lily. We may need you to be a witness in court.'

'Right,' said Lily, a little taken aback. 'Of course, Sergeant – anything I can do to help.' They got up and Lily walked them to the lift.

'How is the questioning going?' she asked casually.

'Everything is moving along nicely. We're all very keen to put this case to bed. The Commissioner, Sir Ian Redmond, has made that very clear.'

'Sure. Well, good luck.' The lift bell pinged and the two police officers stepped in.

145

39

Lily spent the rest of the afternoon researching George Lazarus and his family. There was not a great deal of information available. After surfing the net, scouring *Debrett's* and going through any press cuttings and old copies of *Society*, she gleaned that he was the elder son of Viscount Lazarus, a retired stockbroker who lived in Hampshire with his wife, in a Queen Anne mansion, twenty minutes drive from Newbury. The family also owned Kinvara Hall, a shooting lodge on the Strathlargan Estate in the Highlands of Scotland. George had two siblings – a younger brother Casper, twenty-seven, who was a lawyer and a younger sister Rose, twenty-one, who was studying medicine at Glasgow University. George had studied economics and politics at St Andrews and, after he graduated, he'd joined American megabank F L Norton's in their private client division. He'd left in 2003, when he was twenty-nine, to set up his own fund, Lazarus Investments. He had blazed a trail and, in the last couple of years, had obtained extraordinarily good results that were markedly above the market average. As a result, he now looked after the money of a number of major high net worth individuals.

Lily picked up an old pile of *Society* magazines and began flicking through the social pages at the back of the magazines. There was George with the usual suspects – Henry Marmsby, Sophie Hamilton-Bruce, Rocky Star, Sébastien and Veronique Lapin. There were a number of pictures of him with a skinny blonde called Vanessa Codrington but the pictures of the couple stopped around 2005. Lily discovered that Vanessa was a management consultant, who had moved to New York around that time. She'd found nothing contentious or anything that linked him with Mo, apart from the fact that she knew he had a serious cocaine habit – but she couldn't prove that. He had the cocaine sniff and was regularly spotted coming out of loos at parties but that was hardly proof of anything.

Patrick got up from his chair to make a cup of tea. He was wearing a dark green sweatshirt that he had been given while reviewing a golf hotel in Spain. It amused Lily that such a proper and exact person was so scruffily dressed most of the time.

146

'Patrick, do you know anything about the Lazarus family?' He strolled over to her desk, happy to be distracted from the 'How to achieve the perfect eyebrow' article he was editing.

'They're an old family whose influence has waned in the last century. The Viscount had to sell the family seat as his father ran it into the ground. Not much cash but they're old school. I can't say I know them. I think I've met Lord Lazarus once – not much to report.'

'The son's a ghastly snob,' said Claudia, who had just emerged from Jonty's office. 'The kind of person who really cares who your grandmother's great-aunt was and what brand of shoes you're wearing. I met him again with Minty and he's truly awful. I'm sure she's only with him because he's stinking rich.'

'Well he must have some money to date Araminta,' observed Patrick.

'He's whisking her off everywhere. They have been staying in luxury hotels around the globe and taking private jets like buses. She's over the moon,' said Claudia.

'His fund looks like it does very well. It performs way above the market,' said Lily.

'How much?' asked Patrick, his interest piqued.

'Fifteen-to-twenty per cent.'

'Impossible. Go down to Companies House and get the records Lily. I'll give you a hand. It sounds too good to be true even in the current market.'

'Thanks,' said Lily.

'Why are you so interested in him?' asked Claudia. 'Oh, I know, Mo's rant at the memorial service. Lily, you don't let go on this story do you?'

'Just nosy,' replied Lily, trying to brush it off.

At five o'clock, Lily's phone rang – it was Ricky. She headed out of the office and down to Starbucks to take the call.

'Lily, it's all closing in for Moses Brown.'

'What?'

'I've been outside his flat all afternoon. Dr Philips and his team are here – doing yet another forensic search. Philips told me Mo's fingerprints were on the cocaine in Sophie's bag. That links the two cases as we know he was Zuleika's dealer. The phone records

147

prove they were in constant contact, there were four calls on the day before she died and we are assuming he sold her the drugs on that day.'

'It doesn't prove he strangled Sophie. None of his DNA was found on her body, was it?'

'But, if he gave her the coke, it isn't looking good. I think they'll at least get him on manslaughter for Zuleika, if not murder, as the strychnine was added to cause death. Anyway, what are you – his lawyer?'

'No. I just have a gut feeling about it – I need convincing. I know the evidence is pointing in his direction.'

'You're not in an Agatha Christie novel, Lily. Murder is usually quite straightforward. Anyway, the breaking news is that Mo has a lock-up in Tooting. The police have had an anonymous tip-off, probably by a disgruntled competitor, and they're checking it out now. I think the case is finally coming to a head. The police are excited – I can sense it.'

'Wow. If they get his stock then he's certainly going down.'

'All going well, he'll be in the magistrates' court being charged for the drug offences and Zuleika's death, if not Sophie's, by the end of the week. This will move fast now, Lily.'

'I think I'll still keep going with my investigation into George Lazarus's affairs. Mo's comments were odd. I think there's something fishy with that fund.'

'Sure – keep going with it but, Lily, I'm pretty sure the police have got the right guy. It's a good side story, though, so go ahead.'

Lily walked out of Starbucks and began making her way back to the office. She was about to enter the building when she heard a 'psst' behind her. She looked around but there was no one she recognised on the pavement.

'In here,' whispered a voice and she noticed a black BMW saloon with blacked out windows. The back window came down a little and she saw Flavia inside.

'Get in,' she ordered. Lily opened the door and saw that Zuleika's ex-husband Peter Paul Anderson the IV was sitting beside Flavia. Flavia was still wearing the black, Alexander McQueen suit that she had worn to the memorial service. She had removed the waterfall hat that was resting on the front seat next to Peter Paul's chauffer.

'Bert, drive round the block.'

'This is very exciting,' said Lily, slightly bemused.

'Have you met Peter?'

'No,' replied Lily. 'Nice to meet you,' and she held out her hand. The handsome American shook it. Lily noticed that he wore his vintage Cartier watch on his right hand.

'Hi, Lily,' he said in his East Coast accent. He, too, was still wearing his suit from earlier but he had removed his tie and his crisp, white shirt was unbuttoned at the collar.

'Lily, we think you can help us. We know you know more about these murders than you're letting on,' said Flavia.

'What do you mean?' said Lily.

'Oh, come on, you're still working for *The LEN*. We have contacts too you know. Look it doesn't matter. We're not telling anyone. We just want to pick your brains and pool resources.'

'Right,' said Lily, admitting nothing.

'Do you think Mo murdered Zuleika?' blurted out Flavia.

'I'm not sure. The evidence points that way but I have reservations.'

'Why?' asked Peter Paul, jumping in. He ran his hand down the side of his head, his well-groomed fingers touching the splattering of grey hairs that gathered at his temple. The rest of his hair was jet black and Lily could tell that he must have been a real looker in his youth.

'I just don't think he would have killed Sophie at the Serpentine Party and I doubt he would have arranged her body in that sadistic way. Also, he had a good business with this society crowd so why would he kill his clients? There was no evidence he despised them, in fact, if anything, he idolised them. He loved going to all the trendy parties and he hung out with his clients all the time.'

'He'd kill Sophie to protect his skin, if she was going to go to the police.'

'Sure – I understand the motive, Flavia. It's just a niggling feeling I've got. But, look, I'm not sure myself. He's the obvious guy.'

'Why are you so interested in George Lazarus?' asked Flavia. Lily was completely taken aback.

'What?'

'You're not the only one who's good at detective work round here, Lily,' said Flavia smugly.

149

'It's probably nothing – it was Mo's comment about George in the church that made me think he warranted some investigation, coupled with the fact he looked after both the victims' money. Also, his figures look a little too good to be true.'

'Exactly,' said Peter Paul, who was suddenly very animated.

'Did he get brilliant returns for Zuleika?' she asked.

'My lawyers and accountants are going through her finances with a very fine toothcomb. Yes, he did get the returns but I'm not sure where the original money is. She invested over £30 million with him and I am beginning to get suspicious.'

'I'm off to Companies House tomorrow to get the records,' said Lily.

'I can spare you the trouble. I've got copies. I've now got all of Zuleika's papers and I've managed to get hold of Sophie's bank details. Let's go back to my house on Chester Row and I'll show you what we've got.'

'Great,' said Lily. 'Let's go.'

40

Lily walked into the living room of 5 Chester Row and took a deep breath. It was covered in fabulous art.

'That's a Munch isn't it?'

'Ah, Lily, it's nice to be with someone cultured,' said Flavia, throwing herself back on to one of the plush oyster-coloured sofas. 'I must say, I don't want to go home. I have been staying here for a few days, while Peter and I try and work out what happened to Zu and I could get used to this. I, after all, was born to have staff.' Lily walked over to the other side of the room to admire a Keith Haring painting of a red figure doing a crab with four green men running over his prostrated body.

'Love, love, love Haring. I recognised this one. It's wonderful to see the original.'

'Oh good,' said Peter walking in. 'I've got a Warhol and a Koons sculpture downstairs – if you're interested.'

'Oh yes,' said Lily.

'I'll show you after we've looked at these accounts. Mark, my PA, is just gathering everything together. What can I get you ladies to drink? How about a martini?'

Lily looked at her watch: it was quarter past six. 'Sounds a tad strong for going through bank statements. I'd love a gin and tonic, please.'

'Tosh, Lily!' exclaimed Flavia. 'Peter makes an excellent martini – proper American measures. He can't drink them any more but he sure likes mixing them up.'

'A wild past,' said Peter smiling. 'Flavia, you'll have one?'

'Absolutely: make mine dirty.'

'Do you mind if I smoke?' asked Lily.

'No, not at all,' said Peter, 'I like a girl with a vice,' he winked at her and handed her a beautiful, hand painted Hermes china ashtray with a leopard on it. Lily took a ten pack of Marlboro Lights out of her bag and removed one. Before she had time to light it, Peter was by her side baring a flame from a chic, black enamel and silver lighter.

'I can't abide matches. If you're going to smoke, you've got to appreciate the ritual of it.' A good-looking man in his late twenties came in holding a dark chocolate-coloured leather box file. He put it down on the smoked-glass coffee table.

'When is Michael going into Lazarus Investments?' Peter asked.

'Thursday. Lazarus is away on business but that is probably to our advantage.'

'Thanks, Mark. Can you get Jacintha to send up some sushi, in an hour?' Peter made the two martinis at a discreet, mahogany bar in the corner of the room. 'Try this for size,' he said, handing Lily a satisfyingly heavy martini glass with a swirl of lemon rind suspended in it. Lily took a sip – it was invigorating and strong.

'That is excellent, Peter.'

'Chin chin,' said Flavia, taking a sip. Peter leafed through a couple of documents and then looked up.

'I don't know what Flavia has said to you, but I am not convinced that this Moses character killed Zuleika. I am doing a forensic investigation into Zuleika's affairs.' Lily looked at him quizzically. 'I know it may seem odd and you are probably wondering why I am so interested. The thing is, Zuleika and I were actually on good terms when she died and I want to get to the bottom of this, for our daughter's sake. I do not want people to think her mother was some desperate, drug addict. I think Zuleika was murdered for a reason. What that is, I don't know, but I will find out.'

'My hunch is that this wasn't an accident,' replied Lily, 'but that is not based on anything concrete.'

'Come on, the second girl was killed because she knew who killed Zuleika,' he said animatedly. 'I've only just got my people looking through Zuleika's affairs but we've already found something of interest in here,' and he shook the leather file.

'What is it?' asked Lily.

'Come here.' He patted the sofa beside him. Lily walked over to join him. She caught a whiff of his citrus cologne. He was thumbing through a bank statement. 'OK, this is a bank account for Pandora's Box, which was the production company that Zuleika had just started up. Now, I didn't think she had done anything yet but look: here is a payment of £10,000 to someone. I got someone to trace the account number. Do you know who it is?' Lily shook her head. 'Guess?'

'Moses Brown?'

'No. Try again.'

'George Lazarus.'

'No, but we'll come to him in a moment. The payment is to Sophie Hamilton-Bruce on 27th June.'

'How strange,' said Lily. 'Sophie said she didn't know her that well. She said she only knew her from *Fashion Fix*.'

'I think they must have cooked up a scheme while they filmed that. What do you think, Flavia?'

'I think they must have, not that Zuleika mentioned anything to me,' she replied, looking miffed.

'I don't want to burst your bubble but I think it's highly unlikely that anything Sophie was working on would be controversial. I mean, both these women worked in fashion – it was probably something to do with that. I know some of these designers are mad, but I doubt they're insane enough to poison cocaine and strangle someone at the Serpentine Gallery Summer Party. I had lunch with Zuleika's tutor, Dr Bone, and he said she was looking into making documentaries about historical figures – I don't think it takes us anywhere.'

'I hear you, Lily, but I think this money trail is important. The other thing I've found out is that Sophie also had money invested with Lazarus Investments – not nearly as much, but that could be significant. My private investigator is going in on Friday, masquerading as a fixer for a big hitter who wants to invest £100 million. Look, I'm not a genius but I agree with you that the returns on this fund are too good to be true. I'm going to get Zuleika's money out for Lucile's sake.' Peter handed Lily the documents. There were bank statements and some very sparse figures for Lazarus Investments from Companies House. Lily spent the next hour looking over them. She studied the bank statements for the last year of Zuleika's life – her spending was staggering. She'd been withdrawing at least £3,000 a week in cash.

'Flavia, I hope you don't mine me asking, but how bad was Zuleika's coke habit?'

'She usually had it on her,' said Flavia, 'but she wasn't some weirdo junky that looked out of it all the time. She gave loads of it away and often had parties back at her flat.' The Filipino house keeper walked in carrying a tray loaded with sushi, sashimi and edamame beans – she put it down on the coffee table and walked off.

'Dig in,' said Peter, picking up a couple of pieces of salmon and tuna sashimi with a pair of ebony chopsticks and placing them on to an oval, white china plate. Lily and Flavia helped themselves.

'Peter, I agree with you that this large payment to Sophie is odd. Who do we think might know about it?'

'The murderer?' suggested Peter.

'We've got a plan,' said Flavia. Lily looked at Flavia whose eyes were flashing with excitement. 'I'm going to ask the key players down to a house party at my brother's place in Devon this weekend. He's away and I'll have the run of the place. Peter, we'll get invites biked tomorrow – everyone is in town because of the memorial. They'll all come as they'll want to poke round the castle and we are going to observe them, Lily.'

'Great,' replied Lily, 'but I suspect Moses will be charged with Zuleika's murder by the end of the week.'

'Either way, I want to get the measure of Lazarus,' said Peter, 'and it will be much harder for him to refuse my request to withdraw Zuleika's money, if he has to spend a weekend with me.'

'Peter, can I get photocopies of Zuleika's bank balance and the very thin Lazarus Investments figures?'

'Sure. I'll get Mark to make you copies. Another martini?'

'Go on then. One more, then I've got to hit the road.'

41

Lily woke up the following morning with a belter of a hangover. A ray of white morning sun was blasting through the gap in her thick, grey curtains like a perfectly aimed laser. Her mouth was dry and she had a piercing pain, right behind her eyes. She massaged the bridge of her nose and temples and suddenly got flashbacks of the previous night. Rather than heading home after two martinis, she had gone on to have another few. Then Flavia and Peter persuaded her that a nightcap at Annabel's would be the perfect way to end the evening. Lily had never been to the infamous nightspot before and she'd been surprised to find it so homely. She, Flavia and Peter had decamped on to one of the sofas and she felt like she was in the drawing room of an elderly relative, rather than a nightclub, thanks to the paintings and antique furniture. They had spent the majority of the night plotting the forthcoming weekend at Porcarno Castle, Flavia's brother's stately home in Devon. Flavia had declared the 'suspects' weekend would have a fun and frolics theme.

Flavia had insisted on dragging Lily on to the miniscule, dark dance floor. A few middle-aged men swayed unapologetically out of time with the live music. Their WAGs had seriously big hair and were hoofed in sky-high Christian Louboutin stilettos, which meant all they could do was bop up and down to the beat with their feet glued firmly to the spot. Flavia had livened up proceedings by pushing the band's drummer out of the way and giving her own rendition of tribal drumming. At two in the morning, Lily had made her excuses and left – leaving Flavia and Peter ensconced in a corner with Ryan Todd and his latest squeeze.

She was seriously regretting the night now. She stretched her arm out of bed and picked up a large bottle of Evian. She downed half of it and ran her hands through her tangled hair. She looked down at her pillow and saw it was streaked with mascara. She'd been so exhausted and tipsy when she got in, she had just thrown off her clothes and fallen straight into bed. The clothes were in a mound on the floor, just as she had stepped out of them.

She fished her mobile out of her bag: it was dead so she walked over to the charger and plugged it in. She flicked on the radio, the eight o'clock news had just started. The second news item woke her up.

'The Metropolitan Police have confirmed that London cab driver Moses Brown will appear at West London Magistrates' Court tomorrow, to be charged with the murders of Lady Zuleika Winters and Sophie Hamilton-Bruce.' Lily was staggered. She turned on her phone. There was a message from Ricky at six saying the police were going to charge Mo. She called him back immediately.

'Ricky, I just heard the news.'

'What happened to you this morning?'

'I had a late one. I was following the Lazarus trail.'

'They found a load of goodies in the lock-up. All his drug stash and more I'm told. I'm taking Peters out tonight to celebrate. I'm afraid I've used you as a sweetener. He was most insistent that you come along. Says you are key to the whole investigation. So you are going to milk him for every little detail. Flatter, flirt and cajole.'

'I wouldn't miss it for the world. I'm dying to hear everything.'

'Also, Lily, get yourself down for the charging tomorrow. It is only one journalist per publication so you better ring and sweet talk the Magistrates' Court. I doubt they've ever had anyone from *Society* attending before.'

'Will do. Listen, I think Lazarus is dodgy and I've found a money trail between Zuleika and Sophie.'

'What?'

'I spent last night with her ex-husband and Flavia Wilde.'

'Ooh!'

'Not literally, you clown. I'm serious Ricky! I looked through Zuleika's bank statements for the last year and at the figures for Pandora's Box.'

'Eh?'

'Ricky, you remember her production company.'

'Oh God Lily. You're not back on that again are you? What with that pretentious professor? We're not going to find

155

anything looking at the history books and, anyway, they've got their man.'

'Well, how do you explain the fact that Zuleika paid £10,000 to Sophie a week before she died.'

'Really?'

'It's odd, Ricky, come on.'

'It was probably some money for some fashion programme – a coincidence.'

'I thought there was no such thing as coincidence in crime?'

'Hmm. Here we go: I can see the credits rolling. Lily, how many times do I have to tell you we're not in a TV drama now?' Lily ignored this last comment and carried on regardless.

'They both had money invested with Lazarus. Zuleika had £30 million.'

'Look, we'll discuss all this tonight. I'll text you time and place. Also, you better wear something nice for Peters.'

'Ha ha. Only if you wear your prescription sunglasses again.' Ricky laughed and hung up.

Lily was having a cigarette at the back of the Panther Publications building, watching the deliveries arriving for the mailroom. In the five minutes she had been there, four delivery vans had come and she'd spotted dresses from Chanel, Versace, Issa and Gucci for photo shoots. Jonty had agreed to her going to the Magistrates' Court and had asked her to begin writing a piece on the murders. Her mobile rang: it was Sébastien.

'Hello, hello,' said Lily.

'Ello. I've been thinking of you. They have your man,' he said cheekily.

'Yes. It looks like it.'

'You thought it was Mo from the beginning, didn't you? I remember when you called me about it before we had met properly. Maybe you should have been in the police, Lily.'

'Perhaps I missed my calling.'

'I thought I could take you out to dinner tonight to celebrate?'

'That's very sweet of you but I'm busy tonight.'

'Of course – I'm sure you are a lady in demand…What about tomorrow?' Lily hesitated. She wanted to say yes, but her conscience said no.

'What about Veronique?' she said, feeling priggish.

'Do you want her to come too?' He joked.

'That would be perfect.'

'I'm asking you for dinner, Lily, not to get married. But, as you ask, Veronique and I are no longer together. We split up a week ago actually. We went to the memorial together but it is over. We lost interest in each other some time ago.'

'Oh,' said Lily, trying to play it cool.

'I am pleased to see you are such a nice girl,' he teased 'Why don't you come to my flat for a drink first? I'm at 6 Priory Mansions, on Drayton Gardens. Come for eight.'

'If you make a good martini, I'm in.'

'The best. I also have excellent champagne – the stuff the French drink and do not export out of the country, as it's too good to share.'

'Even better. See you tomorrow.' Lily punched the air in excitement. She knew he was so wrong for her but he was also unforgivably hot. 'Sit back and enjoy the ride,' she said, resting her head back against the wall and lighting another cigarette. She felt great – things seemed to be going her way.

42

Lily had a spring in her step as she walked up the steps at St James's Park tube station. She made her way along Tothill Street and entered the Bay Tree House Hotel. She was exhausted after her late night antics but the adrenalin was keeping her going. She sauntered into the washroom and looked at her reflection. The unforgiving, florescent lights exaggerated the dark circles under her eyes. She was wearing a cream, chiffon blouse with small, black cats printed on it. It was slightly transparent and, if you stared enough, you could make out a pale pink, camisole underneath. She had teamed these with a pair of very tight, black, skinny jeans, a studded black belt, a pair of high-heeled, suede ankle boots and ruby lipstick.

She strode out into the lobby, her heels clip-clopping on the hard floor and looked around for the pub dining room. Ricky looked up the moment she walked in and Peters let out a wolf-whistle.

'That's what I want to see after a very busy week. Hello, darling,' and he got up and gave her a kiss. Lily smiled.

'What are you having?' asked Ricky. 'We're on the Merry Maidens Mild, but I'm guessing it will be a dry, white wine for you?'

'Perfect. I was on the martinis last night so I need something to keep me going.'

'Do you want something harder?'

'Absolutely not.' She turned to Peters. 'So, you got him,' she said.

'Oh yeah,' he said, his chest puffed out in pride.

'Wow. Huge congratulations, Jeffrey. Can you tell me how you got him?'

'It was the lock-up. We got a tip-off. An anonymous caller rang in and said he had a lock-up on Garrat Lane. The bugger wouldn't admit it, of course, and he had an arsehole of a lawyer. Hey Flynn, guess who Mo's lawyer is?' Ricky was standing by the bar, waiting for the drinks. Peters was basking in his success and enjoying playing the big cop. Ricky paused to think. 'Come on, Flynn, my boy, you know the lawyer who represents the South London drug gangs.'

Ricky clicked his fingers. 'Leonard Bruck.'

'That's him. He's been a right pain in the backside, as always. He did his usual trick of arriving late to lessen our questioning time. Then, he took two hours to be briefed – all the usual dirty business. But you should have seen his face when we found the lock-up. There was nothing he could do about that. He had to completely change his advice. Then, Mo sang like a canary and suddenly admitted to selling the drugs to Zuleika.' Ricky handed Lily a large goblet of chilled, white wine. She took a sip and leaned back in her chair.

'Wow. So what did you find in the lock-up?'

'Come on, you know there is only so much I can tell you. I don't want to prejudice the case. We want this guy to go down.'

'What can you say on the record?'

'We found 150g of cocaine.'

'Brilliant. Where was it?'

'Oh shit. I want to tell you but I can't.'

'Well, let me tell you about my discoveries,' said Lily, changing the subject. There would be plenty of time to press Peters again, once he'd had a few more drinks.

'You don't let it go, do you, Lily? If you get bored of journalism you can always come and work for me. You're a terrier.'

Lily smiled, 'Thanks, Jeffrey. I have found out that Zuleika paid Sophie £10,000 a week before she died.'

'What?' exclaimed Peters.

'That is the reaction I wanted from you, earlier,' she said, wagging her finger at Ricky. 'Look and learn.'

'What was the money for?' asked Peters, draining his pint. Ricky got up and ordered him another one.

'It was from the production company Zuleika had set up.'

'Jeffrey, Lily's slightly obsessed with this. I don't think it means anything other than the two women were going to work on some fashion programme together.' Lily glared at Ricky. 'I'm sorry, Lily. I think the police have their man.' Lily ignored Ricky and carried on regardless.

'Did Mo say anything to you about George Lazarus?'

'Why?' asked Peters.

'You heard him in the memorial. Why would he say Lazarus was his only friend, if he hadn't helped him?'

'I suppose Lazarus could have helped him hide...But why would he do that? I hardly think it is in his interest to hide Rastafarian drug dealers, who are wanted by the police. Moses won't say where he was, other than that he was scared and he was in Scotland.'

'Scotland,' said Lily, noting it down. 'What exactly did he say?'

'"I took some time out in Scotland to get my head together."'

'Lazarus's family have a shooting estate in Scotland. I doubt Mo knows anyone else there. I bet he's never been there before. I'm telling you two, Lazarus has something to do with this.'

'I'll get someone to question Lazarus,' said Peters, placating her, enjoying being the big man.

'Well, you'll have to wait: he's out of the country at the moment,' said Lily sharply. Ricky and Peters exchanged looks.

'Lily, you got lucky with your hunch on Moses Brown but you can't just go around assuming people are guilty of aiding and abetting criminals,' said Peters.

'You'll see,' said Lily confidently. 'Right, let's get this party started. Tequila shots all round?'

'You're kidding me,' said Peters. Ricky rolled his eyes but Lily knew he was delighted with her plan.

159

'Man or mouse?' she said, getting up and walking to the bar.

'Here we go,' said Ricky.

'Go on then,' said Peters.

After three tequila shots Peters was much more loose lipped. Lily had flattered him so much about his investigative skills that he was eating out of her hand.

'You must have been so excited when you found out about the lock-up. Did you know then you had a breakthrough?'

'Yeah,' said Peters confidently, 'I could smell it. I knew his stash would be hidden somewhere, it was just a question of finding it.'

'One hundred and fifty. Is that a lot?'

'Yes and no – it's category three in volume but because it's a class A drug that makes it more serious. Even before the fact it killed someone, he's looking at about eight-to-twelve years, depending on the judge.'

'Does he work for anyone?'

'No, we don't think so. He seems to be a one-man show, which is quite unusual. He doesn't appear to be in with any of the big drug bosses. Those guys are bringing kilos of the drugs in and then they get the kids on the estates to deal it. Mo didn't operate like that. Sensible chap, he had a lot to show for it.'

'Really?' said Lily. Ricky was listening intently.

'Let's just say he was very James Bond.'

'You're kidding me. He had an Aston Martin?' asked Ricky, 'Don't tell me he hid the gear in the Aston Martin. This guy's got style, Peters. I like it.' Peters nodded.

'Off the record, Ricky – we want this guy to go down. How could a cabbie afford a DB Vantage GTA Coupe, with fifteen thousand miles on the clock? He bought it second-hand and paid thirty-nine grand for it in cash. He couldn't do that on his cabbie salary – he is only claiming to earn £17,000 a year on his tax return. Also, he had a state of the art TV and sound system in his flat. Bang and Olufsen, don't you know! Those entertainment systems are eye-wateringly expensive. We can merely dream about them, Lily. Oh, and he had no mortgage on his flat – this guy was raking it in.'

'You've got him on the drug dealing fair and square,' said Ricky.

'Oh yeah,' said Peters.

'Come on, one more tequila shot,' said Lily, going to the bar. She tottered back carrying six shot glasses.

'Jesus, Lily! What are you doing to us? We're not in our twenties like you! I've got a big day tomorrow – we're taking this fucker to the Magistrates' Court.'

'Exactly. Something to celebrate. Bottoms up!' said Lily, sprinkling some salt on the space between her thumb and index finger. She licked it off and downed the tequila shot in one. 'How did you get from drug dealing to the murders?' she said, slurring her words slightly. Ricky took one look at Lily and ordered a couple of bowls of chips and a jug of tap water.

'Well, his fingerprints are on both wraps of cocaine. So we can prove he sold it to them. We have the phone records. He and Zuleika had a couple of missed calls and a conversation the day before she died, so we can assume they were arranging the sale of the drug. He has admitted to selling Zuleika drugs. Then, we know he had an argument with Sophie and Araminta about the drugs he supplied Zuleika at the Serpentine Party.'

'Has Araminta remembered that now?' asked Lily.

'Once she realised how serious this all was, Lily. She admits there was an altercation with Moses Brown about the drugs he supplied Zuleika. Although, all agree he claimed they were fine.'

'Did he admit to supplying Sophie with drugs?' asked Lily, who had downed a couple of glasses of water to try and sober up.

'No. He is adamant about that. He says he hadn't sold Sophie any drugs for years. He claims the killer slipped it into her bag to frame him. Lily, he knew Sophie really well he could easily have persuaded her to go into the booth to discuss it further and then bang.' Peters mimed strangling someone with a scarf. 'Witness statements corroborate that he wasn't on the dance floor at the end of the evening either. He says he was hanging with Lazarus.' Lily's ears pricked up.

'Lazarus eh?'

Ricky groaned.

'They're charging him with both murders. We have circumstantial evidence and the prosecutor will have to build a case. Anyway, he'll go down for the dealing and Zuleika's death whatever.'

'There's still no credible motive,' said Lily.

'Well, we'll get to see him in the dock tomorrow,' said Ricky.

'Until tomorrow then,' said Lily, raising the next tequila shot, they all clinked glasses.

43

It was a hive of activity outside the City of Westminster Magistrates' Court. Lily took in the nondescript seventies red brick building – it was completely devoid of character. A crowd of twenty or so onlookers had joined the paparazzi, who were waiting to catch an image of their victim. Shots of Moses entering and leaving the court would sell for thousands and the paps were jostling for prime position. Lily pushed past them and walked towards the entrance. The doors looked like those at a rundown airport rather than those of a courtroom. Above the door was a slim, bright blue banner, which had City of Westminster Magistrates' Court printed on it in white. The lobby was as unappealing as the exterior – Lily strode in and immediately spotted Ricky standing with a gaggle of crime reporters. Lily recognised Sean from *The Post*, from the first Scotland Yard press conference she had attended on the murders. He'd had a severe buzz cut and was ribbing Ricky, as per usual.

'I'll give you this one, Ricky. Probably the first time you've ever been ahead of us,' he goaded.

'As I've said to you many times, Sean, we rely on good old-fashioned, investigative journalism and not your dark arts – we all know about your phone tricks and *The Post*'s credit card bill.'

'We're above board, Ricky. Clean as a whistle,' he said, smirking. 'You're just jealous of the expense account! You should get yourself to a proper paper with a decent entertaining budget. I can't think why this guy turned up at the memorial service. If I'd been him, I would have slipped back to Jamaica and would be smoking a reefer on a remote beach somewhere. He'd have got away with it as well. Let's face it, the police haven't come out of this smelling of roses. It's as big a story as the murders themselves.'

'You mean that's the story *The Post* is going with, as they've not got the main scoop,' said Ricky, rubbing his eyes and letting out a huge yawn.

'Late night?' asked Sean.

'Not late, just heavy.' Ricky realised Lily was hovering next to him. 'And here's the culprit! If it isn't the tequila slammer herself! How are you doing?'

162

'I feel fine actually. It's called youth, darling,' she said, giving him a cheesy grin and doing a twirl. Ricky scowled. 'Joke! I feel ghastly just like you. Do you want some Alka Seltzer? I've got some in my bag.'

'I'm hard, me. I'll ride it out.'

One of the court attendants told them to proceed to court one. There were thirty journalists who were being permitted in the court, all of them were male apart from Lily, a reporter from the BBC news website and a crime writer from *The Independent*. They walked down the corridor to the court and took their seats in the public gallery. Lily hunkered down next to Ricky. It was absolutely packed. Some members of the public had queued for hours in order to be let in.

'It's not nearly as exciting as you think, Lily. He'll just confirm his name and address.'

'I know,' said Lily. 'It's still thrilling. Your job is amazing. I can't go back to features after this. I feel like I'm in a TV series.'

'I hadn't noticed.'

'Shut up. I've been professional. Peters offered me a job yesterday.'

'Hmm, that I would like to see, Constable Cane.' Ricky looked round the gallery and made a note in his notebook. He nudged Lily. 'Mo's sister, Hortense, is here.' He glanced over in the direction of a highly respectable looking, middle-aged lady who was wearing a navy blue suit. She had a red, blue and white silk scarf tied round her neck and large gold earrings hanging from her ears. 'She must have flown over from Jamaica.' Lily craned her neck to take a look.

There was an intake of breath when Mo walked into the dock flanked by two security guards. He stood behind the glass court screen, happy to have that barrier between himself and the people gathered in the court. He was immaculately dressed in a dark blue pinstripe suit, a pale blue shirt and navy tie. His dreadlocks were scraped back off his head and held in a ponytail by a black, woven, hair band. He was clean-shaven and had obviously made an effort to look respectable. He was not handcuffed but he held his hands behind his back. He stared straight ahead into the middle distance. He looked proud and tall and not remotely remorseful.

'He's scrubbed up well,' whispered Ricky.

'A designer suit won't get him off,' said Sean. 'Interesting that he's made the effort though. Where do you think that suit is from, Lily? Can't say I'm a fashion man.'

'I'm not sure. Paul Smith perhaps?'

'He's got a better wardrobe than me,' quipped Sean.

Lily ran her eye up his cheap, shiny suit and thought that was the most honest statement Sean had made since she'd met him.

All but five seats – which had been reserved for the victims' families – were taken. The only person who had turned up was Peter Paul Anderson IV, who was sitting there, fixing Mo with an intense stare.

The court clerk stood up. 'Case thirty-nine,' he said. The district judge nodded. The clerk looked at Mo and said, 'Can you confirm that you are Moses Dexter Brown?'

'That is correct,' said Mo, still staring ahead, not fixing anyone with his gaze.

'Is your address 12 Triangle Place, Nelson's Row, SW4 7JT?'

'That is correct.'

'Can you confirm your date of birth as 27th February 1966?'

'That is correct,' said Mo, looking at the clerk.

The district judge looked at Mo. 'Moses Dexter Brown, you are charged with the unlawful supply of cocaine to Lady Zuleika Winters on 4th July 2007. Do you understand the charge?'

'Yes,' replied Mo.

'It is said that on 5th July you unlawfully killed Lady Zuleika Winters. Do you understand the charge?' Mo bristled. 'Do you understand the charge?' repeated the judge.

'Yes,' said Mo, with a thunderous look on his face.

'It is said that on 11th July you unlawfully killed Sophie Hamilton-Bruce. Do you understand the charge?' Mo looked like he was about to explode with anger. He squeezed his hands behind his back.

'Yes.'

'Finally, you are charged with possessing 150g of cocaine with the intention of supplying it. Do you understand the charge?'

'Yes,' said Mo, looking down at his hands.

Mo's barrister, Leonard Bruck, stepped forward. He was a small, stout man in his forties. His brown hair was combed over to the left side of his head to cover a bald patch. He had a large tan-coloured liver spot the size of a fifty pence piece, on the right

164

side of his cheek, below his eye, and was wearing a grey suit with sleeves that were slightly too long. It had the effect of making him look even smaller then he was. Lily estimated that he was 5' 4" at most.

'My client requests a bail hearing slot,' said Bruck in a nasal voice.

The judge looked at Mo and Bruck and said, 'A bail hearing slot is refused.' Mo and Bruck exchanged glances. Lily looked over to Hortense, who was wringing the handle of her navy blue handbag. 'Your case is sent for trial at The Central Criminal Court. You are remanded in custody until the trial.' Hortense bit her lip. Mo and Bruck looked disappointed. The two security officers stepped forward. This time they handcuffed Mo and began to lead him out of the court. He looked up at the public gallery, searching for his sister. When his eyes found her, they softened. She smiled at him and put her hands together as if she was praying. He closed his eyes in despair, and was hurried out of the court by the two guards.

44

Lily was filled with nervous excitement when she pressed the bell for 6 Priory Mansions. She rearranged the red, Miu Miu dress Genevieve had called into the fashion department for the date. She had loved it when she tried it on in the *Society* office, but now Patrick's comment that it looked like an apron ran thorough her head. 'What does he know about fashion?' she told herself.

'Hello Lily,' Sébastien said over the intercom.

'Hi.'

'I'm on the second floor. There's a lift if you're feeling lazy.' The black front door buzzed open and Lily made her way into the building. She took the stairs in order to delay her arrival. The hall was light and airy, the cream paint on the walls was pristine and crisp, and there was a large, purple glass vase filled with fresh lilies on an antique table with majestic lion-paw feet. The scent of the lilies wafted up the stairs, which were covered in an expensive-looking, thick, dark blue carpet. As Lily got to the second floor, she swallowed – the nerves were getting to her. The door to flat 6 was open, so she tapped on it and walked in. She walked along a corridor and turned into a big sitting room with ebony, wooden floors and light furniture. A tall, oversized, silver sixties floor lamp bent over the end of a white leather sofa. A pony skin rug lay on the floor between the sofa and two very cool, red, art deco, leather armchairs. At the end of the room was a white lacquer shelving unit with uneven cubbyholes and shelves in it. In these photographs, objects of art and books had been carefully arranged. A large black and white photo of a very beautiful blonde woman, who looked strikingly like Sébastien, had pride of place on one of the centre shelves. To the left of this was a beautiful photograph of Sébastien in front of the Taj Mahal – he was indecently good-looking in it. On the shelf below there was an exquisite, contemporary, hand-carved ebony and mother-of-pearl chess set. The pieces were fluid and solid, like miniature Henry Moore sculptures. Lily's eye was drawn to an oversized coffee table book of Helmut Newton's nudes that was placed on a shiny, black leather Ottoman under the large window.

Sébastien entered through some double doors on the right-hand side of the room. He walked straight over to her and kissed her on the lips. He was wearing a pair of dark blue Levi's with a soft, grey, V-necked T-shirt. His arms looked muscular and strong and his skin was still tanned from his various summer holidays. His cologne smelled of lemons and leather – Lily buried her head in his neck and inhaled. He stroked the side of her face and began to kiss her again.

'I have thought about you a lot today,' he said. Lily looked him in the eye. God, he was sexy! She said nothing. 'Champagne or something stronger?'

'Champagne, please.'

'I'm glad you said that. Have you had Ruinard before?' he asked, walking to his kitchen.

'No, I haven't.' He emerged with two full, shallow, circular champagne glasses. He handed her one.

'This is my favourite and these are the best glasses for drinking champagne. I hate the tall ones – it tastes better in these. Did you know this style of glass was modelled on Marie Antoinette's breast? They could easily have done them off yours,' Lily gave him a wearisome look and he laughed. 'Sorry, I couldn't help it. Santé.'

'Santé.' Lily sat down on the white leather sofa. 'How are you?'

'Great. I know it doesn't sound very nice but I am glad Veronique and I are finished. I feel a weight has been lifted. The relationship reminded me of one of my father's old whippets just before we had him put down. He was old and cranky and his limbs and eyes didn't work. He'd drag himself into the corner of a room and just lie there, waiting to die. Veronique and I should have ended a long time ago but we clung on to each other. She is having a fling with that musician, Andy Blake – I am happy for her. It seems we were both misbehaving in Ibiza,' he said, giving Lily a flirtatious look. Lily smiled. 'It's much better this way. I feel young and free again.'

'I'll drink to that. To Sébastien's freedom,' said Lily, taking another gulp of the delicious champagne.

'What have you been up to?'

'I've had a pretty heavy week actually. You're lucky I'm here. I was on tequila slammers last night and martinis the night before.'

'You English girls like to drink,' he said, shaking his head.

'Do we, oh half-English one?' teased Lily. 'Actually, I went to the Magistrates' Court today and saw Mo being charged with the murders.'

'For *Society* magazine?'

'Yes.'

'Really? I can't imagine that.'

'We are journalists, Sébastien.'

'I'm sorry. I just thought it was more socialites and fashion shoots. Come on, you were in Ibiza interviewing Rocky and Veronique a few weeks ago – that's hardly a serious news story.'

'True. Well I'm writing about it for them, so I called the court and got a press slot.'

'Wow. What was it like?'

'The bit in the court was pretty uneventful – it wasn't the trial. There were a lot of people outside and the public gallery was packed. Do you know the only person who attended from the families was Peter Paul Anderson?'

'Not that clown! He's a waste of space. He split up with Zuleika years ago. He probably just wanted to grab some limelight.'

'Do you know him?'

'He's a dreadful man. He used to know my mother years ago.' Lily looked interested. Sébastien brushed the comment away with a wave of his hand. 'I don't want to talk about him. What else happened?'

'Mo's sister was there. And he has some slippery lawyer that all the big drug guys use.'

'Wow, Lily, you do have all the information. How do you know this?' Lily realised she was giving away far too much.

'I overheard one of the crime reporters saying it to his junior. Anyway, they've charged him and now his case will go to the Old Bailey. He applied for bail but his request was refused. He's in Wandsworth prison.'

'Who would have thought it? As I said to you, I didn't really know Mo.'

'Yes you did, Sébastien. I remember the way he greeted you at the Serpentine Summer Party. He seemed very in with your group.' Sébastien frowned, his olive-green eyes darkening. He gathered himself and smiled.

'You were watching me, were you? He was Veronique and Rocky's friend. I'm not one for drugs, Lily. I don't know if you know but my mother died of an overdose,' he said, looking over at the black and white photograph of the beautiful woman.

'Oh I'm sorry, Sébastien,' said Lily, taken aback. She'd forgotten that his mother had died that way but, at the same time, she knew she'd seen him hanging with Mo at the party.

'It was a long time ago now.' He got up to get the champagne from the kitchen. There was now a slightly tense atmosphere in the room. Lily walked over to his modern designer fireplace. There was a mirrored side table beside it on which Flavia's invitation for the 'fun and frolics' weekend rested. Sébastien crept up behind her and ran his hand up the side of her dress. Lily jumped slightly.

'Great dress. It really suits you.' He poured more champagne into her glass. 'Are you going to Flavia's little gathering at the weekend?' he asked, clocking Lily looking at the invitation.

'Yes, I am.'

'Oh good. I wonder who else will be going?' Lily shrugged. 'I've booked a table at Eight Over Eight for quarter to nine. Do you like sushi?'

'Absolutely.'

'I thought we'd walk. How high are your heels?'

'I'll manage,' said Lily, looking down at her black, Rupert Sanderson platform sandals.

'No, absolutely not. If the heels were put on for my benefit the least I can do is not make you walk. They are serious taxi shoes. I like them,' he said, his eyes flickering with excitement. 'It's only down the road. Let's go on my scooter.'

'Perfect. I bet you're not as fast as me. I'm a bit of a petrol head,' teased Lily.

'I'll race you next time. I play polo; I would whip your ass. I love speed.'

'No way! Polo schmolo! I'd beat you ten times over.' They finished their glasses of champagne. Lily was beginning to feel a little light-headed.

'I'll save the rest for later. Put this on,' he said, handing her a chic, black helmet with a white stripe on it.

'These rock shrimp tempura are delicious,' said Lily, savouring the taste.

'Try this soft shell crab,' said Sébastien, picking up a piece with his chopsticks and seductively feeding it to her. 'It's nice to see a woman with an appetite. I think it correlates with what they are like in the bedroom.' Lily almost choked – he was ridiculously corny.

'What are you saying? That you like a fat girl?' she laughed.

'No, not at all,' said Sébastien laughing. 'I am French, Lily. French women aren't fat. You have restraint but you enjoy your food – that is good. There is nothing worse than taking someone out for dinner and they just pick at a salad.'

'Do you really think you can tell what I'm like in bed from the way I eat tempura and soft shell crab?'

'I know what I want you to be like in bed,' he said, staring into her eyes. He flicked a lock of thick, chestnut hair away from his face, revealing his perfectly sculptured cheekbones in the process.

'What about you? Should I be able to guess what you're like from the way you feed me the soft shell crab?'

'You tell me, Lily.'

'I will reserve judgement. I don't like to make assumptions,' teased Lily. He shrugged nonchalantly. 'Are you good friends with George Lazarus?' she asked casually.

'I know him quite well.'

'Nice guy?'

'Yes,' said Sébastien, giving her a quizzical look.

'He's very successful isn't he?'

'He's doing well, yes. Why?'

'It's just Minty was saying he gets the best results in the industry. Is that true?'

'He has had very good returns the last couple of years. He has a very affluent client base.'

'All the society crowd?'

'Yes, and then he's got some big hitters too. It's quite amazing what he's done, actually.'

'Good for him. He certainly lives the life, doesn't he? It's private jets here, there and everywhere. He's whisked Minty off to swanky hotels and fabulous villas around the globe. Money seems to be no object. He even bought her a ring from Cartier last week – they've only been dating six weeks.'

'He has a bit of a chip on his shoulder.'

'Really? Why?' said Lily interrupting.

'He is stuck in the past. He really cares who people's families are. He's a bit of a snob. Who cares that his family used to have influence and a big estate? But he's fun too.'

'He's a throwback?'

'Exactly. So he splurges cash to show he's still a player and he's hugely ambitious. I think he's a gambler personally.'

'Really? Do you think his fund is unsound?'

'Just between us, I think it's a bit too good to be true. I looked into investing in it and he wouldn't give me the figures. He just wanted to show me the returns and the size of the fund. He said it was a privilege to invest in the fund and it wasn't open to normal members of the public. It is apparently invitation only now. He only takes people who will invest £10 million or more. It's crazy. He expected me to convince my clients to invest millions of pounds blindly, with no details of where their money was going.'

'You know both the girls had money invested in it?'

'Where is this going, Lily?'

'I'm just saying.'

'How do you know?'

'I did a bit of research. I couldn't understand why Mo said George was his only friend at the memorial, so I thought I'd check Lazarus out.'

'For your article for *Society*?'

'Yes. Come on, Sébastien, you can see this is prime *Society* subject matter.'

'I hadn't thought of it like that. My cousin didn't have that kind of money. She must have invested in it at the start as a friend. She wouldn't have put more than £15,000 in it. Zuleika would have had substantially more. She had money to burn. I tried to get her to invest with me.'

'Really?'

'I didn't really know her, so that didn't come to anything. On the fund, all I'm saying is that I think the returns are too good to be true – but that is off the record. It's true, George has been haemorrhaging money this summer. He spends like crazy. The villa he took in Ibiza was 18,000 euros a week and he's been a couple of times this summer. That's before the private planes and the rest. He's too grand to get on a commercial flight these days.'

'He must have kept Mo in business.'

'I'm sure,' said Sébastien. 'They were very close. You should talk to him about Mo.'

'He's in Zimbabwe but Flavia said he's coming back a day early to come to the weekend with Minty.'

'Do you want coffee?'

'No, thanks.'

Sébastien paid the bill and they made their way on to the King's Road. He looked at his watch.

'Eleven o'clock, do you want to come back for a nightcap?' Lily wanted desperately to go back with him but she decided to play it cool. It was moving too quickly.

'I should be getting back. Thank you for dinner.'

'My pleasure, Lily,' and he bent down and kissed her. He began to kiss her more urgently and he ran his hands up and down her body. 'Come here,' he said, taking her down the alley leading to Park Walk. 'If I can't take you home, I'll have to ravish you here.' The attraction was animal. He pressed her back against the wall and began kissing her neck. He put his hands between her legs and forced his tongue into her mouth. She opened her eyes and saw his beautiful face looking down at her. It took all of her strength not to cave in and go back to his flat immediately and rip off all his clothes. She kissed him back and then pushed him away.

171

'Good night, Sébastien,' she teased, walking back on to the King's Road and hailing a taxi. He sauntered over to his moped and sped off into the distance.

45

'Hello, stranger,' said Billy, throwing a packet of Marlboro Lights at her. Lily walked over to the sofa where he was reclining and ran her hand through his mop of brown curls affectionately.

'Yo!' She opened the packet of cigarettes and took one out, lighting it with a match. Peter Paul Anderson's comment about the ritual of smoking ran through her head and she smiled.

'What are you grinning about? Your date with the most pretentious man in Europe?'

'I wasn't actually. I was thinking about Peter Paul Anderson the IV's comment about how important it is to use a lighter, in the art of smoking.'

'Man, you've got to begin hanging out with some normal people again. So, how was your date with Count Bolognese?'

'Bourgogne you mean?'

'With the smooth French man, yes.'

'Good, actually.' Billy raised an eyebrow.

'How come you didn't go back to his? That's not like you,' he teased. Lily threw a cushion at his head. 'Has he dumped the seriously hot Veronique Lapin for you? I love you, Lil, but no one would be that stupid, surely?'

'Ha ha. They've split up. You will be delighted to hear she is now shacked up with your hero Andy Blake. I told you they were getting it on in Ibiza. I saw them.'

'That Irish Leprechaun! What does she see in him? He's about 5' 5" and his music is one long whine.' Billy picked up his guitar, did a puppyish face and began singing, 'you're the only one for me, baby. I don't care who knows it, I love you,' in a high, reedy voice. 'There's no accounting for taste. As for you, Lily, your count is good-looking, I grant you that, but he's not going to win personality of the year. Never again can you rib me for dating people for just their looks.'

'Actually, he is quite amusing. He's more interesting than you think Billy.'

'Hmm. I don't trust him.'

'It's a good thing you're not dating him then, isn't it?'

'Drink?'

'I'm knackered, Bill. It's been a heavy week and God knows what this weekend is going to be like.'

'When are you off?'

'Saturday morning. Peter Paul is giving me a lift in his chauffeur-driven car, don't you know.'

'Be careful, Lil. There will be a wandering hand, a yawn in the back of the car and then bingo: his arm will be round you and you'll be trapped.'

'I don't think so, Bill.'

'Is he married?'

'No.'

'He'll be looking for a nice, young wife.'

'He's more interested in finding out who murdered his ex-wife and on confronting George Lazarus about his dodgy fund.'

'Be careful, Lil. Anyway, they've charged this Moses character now. You'll be back at *The LEN* the week after next. This episode is nearly over. I'm almost looking forward to hearing your whinging about Kate again.' Billy lit a cigarette and exhaled three perfect smoke rings into the room. He walked over to his ancient stereo and put on *A Kind of Blue* by Miles Davis. He poured himself a generous glass of whisky and returned to the sofa.

'I don't think it's over yet, Billy, I really don't.' With that, she got up and walked along the corridor to her bedroom and her much-needed bed.

46

The black BMW saloon made its way slowly up the mile long drive of Porcarno Castle. The castle and its parkland were set in the middle of the rolling, Devon countryside. Lily felt weird being in the West Country, knowing she wasn't going on down to Cornwall to see her dad. She'd tried to explain what she was doing down in Devon and he had just got confused and upset she wasn't coming to visit. His rational brain was slowly slipping away.

'Remember, Lily, keep your eye on Lazarus. I've got some evidence about the fund. I'll probe him at dinner tonight, in front of everyone and then we'll get him on his own for the really tough questions. I think your hunch about him hiding Mo in Scotland is correct. I got my people to do a little investigation and it is very remote – the perfect place to stowaway a felon on the run. We'll press him on that too.'

'Right. Thanks for the lift Peter – it beats the train.'

'My pleasure, Lily.' The chauffeur came round and opened Lily's door, she stepped out and took in the magnificent, fourteenth-century castle. One of the original towers was still standing and fitted seamlessly to the Georgian manor house.

'What a cool house! I'm loving the turrets.' Flavia threw open the heavy, studded front door.

'Welcome!' she boomed. She was wearing a cream, brocade coat and a headdress with stuffed, tan leather antlers. Lily noticed the family coat of arms above the door.

'A griffin and a lion,' said Flavia, following Lily's gaze. 'Wilde's my married name. I'm a widow, Lily. My maiden name was Willouby. How are my two sleuths? I feel like I am in a real life Agatha Christie novel – it's terribly exciting.'

'We've got our eyes and ears open, haven't we, Lily?' said Peter. Lily nodded but she wasn't really listening. She was far too engrossed in the architecture.

'Flavia, this house is amazing. I love the juxtaposition of the rugged tower and turrets against this pristine, manor house. It's brilliant.'

'You're quite the little Pevsner, Lily! My family is a bit mad and I think the house reflects our spirit perfectly. I grew up here and it certainly influenced my aesthetic. You two are the first to arrive. I've asked the others for tea. I hope this weekend is a good idea. We don't want to send Minty over the edge, Peter.' He dismissed this comment with a wave of his hand.

'We're going to find out what happened to Zuleika. Screw that money-grabbing half-sister of hers. She's already filched some of Zu's clothes and keeps asking about the will,' growled Peter. Lily was taken aback by this temporary lack of composure from this immaculate and usually controlled man. Flavia wasn't remotely fazed by the remark and she laughed.

'Come in, come in,' said Flavia, ushering them through into a beautiful, oak-panelled entrance hall. Two mounted stag heads hung on the wall, their cold glass eyes stared down at them. 'I've put you two in the Georgian side of the house. Some people think there's a ghost in the tower – I've never seen it, sadly. I've put Lazarus, Minty and the boys up there.' Lily and Peter followed her up a sweeping oak staircase, their every move watched by a collection of Flavia's stony-faced ancestors, whose portraits hung on the walls.

47

Lily lay back on the large double bed and took a sip of Lapsang Suchong from a blue and white, willow patterned teacup. Her room managed to be both cosy and grand; the walls were covered in warm, pink silk wallpaper. A collection of nineteenth-century French plates hung on either side of the mahogany dressing table. Tasteful watercolours of roses and peonies, painted by Flavia's great grandmother, hung over the bed and a hardback copy of *Very Good Jeeves* rested on the bedside table, along with a glass bottle of Blenheim mineral water and a cut glass tumbler. The long, black, Temperley gladiator dress, that she was going to wear that evening, lay at the foot of her bed. She'd borrowed a red, black and white feathered Native American style headdress from Jazz and hoped that would be suitably wild for Flavia. She wondered how Peter was going to embrace the fun and frolics theme – she didn't have him down as the dressing up type.

Most of the guests had arrived, apart from Sébastien and the fabulously named Tabitha Monkton-Miller, a local aristocrat, who Flavia had asked at the last minute when she realised there were going to be thirteen of them for dinner. The frightful Oscar Rutherford had deigned to say hello to her at tea but had then pointedly said to Ryan Todd 'That journalists were getting

175

everywhere these days.' Sébastien wasn't arriving until seven but he'd texted saying he hoped she liked men in uniform. There was a knock on the door and Minty burst in carrying two dresses: one was purple, the other gold.

'Lily, I need your advice. Shall I wear the Prada or the Lanvin?'

'Did Genevieve call those in for you? They're fabulous.'

'No, they're mine. George brought them for me. Isn't he a darling? I am hoping my days of wearing designer samples are over. I should really have a few pieces of couture by now. I've also inherited some of Zuleika's clothes – well, to be more honest, I liberated them. I've been down to her country pad and had a dig round in her monumental wardrobe – she had a converted barn full of designer clothes that are screaming out to be worn. Well, Lucile can hardly wear them at school,' she spat. 'Such a waste on that tomboy. She's not interested in fashion at the moment. Zuleika would have been delighted someone's wearing them – well, at least until Lucile wants them. I just go and help myself, it's awesome!' Minty threw off her clothes and slipped into the dark purple, Lanvin dress. It clung to her skinny frame. She fluffed up her light blonde hair and pouted at Lily. 'So what do you think? Sexy or what?'

'Beautiful,' said Lily.

'I love Lanvin. I think it's a bit grown up for this weekend. I'll save it for Paris. George and I are going next weekend.' Minty wriggled out of it and began to shoe horn herself into a gold Prada number. 'What's all this about you and Sébastien? You didn't waste any time did you, Lily! You dirty bitch! He's only just split up with Veronique. I cannot believe she ran off with the monkey-faced Andy Blake. Tell me is Seb amazing in bed? He looks like he should be.'

'I don't know, Minty,' said Lily. Minty walked over to her and turned round so Lily could do up her zip.

'You better hurry up, darling! Men like him don't hang around. He's a catch. I bet he's amazing – it's true what they say you know, French men are better in bed. I know,' and she gave Lily a knowing wink. 'All of London will be after him. I'm feeling this one, baby,' she said running her hands up and down her body seductively. She stepped backwards and struck a model pose. 'Do you want to fuck me in it Lily?'

'Absolutely! I'm sure George will bend you over the dining room table and bang you senseless.'

176

'Not with all Flavia's ugly ancestors staring down at us. Yuck! I think we'll stick to the four-poster in our room. He's very good in bed you know. I've never had so many orgasms.' Lily gave a weak smile. She just didn't want to think about George and Minty at it hammer and tongs. 'Did you come down with Peter Paul?'

'Yes.'

'He's so monosyllabic. I was trying to chat to him over tea and he kept ignoring me and asking George about his fund. Doesn't he realise that is just not the done thing, on a country weekend?' She looked at herself in the mirror and rearranged her small, pert breasts. 'Bra or no bra? Do I go for bigger tits in a push up or nipple action with no bra?'

'It depends on your underwear, surely?'

'I've got options. I wonder if I should have a boob job – I'm sure George would pay. Although I just hate the idea of surgery. Am I vain enough to do it? Hmm, I probably am. Who are those weird Dutch artists?'

'Friends of Flavia's. They were at the Serpentine Party, remember?'

'Were they? Are they performing later? God, how tedious! I hate performance art. Art? It's just weirdos with halitosis trying to be clever. Yawn, yawn, yawn.'

'I doubt they're performing. They're guests, Minty.'

'Thank fuck for that. Watch out for Ryan Todd by the way, he's a serious corridor creeper.'

'He won't creep in here – he hates journalists.'

'Anyway, you'll have Seb to fend him off. Lily and Seb K.I.S.S.I.N.G. in a tree,' she chanted, as she shimmied out of the room, swinging her hips in the gold, Prada dress.

Lily walked into her en suite bathroom and looked in the mirror. The gladiator dress fitted perfectly. She lined her eyes with black kohl and fixed some feline, fake eyelashes. Then, she put some scarlet lipstick on her full lips and two straight lines on either cheek and tied the Native American headdress around her head, the multi-coloured, feathered strings cascaded down her back. She walked back into her room and gasped. Sébastien was lying on the bed, wearing a Wedgewood blue RAF uniform, with three stripes on the sleeve. He looked offensively handsome. Lily did a little salute.

'You really shouldn't creep into people's rooms uninvited.'

'Hello,' he said, pulling her close to him and kissing her. 'It's always important to get the lay of the rooms before darkness falls. I'm sharing a room with Oscar Rutherford, which I am not happy about. He keeps walking around topless, flexing his muscles and giving me lingering glances.' Sébastien did an imitation of Oscar drooling over him. 'I know where you are now.' He pulled Lily down on to the bed and they began kissing. He put his hand up her dress, caressing her legs and working his way gently up her thighs. 'I was a little upset you didn't come back with me the other night. It was most disobedient of you. This RAF officer punishes disobedience,' and he smacked her bottom. Lily arched her back. She was excited but she didn't want him to see it. Not yet.

'You won't tame me, Sébastien. It doesn't matter how handsome you look in that uniform,' said Lily, pushing him off. 'Come on, we'll be late,' and they began making their way downstairs.

'Is that journalist supreme Lily Cane?' said a cocky, street, female voice. Lily turned round to see Rocky Star wearing a Wonder Woman outfit. 'Hi darling!' gushed Rocky and she gave her a big hug. Behind her stood Matthew Miles, a gorgeous, black actor who had become a teen heartthrob when he starred in the *The Galactic Crusades* trilogy. He was dressed in a red and white leather, Formula 1, driver's outfit. 'Do you know Matthew Miles?' she asked. Lily and Seb held out their hands. 'He's a fabulous actor. Aren't you, my sweet?' Matthew looked faintly embarrassed and quickly changed the subject. 'Well he is. Remember you met him with me. Come on guys, let's go party with Ryan Todd and Henry Marmsby – rock on! They're only thirty years older than us.'

'I'm glad Henry is here. He's good fun,' said Sébastien, stroking Lily's bare back as they walked down the stairs. They walked along the corridor to a beautiful drawing room that had pale green walls with flat marble pillars running up them and inviting, plush raspberry sofas.

'Good evening,' said Flavia, looking striking in a snake headpiece and a long peach-coloured dress.

'Great hat, Flavia,' said Rocky.

'Thank you, Rocky. I've come as Eve tonight. I've *always* succumbed to temptation.' Ryan Todd and Peter were standing next to her. As Lily had predicted, neither of them had adopted the 'fun and frolics' dress code. Peter Paul was wearing a red velvet, smoking jacket and Ryan a well-cut black tie. George Lazarus and Minty walked in arm and arm. Flavia whistled at them.

'If it isn't love's young dream.' George looked like a rap star in a sharp, white jacket with jeans and a pair of aviators. His bouffant, blonde hair had been styled into a perfect quiff.

'Hello everyone,' said George in his clipped, eager voice. He sounded as if he couldn't get the words out quick enough.

'Good jacket, darling,' said Oscar Rutherford, entering the room. He looked suitably flamboyant in a cropped, black, silk jacket with plumed red feathers on the shoulders and very tight, black, snakeskin trousers.

'Touché,' said George.

'You look like Mephistopheles, Oscar. I love it,' said Flavia, admiring his outfit.

'You're all so delicious,' said Henry Marmsby, who had slipped in behind Oscar. The veteran socialite and art dealer looked dapper in an oversized, check tweed suit and a large, velvet, top hat. 'I'm the mad hatter. The question is who is Alice and who is the Red Queen? These two are Tweedledum and Tweedledee.' The two Dutch artists Adalind Janssen and Hanneke Brouwer stood on either side of him smiling. Adalind was dressed all in yellow and had painted a smiley face on her dress, and Hanneke was wearing a tight, bottle green dress and a gold paper crown.

'I'm ecstasy and she's champagne,' said Adalind, in her harsh Dutch accent that grated with her innocent, girlish looks.

'Everyone's here apart from Tabitha. Daphne, pour the champagne,' ordered Flavia. A small woman, dressed in black, handed the champagne round. 'It's so nice you could all make it, at such short notice. George, I gather you and Seb want to DJ later. I got Browning to set up some decks in the music room.'

'Fabulous,' replied George. 'Seb, I bought lots of great house discs in Ibiza and Berlin. Get ready to party, guys.' He was so overexcited that he bounced up and down as he spoke like a small child.

'Mine's all on my iPod, George,' said Sébastien drolly.

'This chat is so boring, George. They're such music boffins,' said Minty, dismissively.

'Rocky and Ryan are the real stars,' said Flavia. 'We'll get you both singing later. Who needs discs when you have the real McCoy?' George looked pissed off. 'Rocky, tell me how is our

179

little friend Veronique. Is it true she is now dating Andy Blake?' There was an awkward silence and Rocky glared at Flavia.

'It's fine,' said Sébastien, 'we're all on good terms.'

'I got a text from Ronnie saying she was having a wild time in Ibiza with Andy at his villa. I thought he was touring at the moment but I must have got it wrong.'

'She texted me as well,' interrupted Oscar. 'She's one loved-up girl.'

The room began to break off into small groups and Sébastien and Lily found themselves talking to Henry and Ryan. They were chatting about Zuleika's memorial service.

'It was a beautiful service but we will all remember it for one thing, won't we?' said Henry.

'I thought it was outrageous that that murderer came into the chapel and ruined the service. He wouldn't even let the families and friends of the dead women celebrate their lives and remember them in peace. Absolutely appalling.' All three of the men suddenly looked up and stared: a beautiful, auburn-haired girl had entered the room. She was tall and willowy and looked like she had stepped out of a pre-Raphaelite painting. She was wearing a long, floaty white dress with gold edging and had a white flower headband resting like a crown on her head.

'What a beauty! Here is your Alice, Henry,' said Ryan Todd.

'Everyone, this is Tabitha Monkton-Miller,' said Flavia, introducing the girl.

48

The dining room at Porcarno Castle was dark and majestic. A hand-carved, gilded chandelier with five, large, cream candles hung over the very long, Tudor, oak dining table. At the far end of the room, a huge portrait of one of Flavia's ancestors, mounted on a dark steed, had pride of place over the fireplace. He had long, dark brown ringlets and an impressive moustache.

'He was an earl. Sébastien, we have Gallic blood. We came over from France in the 1400s.'

'You have been here quite a long time. Perhaps you can now consider yourself English?'

'Of course! Take your places everyone. Peter, you're here next to me.' Everyone walked around the table looking for their place names. Flavia took her place at the head; she'd put Peter on her right-hand side and George on her left. Lily was one down, next to Peter and Henry Marmsby. Sébastien was sitting at the other end of the table, sandwiched between Tabitha and Rocky. Minty was opposite the intoxicating Tabitha; she looked miffed that Sébastien, Ryan and Matthew hung off Tabitha's every word, utterly entranced. Lily was too busy observing George to notice.

The first course was a delicious, cold pea soup with garlic croutons and everyone tucked in. Peter began to interrogate George the moment people picked up their spoons.

'So, George, I hear you've been in Zimbabwe. I didn't know Lazarus Investments had interests there?' George looked taken aback.

'I have a lot of interests in emerging markets, actually, Peter.'

'What kind of thing?'

'Mines, construction – that kind of thing.' Minty looked over at him and beamed proudly.

'George is quite the entrepreneur. He has the Midas touch – or should I say the diamond touch? He brought these back for me,' she said, flashing a pair of large, pear-shaped, diamond earrings. George basked in his own generosity.

'Despite the negative press, Zimbabwe is actually good for business.'

'So, how much money do you have invested in emerging markets?' carried on Peter.

'A fair bit,' said George dismissively. 'Flavia, this soup is delicious.' Flavia smiled. George thought he'd successfully changed the subject.

'The returns on those markets aren't fifteen-to-twenty per cent a year yet, are they? How do you make up the shortfall?' George's mask of tranquillity slipped and he looked vexed.

'Let's not talk shop now, old chap,' he said. Peter nodded.

'Your family have a place in Scotland, don't they?' he asked, trying another tack.

'Yes, we do,' said George, delighted that the conversation had turned. 'It's a shooting lodge up in the Highlands, nothing fancy.'

'Do you get up there, often?' said Peter bullishly. George looked confused.

'As much as I can, Peter. It's hard with work and I'm more of a warm-weather animal. I prefer to charter a private plane to Ibiza and off I go. Isn't that right, Seb?' Sébastien was engrossed in a conversation about French vineyards with Henry and Tabitha. Minty mouthed what George had said across the table.

'He's obsessed with Ibiza,' said Sébastien. 'He dragged us out three times over the summer. You went six times, didn't you?' George nodded enthusiastically.

'Is it remote?' asked Peter Paul, like a dog with a bone.

'It's on the Strathylan Estate. It's in the heart of the Highlands about half an hour from Loch Ness. I'm sure you've heard about the monster.'

'Oh yeah,' said Peter smiling. 'I'm sure he's not the only monster up there.' George looked confused.

'We do hire it out, if you're interested in a spot of summer stalking.'

'Was anyone there in August? That's prime time isn't it?'

'Yes, it is, but it was empty this year. We've just started some major renovations. Well, I have, it's my baby now. My parents went up in July but that was it.' Peter took it all in.

'Moses Brown admitted that he hid in Scotland.' The whole table went silent. 'He couldn't have known many people in Scotland, coming from Jamaica and being a Londoner.' George flushed scarlet. He was holding his bread knife so tightly that his fingertips turned white.

'Well that has nothing to do with me,' he said, slamming his fist on the table.

'It's just a little odd what Moses said at the memorial service about you being his only friend. I wondered what he meant.' George's eyes blazed in fury.

'Peter, this is turning into a character assassination and it must stop immediately. This is not the way we behave here.'

'Daphne, clear away the plates,' said Flavia trying to defuse the situation. 'Rocky, the rock star, tell us about your tour. Did you go everywhere? Tell me do rock chicks have groupies?' Everyone resumed their conversations. A semblance of normality was restored but there was now an unmistakable undercurrent of tension. Peter had thrown the dice. Lily prayed his gamble would pay off but she felt like they were dancing on a knife edge.

49

When the pudding arrived, Flavia insisted on changing the placement. 'Rocky and Sébastien, why don't you come up here and sit where George and Hanneke were?' George jumped up immediately and made his way down to the other end of the table. Hanneke followed closely behind him, relieved to be joining Adalind.

'Think I rattled his cage?' Peter Paul whispered to Lily.

'Definitely.'

'You haven't seen anything yet. Just wait until I get my figures out.'

'Choose your moment,' said Lily. Sébastien and Rocky took their seats opposite. Sébastien began to play footsie with Lily under the table. She indulged him for a minute and then dug her heel into the top of his foot. He looked her in the eye. A shiver of excitement ran from her stomach to straight between her legs. She stared back at him. He raised an eyebrow and turned to look at Flavia.

'Rocky, I like Matthew,' said Flavia. 'He reminds me of a young Sidney Poitier.'

'He's as good as Poitier, too. *The Galactic Crusades* days are over. He's in the next Mike Leigh film.'

'Fabulous! But I know you Rocky: flitter-flutter,' Flavia imitated a butterfly with her hands.

'What do you sing about Rocky?' asked Peter Paul.

'Life. Heartbreak, lust, sex, money, feelings – whatever takes my fancy really.'

'What are you feeling at the moment?'

'I'm feeling like you're stirring things up, Peter, and I'm loving every minute of it. You're a troublemaker, Peter Paul Anderson the IV,' said Rocky, over-pronouncing the IV. Peter gave her an indulgent smile.

'Sébastien, I have not seen you for years. How are you, my friend?' Sébastien bristled, he obviously objected to being referred to in this way by Peter.

'I am well, thank you.'

'I miss your mother.'

'Me too.'

'She was like Zuleika: very misunderstood. Beautiful, charismatic women often are. People here are jealous and so quick to judge,' said Peter. Sébastien looked very uncomfortable. 'You know, I was never convinced about the coroner's verdict on her death either. I think it was all a little too convenient for the sheikh, if you get my drift.' Sébastien rolled his eyes in exasperation and then his mood changed and he looked serious.

'No, not now, Peter. In fact, not ever,' he said, his eyes blazing with pure, unadulterated hatred.

'Enough Peter,' said Flavia. 'You have been quite the agent provocateur tonight.'

'Flavia, this chocolate fondant is delicious,' said Rocky, taking a big mouthful and licking her lips.

'Who is the beautiful Tabitha?' enquired Rocky.

'I thought you'd like her,' said Flavia, giving her a conspiratorial look. Rocky smiled knowingly. 'She's rather wonderful, isn't she? She's an artist but I'm about to shoot her for *Society* – naked. I think Jonty will go for it – all the men are drooling over her down here. She's got a wonderful, ethereal quality, don't you think?'

'A true English rose,' said Sébastien giving her a lingering sideways glance. Lily felt a pang of jealousy.

'Lily, what's the latest on the murders?' asked Rocky.

'She went to see Moses being charged in the Magistrates' Court last week,' said Sébastien. Henry Marmsby leant over to join in the conversation.

'How thrilling, Lily! How was it?'

'Weird. He stared blankly ahead and just confirmed his name and address. I felt sorry for him, I don't know why.'

'Because he didn't do it,' said Rocky. 'We all know that, right?'

'Exactly,' said Peter Paul chipping in.

'Oh here goes Mr Conspiracy Theory again,' said Sébastien. 'You guys have too much time on your hands. It was Mo the drug dealer. You think drug dealers are nice guys because they sell you cocaine at trendy parties? Well, hello! Get with the programme, Rocky. The man is a criminal. You saw his respectable face. The truth is, you know nothing about him.' Sébastien got up and walked down to the other end of the table to sit with George and Tabitha.

'Hypocrite,' muttered Rocky. 'I'm going in to see Mo next week. I'm his friend and I don't believe he did it. Sébastien is

184

too much! It's not like he wasn't one of Mo's clients. Veronique always said he had double standards. There is nothing worse than an arrogant Frenchman. He's good-looking but so controlling. He needs to loosen up man.'

'Now he's gone, give us the lowdown on Veronique,' said Flavia.

'It's really weird. I keep getting text messages from her about what a great time she's having with Andy but she never answers my calls. It is so unlike her.'

'Maybe she's too busy fucking,' said Flavia.

'To fucking!' said Rocky, lifting her glass and looking down in Matthew's direction.

Lily, Henry, Adalind and Hanneke were sitting in the drawing room next to the fire, which had been lit while they were having dinner. Lily had settled into a mint-green armchair. The two Dutch artists sat on the embroidered footstool and Henry was leaning against the mantelpiece smoking. Lily took her cigarettes out of her bag and joined him.

'It's quite chilly now isn't it?' said Henry, exhaling a plume of smoke out into the room.

'I had been warned about English country houses,' said Hanneke.

'Oh yes?' said Henry, tapping the excess ash from his cigarette into the fire.

'By Zuleika. She said she grew up in the coldest houses in England and Scotland.'

'Oh, Struthern Castle was freezing. I went there a few times. The late earl didn't believe in central heating. Maybe that's why he got through so many wives,' mused Henry. 'Did you know Zuleika well?'

'We were getting to know her,' said Adalind, stroking her yellow dress. 'We knew her from the art world. We'd just done a shoot with her and she was commissioning us to do something for a documentary she was making.'

'Really? What was it?' asked Henry.

'She wanted to see if we could do a piece of video art that ran a portrait of a historical figure with modern images of a contemporary person.'

'Who were the people?'

185

'She was cagey about the modern person, but it was an aristocrat called Lady Jane something.'

'That narrows it down,' joked Henry. 'There are lots of Lady Janes, Adalind! Zuleika was thoroughly misunderstood. She was much cleverer than people gave her credit for. Sophie was fun, too. Both of them had demons, but who doesn't? I can't think why Mo would have wanted to murder either of them. But I suppose once he'd sold Zuleika the dodgy cocaine it became like a runaway train. Life can be like that sometimes, especially with murder and crime, one imagines. It just snowballs.'

Ryan Todd came in and sat down on the raspberry-coloured sofa. 'Hopefully, everyone will begin putting it behind them, especially once the trial's happened.' At that moment, Minty stalked in followed by Oscar and Tabitha.

'I can't believe it. Peter has shut George in the study and is grilling him about his fund again. It won't be pretty, I can tell you. George hoovered up three lines of marching powder after supper to get over the first interrogation. Sébastien has gone in to try and defuse the situation. Peter needs to take a chill pill.'

'He's seriously sexy – quite the silver fox,' said Oscar, stirring things up.

'Shut up, Oscar,' said Minty.

'I agree,' said Henry, winking at Oscar. 'Very suave.'

They heard a door slam followed by Peter shouting, 'You're a liar, George, and I'll prove it in court if necessary!'

A minute later Peter Paul walked in looking calm. The only giveaway to his true state of mind was a small, pulsing vein in the left side of his temple. He went to the drinks tray, poured himself a Diet Coke and sat down in the armchair on the other side of the fireplace. After a few minutes Lily and Flavia went over to him.

'I laid the cards on table,' he said triumphantly.

'How?' asked Flavia.

'I said I had evidence that his fund was a ponzi scheme, that I wanted all of Zuleika's funds returned next week and that I would be in touch with the FSA. He went as white as a sheet and walked out. He's not defrauding my daughter out of £30 million.'

'Right. Well, now you've done it, can you stay away from him and let's try and enjoy the rest of the weekend?'

'Absolutely. Mission accomplished.'

50

The music room was long and narrow with pale blue walls and a dome in the middle of the ceiling. The inside of the dome was painted with plump, little curly-haired putti playing various musical instruments. Flavia had got Browning, the butler, to set the decks up right underneath the dome. George was standing behind them wearing his aviator sunglasses and a pair of oversized silver earphones. House music was pumping out of the speakers and reverberating around the room. Rocky had given everyone, apart from Peter Paul, several vodka shots and the mood had lightened significantly. George put on 'Love Generation' by Bob Sinclar and pumped up the volume. Rocky, Sébastien, Tabitha, Adalind, Hanneke, Flavia, Ryan, Oscar, Matthew and Lily took to the dance floor. George bobbed up and down behind the decks shouting 'yeah' and 'tune'. Every so often he would do a little affected turn while DJing. Lily could see that Ryan had the unsuspecting Tabitha in his sights; he kept dancing near her and 'accidentally' brushing her with his gangly arms.

Peter Paul and Henry were deep in conversation in the drawing room. Matthew and Rocky began snogging, in the middle of the dance floor. Flavia fanned herself down in mock indignation.

'Get a room!' shouted Minty, who went and wrapped her arms around George. He sniffed and wiped his nose. Minty slipped her hand into his pocket, took something out and put it in her bag. She walked out of the room followed by Rocky and Matthew. Sébastien walked over to Lily and put his arms around her. It was the first time he had ever done anything like that in public.

'I'm sorry I stormed off. I just found Peter's amateur sleuthing unbearable. He's rattled George's cage. I think you're right about the fund. I've always suspected it was too good to be true. Peter Paul has demanded all of Zuleika's money back and has threatened to go to the FSA with evidence. George is denying it, of course, but he is in a state and is getting seriously off his face. It's as if he has a nihilistic attitude to the whole affair.'

'Do you think he hid Moses?'

'Not you, too! Listen, the police have their man. This George affair is completely separate.'

187

Adalind and Hanneke were dancing with Ryan, who kept glancing over to the door looking for Tabitha who'd gone to find Minty. Ten minutes later, the others returned laden with a chilled bottle of Bollinger and a litre of vodka.

'Let's get this party started,' said Rocky, rushing round topping up everyone's glasses. George put on some electro house. Flavia, Ryan and the Dutch artists groaned.

'I agree. I hate this music,' said Lily. Sébastien smiled and shrugged his shoulders.

'George, there is a rebellion against your trendy music,' he joked.

'What! I got this in Berlin, man,' said George, looking genuinely insulted. 'This is great, give it time.' He began doing a dance that made him look like a chicken.

'You're clearing the dance floor, mate, which is a serious crime,' said Rocky. Everyone booed. 'Seb, do you have the playlist Veronique made in Ibiza?'

'Hmm, I'm not sure,' said Sébastien.

'I'll have a look,' said George, picking up Sébastien's iPod. Sébastien watched him scrolling through his iPod and frowned. Tabitha wafted over and asked Sébastien for a light.

'What are you smoking?' he asked, transfixing her with those almond-shaped green eyes.

'Lucky Strike,' she replied.

'Interesting,' he said, leaning in to give her a light. He took a packet of Gauloises out of his pocket and put one in his mouth and gave another to Lily. 'What do you think, Lily?'

'They're all fine. I'm a Marlboro Light girl myself.'

'You'll convert to Gauloises,' said Sébastien. 'Give me time.' Lily smiled.

'Where is this playlist?' demanded Rocky. George was staring intently at the iPod.

'I can't find it,' he said. 'Look, I've got some great stuff on my laptop.' He bent down again and began looking at his computer screen. A few seconds later the room was filled with funky house beats. They all began dancing, apart from George, who had left the room in a hurry.

'Rock star, sing over the top,' said Matthew. Rocky looked at him and grinned. She went over to George's complex sound system and fiddled about.

'George!' she shouted.

'He's not here,' said Minty.

'Probably gone for another line,' Flavia hissed at Lily. 'I'm all for people having fun but with him it's too much! He doesn't know when to stop.'

'Seb, can you help me?' Sébastien went over and helped her plug in the microphone. 'Thanks, sweet cheeks,' she sang over the microphone. Sébastien laughed. 'This is for you, baby,' she said, pointing at Matthew. 'We're in Devon and you're going to take me to heaven. Here, tonight, under the light of the moon you make me swoon,' she belted out in her bewitching husky voice. Everyone cheered and began dancing. Ryan Todd came up behind her and began ad-libbing: 'She's dangerous, I know it, but I can't help falling under her spell, it won't end well.' He looked at Tabitha as he sang. She found it hilarious and threw back her head and danced – loving all the attention. Matthew danced with her – his moves far outshone everyone else in the room.

'Now that's what I call music,' said Flavia, lifting her full glass of champagne in the air and doing an arabesque. Sébastien walked out followed by Oscar and Hanneke. Lily suspected that they were all going to join George for a line of cocaine. He did seem to have an endless supply.

Ryan Todd was now in full flow and began singing his classic eighties hit, 'Sugar Coated Lies'.

'Fucking brilliant,' said Rocky, giving Matthew a high-five. 'This man is pure genius. You're one of my heroes, Ryan!' and she got down on her knees by his feet and began praying in supplication. Ryan looked slightly embarrassed. Henry and Peter Paul walked in.

'Ah, some music I recognise,' said Peter Paul.

'Ryan is amazing. He'll be forever young,' said Henry.

'Just like me darling,' said Flavia. 'Let's have a toast to eternal youth – let us bask in its glory forever.' They clinked their glasses in approval.

Lily walked along the long, cream corridor, her heels clip-clopping on the flagstone as she went. There were six elegant watercolours of Porcarno and its gardens and then numerous framed photographs of Flavia's brother William show-jumping. Coloured rosettes were fixed to some of the photos and Lily spotted one photograph of Princess Anne presenting William with a silver cup. Lily carried on past the large, yellow kitchen, where she spotted two black

189

Labradors snoozing in front of a cream Aga, basking in its warmth as if they were sunbathing. At the end of the corridor was a white door. Lily opened it and walked into the most magnificent library she had ever seen. Three of the four walls had floor-to-ceiling shelves, which were packed with hardbacked books. A fire burnt in the hearth and next to it stood an inviting, brown, weathered leather armchair. Lily walked over to the nearest shelf and pulled out the first book she saw: it was a first edition of *The End of the Affair*. She opened the pages and inhaled – it smelled musty and smoky. Inside there was an inscription, 'To my dear friend Badger, whose affairs of the heart never ran smoothly, Graham.'

Her eye was drawn to rows and rows of large, red leather-bound books on the other side of the room. There were hundreds of them. Lily walked over to them and laughed – they were bound copies of magazines. William and his wife were obviously avid readers of *Decanter*, *Horse and Hound*, *Country Life* and *Society*. She climbed a dark antique wooden stepladder and took a bound volume of *Society* magazines from the first half of 1990 off the wall. She flicked through it, amused to see pictures of Flavia, Ryan and Henry in the social pages. They really had been on this merry-go-round for years. She put it back and took out the bound copies for the second part of 2000. She perused it while balancing on the stepladder in her heels. There was an interview with Jerry Hall about life after Mick Jagger, a sexy cover of Kylie Minogue dressed as a ballerina and a big article about Hugh Grant and Liz Hurley's split. The November issue had a striking cover of Lady Zuleika Winters in a huge red ball gown, wearing a gold and diamond crown, with the cover line 'Fashion Royalty – Lady Zuleika Winters Undisputed Queen of Couture.'

Lily leafed through the issue and on to the December one, then she stopped in her tracks as there, staring out at her, was the photograph of Sébastien's mother that had pride of place in his flat – emblazoned across it was the title:

Was Anoushka Hamilton-Bruce the most scandalous female aristocrat ever? The spectacular downfall and death of the original 'It' girl...

Lily turned the page and saw a collage of photographs of Anoushka with various husbands and lovers. A picture of a young Anoushka, with a handsome man and two young boys, caught her eye. It was

Sébastien and his brother Guillaume. Lily thought it was strange that Sébastien had never mentioned him. There was a picture of Anouskha on the arm of famous film star Donald Caraway, another with Peter Paul Anderson IV and one with a handsome Arab called Sheikh Rashid Al Shamie. On the next page there was a copy of a tabloid front page from July 1984 with the words 'Home Wrecker' and a pap shot of Anoushka with Tory MP Richard Wallingsford. Opposite that was a picture of Anoushka's nude, *Playboy* cover from March 1983 and, underneath, was a splendid photograph of Anoushka playing lady of the manor at Gunnerston Park, the magnificent stately home of the Earl of Northian.

'Wowza,' said Lily, walking over to the armchair. It was even more comfortable than it looked. She snuggled down into it, kicked off her heels and began to read the article.

> *Badly-behaved women might not make history but they certainly make headlines, and none more so than socialite Anoushka Hamilton-Bruce. When the beautiful goddaughter of the Queen came out as a debutante in 1975, she was immediately identified as 'the' catch of the season. Beautiful, witty, moneyed and fun, she soon caught the eye of the most eligible men in the land. In the first week she bagged the much-desired Duke of Buckingham, who proposed marriage two months later. It was set to be the wedding of the year until she was caught, in flagrante, with the gardener at his parents' pile Sittingham Hall. It caused a huge scandal and everyone in the Hamilton-Bruce family was embarrassed by the incident, apart from Anoushka, who thoroughly enjoyed her notoriety.*
>
> *A few weeks later she was stepping out with English cricketing hero, Martin Sherman, before falling under the spell of the dashing and suave Count de Bourgogne. The charismatic, French aristocrat seemed to have her in check and even managed to get his bride to the altar – convincing her to convert to Catholicism in the process. It would be the first of many religions and marriages – she would go on to marry an earl and a sheikh, converting religions each time, as well as having affairs with a married Tory MP, a priest, various film stars and millionaires along the way.*
>
> *She caused even more outrage when she posed naked for Playboy, wearing mock crown jewels and talking*

about her special, royal connections. She joins the ranks of the Duchess of Argyll, the Duchess of Cleveland and Vita Sackville-West as being one of the most scandalous female aristocrats in history. She lived entirely for herself, abandoning all of her children in pursuit of her next paramour and sexual adventure. In July she plunged to her death after falling from the balcony of her Chelsea town house while high on cocaine. Friends question whether it was suicide or a terrible accident, stating how the society beauty was finding it hard to come to terms with ageing.

The library door opened and Sébastien walked in wearing a blue polo neck. 'I've been looking for you everywhere. What are you doing in here on your own?' Lily immediately closed the book so he couldn't see what she had been reading.

'It's so amazing in here. I got engrossed in the books and then I found these old copies of *Society* bound in these red leather books.'

'You are such a bookworm, Lily. Are you always at work?'

'No, just nosy! Why did you change?'

'I spilled vodka and cranberry down my uniform. We've been dancing in the music room. Rocky and Matthew have been doing some crazy breakdancing. He is a serious, cool dude. Then we noticed you and George had gone missing. We got suspicious! So we came to have a look for you but you're not together. Have you seen George?'

'No. You should look in a bathroom, shouldn't you?'

'Ha ha. We've tried all of them! He's been gone for a while. We were worried Peter had cornered him again but he went to bed hours ago.'

Lily walked over to the steps and popped the book back in the shelf, incredibly relieved that Sébastien hadn't clocked what she was reading. In the silence, she could hear the ticking of the elaborate, rococo mantel clock. She looked over to see the time – quarter to three in the morning.

'Bedtime.'

'I agree,' said Sébastien holding out his hand. Lily walked towards him but was interrupted by a blood-curdling scream that sounded like it was coming from the garden. They ran through the kitchen into the utility room, flinging open the back door and hurrying out into the dark night.

192

51

Sébastien and Lily followed the sound of the scream round the garden, to the old part of the house. There beneath the fourteenth-century tower was the spreadeagled body of George Lazarus. Minty was by his side holding his hand and sobbing. A pool of crimson blood surrounded his head, breaking off into little rivers that ran down the paving and into the gully, between the path and the manicured lawn.

'He's dead,' she said, sobbing uncontrollably. 'That bloody American made him jump to his death. He has blood on his hands. Do you hear me, Peter? Murderer!' Lily put her arm around Minty.

'Does he have a pulse?' asked Sébastien.

'I can't find one,' said Minty, breaking down again.

'Let me see,' said Sébastien, feeling around his neck. 'Nothing,' he said, shaking his head. At that moment, Flavia, Henry and Oscar appeared.

'What's happened? Oh my God!' shrieked Flavia. 'Is he alive?' she asked, seeing Sébastien feeling for his pulse.

'No,' said Sébastien. Minty sobbed uncontrollably.

'Let me try. I've got some medical training,' said Oscar, pushing him out of the way. He felt around for a pulse, 'Nothing. He's broken his neck and with this amount of blood loss, he's a goner.' Flavia glared at him. It began to rain.

'I'll call 999. Oscar can you go and get Browning? His house is the cottage by the stable block. He can stay out here with the body while we wait for the police inside.' Flavia hurried inside and Oscar ran off, towards the stables.

'I'm staying here,' said Minty. She was sobbing and burying her head in George's chest. She was covered in his blood, which was now all over her gold Prada dress.

'Minty, I don't think you should touch him, my dear,' said Henry. 'The police need him to be left just as he is.'

'Come on, Minty. Let's go inside,' said Sébastien soothingly.

'Didn't you hear me?' she spat. 'I'm staying out here with him until the ambulance arrives. It's the least I can do.' She began sobbing again and Lily noticed she was shaking uncontrollably. 'We were in love. He was my soulmate.'

'I'll go and get you a coat and hat,' said Lily. 'Henry, will you stay with her until Browning arrives?' Henry nodded. Flavia threw open the dining room doors and turned on the light.

'Come in this way!' she shouted. Lily and Sébastien walked over. She came out to join them. 'The police and ambulance are on their way. We've got to get Minty inside. It's doing her no good clinging to him like that – she'll catch pneumonia in this rain. She's not going to bring him back to life. You go inside and tell the others what's happened. Those that are still awake are in the drawing room. I'll go and comfort Minty. What a bloody mess.'

Detective Chief Superintendent Parker walked into the drawing room and introduced himself. He was a tall man in his late forties with thick, sandy hair and an impressive pair of eyebrows that curled up at the edges in a comedy flick. Oscar, Adalind and Hanneke moved from the window to join Lily, Sébastien and Rocky, who were sitting by the fire. Flavia and Henry were still outside, trying to persuade Minty to leave George's side.

'I think you should all go to bed,' said Parker. 'We won't do any interviews until the morning and I know you'll be wanting to get back to London. What time did you last see Mr Lazarus alive?'

'When he was DJing in here,' said Rocky.

'When was that?'

'After supper,' said Rocky.

'I don't remember seeing him after you and Ryan began singing,' said Lily.

'You're right, Lily,' said Adalind. 'He never came back in.'

'How did he seem?' asked Parker.

'Jumpy,' said Sébastien. 'He'd had a run in with one of the other guests about his fund. He was excitable.'

'Thank you. As I said, we'll be doing full interviews in the morning.'

Henry walked in holding a mug of steaming cocoa.

'Hello, Henry Marmsby,' he said, holding out his hand to Parker.

'Detective Chief Superintendant Parker.'

'Araminta has finally gone upstairs with Flavia. She's in a terrible state. She's going to sleep in Flavia's room tonight. What a thing to happen. The poor girl has lost her sister and now her boyfriend. It's heartbreaking.'

194

'What did the doctor say?' asked Lily.

'He's been dead for at least an hour, probably longer. He would have died on impact apparently, so at least he didn't suffer. It's a long way down – nobody would survive that fall. Not that he intended to survive, of course.' The others nodded. 'There is hot chocolate in the kitchen. Flavia said to help yourselves,' said Henry.

'I'll be seeing you all in the morning. Goodnight,' said Parker. He went outside to join his colleagues, who were collecting evidence and taking photographs.

'It's just so weird,' said Rocky. 'What a way to go. I knew he was off his face but was he *that* off his face?'

'It wasn't just that, Rocky, it was the fund. He knew it was going to be exposed as a con. Peter was right,' said Sébastien.

'How bad was it?' asked Henry.

'He half-admitted to me, after Peter confronted him again that it was a ponzi scheme. That was how he got those amazing returns. It was a house of cards. I suspect Moses knew and blackmailed him into hiding him in Scotland.' Henry whistled. Lily wished that Ricky and DCS Peters were here to hear this. She knew she'd been right.

'What a tragedy,' said Henry. Everybody nodded in agreement. It was a natural break in the conversation and they began to make their way out of the drawing room. Lily and Hanneke headed to the kitchen. There, on the Aga, was a large pan of hot chocolate. Hanneke filled three mugs and handed one to Lily. She thanked her and walked upstairs, watched by all of Flavia's ancestors. Sébastien was lurking in the corridor outside her bedroom. He moved towards her and tried to kiss her on the mouth, hoping to be invited in.

'I'm going to go to bed,' she said, appalled that he thought he'd come in for some nookie. 'I'm very shaken up by what's happened. I don't think it's appropriate Sébastien.'

'Goodnight, my angel,' and he kissed her cheek. Lily closed the door firmly behind her and walked over to the window and looked outside. She could see the paramedics carrying George's body away on a stretcher in the lashing rain. What on earth was Sébastien thinking? His good friend had just died, could he just block it out and carry on regardless? When she was sure there was no one in the corridor, she picked up her phone and called Ricky.

52

Lily was woken at half past seven in the morning by her mobile ringing. It was Ricky.

'What time do you call this? We only spoke three and a half hours ago.'

'Your quotes on the email are dynamite Lily! I've got a major story hard on!'

'It is almost unbelievable.'

'I owe you an apology. You were right about George Lazarus. We've got our fraud people on it and their preliminary investigations show he was up to his neck in it. I've been on the phone to Peters and he's in contact with the Exmouth Police enquiry team. He's on his way down. Do you think it was an accident?'

'I think it probably was. The guy had nowhere to run. He harboured a criminal and had defrauded a lot of very rich and important people out of millions of pounds. I don't think he was the type to take a jail sentence on the chin. I'm surprised he didn't do a runner last night.'

'I've spoken to Sam. He's delighted. We're running the story big tomorrow. I will write it but with all your quotes, to give us the inside track. We'll just quote you as a guest at the castle. This is one mother of a scoop. Sean at *The Post* can suck on it.'

'Fuck that, Ricky. Everyone will know it was me who spoke to the press. I'd rather just have a joint byline and be done with it. I'm not part of this castle set.'

'Sam was adamant that you keep your cover until this is all over.'

'Great,' said Lily, feeling utterly pissed off.

'Everyone knows the hard work you've put in.'

'I hope so. Look, I better go down to breakfast. The police are turning up at nine to begin interviewing people.'

'Keep me posted.'

'Will do.' Lily hung up and walked over to the window. An incident tent had been erected over where George's body had been and the area was cordoned off with blue and white tape. The paving stones were stained crimson, as was the soil in the gully and the surrounding grass on the lawn.

Lily walked into the dining room. Flavia, Peter Paul, Ryan, Rocky and Toby were sitting at the far end of the long dining table. Even on a day like this Flavia looked majestic. She was dressed in a black and white checked McQueen jacket, a black pencil skirt and had a small, black, signature Percy Drawing pill-box hat on her perfectly groomed head.

'Lily! Come in and help yourself to breakfast,' said Flavia, waving her arm in the direction of the mahogany sideboard, which had a hot plate with bacon, scrambled eggs and grilled tomatoes on it, as well as blue and white striped jars of cereal. Lily helped herself and walked over to the table.

'Coffee?' asked Peter, passing her a large stainless steel cafetière.

'I'll definitely be needing that,' said Lily, pouring the steaming dark liquid into a green and white china cup decorated with birds.

'The police are arriving at nine to interview everyone. Although I don't think they are treating the death as suspicious.'

'What a bloody mess,' Peter drawled in his strong East Coast accent.

'How is Minty?' asked Lily.

'I dosed her up with tamazepam. She's still asleep. I am very worried about her. This will be very hard for her; she's not a strong person.'

'Browning and I had to prise her off George's body last night. It was heartbreaking,' said Henry.

'I'm surprised he jumped,' said Rocky, 'I always thought his sense of self-preservation was greater than that.'

'I didn't know him well but I thought he'd be a bolter,' agreed Lily.

'Me too,' said Peter emphatically. 'I feel terrible if I was the catalyst to his suicide. I didn't have him down as the excitable type, who would jump off a turret in the heat of a moment. I thought he was more headstrong. All I was trying to do was get some answers. The guy was off his head but I gather that was a normal state of affairs for him. At the end of the day, we are all responsible for our behaviour. Christ, I of all people know about that,' he said, smiling. Ryan Todd, Henry and Flavia nodded. Lily knew he was referring to the publicity surrounding his indiscretion with a transsexual in a Brooklyn cinema that had resulted in the breakdown of his marriage to Zuleika. 'I still maintain he had a lot to answer for. Sadly, he couldn't face up to

197

it. It's an awful thing that has happened but he was going to have to face the music sometime. Deep down he must have known the party was over.'

'Of course he did,' said Flavia, patting Peter's arm. 'It was only a matter of time, Peter. Minty admitted last night that, after dinner, George confessed that he had hidden Moses in Scotland. She said he knew about the fund and blackmailed George into hiding him. She said George didn't believe Mo was guilty – whether that is true or not we will never know.'

'Look, both of them were probably guilty – Mo of murder and George of fraud. Hopefully, this will be the end of this sordid scandal. I just want to get the police interview out the way and back to London as soon as possible,' said Ryan. 'I don't want my name associated with this in any way at all. It's a bloody nightmare.'

'I agree,' said Henry. 'How on earth did George get a murder suspect up to Scotland unnoticed?'

'Helicopter,' said Flavia. 'He got him out of Battersea Heliport on the Friday night before he was a suspect. He travelled with him. They went straight to the shooting estate.'

'It's so James Bond, it's almost wonderful,' said Henry.

'I'm going to see if I can go and visit Mo. I still think he's innocent,' said Rocky.

Sébastien and Oscar walked in. Sébastien was wearing the blue polo neck he had been wearing the night before.

'It's a bit warm for that jumper, isn't it?' said Flavia. 'It looks like a skiing jumper, Sébastien. It's most unlike you to wear such a thing. You normally have such good style.'

'I'm cold,' said Sébastien, giving a mock shiver. 'I think I might be coming down with something. Also, I know about English country houses and their central heating systems. How is everyone?'

'Shell-shocked,' said Flavia.

'Poor George,' said Oscar. 'The only good thing is he would have died the moment he hit the ground. It looked like his neck had completely snapped.'

'Are you sure about his neck, Oscar?' said Rocky.

'Yes I am actually, Rocky. I spent two years studying medicine before I realised fashion was my true calling.'

'Poor chap. At least it was quick,' said Henry getting up from the table. 'I'm just going to freshen up before the police arrive.'

'Good point,' said Flavia, standing up. Lily noticed she was wearing an impressive pair of black, lizard-skin stilettos. 'I better check on Araminta. I think I'll leave her to sleep. The police can interview her last.'

'They're not treating this as a suspicious death, are they?' asked Sébastien.

'They have to look at all possibilities but I think the general consensus, in the circumstances, will be suicide. The police went up on to the tower last night after they'd attended to the body. As you know it had been raining heavily so I don't know what they found. The water just gushes along up there.'

'They will be looking for evidence that he jumped,' said Lily. 'They will want to establish that beyond reasonable doubt.'

'There you go.'

'Was there anything up there?' asked Sébastien.

'They took a glass of champagne and a cigarette butt away for analysis,' said Flavia.

'Looks like he had a last snifter and then, poof, off he went,' said Henry throwing his arms in the air dramatically.

'What champagne were we drinking?' asked Oscar.

'Bollinger,' said Sébastien.

'Least he went in style,' said Oscar.

53

Everyone except Minty was gathered in the drawing room. The atmosphere was tense and so markedly different from that of the previous evening, when they were in their fancy dress. Flavia was in the mint-green armchair, Peter was facing her on the long, embroidered footstool and they were talking in hushed tones. Ryan Todd was opposite in the other armchair, deep in conversation with Tabitha Monkton-Miller, who had driven over for the police interviews. The sunlight bounced off her rich, russet hair making it the colour of a vintage malt whisky. The others sat on the raspberry-coloured sofa and a few antique chairs that had been drawn up beside it. Lily and Rocky were sitting in the window seat looking out at where George's body had fallen. Lily had chosen not to sit next to Sébastien – she couldn't quite get over his advances the night before, when he knew George was dead. Rocky fiddled with the ties of a tan leather bracelet on her left arm. She had bitten her nails right down to the nub. A small tattoo of an eagle peeked out from underneath the bracelet on her left wrist.

DCS Parker walked in accompanied by DCS Peters and a junior officer. They stood in front of the fireplace. Everyone stood up to greet them.

'Please sit down,' said Parker, making a sitting down motion with his hand. Lily and Rocky got up and walked over to the others. They both squeezed on to the footstool, beside Peter Paul. Lily nodded at Peters who smiled. 'This is Detective Chief Superintendent Peters of Scotland Yard, CID,' said Parker introducing Peters. There was a collective gasp.

'This isn't being treated as a murder is it?' asked Flavia, looking horrified.

'It's too early to comment on that,' said Parker. 'The initial findings suggest suicide but we can't rule it out until we've studied the evidence. My esteemed colleague is here because George Lazarus has a connection to another case he is working on. We will be interviewing you all individually. If I could ask you to be patient and, please, do not leave the premises without checking with one of our team first. We will be conducting the interviews in the library, starting with Mrs Wilde. Constable Cousins here has the order in which we wish to see you. If I could ask you not to go up to the tower or near the path where George's body was found, as forensics are carrying out more detailed investigations. Thank you.' Parker strode out of the room with purpose followed by Peters and Constable Cousins.

'I was hoping I'd wake up this morning and realise it was just a ghastly nightmare,' said Flavia.

'Well it's all very real now,' said Henry.

'What a thing to do,' said Sébastien, rubbing his eyes.

'Everyone will know about it soon,' said Flavia.

'They do already,' said Rocky. 'I got a text from Veronique this morning saying how awful it was.'

'There is no mystery there, Rocky. I let her know,' said Sébastien. 'George was a friend.' Lily felt irked by this. She knew she had no reason to be irritated but she wondered how much contact Veronique and Sébastien were really having.

200

The youthful Constable Cousins walked back in and towards Flavia.

'Do they want me?' she asked dramatically.

'Yes, Ma'am.'

It was half past twelve when Constable Cousins knocked on Lily's bedroom door to say that they were ready for her in the library. She followed Cousins down the stone staircase and came to the conclusion that this death, at the castle, was the most exciting thing that had happened to him since he'd joined the police force.

'What a horrid way to go,' he said in his lilting Devon accent.

'Awful,' agreed Lily.

They walked along the corridor towards the library. Sébastien was walking towards them in the other direction. He looked utterly pissed off.

'Get ready for a grilling. It is outrageous! Your friend dies and you're treated like a murderer. Appalling!'

'I'm sure they're like that with everyone,' said Lily.

'Of course,' said Sébastien, 'Do you want a lift back?'

'Ooh, yes please.'

'Let's go after your interview. Don't be long!' He walked up the corridor in the direction of the drawing room. Constable Cousins knocked on the library door.

'Come in,' said a voice through the door. Lily and Cousins walked in. Peters was sitting in one of the brown leather armchairs. He was pulsing with frenetic energy and his blue-grey eyes were alert and piercing. Parker was sitting next to him on a wooden chair with a pale green silk seat. They both stood as she entered.

'Lily!' exclaimed Peters. 'Fancy seeing you here,' and he raised his right eyebrow cheekily.

'Hello, Jeffrey.'

'How do you two know each?' asked Parker.

'We've worked together on these society murders. Lily is a journalist.' Parker looked at her suspiciously.

'It's all right, Tony, she's a good one.' Lily stretched out her hand to Parker.

'Lily Cane,' she said.

'Come and take a seat, Lily,' said Parker, ushering her towards one of the brown leather armchairs. 'Cousins, can you take notes?' Cousins nodded obediently. 'So, how have you two worked together?'

'I'm working on this society murders story for *The London Evening News*. I'm actually working undercover at *Society* magazine.'

'Good Lord!' exclaimed Parker. 'Do you mean to tell me you suspected something like this might happen?'

'No,' said Lily, shrugging her shoulder. 'It is almost unbelievable. To be honest, I have just been trying to get closer to the key characters in this drama.'

'Well, you've certainly managed that,' said Parker, rubbing his forehead, catching one of his sandy bushy eyebrows with the base of his right hand as he did so. 'Do you think George Lazarus jumped from the tower? Was there anything unusual about his behaviour last night?' Lily sat back in the armchair and considered the question.

'I had had my suspicions about George Lazarus's fund for some time, as Chief Superintendent Peters can tell you.' She gave Peters a meaningful glance. She wasn't going to let Ricky and Peters's dismissal of her hunch go unchecked. Peters nodded in acknowledgment.

'Lily had suspected that George Lazarus had been defrauding his clients and had made us aware of these suspicions,' said Peters.

'Did you make him aware of your suspicions?' asked DCS Parker.

'No I didn't. I didn't need to because Peter Paul Anderson confronted him about them over dinner, in a very public way. I would not have approached the matter directly anyway. Also, Peter Paul had confided in me that he was going to confront George over the course of the weekend. He was very angry because George had lost millions of pounds of his late ex-wife's money.'

'How did George react to this accusation?'

'He was most uncomfortable and asked Peter to desist from talking about business at a social occasion. Then, Peter changed tack and asked him if he'd hidden Moses Brown in Scotland. George was furious at that point and Flavia changed the placement, so that he had his pudding at the other end of the table.'

'Do you think George Lazarus was in such a heightened state of emotion that he would have jump off the turret?'

'I don't know. Look, I don't want to land people in it here but as I am sure you are aware he was high on cocaine. I believe he had a serious cocaine habit. He was also a vain man who cared desperately what people thought about him, so maybe the combination of the scale of his fraud, his subsequent downfall in society and the fact he was high as a kite made him decide to fling himself off the turret. I didn't know him well enough to make a call on that. If you're asking me do I think a guest here murdered him? I don't think so but I don't know so.'

'Hmm,' said Parker, rubbing his head.

'The party was about to be over for him in a major way,' said Peters. 'He would have faced jail for that scale of fraud and, quite frankly, assisting an offender in a high-profile murder like this would probably not go unpunished either.'

'Surely the forensics will throw a light on all this?' asked Lily.

'Well the post-mortem findings should be ready tomorrow and we'll see what else the forensics have found,' said Parker. 'Although there was heavy rain last night.'

'All this information will be looked at during the inquest.'

'When will that be?' asked Lily.

'Well, the coroner was informed of the death in the early hours of the morning. We will have a few days to do our investigations and the inquest will be end of the week or the beginning of next week.'

'Gosh,' said Lily.

'It's standard procedure in cases of unnatural death,' said Peters.

'Can you talk us through the evening from beginning to end?' said Parker.

'Of course,' said Lily. She spent the next half an hour recounting the events of the previous night, in minute detail.

54

Sébastien was pacing around on the gravel outside the castle. His silver Ferrari Spider glinted in the sunlight. He looked like a horse chomping at the bit, which Lily thought was wholly appropriate, given his passion for polo. She opened the heavy, pale blue, studded front door. He looked up and frowned.

'There you are, Lily! You've been in there nearly an hour for Christ's sake. What on earth were you talking to them about? You didn't need to give them your life story.'

'They were asking me about the two girls' murders, as well as George's death.'

'Why? How are they connected? They didn't ask me about that.'

'I think because I'd been in contact with Superintendent Peters when I was at *The LEN*.'

'Come on, let's go! I wanted to leave hours ago.'

'I need to pack. Also, have you eaten?'

'Oh Lily come on!' he exclaimed. 'There are some sandwiches on the dining room table. I am leaving in twenty minutes. I'm finding the atmosphere here unpleasantly oppressive. Minty has just woken up and I think we should all make a move so she can have some quiet time with Flavia. She doesn't want all of us hanging around. Ryan, Peter, Tabitha, Henry and the Dutch two all left ages ago.'

'I'll be with you as quickly as I can.'

Lily ran up the stairs and along the corridor to her bedroom. She flung all her clothes into the holdall and did a sweep of the room for her belongings. She knew Ricky would want an update so she texted him.

> *Yo Ricky, I've seen Peters. General consensus is that Lazarus probably jumped. Results of post-mortem should be ready tomorrow afternoon. Inquest later in week. Speak later. Lunch tomorrow? L x*

As she made her way back downstairs, her phone beeped.

> *Defo. 1pm at sushi place we went to last time? R*

Lily walked into the dining room. A large plate of homemade sandwiches sat in the middle of the dining table, along with a couple of bottles of mineral water and some apples. She was damned if she was going to eat her sandwiches in the car. Sébastien could wait and, if he left, it was no big deal. She could always catch the train. She sat down at the long dining table and tucked into a delicious ham, cheese and pickle sandwich.

Flavia walked into the dining room, looking stressed.

'Oh, Lily, I hear you're leaving.'

'I thought it was best if we got out of your hair. How's Minty?'

'Absolutely dreadful. I've got her mother coming over later.' Flavia looked around her and then whispered, 'The mother's pretty ghastly. She didn't always have time for Minty when she was growing up, but she's on her way now, which is something.'

'When will you get back to London?'

'God knows! It depends when they finish the investigations. William is absolutely furious. It's bloody typical this has happened, when I've had friends down. He says it will put people off coming round – it's open to the public one weekend a month. I said "What rot! They'll want to come and see where George went splat!"' Then, she almost broke down. 'Lily, I'm really shaken up by it all. Do you think what Peter said made him jump?'

'Who knows? He was going to have to face the music some time.'

'Quite. Peter thinks he jumped. For once, he doesn't have a conspiracy theory.' Lily had now finished her sandwich. She took an apple for the car and got up and hugged Flavia.

'Poor you! You were only trying to find some answers throwing this weekend.'

'Well it backfired! I fear Peter and my meddling in this affair has had terrible consequences.'

'What's done is done. I better go – Sébastien will be tearing his hair out.'

'He did look cross. He's not used to being kept waiting Lily. Well done – he's quite the catch!' said Flavia, shooting her a mischievous wink.

Lily was roused from her sleep by her mobile ringing. She looked out of the window and noticed they were already on the M4.

'Wow, how fast have you been driving?'

'It's a crime to drive one of these cars slowly,' said Sébastien, looking at the road ahead and putting his foot on the gas. 'This car is one of my only extravagances. I bought it as my thirtieth birthday present.'

'How generous of you!' teased Lily. 'When did I fall asleep?'

'About five minutes after we left.'

'Sorry! I was exhausted.'

'Also, I'm a great driver. We just passed Swindon, not that that means anything to me.' Lily smiled. Sébastien and his flash Ferrari were about as far removed from Swindon as you could get. She checked her phone, there was a message from Jazz asking how the weekend had gone – she texted her back discreetly.

Yo Jazz, Not such a romantic weekend. One of the party
died. It looks like he jumped off a turret. Will call later!
Lx

'How long were you with the police this morning?' Lily asked
Sébastien.

'About twenty minutes. They asked some outrageous
questions. Do you know they asked me if I knew of anyone who
would want George dead? Can you believe it? I mean really! We
weren't in an episode of *Midsomer Murders*.' Lily smiled. She was
amused that *Midsomer Murders* was even on his radar. 'What?'
asked Sébastien, clocking her smirk.

'I just didn't have you down as being into that kind of thing.'

'No, I prefer a slick, serial killer myself. *American Psycho* and
The Talented Mr Ripley are more my style.'

'So you're one hundred per cent sure he jumped?'

'Of course he did! I told you, he as good as admitted to me
that he had embezzled all those funds and he confessed to Minty
that he hid Mo. The simplest explanations are normally the correct
ones – just not in Midsomer!' He smiled at her. Lily looked into
those green eyes and got the thunderbolt in her stomach again.
'Now, are you going to stay tonight?'

'I can't,' she giggled, 'I've got to work.' Lily wondered why she
was rebuffing him in this way. She needed to speak to Ricky but
she could easily stay over. Something was making her hold back,
she put it down to nerves.

'You can't be serious,' he said, laughing. He ran his large,
strong hand up and down her right thigh. For the first time
she noticed quite how long his fingers were. He had a scratch
down the side of his left middle finger. 'I'm not going to beg
you Lily.'

'Oh yes you are. You'll be down on your knees.' He looked
over at her again. A lock of his thick, brown hair caught the top of
his left cheekbone. And even though he was wearing the absurd,
blue, polo neck jumper he looked utterly shaggable.

'Tomorrow night?' he said, staring at the road ahead, the
corners of his generous mouth breaking into a flirty smile.

'OK.'

'Good! Could you light me a cigarette? Mine have finished
so I'll have to have one of your girly ones.' Lily took a pack of

Marlboro Lights out of her bag and pressed the button to wind down her window. She lit Sébastien's first and then one for herself. He inhaled the smoke and breathed it out through his open window. 'I am beginning to calm down. I found the weekend strained even before George killed himself.'

'Why?'

'I just thought it felt very unnatural. George thought the same actually. We had a conversation about it last night. I just wouldn't normally hang out with Peter Paul and I'm not a fan of Oscar Rutherford either.'

'Yes, maybe it was an odd mixture,' said Lily, knowing exactly why they had all been thrown together.

'Do you know the police had the cheek to ask whether I had taken cocaine? That was the final straw. I lost it at that point. How dare they cast aspersions on my character in that way?'

'It's not that odd, given that some guests were partaking with George.'

'I don't want to be tarred with their brush,' he retorted. Lily was puzzled. She knew that Sébastien had taken coke with the others. Was this charade for her benefit? Her phone beeped – it was a text from Jazz.

'You are a lady in demand,' teased Sébastien.

'It's my best friend, Jazz, wondering how the weekend went.'

'Ah. You told her about me did you?' he teased. 'Have you been friends since you were small?'

'No. Since Oxford.'

'I like that you're bright, Lily. And what does this mysterious Jazz do?'

'She's a documentary maker.'

'Oh, not another one,' said Sébastien, the words falling out of his mouth. Lily could see he wanted to swallow them back immediately. She thought about what he had said and her blood ran cold. Was he referring to Zuleika? He always claimed he hardly knew her. Not that many people knew she had set up the documentary company – it certainly wasn't public knowledge.

'Who is the other one?' she asked innocently. Sébastien looked relieved.

'There are so many! A couple of my friends from Brown have gone into it. I find them all so self-righteous and worthy. There they are, with their expensive educations, bemoaning finance, war, commercial farming or whatever they wanted to tub thump about. Pretending to be all down with the people, while taking money from daddy to fund their films and live in Brooklyn and the Meatpacking District. Hypocrites! They were really able guys, too,' said Sébastien, waving his left hand in the air.

'Just because they're not making big cash, doesn't mean what they're doing has no value,' said Lily.

'True,' he said, not looking like he agreed in the slightest. There was an awkward silence, and after a minute of it, Lily reached out for his iPod.

'Let's put some music on. Let's see if you can convert me to house music with your famous Ibiza playlists, Mr DJ.'

'No,' said Sébastien, snatching it back and putting it in his jeans pocket possessively. 'It's just dance music on there. Let's have some of your rock 'n' roll. I think my Balearic days are over. It's all soured after what's happened to George.' Lily looked at Sébastien: a vein was pulsing in the middle of his otherwise perfect forehead.

'Are you OK?'

'I'm really cut up about it,' he replied, stony-faced, 'it's only just sinking in.' Lily opened her bag, got out her iPod and fixed it into the docking station of the car stereo. 'I Can't Get No Satisfaction' blasted out of the speakers.

55

Sébastien drew up outside 8 Nevern Square. He ran his eyes up the building in a dismissive fashion, taking in the rogue electricity cable flapping outside the top window, the rust stains that trickled down from the second-floor balcony railings and the peeling black paint on the front door.

'Do you own your flat?' he asked, undoing his seat belt.

'No, it belongs to my flatmate Billy,' said Lily, stepping out of the car. Sébastien got out and walked to the front of the Ferrari. He lifted the bonnet and bent down to take her overnight bag out of the boot. He handed it to her, then stooped down to kiss her. Even though Lily was beginning to have doubts about him, she kissed him back.

'Are you sure you can't come back with me?' he asked, kissing her up her neck and running his hand up and down her back.

'I told you, I have to work,' she said coyly.

'I could always come up,' he said, drawing her in close again.

'Nice try! Billy's up there. Patience Sébastien! You'll just have to wait until tomorrow.'

'You tease me!'

'It will be worth it,' said Lily.

'I know,' he said, looking her right in the eye. 'I've thought about it a lot,' and, with that, he climbed back into his Ferrari, revved the engine and zoomed off out of the square at high speed.

Lily walked up to the second floor and opened the front door. She felt wired after the weekend and lots of conflicting thoughts were swirling in her mind, but that comment about the documentary makers kept nagging at her. Why would Sébastien be so bothered about documentaries? She went into her bedroom and picked up a large, black Moleskin notebook, in which she kept all her notes about the murders. She flicked to the pages she'd written after the lunch with Dr Bone. There was a list of names.

The Duchess of Argyll
Vita Sackville-West
Jane Digby
Lady Castlemaine
Caroline Norton

'Jane Digby,' exclaimed Lily. 'That's it!' She remembered the Dutch artists saying that Zuleika had commissioned them to make some video art of Lady Jane-someone morphing into a modern person. She went over to the desk in her room and turned on her laptop, the thirty seconds she had to wait before it sprang into action felt like a lifetime. She typed 'Lady Jane Digby' into Google and read the beginning of the Wikipedia entry.

Jane Elizabeth Digby, Lady Ellenborough (3 April 1807 – 11 August 1881) was an English aristocrat who lived a scandalous life of romantic adventure, spanning decades and two continents. She had four husbands and many lovers, including King Ludwig I of Bavaria, his son King

Otto of Greece, statesman Felix Schwarzenberg, and an
Albanian brigand general (the Bulgarian Hadji Christo).
She died in Damascus, Syria as the wife of Arab Sheikh
Medjuel el Mezrab, who was twenty years her junior.

Lily sat back in her chair and ran her hands through her hair. This woman's life had huge parallels with Sébastien's mother, Anoushka Hamilton-Bruce. She had married Sébastien's father, she'd married an earl and a sheikh and they were just the few out of many conquests and scandals that Lily remembered after what Patrick had told her and after reading the beginning of the piece in that old *Society* magazine at Porcarno Castle. She googled Anoushka Hamilton-Bruce: hundreds of entries flicked up. Some were about her affair with married Tory MP Richard Wallingsford that caused an outrage because his wife Cynthia was pregnant at the time; there were a couple of entries about her posing naked for *Playboy* in mock crown jewels; several glamorous paparazzi shots of her on the arm of famous film star Donald Caraway and some mentions in Michael Duster's social column about her marriage to the Earl of Northian in 1985 and then to Sheikh Rashid Al Shamie in 1991. Then there was the illegitimate daughter, Stephanie, who was not the Earl of Northian's, and prompted the end of their marriage.

Lily bent down and picked up a large drawing pad from under the desk. She took a red marker pen out of a steel pen pot and drew a spider gram. She left the middle circle empty and then put Zuleika, Anoushka and Sophie's names in individual circles coming off the chart. If Zuleika had planned to make a documentary about the late Anoushka Hamilton-Bruce, she would have approached Sophie and Sébastien. There was no way she wouldn't consult Anoushka's son. The name that fitted in the centre of the chart was his.

Of course he knew about it, thought Lily. There was nothing that he would have hated more than a documentary raking up his mother's scandalous private life once again. How would he stop Zuleika making it? Lily thought about Sébastien, his power was his looks and charm. He could easily seduce her and she would be vain enough to believe it to be true. Once she was smitten he could try and dissuade her from making it, but what if he couldn't get her to drop it? Lily began to think the unthinkable. If she refused, the only way to stop her would be to kill her. If he was her lover he could easily poison her cocaine – there would be ample opportunity. Lily put her head in her hands. Was she going mad? She phoned Ricky but it went straight to voicemail.

'Ricky, forget sushi tomorrow. Can you come over to the flat tonight? I have a new theory.' She got up from her desk and began pacing round the flat, following her theory through to its logical conclusion. Why would he kill his cousin? Surely he loved his cousin? Did Sophie know he and Zuleika were lovers? Or had Sophie worked it out? She was in on the documentary as she had received money. Was she the only person who knew someone who would want to kill Zuleika? If so, she would have to be got rid of, to protect Sébastien's skin. Maybe Moses Brown was innocent, as he had always claimed. George thought he was. Had George been murdered after all? She phoned Peters but his phone also went to voicemail. She grabbed her motorcycle helmet off the battered pine table in the sitting room, ran downstairs and jumped on her scooter. She whizzed down the Brompton Road and up past South Kensington and Knightsbridge, taking Hyde Park Corner at high speed. She pulled up outside Panther Publications and rang the bell until the security guard came to the glass door.

She couldn't be bothered to wait for the lift, so she sprinted up the four flights of stairs to the *Society* office. She went straight to the wall of bound copies and took down the one for late 2000. She found the issue with Lady Zuleika on the cover and the next one with the piece on Anoushka Hamilton-Bruce and photocopied them. She put the heavy red book back on the shelf and ran downstairs. She jumped on her Vespa and was back at 8 Nevern Square in 7 minutes flat.

Ricky arrived at Lily's flat at seven o'clock armed with two bottles of Good Ordinary Claret. Billy was back and was lying on the light blue sofa, smoking a fag. Ricky was sitting at one of the chairs around the pine table nursing a large glass of wine. Lily explained her theory.

'I told you that Count was a nasty bit of work. I can't think why you got involved with him, Lily,' said Billy.

'Whoa! Whoa! Whoa! I don't know anything about this,' said Ricky looking over at Lily, who blushed.

211

'Oh fuck. I wish I could say I was doing it as part of the undercover operation.'

'Bullshit!' teased Billy. 'She's fancied the socks off him ever since she went to the Serpentine Party. I could see he was handsome but a real arrogant Frenchman. He drove a Ferrari for Christ sake. That's just so eighties.'

'Actually I quite liked the Ferrari, as a fellow petrol head, not as a style statement. I'm not proud of it.'

'Did anything actually happen?' asked Ricky, who was obviously finding the whole thing amusing. Billy looked over at Lily and raised an accusatory eyebrow.

'Yeah it did – but it is very early days,' said Lily dismissively.

'Well, he split up with his girlfriend,' said Billy.

'What?! He dumped that seriously sexy singer Veronique Lapin for Lily? He must be mad!' teased Ricky.

'He didn't! She was boffing someone else. I saw her with Andy Blake.'

'OK this is getting weirder and weirder. And, quite frankly Lily, I am furious you didn't tell me this,' said Ricky. 'Jesus, even if he isn't the murderer – and let's be rational here – this part of the story is hilarious! Peters is going to love this! He was asking about your love life. You really are a dark horse!'

'With terrible taste,' said Billy, taking a big gulp of claret.

'OK look: forget about my part in this story. It is irrelevant.' The other two shot each other conspiratorial glances. 'What do you think of my theory?' Ricky leaned back in his chair and looked into his glass of wine.

'I think it's worth looking into. I agree he has a credible motive and I agree there are a few too many accidents in his orbit.'

'I left Peters a message about getting hold of Anoushka's postmortem. Do you think you can persuade him, Ricky?'

'Yes I do actually. As you know, Lily, the police don't like coincidences.'

'Anoushka fell out of a window high on coke. Zuleika died from a coke overdose. George fell off a turret, also high on coke. They all fit together rather too well, don't they? I still don't get why he would kill George. He liked him didn't he?'

'Yes he did. He was acting weirdly, though. He tried to come to bed with me just after the body had been found.' Billy looked appalled.

'What?! His mate died and he thought, "Never mind, I want some action?" Psycho!'

'George worked it out. Sophie worked it out. It's obvious guys. He had to silence them,' said Lily, pacing around the room like a caged tiger.

'We'll get that report tomorrow, Lily. Is there anyone in Zuleika's social circle you could test this theory on?'

'I'll run it past Flavia tomorrow. I'm also meant to be seeing Sébastien tomorrow night. I'm going to do some gentle digging.'

'Is that wise?' asked Billy.

'He doesn't think I suspect anything. I'll act normal. Also Ricky's *LEN* piece about George will be out tomorrow, with all my insider details. I can distract him with that. It'll be fine. I know what I'm doing.'

'I don't like it either,' said Ricky.

'Tough. I'm going to see him tomorrow. I need to know for my sanity if he did it or not.'

56

The *Society* office was buzzing on Monday morning. Everyone was talking about George Lazarus's suicide and how typical it was that it should happen, quite literally, on Flavia's doorstep. Jonty ushered the features team into his office. His desk was a sea of papers, most of which had his spidery writing sprawled over them in green ink. A row of white, purple and pink orchids in ceramic flowerpots stood on the windowsill.

'Hello, everyone. I'm sure you've all heard about George Lazarus's suicide. Poor Araminta is in a terrible state and, obviously, won't be coming into the office for a while.'

'What about Flavia?' asked Lara. She was wearing a fabulous pair of black high-heeled sandals by Sergio Rossi. Her aubergine-coloured toenails peeked out seductively.

'Flavia is still at Porcarno. The police are still carrying out forensic investigations. She sounded on top of things.'

'She'll be loving every minute of it. She loves an audience; the police are not going to know what's hit them. She'll be recruiting

213

any good-looking ones for fashion shoots. I bet she's dressed up to the nines. When I went to the beach with her, in Santorini, she insisted on swimming in her hat,' said Claudia.

'So, Lily, how was the weekend?' asked Patrick directly.

'Well, it was very tense. It was a strange mix of people, and Peter Paul Anderson insisted on confronting George Lazarus about the legitimacy of his fund, in front of the whole house party, at dinner on the Saturday night – which was awkward.'

'Was that Peter Paul Anderson the IV?' said Claudia in an American accent.

'So we were right, Lily? The fund was too good to be true. I had a little look myself and I thought there was something fishy about it,' said Patrick, pursing his lips.

'Peter Paul discovered that it was a ponzi scheme.'

'Christ,' said Jonty.

'Well I bet he didn't discover it,' said Claudia, looking sceptical.

'He hired some private investigators to look into it,' said Lily. Claudia laughed.

'Don't you just love the super rich?'

'This is huge,' said Jonty. 'Is this in the press yet?'

'I'm sure it will be today,' said Lily.

'Guys, we need to run on this. Lily, are you telling me the people who have invested in this fund don't even know about this yet?'

'That's right.'

'My God! A lot of rich and influential people had money with this guy. He was delivering them returns like they'd never seen before. Ron Smile and Herbert Lowerstein were both raving to me about it at a private view at Red Triangle the other day.'

'Well the now not-so-gorgeous George courted the super rich didn't he? He had the access and he milked it. Minty was living like a princess. No wonder she's so blindsided,' said Claudia.

'So, how did George react to Peter's interrogation?' asked Lara.

'Terribly. He tried to change the subject, which didn't work, because Peter Paul then accused him of hiding Moses on his family's shooting estate in Scotland.'

'You couldn't make this up,' said Jonty, loving every minute of it.

'George was furious at this point and Flavia changed the seating plan. Minty admitted to Flavia that it was true, after George had thrown himself off the turret.'

'Hang on. That poncy-haired George harboured the murder suspect in this summer's biggest police enquiry in a family pad in Scotland! Why the hell would he do that?' said Claudia. Lily thoroughly enjoyed all of their different reactions.

'Blackmail,' she said triumphantly. Claudia whistled, Lara was wide-eyed and Patrick and Jonty shook their heads.

'Unbelievable. This is going to make a fantastic feature. Lily, can you write up your weekend as you experienced it? Patrick, I am going to put you on Lazarus Investments. I want to know exactly what happened and how he managed to pull the wool over everyone's eyes.'

'Absolutely!' said Patrick, rubbing his hands with glee.

'Claudia, can you write fifteen hundred words on George? And then we'll see where we are at the end of the day. If you discover any more bombshells, come and tell me immediately.'

Lily offered to do a Starbucks run for everyone, which gave her the perfect excuse to pop out of the office to make some calls. First she tried Flavia. It went straight through to voicemail.

'Flavia, it's Lily. Can you call me urgently? I don't think Moses Brown killed Zuleika or Sophie. I have a theory to run past you. Call me!' Next, she called Peters. The phone rang four times before he picked up.

'Hi, Lily, I hear you've got a new theory. You've been proved right with your hunches so far, so I can't ignore it. I've got someone pulling up Anoushka Hamilton-Bruce's post-mortem for you. All being well we'll have it this afternoon.'

'That's great. Thanks Jeffrey. What do you make of the Lazarus suicide?'

'Well, we've started looking into Lazarus Investments and the whole thing is a sham. The Serious Fraud Office are on it now. It's a huge scandal, Lily. He's lost millions and millions of pounds. Off the record, I can tell you that Mr Lazarus did hide Moses Brown in Scotland. Brown says it's because George knew he was innocent but I suspect he blackmailed him. He says he wasn't aware of the fund but he's hardly going to admit that he knew about it and did nothing. He's in enough trouble as it is.'

'Do you think George committed suicide?'

'Yes I think so, although my gut says it's one coincidence too many. He's too connected to the other women. Also Lily, what

215

were all the main players in the murder cases doing spending a country weekend together.'

'I'll come clean on that. Peter Paul Anderson had the evidence on Lazarus. He was furious that George had lost £30 million of Zuleika's money and wanted to grill him about it. Also, he didn't think Moses Brown was the murderer. He wanted to question Lazarus and observe the people who were hanging around with Sophie at the Serpentine Summer Party. He thought she was murdered because she knew something about Zuleika's murder.'

'And you now think the same? Peter Paul is pleasant enough but I wouldn't believe everything he says, Lily. He's probably trying to compensate for his failed marriage by finding the killer single-handedly.'

'I hear you, Jeffrey, but the problem with these murders has always been motive. I don't think Moses would have killed Sophie to shut her up. You have to admit that the Count de Bourgogne has a connection to everyone and a motive. He is seriously private.'

'Well you'd know!'

'What? Oh. Ricky's told you, has he?'

'Yes and it's important.'

'Oh look, it's nothing serious. It certainly won't be continuing now! Although I am going round tonight to do some digging.'

'Christ, Lily! Well, you'll probably get more out of him with pillow talk than we did. He's an arrogant little shit, if you don't mind me saying so.'

'I know. He said he got cross when you asked him if he took cocaine.'

'He lost it! Please be careful. He has a nasty temper and, if your theory is right, you're putting yourself in danger. Lily, no one is going to buy this until we have some concrete evidence. Saying the guy has a mummy complex isn't going to wash in court. There's also a lot of evidence to suggest Moses is our man. We've got the phone records, the finger prints, the drug stash and the altercation with Sophie and Araminta.'

'I know, I know. I'll keep you in the loop.'

'Make sure you do.'

Lily spent all morning and most of the afternoon crafting her piece on the fateful weekend at Porcarno Castle. She wanted the reader to experience the excruciatingly tense atmosphere at dinner and, then, the highly charged volatile energy on the dance floor

216

afterwards. She was in full flow typing like a whirling dervish, when Flavia called.

'Good afternoon. How are you?'

'Harassed. They're saying the scene at the top of the tower is too clean. Whatever that means. Hit me with your theory.'

'First of all, did Zuleika have a younger lover at the time of her death?'

'Yes, I think she did, but she always had younger men. That was the norm.'

'Do you know who she was seeing?'

'No. She was very secretive about it. He must have been married or had a girlfriend.'

'That figures. Don't think I'm mad, Flavia, but could it have been Sébastien?'

'I doubt it. He was glued to Veronique's side.'

'Well, not really, she lives in Paris.'

'Why? You can't be possessive already Lily.'

'Don't be absurd! Did Zuleika ever mention anything to you about a documentary about Anoushka Hamilton-Bruce?'

'No.'

'Well it looks like she was planning on making a series of programmes about scandalous women – kicking off with one comparing Anoushka Hamilton-Bruce and Jane Digby.'

'Right. Is that what that £10,000 payment to Sophie was for?'

'Exactly! You know how Sébastien hates any kind of publicity, especially about his mother. What if he had a fling with Zuleika to try and dissuade her from making it and then, when she refused, he took matters into his own hands?'

'And you think Sophie was murdered because she knew about the documentary?'

'If this theory is right, I think Sophie worked it out that evening at the Serpentine. Maybe she thought Anoushka's death had been suspicious too.'

'Holy Moly, Lily! Do you know what you're suggesting?'

'Yes.'

'He hasn't dumped you has he?'

'No. He has no idea I suspect him.'

'Speak to Peter Paul. He dated Anoushka for a while. He says Sébastien never forgave his mother for the death of Guillaume and for leaving him and his father.'

'What?'

'His little brother drowned in the swimming pool at their chateau in Burgundy. Sébastien was six at the time and poor little Guillaume was three. His parents split up months after. I think Anoushka was off her head.'

'How dreadful.'

'Sébastien's had a tough time. His father died about five years ago in a car crash. Peter Paul was good friends with Anoushka, right up until the end of her life. He thinks Sébastien has issues but they've never seen eye to eye. What has brought all this on?'

Lily's mobile bleeped. A text message had come through; she ignored it and carried on with the conversation.

'Something he said in the car. Do you think George jumped?'

'The police and medics have been asking a lot of questions. I sense there has been a shift in opinion, not that they've said anything. They're doing the post-mortem today. Personally, I think George jumped and I'm not sure about your theory, Lily. I need to think it over. It sounds a little far-fetched. I've got to go, Parker wants me.'

Lily rang off and opened the text message: it was Sébastien.

Can't wait to see you tonight. What time are you coming over? Sxx

Lily stared at her phone. Had she got it all wrong? Was she getting swept up in her own imagination because she wanted the ultimate story? What was she planning on doing anyway? She could hardly just confront him with her theory that he was the murderer. She replied.

7.45? Lx

She'd thown the dice, now she'd just have to handle it. A second later her phone beeped again.

Perfect. Sx

57

Lily's hands were shaking when she rang the bell of 6 Priory Mansions. Pull yourself together, she told herself. She'd texted Sébastien's address to Billy and Ricky, who thought she was crazy going over to his flat given her suspicions. Sébastien's voice rang out over the intercom.

'Good evening, Lily.'

'Hi!' she said chirpily. She pushed the door and walked into the hall. The large, purple, glass vase was filled with the usual fragrant, white lilies – she hoped they weren't a bad omen. She ran her hand over the black and white silk Chloe blouse she'd liberated from the fashion cupboard. She'd dressed up for the date because she wanted everything to appear normal – jet-black skinny J Brand jeans, and a very sexy pair of black suede Christof Canaletti platform boots. It seemed appropriate that she was wearing Zuelika's favourite shoe designer. She walked up the stairs as slowly as she could.

Sébastien was standing in the doorway waiting for her. He pulled her close to him and began to kiss her. She kissed him back – she never thought she would enjoy kissing anyone less. His cologne, once so sexy, now made her feel physically sick and caught in the back of her throat. He took her hand and walked her along the corridor. Rather than going straight on to the sitting room, he took a right and pulled her into his bedroom. A huge Julian Opie painting of a girl pole dancing hung above his king-size bed, dominating the room. The walls were painted a green-grey colour and blood-red velvet curtains hung across both windows. He threw her back on to the bed, which was covered with a fake fur throw. He was supporting all his body weight on his strong, muscular arms, which were covered up by a soft, black cashmere jumper.

'You look like the man from the Milk Tray ads, if you don't mind me saying so,' teased Lily.

'Hmm,' he said, ignoring her and continuing to kiss her. Lily looked into his eyes, trying to read him. He stared back at her seductively. She rolled off the bed and walked out into the corridor.

'What's a girl got to do to get a drink in this joint?'

'I can think of a few things,' said Sébastien, joining her in the corridor. 'You are a prick tease Lily! But you know I love the thrill of the chase. What would you like?'

'A gin and tonic, please.'

'Coming up.' Sébastien walked into the kitchen and took a bottle of Tanqueray gin out of his kitchen cupboard. He then picked two heavy crystal highball tumblers off a brown leather drinks tray, and proceeded to mix two very strong gin and tonics.

'Are you trying to get me drunk?'

'Well, you're clearly nervous,' he joked, handing her one of the glasses. They walked into the sitting room; low-level house music was playing in the background.

'You're back on the house music?' joked Lily.

'Until I update my iTunes library. What do you want to do tonight? Shall we go out or I could get a Vietnamese from round the corner?'

Lily weighed up the options in her mind: if they went out it would be easier to escape at the end of the evening, but if they got a takeaway, he would have to go and collect it, which would give her a bit of time to snoop around.

'I'd love a Vietnamese.' He strolled back into the kitchen and returned with a leather restaurant menu from Nam Long Shaker; Lily shot him a quizzical look.

'They know me in there. They do great cocktails. We'll go one time. What are you having?'

Lily scanned the menu. 'I'd like some dumpling rolls and the chicken with chilli and lemongrass.'

'Chilli, eh? You're hot enough already,' said Sébastien, thoroughly enjoying his bad joke. He phoned through the order. Lily saw a copy of *The LEN* on the white, leather sofa. A photograph of George Lazarus stared out on the front page with the headline:

Aristocrat plunges to death at country weekend after his exclusive fund revealed as ponzi scheme

'Did you see that?' said Sébastien, pointing at the paper.

'Yes I did.'

'Someone beat you to the scoop, Lily! One of the guests at the weekend really dished the dirt. They've broken the story on the fund and about George hiding Moses Brown. This Ricky Flynn is stealing a march on you.'

'He certainly is,' said Lily, thinking exactly the same thing.

'Poor George, he would have hated all this. It is exactly why he jumped: so he didn't have to see his reputation ruined. I saw all this with my mother.'

'If he jumped,' said Lily. 'It says in the piece that the police haven't confirmed it was suicide yet. I spoke to Flavia this afternoon and she said the forensics thought the scene at the top of the tower was too clean.'

'What does that mean?' asked Sébastien.

'Maybe someone cleared it up.'

'They'd leave traces doing that. It rained very heavily on Saturday night. Did Flavia have any other news?' he asked nonchalantly, but Lily could tell she'd piqued his interest.

'She said the police are getting the post-mortem results today.'

'I'm sure that will clear everything up. George was a clever guy. He knew what he was doing. I told you he had a nihilistic attitude that night. He knew his number was up, so he weighed up the consequences and took his decision.'

'It's very sad.'

'It is. I feel sorry for Minty. I think she genuinely liked George.'

'Poor thing.'

'I'm going to get the takeaway. Don't go anywhere.' He picked up his mobile and his thin, black leather wallet from the mirrored side table and walked out of the room.

Lily waited until she heard the front door slam shut and then she scanned the room. There in the designer shelving unit was the glamorous picture of Anoushka Hamilton-Bruce. Lily walked over to it and picked it up. Could Sébastien's hatred of his mother's behaviour really send him on a killing spree? She ran her eyes over the books and ornaments, stopping to look at a stunning ebony and mother-of-pearl chess set. She remembered Dr Bone saying that Zuleika had developed an interest in chess. She walked over to the board and picked up the Henry Moore-style hand-carved, stone chess pieces. It was a beautiful set. She lifted up the board and there on its base was the Linley brand logo. She remembered someone mentioning a Linley chess set but she couldn't think who it was. She took out her phone and photographed it then she put it back exactly as it had been.

She walked through the double doors into a study. A light blonde oak, art deco desk stood in front of the window. Sébastien's iBook was placed in the centre with its lid down. There was a floor-to-ceiling cupboard in the left-hand corner facing the window and a grey, art deco armchair in the opposite corner. Lily walked over to the desk and opened the top left-hand drawer – it had a box of Smythson stationery and some business cards. She rifled through all the drawers on that side and found nothing of consequence. As she was searching the right-hand drawers she heard the beep of a phone receiving a text message. She could have sworn Sébastien took his mobile with him. She pulled her phone out of her pocket and checked if there were any messages: the screen was blank. She opened the cupboard. Half of it was taken up with clothes but there were five inbuilt cubbyholes down the right-hand side. They were filled with books, files, boxes and general clutter. Lily scanned them, working from the top to the bottom. There, lodged on top of a photo album in the middle row was an iPhone. Lily picked it up and opened the text message.

> *Ronnie, How is touring with Andy? Want to hear ALL about it! Need cheering up after the weekend. Stop texting and pick up the phone girl! Love, Rocky x*

Lily scrolled down the text messages, there were tons of messages from a variety of contacts including Sébastien up until 4th September. Lily scrolled over to the sent box. On Wednesday 5th September Veronique had sent two text messages to Rocky and one to Oscar Rutherford. Lily read the messages.

> *Rockstar, I'm in Ibiza with Andy. Sex surprisingly good... Vxx*

Rocky had texted her back.

> *OMG! What the fuck? Thought that was a one off.*

Veronique had replied.

> *I lied. Was all too complicated with S. Am now free :)*

Lily opened the one to Oscar.

Hi baby face. Seb and I have split up. Having a blissed up time with Andy Blake. You were right he is good in the sack. Love Vxx

Oscar had replied.

You CRAZY girl. Seb way more beautiful than Blake. Maybe I can turn him! Glad you're getting some – you sexy beast. Osc x

Lily found another message, which had been sent to ten friends in reply to their messages.

Seb and I have split up. I'm fine! I'm in Ibiza. Miss you. Call you when back. Vxx

Then there were two other text messages to Rocky: the first one was sent on Saturday night at around ten, the second on Sunday morning at twenty-five to nine. Lily read the first one.

Rockstar, I've joined Andy on his tour. It's wild! Miss you. Vxx

She couldn't quite believe her eyes. It was obvious Sébastien had sent these messages pretending to be Veronique. She remembered Rocky commenting that she thought Andy Blake was on tour. Sébastien must have headed upstairs and sent a text from Veronique to allay Rocky's suspicions. Lily opened the last sent message.

Rocky, Seb has let me know about George. I'm so sorry. I hope you're OK. Must have been awful seeing it all. Call you next week. Vxx

It was clear that Veronique didn't have her phone and Lily figured that if they'd split up, Veronique would have got her phone back, or if relations were so hostile she felt she couldn't get it back, she would have cancelled it. Her blood ran cold. No one had missed her because Sébastien had been texting all her friends. The real question was, where the hell was she? Lily began to take photos of the text messages with her iPhone, but it was difficult because her hands were shaking so much. When she'd finished she put the

223

phone back in its hiding place and as she did, something caught her eye. The end of another mobile was poking out off a red box file next to the file where Veronique's phone had been. Lily took the file out and a silver Nokia fell out. She turned it on. It had been wiped clean of all messages and numbers. Lily called herself with it and then texted the number to Ricky and DCS Peters. She was halfway through typing 'Is this the mystery number on Zuleika's phone?' when she heard the front door slam. She sent the text message unfinished, slipped the Nokia into her back pocket and put Veronique's mobile back in the cupboard, closing the door and making her way back into the sitting room.

58

Sébastien walked into the sitting room carrying a white paper bag; he put it down on the glass coffee table, and looked up at Lily.

'Sorry about the wait.'

'No worries,' said Lily. 'I had to make some work calls.'

'Did you have a snoop around?'

'No,' said Lily, looking taken aback. 'Why? Do you have something to hide?'

'You tell me?' he said, fixing her with those green eyes, which now looked cold and menacing.

'Sébastien! Don't be weird.' Her phone beeped. She took her mobile out of her side pocket. There was a message from Ricky.

> That's it! Get out of there now! It looks like George was pushed. Someone else's DNA found under fingernails and it's not Araminta's. They're going to test all the guests from weekend ASAP. Anoushka's suicide suspiciously similar to George's. R

Lily took the message in and wondered how she was going to extract herself without arousing suspicion. She put the phone back in her side pocket.

'Everything OK?' Sébastien asked.

'They've found DNA under George's fingernails. He may well have been pushed. Look, I'm really sorry but I've got to go back to the office. That was from Jonty.'

Sébastien walked over to her. 'Not so fast,' he said. He put his arms round her and ran his hands down the back of her jeans and took the Nokia phone out of her back pocket. 'You found my phone collection?'

'Yes,' said Lily, trying to break free of his grasp.

'Where is Veronique?' demanded Lily.

'I find it amusing that you suddenly care about her. That wasn't the case in Ibiza.'

'Fuck you, Sébastien. That's not even funny.'

'It is quite,' he said, the corners of his generous mouth turning up in a cruel snarl. 'I've been waiting for this moment for some time. What's taken you so long? I thought you were meant to be intelligent?' As he said 'intelligent' he made two quote marks with his fingers. 'The funny thing is that you thought you were playing me. You thought you were so clever, making me wait to sleep with you. I have far more exciting things in store for you,' he said, his eyes flashing with sadistic excitement.

Lily lifted up her right foot and plunged her Chrisof Canaletti heel into his foot as hard as she could.

'You bitch!' he screamed, loosening his grasp. Lily elbowed him in the side but he still clung on to her. 'It's too late, Lily.'

'The game's up, Sébastien. I know you killed Zuleika, Sophie, George and probably Veronique and your mother as well, you sick bastard.'

'Leave my mother out of this!' he shouted at her, his eye blazing in anger. Lily's mobile rang. Sébastien dragged Lily over to the coffee table. She began to scream. He reached around behind him and took a black and silver Smith and Wesson revolver out of the takeaway bag and held it to her temple. 'Shut up! Who is it?'

Lily took her phone out of her front pocket her hands were shaking uncontrollably, 'Ricky Flynn.'

'I knew you were in cahoots with him. You've really helped his career Lily. I'm hoping he will be eternally grateful for your sacrifice. Answer it and tell him you've left the flat. Any funny business and I'll pull the trigger. And I will, Lily, you know that.'

Lily answered the phone.

'Lily, tell me you're out of there,' said Ricky, sounding concerned. Lily felt the nose of the pistol digging into her temple. Sébastien tightened his left arm round her neck.

'Yes, I'm out.'

'What happened?'

Sébastien bent down and whispered in her ear. 'Tell him you can't speak now. You'll call back in ten minutes. Make up a credible excuse. Show me you're cleverer than the others.'

'I'm going to have to call you back in ten. Sébastien's calling on the other number and I don't want him to suspect anything.'

'OK. Make sure you do.'

'I like it, Lily. You see you can think on your feet when you put your mind to it? Now, let's do this in a more civilised fashion.' He moved the revolver into the small of her back and took his arm away from her neck. 'I think we need some music. You mentioned an Ibiza playlist but I have one that I've made specially.' They walked over to the docking station: a black iPod stood in the centre. 'Now scroll down the playlists.'

Lily saw the Ibiza playlist and then, beneath it, one called Mother Dearest.

'What is this?'

'Have a look.'

Lily clicked on the list:

> 'Cocaine Blues' – Johnny Cash
> 'Cocaine' – Eric Clapton
> 'No Mercy' – Stranglers
> 'Bang, Bang (My Baby Shot Me Down)' – Nancy Sinatra
> 'Jump Around' – House of Pain
> 'Russian Roulette' – Killer Lords

'George found the list. That's why he had to go. I never intended to kill him. I updated the list last night to add George and you.'

'So, you shot Veronique?'

'Yes. She finally worked it all out.'

'Where is she?'

'On the Eurostar, she always preferred that to flying.'

'What?'

'I shipped her off. I think the DHL crate I sent to Paris should be on the Eurostar by now. She looked great. She was wearing the

Ruby Woo red lipstick and Sophie's scarf. I was going to save the scarf for you, seeing as you worked it out, but then I thought it was best to get it out of the country.'

'You won't get away with this, you know,' spat Lily.

'It has got a bit out of control thanks to you. That's why I want to make your death extra special. It's your story and I know you'd like to make the front page at least once in your career.'

'I already have, arsehole.'

'But, you'll be on every front page in the country.'

59

Sébastien flicked the iPod on to 'Russian Roulette'. The soft rock ballad began to reverberate around his flat. He upped the volume and ushered Lily into his study, the revolver still placed firmly in the small of her back.

'No one will hear your screams. The Verities in the flat opposite are on holiday, the old lady in the flat above is deaf as a post and Kieran in the flat below works every hour God sends at Morgan Grenville.'

'Don't think that will stop me.'

'One scream out of you and I will pull the trigger.' He took something out of his pocket. Lily recognised it as Sophie Hamilton-Bruce's missing Ruby Woo Mac lipstick.

'I'm not putting that on,' she said.

'Oh yes you are. I think it will look better on you than it did on Sophie. She never really knew what suited her. Which was ironic, given her profession. Red works best on blondes.' He burrowed the pistol further into her spine and frog-marched her over to his desk, swinging his hips to the music as he went. He turned the chair around and pushed her down on to it. He drew the curtains, took a small hand mirror from the top-left drawer of the desk, and handed it to her. She applied the lipstick slowly. He moved over to the left-hand corner of the room and dragged the armchair over, so it was opposite her chair, all the while keeping the gun trained on her chest.

'Perfect. I was right: it is your colour.'

'Can I have a drink?' asked Lily, trying to buy some time.

'Yes,' said Sébastien, smiling. 'What would you like?'

'Vodka.'

'I'll join you in a drink.'

'No, you won't. You might be drinking at the same time as me but don't think for one moment you'll be joining me. That's what friends do.'

'Ah, if only one of your little admirers could be here now. Where are Billy or Ricky when you need them? They'd love to come and save their damsel in distress.' Sébastien took off his belt with one hand, bent over Lily and strapped her to the chair. He stood back up, took off his polo neck and bound her hands, as tightly as he could, to the back of the chair with the sleeves of the jumper. Lily saw that he had scratch marks all down his neck. So that's why he'd worn polo necks since the early hours of Sunday morning. He saw her looking at them.

'George tried to fight me off. He just didn't have the upper body strength. People dismiss polo as a sport but they do so at their peril. I find it keeps me in condition. I took a gamble when I tried to seduce you after we found George's body. I knew you wouldn't go for it and I thought it might be useful, if I got taken to court, as I could say "how could I seduce her if I was covered in bruises and scratches?" But I see we're beyond that now.' He walked out of the room to get the vodkas singing, 'Gimme, gimme, gimme some Russian roulette.'

Lily tried to wriggle free but the knot was too tight. Sébastien had been tying up polo ponies for too long. On his way back to the study he put the song on repeat on his iPod.

'Here you are,' said Sébastien, putting two shot glasses and a bottle of vodka on the desk. He poured two out and then untied her hands, quickly sliding the jumper down the chair and using it to tie her ankles tightly to the wooden legs. 'Chin chin,' he said, handing her the glass. She looked at him coldly and then downed the vodka.

'I know you're an adrenalin junkie. You boasted to me about how fearless you were on your little scooter. So Russian roulette seemed appropriate for you. Now, let me explain how this works.

'I know how it works, Sébastien.'

'Excellent.' He flicked open the gun cylinder and showed her the six empty chambers. He took a gleaming bronze cartridge out of his pocket and flaunted it at her. He held it up to his lips, kissed it and then turned his back to her and slipped the cartridge into one of the chambers.

'Poor Lily! She's so alone – a dead mother and a father who's hardly there. I have no family. We have that in common, but of course, you are unlucky in love as well. The war journalist who doesn't quite love you enough, yet you loyally hang on in there, just in case he changes his mind. Then I come along, the handsome, rich, Count de Bourgogne. I was quite different from your dreary, little, middle-class, professional circle.'

'I am ashamed of my attraction to you. I don't know how you live with yourself and what you've done. I wouldn't wish that on anyone.'

'You couldn't be further from the truth, Lily. I know you would like me to hate myself but I'm very happy with who I am. There will always be women who throw themselves at me. I'm irresistible to them – as you know. When you were reading up on my mother in the library at Porcarno Castle, I was having my way with Tabitha Monkton-Miller, we found it most amusing.'

'I really don't care about your sex life. And I know you're lying. What you did to your mother has defined your whole life. You couldn't bear for her past to be raked up again. You thought it had gone away but it will never go away. It's in here,' she said, pointing at his head.

'Your armchair psychology is touching, Lily, but it's time to play,' said Sébastien sadistically, playing air guitar to the music. 'Now, as I'm being kind and giving you a fifty per cent chance of survival, there needs to be a payoff for me. I thought you'd pull the trigger for all the shots, so you either kill yourself or me. I know how much it will damage you to have blood on your hands. I'll hold my hand over yours so there's no funny business. Let's flick a coin to see who starts. Heads or tails?'

'Tails,' said Lily.

Sébastien took a pound coin out of his pocket and flicked it into the air with his thumb and forefinger. Lily watched the coin rise and then flip four times on its way down. The coin was in free fall just like her life. It landed on tails.

'You first,' she said defiantly.

Sébastien positioned the gun on his temple his hand was tightly clamped over hers. She took a gulp and pulled the trigger. Nothing happened.

229

'Fun, isn't it? What are you thinking?' he asked, his eyes flashing with excitement.

Lily stared back into them and replied drolly, 'That journalism was a bad career choice.'

'I couldn't agree with you more. Ghastly profession,' he said, shaking his head in mock disapproval.

Sébastien moved the gun so it was resting on Lily's temple. He smiled at her. She shut her eyes, said an internal prayer and pulled the trigger. Nothing happened. She was finding it very hard to keep it together but she was not going to let him have the satisfaction of seeing her lose it.

'Now, now,' said Sébastien, stroking her hair. He poured two more shots of vodka. Lily downed hers immediately. 'Round two?' he said, raising a perfect eyebrow.

The lyrics blasted out from the other room and Lily could hear 'Outta my mind, can I come to play. Hey, hey, hey we're in the movie. I feel up and I feel groovy. Let's go out and get some of that. Gimme, gimme, gimme some Russian roulette. La la la.'

'I don't want to die to this shit,' said Lily.

Sébastien grinned at her. 'I thought you'd like it. It's ironic and I didn't think you'd like rap.' He moved his armchair so it was as close as it could be to hers. He stared into her eyes and put the gun up to his temple. Then he dared her to pull the trigger. She pulled it – nothing happened. He laughed in her face, his sour breath lingering like early winter morning mist.

'Luck seems to be on my side today,' he taunted. He poured two more vodkas. 'This is so much more exciting than making love, don't you think? I admit it is a small regret that I didn't have you before you died. To give you credit, I thought you would be easier than you are.' He moved the gun back to Lily's temple drawing little circles with the tip. 'Your turn.'

Lily didn't pull the trigger. He looked at her, his eyes cold and hard.

'Don't cheat, Lily,' he said, and he tightened his grip on her hand so it was excruciatingly painful, then he yanked her fingers back over the trigger sharply and pulled it. 'Sometimes one just needs a helping hand. Your luck is holding for now.' He poured two more vodka shots and handed her one. He stared right through it. 'I'm a little nervous, too. You seem to have forgotten that I'm putting my life on the line here as well. In another setting it might almost be romantic.'

'Your life is over. You pretended George couldn't bare the publicity of the shame of the embezzled funds. The truth is, you will hate all the publicity around this. You've probably rigged this so you die,' she spat.

Sébastien turned the gun back to his temple. He was tickling Lily's trigger finger.

'Ready to commit your first murder, Lily?'

'Don't kid yourself into thinking I'll have sleepless nights about this, Sébastien. I'm happy to pull the trigger. It's an honour to avenge the deaths of those poor women. Just tell me one thing: what did it feel like killing your mother?'

He looked at her and hissed. His eyes burned with pure evil as they bore into her soul. A cold shiver ran down her spine. He brought his face as close to hers as possible and pulled the trigger.

'Bad luck,' he said, 'best to get it over quickly, I find. Goodbye, Lily Cane.'

BANG! BANG! BANG!

60

Lily came round a few seconds later. A female paramedic was patting her face.

'Lily, Lily are you with us?'

Lily lifted her head. 'Yes,' she replied.

A male paramedic and two police officers lifted Sébastien's limp body off her and carried it into the sitting room.

Lily noticed some of his blood had splattered on to the silk Chloe blouse she had borrowed from the fashion department. She put her hand up to her face, felt something sticky down the right-hand side and gasped. It was covered in blood.

'Don't worry. It's his,' said the paramedic, smiling. 'I'm Jane by the way. Hello, Lily. I want you to know you are going to be fine. You've had a traumatic experience, but you're not physically hurt.' Jane unfastened the belt and began to untie the jumper that was binding Lily to the chair. Her legs had gone dead and Jane rubbed them to get the circulation going.

Lily began to take in the enormity of what had happened. Everything seemed to be playing out in slow motion, as if she was waking up from a nightmare. She saw DCS Peters, standing by the double doors leading into the sitting room; he was saying something to the officers who were by Sébastien's body.

'Is he dead?!' shrieked Lily hysterically.

'Yes,' said DCS Peters walking over and rubbing her shoulder.

'What happened? Why didn't I die?'

'Because our marksmen took him out. We got here in the nick of time. You've got Ricky to thank. He knew something was up and called me and 999.'

'Was there no way of getting us both out alive? Death is easy for him,' she said, pointing her head in the direction of Sébastien's corpse. 'He would have found the trial and the shame far, far worse,' she muttered, breaking down again.

'He'd have turned the gun on you, Lily. He'd already killed four people and probably his mother as well. By the time we were in position there was only one objective and that was to get you out of here alive. Do you want a brandy or something?'

'No. I've been downing vodka shots with that psychopath.'

'You need to have some rest,' said the paramedic. 'Is there someone who can take her home?'

'Yes, there is. Your friend Billy is waiting downstairs. He was in the street, you know. He was about to come up.'

Lily looked up at Peters and smiled. 'Dear Billy.'

'I have to hand it to you, Lily. You were right. Those feminine hunches, eh?'

'He did kill his mother.'

'I really think you need to go home now, Lily,' said Jane.

'Don't you need to take a statement?' asked Lily, completely ignoring her.

'We can do that tomorrow, Lily,' said Peters, patting her shoulder once again.

'I'm not going home to rest, doctor. I'm going to go and write this up. I risked my life for this story and I'm going to get my scoop. What I need is a cigarette.'

'Where are they?' asked Jane.

'In my bag, in the other room.'

Jane came back with Lily's bag and took out a cigarette, lit it and handed it to her. Lily inhaled deeply and then exhaled huge plumes of smoke out into the room. It was as if she was expelling all the bad things that had just happened with the smoke.

'Finish that and then we'll go down to the station,' said Peters.

'I don't think she's in the right state of mind,' interjected Jane.

'I'm fine,' snapped Lily. 'I've been living this case for the last two and a half months. I want to give my statement while it's fresh in my memory and then write my story. I don't want to go home and drink tea or take some sleeping pills to knock me out. If you think I'm going to sleep tonight, you're very much mistaken. I'm happy to be alive! I need to write this in order to make sense of it and to exorcise all these awful emotions. I'll rest later.'

It was past ten when Billy and Lily returned to the flat. Billy went into the kitchen and poured two large glasses of red wine. He handed one to Lily and took a gulp out of the other.

'Are you hungry?'

'I am actually. All that adrenalin has taken everything out of me.'

'I take it you don't want takeaway?' joked Billy.

'Ha ha,' said Lily, raising a smile. She took a sip of wine and then lit a cigarette.

'I'll make a tomato pasta,' said Billy, looking in the half empty cupboard.

'That would be lovely. Thanks, Bill.'

Lily stared down into her wine glass. A silence hung in the air.

'Go on, I know you're itching to start writing. Promise me that this will be the best piece you've ever written.'

Lily threw her arms round Billy and he hugged her back.

'I knew you'd understand.'

'It doesn't mean I approve. I think you were incredibly stupid to go round there when you thought he was the murderer. I guess I didn't take it seriously; otherwise I'd have tried to stop you. I told you that guy was a wanker.'

'He was more than that, Bill.'

'I know,' said Billy, shaking his head. 'Please listen to me next time. You really do have the most appalling taste in men.'

Lily nodded and then walked out of the kitchen. She grabbed everything she needed from her desk, set up her laptop on the dining table and began typing. The words came thick and fast, pouring out of her, but when she came to write about the Russian roulette she stopped. She looked at her watch: past two in the

233

morning. She lit a cigarette and walked over to the window, staring out into the empty dark square.

Tears poured down her cheeks. She wiped them away with the back of her hand, before inhaling deeply. When she'd finished the cigarette, she returned to the laptop and carried on typing.

61

It was ten o'clock when Lily woke. She'd finished her piece at five o'clock and had filed directly to Sam and Ricky. Never before had she got so much satisfaction from pressing the send button. She wanted Sam to see the raw, rough, unedited version and to feel like he was in the room with Sébastien and the pistol. She'd then collapsed into bed and had finally fallen asleep at six. Lily stretched her arm out of bed and felt around on her bedside table for her phone. There was an email from Sam.

> Lily,
> You have more balls than any of the men on the paper. I salute you. Brilliant work. Come and see me tomorrow in the office.
> Yours,
> Sam

Lily immediately replied.

> Hi Sam,
> I'll be in around 12.
> L

He replied.

> Great. See you then.
> Sam

She also had an email from Ricky.

Lily,
You 'canned it' – excellent journalism.
I hope you're OK.
Love
Ricky
X

Lily read the message and smiled. Then she thought of Sébastien goading her about pulling the trigger for that last shot, his eyes dancing at the thought of her blowing her own brains out. She shuddered and cursed herself for taking so long to work everything out. How could she let herself be taken in by him? Her dad was right – vanity was a sin. She'd been vain enough to be swept along by him. She picked up her mobile and jumped out of bed. The phone rang and rang. Eventually an elderly, male voice answered.

'Hello.'
'Dad!'
'Who's there?'
'It's Lily.'
'Elizabeth?'
'No, Dad. Mum died thirteen years ago. It's Lily, your daughter.'
'Of course I know who you are,' he snapped.
'Is Francis there?'
'Yes, she's upstairs having a shower.'
'Great. Dad, I just wanted to let you know that I'm OK.'
'Good. Good. Why wouldn't you be?'
'Well, you know I've been reporting on these murders in London.'
'Who's been murdered?'
'Dad, you remember we've spoken about it a few times.'
'Have we?'
'Anyway, look, I actually solved the case.'
'Are you talking about a film?'
'No, Dad. I worked out who the murderer was.'
'I'm confused.'
'Anyway, in the process I nearly got murdered myself.'
'What are you talking about, girl! Have you been drinking?'
'I don't want you to be alarmed by anything you read in the papers as there will be some publicity.'
'OK. I hardly read the papers any more.'

'I'll come down this weekend. Can you get Francis to call me when she's out the shower? Write it down, Dad.'

'I'll remember. Don't fuss.'

'No, you won't, Dad. Write it down while I'm on the phone.' Lily heard him crashing about the kitchen.

'All done.'

'See you at the weekend.'

'Did you?'

'No, this coming weekend.'

'OK.'

'Love you,' said Lily. As she put down the phone she was hit by an immense feeling of sadness. She lit a cigarette and walked into the kitchen to make a coffee. Billy had left her a note.

> *Lil,*
> *I can't wait to read all about it.*
> *B x*

Lily inhaled on her cigarette and then laughed out loud. It suddenly hit her – she was ALIVE! She took in what had happened in the last forty-eight hours. She'd not only survived, but also revealed who the murderer was. The enormity of what had and hadn't happened sunk in. She walked over to Billy's old stereo and played the LP of 'Lovely Day' at full volume. She began dancing around the room, belting out the lyrics enjoying this private moment of satisfaction.

62

Lily walked through the revolving door of *The LEN* offices with a swagger, swiped her card over the security pad, winked at Barry the doorman and then ran up the escalator taking two steps at a time. Rather than go straight to Sam's office, she decided to take a detour through the news floor, past the features desk. She strode through the office, past the sports desk, past the subs and news team. Sylvester was the first to see her. He was wearing a mustard-coloured sleeveless jumper.

'Lily!' he exclaimed. 'What are you doing here?' He got up to give her a kiss.

'I'm here to see Sam.'

Nick Weston looked up and walked over.

'How's life at *Society* old girl?'

'Dangerous.'

'What?'

Kate Pollock strode over. She was wearing a grey shirtdress and black L K Bennett heels; she looked as middle-of-the-road as ever.

'Lily!' she exclaimed. 'What a surprise! Are you missing us?' Kate reached up and gave her an affected kiss.

'I'm back.'

'What?' said Kate, her face changing from mock sincerity to pure fury.

'I never left, darling,' said Lily, savouring the moment.

'What do you mean?' spluttered Kate.

'I was undercover on a special assignment for Sam.'

'Why didn't I know about it?'

'Only the top brass and Ricky knew about it,' Lily looked at her watch. 'I'd love to chat but I've got to see Sam.'

'What's all this about?'

'You'll find out soon enough.' Lily smiled at Kate and then walked off in the direction of Sam's office.

As she was walking along the corridor, Lily heard a familiar voice.

'Lily!' shouted Ricky. 'Are you OK?'

'Just about.'

'Thank you for calling the police last night, you saved my life,' said Lily looking him straight in the eye.

'I should never have let you go.'

'Rubbish. I would have gone anyway.'

'Sam's bidden me to his office too. Come on.'

Tracey, Sam's PA, ushered them both through with a motherly grin.

'Lily!' exclaimed Sam, getting up from his desk and giving her a bear hug. 'You're a wild card. What the hell were you doing taking on a murderer single-handed?'

'I needed to know.'

Sam laughed out loud. 'It's in your blood, Lily! I can see it. You're hungry and you only stop at the truth. This is a bloody brilliant piece,' he said waving around a printout of Lily's story.

'We're going to run pages of it. You've delivered us the best scoop we've had in years.'

'Thank you,' said Lily.

'Listen. I'm going to go over some details on the story with you and then I want you to take a week off. Wrap up your loose ends at *Society* and come back to us pronto.'

'OK,' said Lily. 'Will I still be working on features?'

'I was testing you!' teased Sam. 'No, you won't be on features. Please meet the new head of special projects,' he said, waving his arm in Ricky's direction.

'Thank you, Sam,' said Ricky, puffing out his chest.

'And you, Lily, are his chief reporter. I want you two to cause mayhem. You are going to be my bloodhounds, investigating the most explosive and top-secret stories. Lily, you've shown you are more tenacious than anyone else on this paper. I'm expecting great things.'

'Fantastic news. Thanks, Sam,' replied Lily. 'We won't let you down!'

French Aristocrat Revealed as Society Serial Killer

By Ricky Flynn
TUESDAY 11TH SEPTEMBER 2007

Thirty-year-old hedge funder, Count Sébastien de Bourgogne, was shot dead by the Metropolitan Police yesterday evening, when it was discovered that he was holding LEN journalist Lily Cane captive, forcing her to play a deadly game of Russian roulette, in his luxury Chelsea apartment in Drayton Gardens. Miss Cane, who was dating Bourgogne, suspected he was guilty of the crimes and discovered two mobiles in his flat. The first was that of his ex-girlfriend, singer Veronique Lapin, whose body was discovered last night in a DHL shipping box on the Eurostar. She was wearing the missing Louis Vuitton scarf, the missing murder weapon in the killing of TV presenter Sophie Hamilton-Bruce, at the Serpentine Summer Party. *Continued on page 3.*

LEN EXCLUSIVE
How I escaped death – My night of hell playing Russian roulette with Sébastien De Bourgogne
By Lily Cane
TUESDAY 11TH SEPTEMBER 2007

The first time I met the Count de Bourgogne was at the Serpentine Summer Party in July. He was a striking figure who exuded an air of success and suavity. The elder son of the late Count de Bourgogne and the late British socialite Anoushka Hamilton-Bruce was a regular fixture on London's social scene. He appeared to have the perfect life – he worked for Tibera, one of the city's most profitable hedge funds, played polo with Prince William and Prince Harry and was undeniably handsome.

On his arm hung the beautiful Gallic pin-up, popstar Veronique Lapin. They were the golden couple, who lived a glamorous jet-set existence, partying across Europe. However, beneath Sébastien de Bourgogne's charming and cultivated exterior lay a disturbed, damaged and sadistic person.

Continued on Page 5...

239

Acknowledgements

I am very grateful to the team at Quartet for their friendly encouragement and support. Thank you to Naim Attallah for publishing this and to Gavin James Bower and Grace Pilkington for all their hard work. Thank you to my agent, Pat Lomax, who is patient and wise and who always gives me great advice. I am indebted to my mother and Dan who both got bloodshot eyes reading this over and over again. To my glamorous proofreaders Flora Astor, Pinny Grylls and Andrew Pirrie - thank you for taking the time to read it. I'm most grateful to Steve Bird for giving me the lowdown on the politics of crime reporting. Thank you to Simon Rowell whose industrial printer knew many versions of this book. I'm truly grateful to Katarzyna Racjan, Sue Phillips, Olla Cholewa and MariCruz Orihuela, who looked after my son so well and enabled me to write the novel - I couldn't have done it without you. And lastly to my dear friend, the late John Graham, who is hugely missed and whose generosity helped me write this book and fulfil an ambition of a lifetime.